NEW YORK REVIEW BOOKS
CLASSICS

THE MANGAN INHERITANCE

BRIAN MOORE (1921–1999) was born into a large, devoutly Catholic family in Belfast, Northern Ireland. His father was a surgeon and lecturer, and his mother had been a nurse. Moore left Ireland during World War II and in 1948 moved to Canada, where he worked for the *Montreal Gazette*, married his first wife, and began to write potboilers under various pen names, as he would continue to do throughout the 1950s. *The Lonely Passion of Judith Hearne* (1955, now available as an NYRB Classic), said to have been rejected by a dozen publishers, was the first book Moore published under his own name, and it was followed by nineteen subsequent novels written in a broad range of modes and styles, from the realistic to the historical to the quasi-fantastical, including *The Luck of Ginger Coffey*, *An Answer from Limbo*, *The Emperor of Ice-Cream*, *I Am Mary Dunne*, *Catholics*, *Black Robe*, and *The Statement*. Three novels—*Lies of Silence*, *Color of Blood*, and *The Magician's Wife*—were short-listed for the Booker Prize, and *The Great Victorian Collection* won the James Tait Black Memorial Prize. After adapting *The Luck of Ginger Coffey* for film in 1964, Moore moved to California to work on the script for Alfred Hitchcock's *Torn Curtain*. He remained in Malibu for the rest of his life, remarrying there and teaching at UCLA for some fifteen years. Shortly before his death, Moore wrote, "There are those stateless wanderers who, finding the larger world into which they have stumbled vast, varied and exciting, become confused in their loyalties and lose their sense of home. I am one of those wanderers."

CHRISTOPHER RICKS teaches at Boston University and is a former president of the Association of Literary Scholars, Critics, and Writers. From 2004 to 2009 he was Professor of Poetry at the University of Oxford. His most recent book is *True Friendship: Geoffrey Hill, Anthony Hecht, and Robert Lowell Under the Sign of Eliot and Pound*.

THE MANGAN INHERITANCE

BRIAN MOORE

Introduction by
CHRISTOPHER RICKS

NEW YORK REVIEW BOOKS

New York

THIS IS A NEW YORK REVIEW BOOK
PUBLISHED BY THE NEW YORK REVIEW OF BOOKS
435 Hudson Street, New York, NY 10014
www.nyrb.com

The introduction by Christopher Ricks originally appeared, in slightly different
form, in the *London Review of Books*.

Library of Congress Cataloging-in-Publication Data
Moore, Brian, 1921–1999.
 The Mangan inheritance / by Brian Moore ; introduction by Christopher
Ricks.
    p. cm.
 ISBN 978-1-59017-448-7 (alk. paper)
1. Mangan, James Clarence, 1803–1849—Family—Fiction. 2. Inheritance
and succession—Fiction. 3. Poets—Fiction. 4. Ireland—Fiction. 5. Domestic
fiction. I. Title.
 PR9199.3.M617M3 2011
 813'.54—dc22

                    2011020447

ISBN 978-1-59017-448-7

Printed in the United States of America on acid-free paper.
10 9 8 7 6 5 4 3 2 1

INTRODUCTION

Jamie Mangan, left at thirty-six by his wife and then suddenly left all her money, takes it into his heart to go off from New York to Ireland to find out whether or not he is the great-great-grandson of the poet James Clarence Mangan. Jamie's father had once half-heartedly tried this, but he wasn't prey to a sufficiently insatiable hunger for the quest. But then it is Jamie, not his father, who bears an uncanny resemblance to the man in an heirloom daguerreotype which has "J. M. 1847?" on the back of it. The resemblance—a newly missing tooth, for instance—eerily increases once Jamie is in Ireland, entangled with disreputable Mangans who are probably his cousins (ah, how treacherously and sluttishly lovely, and how erotically practiced, is eighteen-year-old Kathleen Mangan), and likewise with respectable Mangans who are very guarded (and what are they guarding?). Jamie starts to sense that the daguerreotype is not so much a passport to a past world as a death-warrant in a present world.

"We are the same, all of us. We look the same, we write poetry, and we come to a bad end." For his double or *Doppelgänger* monstrously multiplies. It is not just that Jamie has the face of James Clarence Mangan (and the poetic aspirations, and so the bad end?), but that the face is also the face of two more Mangans along the line, a line which is cursed with their lineaments, with their versifying lines, and with their palm-lines of violence and death. What, will the line stretch out to the crack of doom? Jamie, though, looks like being the end of the line. Meanwhile the double-goers double into triple- and quadruple-goers. What the Mangan face beseeches is recognition, of itself and for its writings.

At the center of *The Mangan Inheritance* is a person who has—as yet?—no center. As long as Jamie Mangan was married to the very famous filmstar Beatrice Abbot, he had no other identity than that of her husband. Karl the doorman equably calls him "Mr. Abbot," and in the anger of a quarrel Jamie rams the truth of Beatrice's words into his head: "I'm your husband. That's it, isn't it? That's what I am. That's exactly what I am. In fact, it's all I am." Yet when she walks out on him, he is released only into a different sense of the same vacancy of self: "Nothing happens. It's as though I'd ceased to exist." And what has he ever achieved? "At thirty-six I'm nothing." But then the quest to Ireland cannot simply restore him to being someone. "Like the man in that photograph, he had once been someone, was now no one, and might here, in this small wild country on the edge of Europe, discover who and what he would become." Yet to find oneself the latest incarnation of the Mangan face, the Mangan ill-fortune, and the Mangan poetic itch: this is to find an identity, perhaps, but not to find one's own identity or individuality, even apart from the fact that the face which later beetles into his, the face of his aged double, is that of a wheedling pervert and poetaster.

When Mangan arrives in Ireland, he thinks of himself as "reborn but not renamed, searching a new identity." At first, comparatively blithely, that *searching* means "searching for" or "seeking": the climax of his search, though, is not his searching *for* a new identity but his searching it. He searches it, through and through, and what he then diagnoses looks like a disease in his blood. Perhaps he will be saved. For, off the end of the book, beyond its chastened close, there is at last a duty for Jamie Mangan, and duty is nothing like so stern and jealous a god as is the dearth of duty. Someone yet unborn is going to need this man who, now knowing what is the blight Mangan was born for, might otherwise wish that he had never been born.

It cannot be simply a stricture on this novel, then, that its hero is something of a zero. Nothing in himself, he yet multiplies into other selves; and he multiplies the scale and the stakes of all those with whom he engages. If he is a cipher, this, too, he multiplies into both of the senses of a cipher. Certain honorable satisfactions are therefore honorably not forthcoming from this novel, and the would-be poet Mangan is not himself a center of interest in the way in which the would-be novelist Brendan Tierney is, in Moore's earlier superb novel *An Answer from Limbo*. Yet this isn't a defect in the book, it is the ground (grounds constituting limits, true) of its success. The nature of that success can be glimpsed within the "glassed-in bookcase with leather-bound books on its shelves," there within the scrubbed cottage which belongs to the respectable branch of the Irish Mangan family. Pride of place within that sentence, and so within the bookcase, is given to "the Waverley novels of Sir Walter Scott."

It is *Waverley* itself which defines the kind of success gained here, for it is Waverley which Donald Davie celebrated in these terms in *The Heyday of Sir Walter Scott*: "The hero in the lost-father fable has *to be* what Scott and the others have made him—wavering (there is a sort of pun with 'Waverley'), inconstant, mediocre, weak. How else should he behave, since, not knowing his father, he does not know who he is, nor where his allegiance lies?" For *The Mangan Inheritance*, too, is a lost-father fable. Jamie is credulous when he finds the demonic hermit, "this poet who bore his face, his true spiritual father." Yet he is inconstant—fortunately, since he is thus able to recognize where his allegiance lies, acknowledging that his true spiritual father is . . . his father. In the words of the book's last page: "Through his father—who knew nothing of Gorteen, Duntally, Norman towers, and lonely headlands—the uncanny facial resemblance, the poetry, the wild blood had been transferred across the Atlantic Ocean to this cold winter land, to this, his father's harsh native city in which he now lay dying. He looked at his father's face and wished that those features were his own."

Much of Davie's spirited salute to *Waverley* ("one of the greatest novels in the language") would constitute a firm basis for a true reading of Mr. Moore's markedly good novel. Like *Waverley*, *The Mangan Inheritance* "shows the victory of the un-heroic over the heroic": "'Heroic' and 'un-heroic' may both be misunderstood, unless we admit that for 'heroic' we may substitute 'barbarian,' for 'un-heroic,' 'civilized.' The second pair of terms tilts the scales of approval towards the English, as the first pair towards the Scots; the novelist's achievement is in tilting neither way, but holding the balance scrupulously steady." For "English," we may substitute "North Americans," and for "Scots," "Irish."

Likewise, if Mr. Moore's presentation of Mangan is, like Scott's presentation of Waverley, "a strong portrait of a weak or weakish character," the perceptive critic has brought out what the strength is for:

> Thackeray, when he subtitled *Vanity Fair* "a novel without a hero," meant by that something very interesting but quite different from what it may mean as applied to *Waverley*. The formula fits the Scott novel just as neatly. And the enormous advantage of the Scott method in this particular

is that it makes of the central character a sounding-board for historical reverberations, or else, to change the metaphor, a weathervane responding to every shift in the winds of history which blow around it. This device, and this alone, of a weak hero poised and vacillating between opposites allows the historian to hold the balance absolutely firm and impartial, giving credit everywhere it is due. If the central figure is exempted from judgment, this is not from any moral laxity in the storyteller; but is designed to permit judgment of the parties, the ideologies, the alternative societies which contend for his allegiance.

Jamie Mangan is the precipitator, not the passer, of judgments. He is no longer the person he was: "That person would have made guilty judgments on this girl"—a beautifully equivocal use of "guilty," one which is the disconcerted counterpart to Beatrice's hideously undisconcerted use of the word when she announced her defection: "I realize that I'm the guilty party, so to speak." Jamie in the end believes himself incapable of judging his odious double's poetry, but he judges it all right: "I can't judge it. I'm completely hostile to its content." Poetic justice? The phrase is one which the blackguard poet uses twice—"If there was any poetic justice, which there's not, I'd be as well known as James Clarence himself": this, with a smirking disregard for the nemesis which is part of this locution for ideal rewards and punishments.

Henry James said that "*Waverley* was the first novel which was self-forgetful." No modern novel can be thus self-forgetful, and *The Mangan Inheritance* is instinct with conscious memory of itself, and of its proceedings. But its life as a novel is a matter of its having at its heart a strong portrait of a weak character, naggedly unable to be self-forgetful, the more so as his doubts increase as to whether he even has a self to forget—and yet finally becoming capable of the strong form of self-forgetfulness which is self-abnegation.

The Mangan inheritance is a double one, as befits its involving a search for a double. The literal inheritance of money is what makes possible the search for the heritage of blood. But it is one of the lacerations within the book that though "the Mangan inheritance" is a straight description in that it is Jamie Mangan who inherits all that money (about $800,000), it is askew in that the money could as well be called the Abbot inheritance: Mangan inherits it from his wife Beatrice Abbot (who assuredly is not known as Mrs. Mangan), and moreover she had inherited half of it from her father. Mangan knows that the honorable thing to do would be to renounce the money, left to him by a wife who was cutting him dead but who had not yet had time to cut him out: but his urge to discover his forbear makes forbearance impossible. In the bitter end, though, he cuts his ill-gotten losses. The vital and honest spending of the Mangan inheritance will be its caring, not for Mangan, his father's child, but for another child of his father. Jamie Mangan has inherited, from someone not of his blood, blood-money. He has inherited too the wild blood and the poetic lust of the Mangans, the line running back to "the first *poète maudit*." For James Clarence Mangan "was the prototype of that sort of poet. Before Baudelaire or Rimbaud. Before the term itself was invented."

Jamie often wonders what to wear, and Beatrice used to unleash a psychiatrist on to this: "Narcissistic, wouldn't you say? Or perhaps, said Dr. H., some deeper problem of identity. Beatrice could quote an analyst to suit her purpose." Devilish. But then someone is citing Shakespeare to his purpose. The book's purpose brings out the way in which quotation and allusion are intimate with the deep problem of identity. An earlier novel of Mr. Moore's, *The Emperor of Ice-Cream*, had made serious play with the Wallace Stevens poem, gravitating from the delicious chill to the coldness of death. But it is inheritance which makes allusion central and indispensable, since literary allusion is itself an act of

And pawned his soul for the devil's dismal
  Stock of returns.

Abysmal, yes, and dismal; the rhyme has something of the demented unignorability of Tennyson's rhyme of "abysm" with "Zolaism."

  The first page of the introduction to John Montague's *Faber Book of Irish Verse* moves at once from saying that "the true condition of Irish poetry in the 19th century" is "mutilation," to "Loss is Mangan's only theme," this sentence then speaking of castration in a way which is grimly germane to Brian Moore's novel. But there is another shadowy name which looms unnamedly large in the book, that of the bland charmer who had all the graces which were denied to the *poète maudit* who yet perhaps was man enough for damnation:

Oft in the stilly night,
Ere slumber's chain has bound me ...

The lithe and lying Kathleen sings all of this, with great beauty, at a very important moment of the book. Thomas Moore's lines are alive as part of the Moore inheritance.

—Christopher Ricks

1979

inheritance. To use the wording of previous writers is to acknowledge oneself an heir. But heir to what?

For the Augustan poets, the crucial acts of allusion were those which alluded (with a witty self-reflexiveness which was not narcissism) to inheritance royal, legal and literary. For Wordsworth, the previous poetry which was now his heritage was alive with a sense that the central human inheritance was perceptual, being the human senses, especially the eye and ear. The great achievements of allusion, in this sense of inheriting the words and phrases of previous poets, are precipitated by a coinciding of whatever is seen in life as the central or crucial inheritance with those particular acts of literary inheritance which are allusion itself. *The Mangan Inheritance* is in this tradition—a most intelligent, resourceful and surprising quest for a family inheritance which is at once an uncanny facial resemblance, poetry, and wild blood. The black blood of the Tennysons, you might think of murmuring, except that James Clarence Mangan was secured neither within the laureateship nor within genius.

The first explicit allusion, half a dozen pages into the novel, comes when Jamie reflects from Byron:

Man's love is of man's life a thing apart,
'Tis woman's whole existence.

"He picked up the coffee-pot. By Byron's standards, he was not a man." But is he even an existence? Twenty pages later, and now in that foreign country from which he had emigrated, Canada, his rage splutters into the murder of rhythm:

Time to rewrite Byron's lines:

Her love was of her life a thing apart,
'Twas my whole goddamned existence.

What looked like salvation from this, namely the Mangan quest, turns into the damnation of Mangan look-alikes. "Be damn and you have the look of a Mangan, so you have."

But Byron's wise levity had early been replaced by T. S. Eliot's wise gravity. Jamie does not know how to be himself once Beatrice is glitteringly back in the apartment for some divorce-chat:

Eliot's lines came into his head:

> Who is the third who walks always beside you?
> When I count, there are only you and I together
> But when I look ahead up the white road
> There is always another one walking beside you.

In the three weeks since she left me another one walks always beside us.

It is a great stroke, to turn Eliot's mysterious third person into the adulterous lover who has created a triangle which will now be collapsed back so that it will be Jamie who is to become the third person, left behind. A true stroke, too, not only in that *The Waste Land* is (among other things) a poem of marriage misery, but also in that it is a masterpiece of allusion, including the uncrystallized allusiveness at this very point, with Eliot not altogether sure who is the other one to whom he is indebted for this evocation of another one: "The following lines were stimulated by the account of one of the Antarctic expeditions (I forget which, but I think one of Shackleton's): it was related that the party of explorers, at the extremity of their strength, had the constant delusion that there was *one more member* than could actually be counted." From one point of view, the third person is the poet Eliot himself, who provides Jamie with the painful solace of these lines, with their companionship in grief and loss. Again, given the hideous amputation at the novel's climax, the novel might be seen as a nightmarish perversion of Eliot's italicized words: *one more member*.

Allusion plays throughout the novel, with cunning and versatility. Not only does it embody a great variety of inheritances—guilt, disease, talent, money, physiognomy, property—it also allows James Clarence Mangan's work to figure in the book with a substantial solidity and yet with an acknowledged insubstantiality. What is so right about the choice of the poet James Clarence Mangan is exactly that you can be happy neither simply to grant him, nor simply to withhold from him, the name of poet. Lines of his keep recurring:

> O, the Erne shall run red,
> With redundance of blood . . .

Are they any good or not? Jamie Mangan, goaded by praise of his forbear which comes from lips which he loathes, lips of Mangan's kin and his, is driven in the end to total rejection:

> Oh, for God's sake, you stupid old fool, who in hell do you think Mangan *was*? Nobody ever heard of him, outside of a few English professors and the people who live here on this godforsaken island. Mangan's not a world poet. He never *was*. He's dead, buried, and forgotten. Second-rate, rhyming jingler, doing translations from languages he didn't understand, dull, and pathetic, just like the crap you showed me today.

But the book doesn't endorse the judgment. Not only was there, as it happens, a last-minute revision to the last page of this novel's proof-copy, so that "the bad poetry, the bad blood" became, with studied abstinence from conclusive judgment, "the poetry, the wild blood," but James Clarence Mangan's poetry remains memorably bizarre and hauntingly apposite:

> Would give me life and soul anew,
> A second life, a soul anew...

> My royal privilege of protection,
> I leave to the son of my best affection.

T. S. Eliot is by no means the only poet to haunt the book and the consciousness of Jamie, but it is his art which walks beside all of the art called up, whether actual, like James Clarence Mangan's, or imagined, like that of other Mangans.

> *Mangan, James Clarence* (1803–49), Irish poet and attorney's clerk, whose life was a tragedy of hapless love, poverty and intemperance, till his death in a Dublin hospital. There is fine quality in his original verse, as well as in his translations from old Irish and German.

The entry in *Chambers' Biographical Dictionary* from 1974, and yet how right of it to speak with that touch of archaic falsity about a true suffering, as "hapless love." Mangan himself, in "The Nameless One," was happy to tell of his miseries:

> Till, spent with toil, dreeing death for others,
>   And some whose hands should have wrought for him;
> (If children live not for sires and mothers),
>   His mind grew dim.

> And he fell far through that pit abysmal,
>   The gulf and grave of Maginn and Burns,

THE MANGAN INHERITANCE

For Jean, again

PART ONE

The doorbell.

Mangan went to the front door, looked through the peephole, then unlocked. The apartment super entered, followed by one of his Puerto Rican workmen.

"Hi. You have bathroom trouble?"

He showed them the dripping tap. The super turned it on, then off. "Washer. Something else wrong?"

"No. Everything else is fine."

"How is your missus? I don't see her jogging on the roof." The super laughed, recalling this pleasant eccentricity. Mangan looked at him. Didn't he know?

"She's not living here anymore. We've separated."

"Oh. I am sorry."

How did one answer that? Mangan acknowledged sorrow with a nod.

"I leave now. My man will fix the washer, okay?"

As he went back to the front door, the super paused and peered into the living room. On its white walls like an afterimage were whiter rectangles where her pictures had been. Rugs and most of the furniture had been removed. Books fell about on the looted shelves. How could the super *not* know she had gone? Hadn't he seen the entrails of her belongings heaped on the sidewalk when the mover's truck did not come?

As the super let himself out, Mangan called, "Happy New Year." But he shut the door without replying. Perhaps it was his Christmas envelope? Last year they had given away two hundred and fifty dollars in tips in this building alone. Without Beatrice, Mangan had felt he must economize. But the super had not known that Beatrice was gone.

Alone in the living room, Mangan moved toward the picture window. Snow fell outside. In the Orient, white is the color of mourning. Snow, the voice of silence, shutting off the city's sound track. Tonight in many offices the staff will go home early. In others, people will sit on desk tops, drinking liquor from paper cups, eating cocktail tidbits sent in from the delicatessen down the block. Horseplay, office jokes, smudged kisses. Happy New Year.

For tonight, what should I wear? Do you know what he does sometimes when he's alone in the apartment, Beatrice told her friend Dr. Hopgood. He goes into the bedroom and spends an hour trying on his clothes. Changing outfits, looking at himself in the mirror. Narcissistic, wouldn't you say? Or perhaps, said Dr. H., some deeper problem of identity. Beatrice could quote an analyst to suit her purpose. She did not understand rituals. She would never buy worry beads.

The Puerto Rican workman came from the bathroom. "Finish."

"Thank you."

The workman, unassailable in his monolingual armor, nodded and let himself out. Mangan remembered that he should call early. They had a class of some sort at nine-thirty, their time. He went into the kitchen for coffee to help him with this.

"Ridgewood Convalescent, good morning."

"May I speak to Mrs. Mangan, please?"

"One moment, please, I'll check."

"Art therapy. Joan Mangan speaking."

"Hello, Mother."

"Jamie!" his mother said. "Where are you? How are you?"

"I'm in New York. I just called to say Happy New Year."

"New Year's is tomorrow," said his literal-minded mother.

"Well, I just thought I'd call before the circuits got all jammed up."

"Yes, good idea. What are you doing, are you going to a party tonight?"

"I might, yes."

"Do," his mother said. "This is no time of year to sit alone. Will you be calling your father tomorrow?"

"No, I wasn't planning to. I called him on Christmas Day, remember?"

"Oh, yes, so you did. I must give them a ring myself. I've been so busy. I tell you, you should see this place. It's a madhouse."

But it *is* a madhouse. Still, it was nice that she did not think of it as such. "So, they're working you hard," he said.

"Oh, I tell you. Dr. Edie's on vacation and Dr. Hollins is all on his own, poor man. Matter of fact, I have a room full of customers waiting outside this minute. But it's lovely to hear your voice, dear. Thank you for calling me. I would have called *you*, you know."

"I know. Happy New Year, Mother. And God Bless."

"Oh, Jamie? When you speak to your father tomorrow, would you say hello from me? I'll tell you the truth, I haven't called him because, if I do call, I always get her."

"All right," he said. She had forgotten he wasn't going to call. She forgets quite a bit, Dr. Edie said. "Goodbye, Mother."

"Goodbye. Happy New Year. And Jamie? Next year will be better, you'll see. You'll put all this behind you."

He hung up and went back to the picture window. Large snowflakes sifted down, blurring his view of the East River and traffic on the Drive below. Mother in her cubbyhole in Santa Monica, California, swiveling in her brown Naugahyde armchair, her back to the Pacific Ocean, a phone receiver vised between her shoulder and ear. Beyond, in the big dayroom, people in playclothes waiting for pills and counsel from Dr. Hollins, an old, tall man in steel-rimmed spectacles. *Your mother has been a great help to us here. Her art class is very popular. Art is good therapy for our patients. Besides, it's therapy for her, you know.* The Christmas card she sent this year had a Californian motif, two pelicans skimming over a wave, the drawing delicate and graceful, yet with the touch of kitsch that showed in all her work.

Christmas cards. "You mean you've already done them?" Beatrice had asked. At once he was sorry he'd brought it up. He said he hadn't sealed the envelopes yet.

"All right, I have an idea. I'll have a little notice printed saying we've separated and that from now on my address will be the beach house and that you'll be at the apartment. You could slip the notices in with the cards. It would be a way of letting people know what's happened and how they can reach us."

He thought it a terrible idea but did not argue. Ten days later a package of printed slips arrived in his mail. She had not listed the Amagansett address. The slips read:

WE HAVE DECIDED TO SEPARATE. FROM NOW ON BEATRICE CAN BE REACHED AT 77 EAST 71ST STREET, WHILE JAMIE WILL REMAIN AT 455 EAST 51ST STREET.

Turnbull lived at the Seventy-first Street address. That made it final. Mangan put the slips in the Christmas card envelopes and counted them before mailing. There were ninety-seven cards in all. By Christmas morning he had received only forty-six cards in return, by far the largest number of which—thirty-four—came from tradespeople, press agents, and theater professionals with whom Beatrice had dealings, and were addressed to both of them or to Beatrice alone as though the slips had not been noticed. There were seven cards from friends who had mailed early. These wished them both a Merry Christmas and a Happy New Year. That left three cards addressed to him alone. One was from his mother. There was a card from his friends the Connells bearing a scrawled invitation asking him to come to their annual New Year's party. And there was a card and a long sympathetic letter about the breakup from his friends Jack and Rosa Hutter. The Hutters were now living permanently in London.

Three cards. One from a relative, two from friends. He turned around, walked through the living room and into the bedroom, where the window gave on a view of the street. Below, two professional dog walkers came from Beekman Place, small wiry men, their hands bunched against their chests like charioteers as they gripped the several leashes of the pedigreed pets they were paid to exercise. The dogs, excited by the snowfall, tried to gambol and wrestle and race. The walkers, moving side by side, held them to a fast walk, turning and turning in the small cul-de-sac of East Fifty-first Street which ended at a flight of steps leading down to the East River Drive.

"But why not Beekman Place?" Beatrice had said. "Of course we can afford it. Anyway, this isn't Beekman Place, it's East Fifty-first Street. Where else are you going to get a view of boats passing by when you wake up in the morning? And a location like that is an investment. If we buy an apartment there, it will never go down in value."

She meant, of course, that it was her money. He could use it, but it was her money, made by her. Her presence on a Broadway stage now brought her a weekly salary of four thousand dollars, and on the rare occasion when she acted in a film she was paid ten times that amount. She had insisted on joint savings and checking accounts. She said money shouldn't be allowed to come between people. But it was her money. There was no getting away from that.

In the street, a brown Mercedes sports car rushed recklessly out of Beekman Place and braked to a stop below his window. Kevin, the doorman on duty, came from under the street awning, bent-backed as he fumbled with the clasp of a large umbrella. As the door of the Mercedes swung open, a snow flurry gusted up, obscuring Mangan's view. Tiny tendrils of water trailed diagonally across the windowpane. He heard a noise behind him and, turning, re-entered the living room to find that the day's letters had been shoved under the door jamb. He sifted them with the toe of his loafer, then bent and flipped a few pieces of mail over, reading the addresses. All were for her. He did not pick them up but moved on into the kitchen to pour his fourth cup of coffee that morning. Last week, leafing through an anthology, he had come upon some lines of Byron's.

> Man's love is of man's life a thing apart,
> 'Tis woman's whole existence.

He picked up the coffeepot. By Byron's standards, he was not a man. He poured coffee and at that moment the doorbell rang loudly. He expected no one. He went to the door as to an intruder and through the tiny, wide-angle lens of the peephole, distorted like a figure in nightmare, discerned his runaway wife. His heart hit. He unlocked the door.

"May I come in?"

Wordless, he beckoned. She advanced as though onto a stage, her face assuming the smile which was so much her shield that it came on her unbidden, even in moments of anger. Smiling, she became the Beatrice Abbot who was known and admired by thousands of people she had never seen, a woman by no means a beauty, but attractive, with blond hair cut in a simple bob, nicely offsetting her large brown eyes. Even now, in her thirties, she emanated a pubescent charm and fostered this illusion by dressing in simple clothes—a tweed skirt, a shirt, and, sometimes, a cashmere sweater. Today, however, to Mangan's great surprise, she wore elegant knee-length boots of polished cognac-colored leather, and a long and very beautiful dark mink coat, its rich gloss beaded with melting snowflakes. On her head (she who never wore a hat) was a Cossack shako of the same fur, and while her brown cashmere dress was one he had seen before, it was ornamented by an extraordinary necklace of turquoise beads, large as pullets' eggs. "Happy New Year," she said. Was she being sarcastic? Looking at her, he surmised not. "And how have you been, Jamie?"

"All right."

She smiled at him again, then moved center stage into the living room, opening the beautiful coat, resetting it on her shoulders like a cape. "I thought of phoning to ask if I could come, but I was afraid you'd say no. So I just got in the car and drove over. I hope you don't mind."

"Got in *what* car?"

"It's Perry's."

"And is that his fur coat?"

"His Christmas present to me." She pirouetted as though modeling the coat, then sat down in the one easy chair which remained in the living room. "So," she said. "And how was *your* Christmas?"

"All right."

"What did you do?"

"What do you care?"

She sighed, leaning back in the chair, head lax, booted legs outstretched, looking for a moment like some youthful Regency buck. "I'm sorry," she said. "It would be nice if we could manage not to fight with each other."

He walked to the large window and sat on the long window bench facing her, his hands gripping his kneecaps. Eliot's lines came into his head:

Who is the third who walks always beside you?
When I count, there are only you and I together
But when I look ahead up the white road
There is always another one walking beside you.

In the three weeks since she left me another one walks always beside us. "What did you come for?" he asked. "Did you forget something?"

She ignored this. "Weinberg's been trying to reach you all week. Have you been away?"

"No. I just didn't feel like talking to him."

"Well, there's a problem. I want to go away for a few weeks. But Weinberg says that before I do, you and I should talk about the divorce."

"Where are you going?" At once he regretted asking. What did it matter where she was going?

"Perry's family have a place in Jamaica. I thought we could stay there until my rehearsals start at the Kennedy Center." She stood, letting the fur coat fall back on the chair. "Do you mind if I make a cup of coffee?"

"There's some on the stove," he said, eying her as she

went into the kitchen, her gait slightly unsteady in the unaccustomed boots. The boots would be Turnbull's taste. For a moment he imagined her booted and furred, riding crop in hand, flogging Turnbull's bony naked rump, he squealing in pain and joy. Behind him the expanse of windowpane began to chill his back. He heard her jiggle the percolator and then she came out of the kitchen, a full coffee mug held carefully in her right hand as she settled herself again in the chair with an easy, isn't-this-fun gesture he'd seen her use on strangers. Was he now just a stranger? He turned to stare out the window, saw the river cold under a whited sky. In its choppy gray channel a bulldog tug moved upriver, hauling a funerary file of garbage scows.

"Weinberg's idea," she said, "is to go for a no-fault divorce. He feels that would be by far the best for both of us. I don't know. I've no opinion. I'm just repeating what he told me to ask you."

"Ask me what? If I'll go for a no-fault divorce?"

"Well, remember we sort of decided that day—the day I told you—that I'd take the beach house for now and you'd stay on here?"

"You decided it. Not me."

"All right. But you know what I mean."

He thought of the printed slips she sent to be put in with the Christmas cards. The utter deceit of all that. Anger made his voice hoarse. "You never had any intention of living in the beach house," he said. "You moved straight in with Turnbull."

"What does it matter?"

She was right, of course.

"Look, let's not lose our tempers," she said. "One thing. I want you to keep this apartment. I'm ready to sign it over to you. Completely. I'll keep the beach house. Okay?" She smiled then, a forced smile, the smile of one who is being more than generous. He could almost hear her say it. More than generous.

"No, it's not okay," he told her. "Payments and maintenance on this place come to thirteen hundred a month, in case you forgot. And now that you've left me, I can't afford that. Last month, for instance, I made four hundred dollars. And in November I made twelve hundred. That was a big month for me. Besides, you own both places. We bought them with your money."

"Your money, my money." She kicked out her legs, her heels thudding on the parquet floor. "Tell you what. I'll make the monthly payments here for, say, two years. After that you can continue them, or if you feel like it, you can sell the apartment and keep the proceeds. The thing is, we spent seven years together and this breakup is because I want out. So I'd like to be generous with you. What's the matter? Did I say something funny?"

"No."

"Well, do you want the apartment?"

"I told you. No."

"What about the beach house? Maybe you'd rather have that? At least we own that outright, so you'd have no payments to make."

"I don't want the beach house. I don't want anything from you. And what's this rush about the divorce? Are you going to marry Turnbull?"

She hesitated. "Weinberg said if I told you you might try to hold things up. You wouldn't, would you, Jamie?"

As she spoke she leaned forward, her knees coming like polished ovals out of the sleek brown hide of her boots, her face, smiling now, framed in the three sides of a rectangle formed by her blond, bobbed hair, that face so familiar, yet now the face of a stranger. He felt a slight shiver of fear that this stranger could know so well the winning cards to deal against his resolve.

"Why would I hold things up?" he heard himself ask. Indeed, he had been meaning to make trouble if she wanted to marry Turnbull, but now dead pride invaded him like a dybbuk. "Are you trying to buy me off? Is that it?"

"Of course not. That's mean."

"Anyway," he told her, "there's no settlement that could make up for what you've done to me."

"What exactly have I done to you?"

"Nothing, nothing." Humiliatingly, tears filled his eyes. "Go on," he said. "You can go now. You can tell Weinberg it's okay, you've fixed me. But you'd better warn him you'll have to take over this apartment. Because I'm moving out."

"But there's absolutely no need to do that. It will just be sitting here empty." She got up, came to him, and put her arms around him. "Oh, Jamie, I'm sorry. I am sorry."

And once again he had been the weak one, once again he had confessed to her what he least wanted her to know. A nobody has no pride. The dybbuk left him. He stood, letting her embrace him, a shameful person who had wept to gain her sympathy. "I didn't mean to insult you," she said. "I know how awful all this has been for you." And his voice, controlled now, said he hadn't meant to shout at her. He did mean it about the apartment, though. And he would call Weinberg tomorrow.

"Tomorrow is New Year's," she said, releasing him. "The day after would be better."

Turning from him as she spoke, picking up the long fur coat, slipping into it, her back to him, showing him only the brown fur, the polished leather boots, the fur shako and blond bob, as though she were some animal, all hides and hair. How could he have imagined he could confide his new fear to that furred animal back? Then she turned to face him and for a moment was the girl who had improbably asked him to marry her, who had joined with him in matrimony before a clerk at City Hall, who in Doctors Hospital had delivered the stillborn son he had never seen. All that, that life, was over. Tomorrow would be New Year's Day and Weinberg's office would be closed. *The day after would be better.* She had finished her business here.

"By the way," he said, "you're not going to the Connells' tonight, are you?"

"I don't know. I thought we might drop in for a few minutes, later on. Why? Are you going?"

"Not now."

"Oh, come on, Jamie, that's silly. There's always an enormous mob there. We can easily avoid each other if that's what's worrying you."

"Did Bob Connell ask you? I mean, specifically."

"I don't remember. I suppose there was an invitation."

"Well, they invited me. Specifically. The Connells are my friends."

"I thought they were my friends, too," she said. "But let's not argue about it."

"You and Turnbull must have a dozen other parties you can go to."

"All right. Whatever you like. You go. We won't." She opened the front door, then put her hand on his sleeve and looked up at him. "And listen. Please use the apartment. It's just going to go to waste."

"I don't want it. Clear?"

She removed her hand at once. "Fine," she said and walked off down the corridor, all moving mink and wobbling polished boots. Absurdly, he wanted to call her back and start the encounter all over again. For days he had planned how he would behave if they met. He would be polite. He would make her believe he was better off without her. He would be magnanimous, yet indifferent, for indifference is the ultimate revenge. Instead, he had wept, had lost his temper and had even begged for a favor, asking her to stay away from the Connells' party.

"Beatrice?" he called in a loud, uneven voice. She had reached the elevator. His voice went up to a shout. "I'm *not* going to the Connells' tonight. I'm going to Montreal to spend New Year's with my father. I may not be back for a while. I'll leave the keys with the super."

"What about Weinberg?"

"I'll call him from Montreal."

"Good." She pressed the elevator button. He slammed the door on her image. Polite, magnanimous, indifferent. Didn't that describe *her* behavior perfectly? He went into the living room, saw her coffee mug, and carried it into the kitchen as though to rinse out this evidence of her visit. But, irrationally, was filled with a wish to have one more look at her and so ran to the bedroom window in time to see a movement of fur and boots as she got into the little Mercedes. Kevin, the doorman, shut the door. The Mercedes slewed around awkwardly, then, accelerating, skidded slightly in the snow as it zoomed toward Second Avenue. She'll wreck it, he thought. She never did know how to drive.

> So she would have left
> As the soul leaves the body torn and bruised,
> As the mind deserts the body it has used.

That was her way. Primitives fear the photograph, the shutter click, their image stolen, then given back to them as a lifeless souvenir, entombed in a piece of paper. Beatrice had snapped the shutter, stealing away the man he once had been, presenting him with himself as her useless husband. He took that husband figure into the bathroom, stripped it of its garments and stood it for a time under the shower, the water too hot, reddening the skin. He dried body and hair, then went naked into the bedroom, where, in the triptych mirror she had installed, he saw a face in stasis, eyes which had no light behind them, a waxwork countenance, lifelike, but not alive. The primitive photographed, robbed, abandoned.

He began to dress. He hung up the suit he had taken out to wear to the Connells' party, instead picking out a turtleneck sweater, tweeds, wool socks, and brogues. He did this without premeditation, just as a few minutes ago he had called out to her that he was going to visit his father in Montreal. He had not seen his father in seven months and when he called him on Christmas Day had not felt able to admit to him that Beatrice had walked out. Yet now, suddenly, he needed his father. His father might be the one person who could help him. To his father he was his father's only son, continuance in a line which stretched back to Ireland and their grandfather's claim to be descended from the poet Mangan himself. Fumbling with the address book, he found and dialed his father's number. Our Father Who art in Montreal, please be at home. It rang, it rang. Waiting, he looked out of the window. Gray channel of river under a whited sky; two cargo ships, light in the water, moving downriver toward the ocean.

> I should have been a pair of ragged claws
> Scuttling across the floors of silent seas.

In Montreal someone picked up the receiver. He heard his father's voice.

_____ _"Where do you live?"_
The immigration officer's intonation was French-Canadian.
"New York."
Seven years ago when Mangan moved to the United
States he had applied for American citizenship. Thus, it was
an American passport which he now passed across the
counter to identify himself to the officials of his native land.
The officer gave a cursory look at his photograph and re-
turned the passport to him, saying: "What is the purpose
of your visit?"
"To see my father."
"Do you have any gifts, liquor, or cigarettes with you?"
"No."
The officer stamped a customs form, handed it to him,
and, for the first time in their encounter, smiled. "Happy
New Year, sir."
"Thank you. Same to you."
Carrying his bag, he entered the customs area, handed the
form to a customs officer, and was waved through auto-

matically opening doors to a mill of waiting faces in the arrivals lobby. On the phone, a few hours ago, when he told him about Beatrice, his father had treated it as a true bereavement, saying, "Of course, come on up. And—look—we'll meet your flight." Now, in evidence of this concern, here was Margrethe, "larger than life," in his mother's bitter phrase, pushing to the front of the waiting crowd, tall as Mangan himself, her blond hair falling down about her shoulders, dressed in a blue ski parka and matching stretch pants, her Viking eyes steely with delight as she ran to fold him to her in a warm, moist, kissing embrace.

In the past, during similar displays of affection, Mangan had experienced an illicit sexual thrill at holding and being kissed by this handsome prize of his father's old age, a Danish girl six years younger than himself. But tonight when her warm lips touched his cheek he did not feel his usual *droit de sang* and entertain his fantasy of cuckolding his father. Instead, he felt, suddenly, grateful, glad to be seen at last not as Beatrice's husband, but welcome in his father's house, a son come home.

"Come, I have my car," said Margrethe, speaking in the clipped, English-accented tones she had learned in a Danish school. And so he went with her into the blear vise of a Montreal winter's night, waiting in freezing wind as she unlocked the Volvo. Then, snug beside her, the heater roaring, they drove out onto an access road lined with snowbanks high as horse jumps, pitted with yellow dog piss, great gray dirty slabs which would not melt till spring. Facing them, waving them on, his fur hat and greatcoat hoar as Banquo's Ghost, a Montreal policeman, whistle in mouth, leather mitts pawing the smoking Arctic air. Canada: cruel landscape, its settlement a defiance of nature. Home.

"So," Margrethe said. "When did she leave, exactly?"

"Three weeks ago."

"Maybe you don't want to talk about it?"

"No, that's all right."

"Was it Perry Turnbull she went with?"

He turned to her in astonishment. She ignored his look, her attention on the traffic as she slipped in and out of lanes at high speed, her profile immobile as an image on a coin. "How did you know about Turnbull?" he asked.

"Ah, so it *was* him." She turned for a moment and gave him a warm triumphant smile. "It was something she said when she was here last time."

"But that was more than a year ago."

The Volvo leaped forward as though running away from this dangerous revelation. "I remember," Margrethe said. "She told me this man has a big place in Jamaica."

"Yes. She's going down there with him."

Margrethe laughed. "What an extraordinary person she is. Were you sad when she left?"

"Sad?" Nobody had asked him this question. "I think I felt insulted."

"She must have been a difficult person to know. I mean, to really know. She's such an actress."

CÔTE-DE-LIESSE said the green and white expressway sign leading him back in memory to his boyhood, to a time before Beatrice, to turnings he wished he had not taken.

"And so charming," Margrethe said. "I used to watch her working on your father. Poor Pat, I think he sort of fancied her."

So as I lusted for Margrethe my father lusted for Beatrice. "How *is* Pat?" Mangan asked.

"He's in great form. He's having a party tonight, did he tell you?"

"A big party?"

"Oh, you know." Margrethe leaned forward, concentrating as the Volvo rushed up an off ramp then slowed with a lurch at the approach to Côte-de-Liesse Road. "The old gang. We're having drinks and then, later on, a buffet."

Windshield wipers rose and fell, guillotining the view.

Down Sherbrooke Street past Queen Elizabeth Hospital, where he had been born in crisis, a placenta previa, his mother in danger. Margrethe was silent: the only sounds the roar of the car heater, the wipers' slick downslap and dragging rubbery upsweep. Ahead, a townscape little changed from the years when this was his world, Westmount Park, the public library, the hockey rink, the rows of suburban avenues climbing steeply up to the Boulevard, dividing line on the social Monopoly board between the managers of banks and businesses, who lived, aspiring, on the lower slopes, and the owners of those banks and businesses, who were ensconced on the higher reaches of Westmount Mountain. The Volvo turned in at Lansdowne Avenue, the street on which Mangan grew up, beginning a climb past red-brick Victorian-style houses, their wooden porches silted with old snowdrifts, their walls and steps salted down to break the carapace of winter ice. Halfway up, the Volvo turned in at a narrow driveway, facing the front steps of a semidetached house with a front of gray Scots fieldstone. Mangan and Margrethe got out. To the left of the door, a lighted window, its curtains undrawn. Framed in this window, looking down at him, his father, dressed for a party in navy blazer, royal-blue shirt, red silk foulard. His father inclined his head in a mock-comic bow of welcome, exposing a tonsure of baldness ringed by longish gray hair. "There's Pat," Margrethe said happily, running up the steps, pushing open the front door, beckoning Mangan to follow her.

He waved to his father, then went up into the small entrance hall, picking his way through its familiar winter confusion of scattered rubbers, circulars, and unopened suburban newspapers to enter the living room, a place of contrasts, its wooden Bauhaus chairs and end tables bought in the thirties at great expense, now old and warped as a thrift-shop assemblage. Books furnished the room. In an

Adam-style grate a log fire burned brilliantly. His father, kissing and being kissed by Margrethe, raised a hand to wave to him.

Don Duncan, his father's oldest friend, stood with his back to the fire, glass in hand, smiling and nodding in welcome. His father, releasing Margrethe, came to shake hands. "How was your flight?"

His father's grip was firm. His father's way of dealing with people and crises was to be brusque, cheerful, a little distant, a trait developed in his work as managing editor of *The Gazette*, where people and crises were the daily material of his trade. Possibly he had copied this manner from some managing editor he had known in his youth, but in Mangan's eyes it gave his father a *gravitas* which other men seemed to lack. Incongruously, it occurred to him that to his father he was tonight's top local news story. SON CUCKOLDED BY CELEBRITY MATE.

"What about a drink?" his father asked. "Scotch and water, isn't it?" He nodded. His father went to the pantry.

"I have to go up and change now," Margrethe said. "You know your room, Jamie."

And went off, leaving Mangan alone with Don Duncan, who stood, his back to the fire, immense in a light-gray suit, his thick white hair matted like some badly cleaned sheepskin rug. "So how's it been, Jamie?"

"Oh, so-so."

"Pat told me."

"Oh, did he?"

"Yes, he mentioned it. Well, what can I say."

"How have *you* been, Don?"

"Oh, *comme ci*. Is she in a play or a movie, right now?"

"She's opening in a play in March."

"I only saw her in the one thing," Don said. "It was with Henry Fonda. I must have told you about it. Hell of an actress, though."

"Yes."

"My daughter Deirdre is crazy about her, you know. I remember when she came up here that first time with you, a few years back, right? Deirdre made me get her autograph." Don smiled and shook his head at his empty glass. "Well, it should be a nice party tonight. No celebrities, of course. It's not New York, Jamie. No movie stars." He laughed.

His father reappeared. "Here's your Scotch. Don, how about a refill?"

"That's okay. I'll get it myself. I know the good place."

"Will you? Thanks."

Don went out.

"Are you hungry, Jamie?" his father asked.

"No."

"We're going to eat some supper around ten. Will you be all right till then?"

"Yes, fine."

His father hesitated. "On the phone you said you wanted to talk about something. Was it something special?"

"No, I just wanted to see you, I guess. And suddenly I feel I want to ask you a lot of questions. Family history, mostly."

"Ah," said his father. "Interest in the family tree is said to be a first sign of middle age. Anyway, I have the family records upstairs, such as they are. The Bible with births and so on. And those books about James Clarence Mangan that I once tried to interest you in. Maybe you're ready for them now. You'll stay a few days, I hope?"

"I'd like to."

"Why don't you drive out to the Townships with us tomorrow. You could go out with Margrethe in the morning and I'll join you at suppertime. We'll stay out a couple of days, if that's all right."

"Fine. Where is it this year?"

"We've rented a cottage near Knowlton. It's only fifteen minutes from the ski lifts."

"I thought you'd given up skiing."

"Self-defense. Margrethe."

"Oh, right."

"Good. So that's settled, then."

"Yes. I think I'll go upstairs for a bit, if you don't mind."

"Of course," his father said. "Take your drink with you."

"See you, then."

Drink in hand, he went up the familiar stairs, up to the room which had had no regular tenant since his day and so retained the furniture and look of his boyhood and college years. He did not switch on the lamp but, closing the door behind him, went confidently in the dark toward the single bed. Headlights from a passing car swept the ceiling, bringing back a clear memory of himself at nine lying there, pretending his bed a boat, the car headlights lighthouse beams, the ceiling an ocean. *Longtemps, je me suis couché de bonne heure.* But unlike Marcel, I did not lie here longing for Mama to come up and kiss me good night. I was happiest in those hours, the day done, the door shut, alone, turning beds into boats, an only child who did not want a little brother.

He lay back on the pillows. A second car came up the avenue. Stopping directly outside the house, its headlights' reflections casting long shadows on a Swedish teakwood desk, a present from his mother, his first year at McGill. At sight of the desk, the room seemed the cemetery of his failed ambitions reentered at his peril. Below, he heard the doorbell ring. Arriving guests, shedding their rubbers, stamped heavily on the wooden porch floor. Dreams should not leave this room; they do not travel. But long ago he had decided to risk it, and like a gambler winning the first hand of the evening, an omen for a losing night, his first submitted poem was accepted by *Poetry*. Three months later, *The*

New Yorker took one of his poems, making him, at nineteen, a twice-published poet. His father was pleased but, ever practical, urged him to continue working for a law degree, while he, pretending indifference to his success, was secretly launched in a wild daydream of fame and so settled instead for a lazy B.A. Then something soured. Poems came back. The magazines that had written encouraging letters now wrote regrets. Those that did accept his poems were Canadian, obscure as their contributors. By the time he graduated he had not repeated his early success and, without special talents, was forced to accept his father's offer of a job on *The Gazette*. There he stayed for three years, still writing poetry on the side, until he and his father decided it would be better for his future if he could work for another newspaper. And so, again through parental influence, he was hired by the *Globe and Mail* and left home to live in Toronto.

He heard footsteps on the stairs outside. Someone knocked on his door. "Jamie?" Margrethe's voice. He did not answer. She opened the door slightly, but, seeing no light inside, closed it again. Laughter jollied up from the living room. He stood, switching on the bedside lamp, noticing that the picture which used to hang near the switch, a Laurentian landscape in pastels done by his mother, had been replaced by a poster entitled "The Doors of Dublin."

"Jamie?" Margrethe's voice again. She had knocked on the bathroom door down the corridor.

"Someone here," a woman answered from inside.

"Oh, I'm sorry." Margrethe said.

He went out into the corridor. "Here I am," he told her. "I put the light off and went to sleep for a few minutes."

She accepted his lie. "Sorry if I woke you." She had changed into a long evening dress of some shiny jersey material which outlined her young, sleek good looks. "Your father has taken a fancy to Danish pastry," his mother once said, cattily. "I don't think he can digest it at his age." But it was his mother who could not stomach Margrethe.

"Jamie!" He looked down, saw Mark Magennis semaphoring at him from the hallway below, remembered that Magennis was now a panjandrum at the Canadian Broadcasting Corporation, and thus a person who had the power to give him assignments. "Nobody told me you were in town," Magennis said. "Where's Beatrice?"

"She's not with me."

"Oh, too bad. I've been looking forward to telling her how good she was in that film, the French one, whatsitsname? Anyway, I saw it in New York last September. Did they dub her? She doesn't speak French, does she?"

"Yes, she was dubbed."

"Anyway, she was terrific. Oh, excuse me, Peg. Jamie, do you know Peg Thornton?"

No, he did not know Peg Thornton, a witchlike person whose eyebrows inched together as she focused on him. "Are you Beatrice Abbot's husband? That's who we're talking about, isn't it?"

"Yes, he is," Magennis said. "This is her husband, Jamie Mangan. He's also Pat's son and heir."

"Pat's son! Well, you *are* well connected. I remember now I knew Pat had a son who married someone famous— but Beatrice Abbot! I'm like Mark, I'm a great fan of hers. Your wife isn't with you, you said?"

"No, she's in New York."

"In a play?" Magennis asked.

"No. As a matter of fact, we've just separated."

"Oh?" Peg Thornton looked at Magennis, who looked at Margrethe. All looked at Mangan. "Jamie, what about a drink?" Margrethe said. "Come, let me show you what we've got."

She led him away. And, at once, there was Handelman, his reddish hair framing his skull like a saint's halo, his face loose in a grin of delight. "Hey, Jamie! Happy New Year! Hey, good to see you. Where's Beatrice?"

It was going to be that sort of evening.

Hours later, when the party was at its height and the supper plates had been cleared away, Mangan, at Margrethe's request, carried a television set down from the master bedroom and installed it in a corner of the living room. At ten minutes to midnight his father left his guests and went over to switch on the set. Mangan joined him as he fiddled with the knobs. In a few seconds Bill Lombardo smiled from the screen. The music swelled. A tune ended. Bill Lombardo looked at his wristwatch, then put on a paper party hat. He picked up his baton again and launched his musicians on a new medley.

"Exactly right," Mangan's father said. "They always put on the paper hats near midnight."

People began to crowd around. "Guy Lombardo and his Royal Canadians," Handelman said. "My God, I remember dancing to them at the old Astor back in '41."

Times Square was shown on the screen. Faces in the crowd stared up at the television cameras; people waved, huddled together in the cold wind. Despite the announcer's breathily excited tone, it was evident there was a poor turnout. In the living room, conversations resumed. "People don't care any more," Peg Thornton said, turning her back on the screen. Mangan sat down on the floor, cross-legged, facing the set. "Jamie, let me know when it's midnight, will you?" his father called. He nodded. He felt drunk. Behind him they were talking about the chances of Quebec's separating from the rest of Canada. His father said it was like living in the Weimar Republic. "It's already the end of this province as we knew it," his father told the others. But his father had, all his life, been exercised about politics. This place, these people, this conversation seemed a long way from New York. Last New Year's Eve, he remembered, Beatrice was in a play. He had gone to the Helen Hayes Theatre to pick her up, only to find that a hired limousine was waiting at the stage door. They had three parties to go to and she said they'd never find taxis. When he made some remark about the expense of a limo, she said the play's producer would pay for it.

Something was happening on television. "One minute to midnight!" the announcer cried. Mangan turned and called, "Dad? Here we go." He did not get up. The midnight countdown began. "Happy New Year!" people cried in the room behind him. He watched his father kiss Margrethe. There was a glut of kissing and handshaking, people moving around like politicians at a rally. Then Margrethe bent down and kissed him on the cheek. "Happy New Year, Jamie!" He felt like crying. The Royal Canadians played "Auld Lang Syne" and his father's guests began to sing along. But auld acquaintance *had* been forgot. He remembered that Turnbull was producer on that play. So it was Turnbull who paid for the limousine last New Year's. Beatrice and Turnbull would have a limousine tonight. Probably start off at some Park Avenue address with Turnbull's fellow Republicans. And, of course, they would drop in later at the Connells', making an entrance, people asking, Who's that Bea's with, no, I didn't know, when was the breakup? Everyone agog, everyone loves gossip.

"Happy New Year," his father said, leaning down, putting a hand on his shoulder. "How are you? Are you all right?"

"I'm fine. Happy New Year."

"I think we can turn that off now," his father said, and did.

"Oh, Pat?" someone called. "Do you have any more vodka?" And his father was gone, the set turned off. He stared at his own vague reflection on the dead screen. People would be kissing Beatrice, wishing her a Happy New Year, probably saying nice things about her new romance. She smiling her Beatrice Abbot smile, telling them how wonderful she feels, how happy she is. Her graph goes up and up. Even when a play fails, she gets good notices. She's a winner, one of the All-American winners. And if she ditches you, it's because you're a loser. A Canadian loser.

Time to rewrite Byron's lines:

> Her love was of her life a thing apart,
> 'Twas my whole goddamned existence.

Well, that's over. Happy New Year. He shut his eyes and rocked to and fro on his heels. All around him the roar of talk. "Bitch," he said softly. It was comforting to say it. It was her fault. There was no point in pretending to be fair about her any more. I hate her. I hate her.

came a noise which grew louder until it sounded like a distant chainsaw. It did not come from the small road which led to the lake but from the lake itself. Mangan, who had been dozing in the living room of the ski cottage, got up and went to the window. Behind a scrim of bare winter boughs, the lake, opaque and white, its icy flats circled by snow-covered hills bristled with a stubble of black, stripped elm. Somewhere out there in that frozen world the angry sound grew, until his eyes, narrowed against the blinding whiteness, sighted an object moving on the ice. It came nearer, passing by, close to the window, a bright yellow snowmobile driven by a youth, his vermilion wool cap and scarlet parka giving him the look of a hobgoblin as he hunched over his irritating machine. The noise died to silence.

Beyond, in the kitchen, the old refrigerator went on cycle, beginning its high, tiny whine. Here there was no telephone. Waking in this room, he felt again linked to the shabby summer cottages of his childhood, to that remembered feeling of being at the lake, absolved from all duties, unreachable, on the edge of wilderness. How pleasant it would be to stay on here after his father and Margrethe left, reading, going for walks, cooking his own meals, maybe writing something. But that was another daydream. For although there must be two hundred thousand dollars in their joint certificates of deposit, he felt he could not in honesty touch that. He had only about five hundred dollars in his own account. It was possible that Weinberg had already instructed Beatrice to redeposit the certificates in her own name. It was her money, after all.

Money. "You mustn't worry like this," Beatrice used to tell him. "Worry, worry, worry," she teased him. "I don't want you to make a whole lot of money. We won't need a lot of money. The way I feel about you I could live with you on food stamps in a two-room cold-water flat in the Bronx and be happier than with any other man in the world." And she meant it. Even though, as he later discovered, she didn't know what food stamps were. And he believed her. Because that was in the beginning when it had just happened.

He was twenty-seven at the time and a reporter on the Toronto *Globe and Mail*. A special overnight train had been laid on by Canadian National Railway to bring Zero Mostel and several other Broadway stars up to Toronto to perform in a charity benefit. The *Globe and Mail* was one of the sponsors of this event and so Mangan was sent to New York, to ride up on the train, write a general story on the benefit, and also interview Mostel for the paper's Saturday entertainment page. At the last minute the features editor tossed three extra clippings on the desk. "That's some stuff on Beatrice Abbot," he said. "You might fit her in if you have time. The word is, she may be the next Mrs. René Chandler."

René Chandler, well known in Toronto, was the heir to Algonquin Metals, twice married and in his early thirties. Mangan had never heard of Beatrice Abbot, but on reading the clippings learned that she was twenty-five and in the beginning of her fame, having won a Tony Award that year for her performance in *Major Barbara* on Broadway, and headlines by walking off the set at Warner Brothers on her first film because, she said, "The script is a lot of old rubbish and the star hasn't been sober in three years."

On the show train Mangan did not recognize Beatrice Abbot from her newspaper photograph and had to have her pointed out to him in the parlor car. When he asked for an interview, she said it was too noisy there and invited him to come back to her bedroom. After the interview she offered him a Scotch. He did not keep his appointment with Zero Mostel that night and in fact had to use her intercession to reschedule it for the following afternoon. Mangan and Beatrice Abbot spent the night together in her train bedroom. After that, they were rarely separated.

Mangan fell in love instantly and without reservation. He did not ask himself what sort of person Beatrice Abbot might be. He did not know her views on politics or on a dozen other subjects. Indeed, if at that time he had discovered them to be radically opposed to his own, it is unlikely, given his state of mind, that he would have thought twice about it. He did ask her about René Chandler, but she said that was a gossip columnist's invention. And he did wonder why she slept with him that first night and who were his predecessors. She said she had never been in love before. She had never felt anything remotely like this. She could not believe that this had happened to her but, now that it had, nothing must ever separate them. When she had finished the benefit show, she declared she wouldn't go back to New York until she was forced to go. And when that time did come (she had to report for rehearsals for a play to which she had been committed), they decided, impulsively, that he would give up his job on the *Globe* and join her in New York in a few weeks. Those weeks he spent job hunting in Toronto, finally securing a part-time position in the New York office of the Canadian Broadcasting Corporation. The pay was not enough for him to live on, but it was his *annus mirabilis* when everything seemed possible, when every wish was likely to come true. And so two days before he was due to leave Toronto, *Maclean's* magazine hired him to do four pieces on the U.S. and *Saturday Night* commissioned him to write a biweekly column on New York theater. He moved into Beatrice's Chelsea flat at the end of June, and four months later, on her urging, they got married. The ceremony took place early one October morning at City Hall, with two of Beatrice's theatrical friends as witnesses. The officiating clerk, seeing the name of Beatrice Abbot on the forms, ran into his private office and returned with a camera, asking if he could be photographed with the newlyweds. They went on to a wedding luncheon at the Four Seasons given by Beatrice's agent. There were twenty guests, all of them Beatrice's friends and colleagues. Later they spent the afternoon wandering hand-in-hand among the pictures in the Frick Collection until it was time for tea at the Plaza with Beatrice's lawyer and his wife. That night Beatrice had a performance, and when Mangan went to pick her up afterward, he discovered her fellow actors in the company all dressed and ready to take them both out to a late-night supper at Sardi's.

As the wedding went, so went those first years. He was in love with her. She was in love with him. And the world was in love with her. In *The New York Times* Clive Barnes wrote that she was "the most accomplished actress to appear on the New York stage in the last two decades," and another critic characterized her as "the American dream girl next door." As for Mangan, the CBC seemed satisfied with his work and he began to make regular broadcasts to Canada from the United Nations. In those years he co-edited an anthology of Canadian poetry which was published by McClelland & Stewart in Toronto and widely reviewed in Canada. He also worked on a long poem and simultaneously on a series of "imitations," roughly translated from Cree legends, in the then-fashionable manner of Robert Lowell.

They were in love. When Mangan walked out with Beatrice on his arm, he knew that other men envied him. As for Beatrice, she had said from the beginning that she never realized what happiness was like until she met him. From the beginning it was an article of their private faith that their sudden going to bed together was much more than an overwhelming sexual attraction. It was love, that romantic falling in love one read about but rarely encountered in real life. And the second article of their belief was that as long as they loved each other in this way nothing or no one could come between them. But in the fifth year of their marriage, that belief was tested. Beatrice made a sudden leap to a new level of celebrity. She was nominated for a Motion Picture Academy Award as Best Supporting Actress. At once she was invited to appear on national television talk shows and shortly afterward found that she could no longer go into a New York department store without being recognized and pestered for autographs.

In that year, coincidentally, Mangan's fortunes diminished. *Maclean's* magazine, responding to the new Canadian nationalism, found it editorially inexpedient to run so many American articles. Similarly, *Saturday Night* changed management and dropped his New York column. As always, the CBC job did not pay enough to live on, and his efforts to find assignments in the American magazine market were unsuccessful. He wrote and submitted an outline for a book on the Canadian National Ballet. Fourteen publishers turned it down. When he worried out loud about money, Beatrice became indignant. "But money is *secondary*, darling. It's being together that matters. Things will look up for you, you'll see. Anyway, worrying like this is simple male chauvinism. If *you* were earning it, I wouldn't worry. We have plenty of money. So let's just enjoy it."

But he could not. They had slipped into a style of living which, even in his most optimistic forecasts, he knew he alone could not provide. It also seemed to him that they were spending more and enjoying it less. Why must they always eat at Lutèce, or the Côte Basque, or whichever new and expensive restaurant *The New York Times* had written about the week before? The apartment on Fifty-first Street was in a cul-de-sac inhabited by millionaires. And even when they retired to their beach house in the Hamptons to live the rural life, they wound up giving catered parties which cost a thousand dollars a throw.

There were other things. If he said something witty it would often be quoted back to him as "that marvelous thing Beatrice said the other night." In fact, as it became increasingly clear that people listened more intently when his subject was Beatrice, he had begun to act as her shill, talking of her new projects, giving out the gossip of her days. Worse than those people who wanted only to hear about Beatrice were those to whom she was the only person in the marriage. People like Bloomfield, a producer. Once, while waiting in his outer office, he overheard Bloomfield on the phone. "No, we need first-class transportation for two," Bloomfield told a film company. "No, not her hairdresser. Her husband. Yes, her husband. Yes, Jamie Mangan is his name. No, I'm not kidding. J-a-m-i-e." Or the headwaiter at Sardi's, who would pick up two menus as he approached, nod to him as to a fellow servant, then move past him, his features composing a smile as he greeted Beatrice and led her toward one of the best tables. Or the people who asked, "Where's Beatrice?" when he entered a room alone. None of it mattered, really. It was unimportant. A man who resented his wife's success would be a man who did not love her. And he loved her.

And she loved him. She still said there was no one else she wanted to be with. Trouble was, while he now had more free time than ever to be with her, she was constantly in rehearsal, taking ballet classes, at the hairdresser's, performing, being interviewed, lunching with a producer, attending a business meeting, planning an actors' benefit or some other function at which his presence would be superfluous. He finished his long epic poem. He assembled and wrote an introduction to a book of Canadian stories. Neither of these ventures succeeded in finding a publisher, and so he had a serious talk with himself and decided that Beatrice was right. One only lived once. He should enjoy it. And so, when she was asked to do a film in London, he applied for a leave of absence from his CBC job and flew with her, first class, all expenses paid by the film company. They stayed in a suite in the Dorchester and were surprised to find themselves the only non-Arabs on their floor. When Beatrice finished her work in the film, they flew on to Paris, where the studio had booked them into the Ritz, and their few excursions to the Left Bank were, for Mangan, painful reminders of how much his life had changed since the carefree impoverished summer he spent long ago living in a student hotel in the rue Jacob. But Beatrice did not miss the Left Bank. Her memories were of the Ritz, Ledoyen, Lucas-Carton, schoolgirl outings with her father, dinner parties with his rich friends. She called some of these friends, and they were duly asked over for luncheons and drinks. She shopped and went to the opera and the ballet. She said they must go on to Venice and Rome, but Bloomfield called on the transatlantic phone, asking her to please read a great new play by a young playwright called Frank Fortini. She read the play and pronounced herself excited. They flew back to New York at once. When Mangan walked into the CBC offices on Park Avenue after an absence of nearly three months, no one asked where he had been. His immediate superior told him the new man on the UN broadcasts had done an especially good job. "He has a fresh perspective on the Canadian role," Mangan's superior said. "I'm tempted to let him do a few more. Don't worry, Jamie. We'll find other things for you."

Beatrice went into rehearsals, and at once Fortini, the playwright, began to show up at the apartment at all hours of the day and evening, usually bringing new revisions of his script. He was twenty-eight years old and six feet four inches tall. He was trying to kick the smoking habit by chewing some foul-smelling tobacco plug, frequently spitting the juice into their living-room plants. From the beginning he treated Mangan as though he were a stranger who had wandered in illegally off the street. Beatrice had the only speaking role in the play. The other actors were mimes. So when Fortini would show up at the apartment, he acted out the mime roles himself, while Beatrice spoke his new lines in monologue. Mangan found himself spending a great deal of time in the bedroom with the door shut, trying to avoid the sound of her voice. "Why can't Fortini hold his rehearsals in a theater like everybody else?" he asked her.

"Don't you like him, then?"

"It's not a matter of whether I like him. He's disrupting our life, coming here at ten o'clock at night without even phoning first. I mean, do you like it?"

"Not necessarily."

"Then why do you allow it? You never allowed anyone else to treat you this way."

"Frank is not an ordinary person."

"What's that supposed to mean?"

"I think he's a genius."

"Oh, Jesus."

"No, I do. I really do. And I think it's my job to recognize his genius and help him do things the way that's best for him. Very few people are geniuses. I'm not one. You're not one. So how can we judge the way they behave?"

"I see. All right, so I'm not a genius. And I don't chew tobacco. Come to think of it, what am I?"

"Well, you're my husband, for one thing. So stop shouting at me. It's not like you."

But he could not stop. "I'm your husband. That's it, isn't it? That's what I am. That's exactly what I am. In fact, it's all I am."

"Darling, don't say that. It's not true." She began to cry. "I love you. You're the one who matters. I'll tell him not to come here any more."

At once, he felt foolish and in the wrong. "No, no," he said. "It's okay. I'll buy him a spittoon."

They laughed, kissed, made up. But when Fortini's play opened to good reviews, a gossip columnist wrote that "there's talk of a starring relationship between Beatrice Abbot and Broadway's hottest new playwright." When Mangan read that, he experienced a rage of jealousy. He went to her and held out the newspaper. "Have you read this?"

"Well, what about it?"

"That's my question," he said. "What about it?"

"I'll tell you what about it," she said. "I want to have a baby. Why don't we?"

"But you said you didn't want children. I thought we decided."

"I want one now. I think it's time."

Almost a year later she was delivered of a son, stillborn, at Doctors Hospital. She said they would try again, but soon afterward went off to California to play a cameo role in a disaster movie in which a great many stars were playing similar roles. When she returned, she told him stories about Laurence Olivier, John Wayne, Bette Davis, and others. The baby was not mentioned.

Mangan was relieved. The way he felt just then, he could

see that if they had a child he would end up being father and mother to it. He had the time. She had not. That summer, in the sixth year of their marriage, they bought the beach house in Amagansett. He spent most of the summer out there working with the painters and single-handedly built a deck and a walkway to the sea. Beatrice came out from town every Wednesday and stayed till Sunday night. They worked on the house, gave no parties, and spent long lazy afternoons walking on the beach. It was a good time. They were together. He forgot his worries and resentments. They had only one life. And they were living it.

But that was the summer she met Perry Turnbull. He was to produce the play she would open in that fall. Mangan had met Turnbull only briefly, and when he asked Beatrice about him, he got the impression that she did not like him. She said the play's director called Turnbull "Cubelets" in reference to his family's sugar fortune. And that someone had said of him: "Money talks all right, but this money needs remedial speech therapy."

The play opened in October and got good reviews. It also played to sellout audiences. On the first Saturday in December, when she was playing a matinee, Beatrice phoned Mangan from the theater and asked him to meet her in the bar of the Stanhope Hotel at six. "I have to talk to you," she said.

"What's up?"

"Well, something *has* come up. But it will keep till I see you. Don't be late though, will you? I have to meet someone at the Metropolitan Museum at six-thirty."

"The Met?" he said. "Are you mixed up with that now?"

"I'll tell you about it at six."

When he arrived at the Stanhope, she was already sitting in the bar and had ordered drinks. He was surprised. The matinee got out at five-thirty so she must have jumped in a cab right after the final curtain. She was wearing her usual daytime uniform of pink Brooks Brothers shirt, tweed skirt, penny loafers, and a loosely tied camel's-hair overcoat. "Is Scotch all right for you?" she asked.

"Yes." He was surprised, too, at this ordering drinks in advance.

"I didn't want to waste any time," she said, smiling the Beatrice Abbot smile, but in a willed way, as though she was having difficulty with it. "I have to tell you something," she said. "I want to tell it to you quickly and then I want to go. Will you promise I can do that?"

"What is it?"

"I've thought of all kinds of ways to say this, but there isn't any way that's going to make it easy. So I'll just tell you I'm in love with Perry Turnbull and he's in love with me. I'm going to leave you. And you won't believe this, but I'm sorry. I'm very sorry."

"Perry Turnbull? But you said he was a fool."

"I did not."

"You made jokes about him."

"Other people did," she said. "I just told you what they said."

"But Turnbull? It doesn't make sense."

"It didn't make sense when you and I met," she said.

"Jesus Christ."

"Jamie, I'm sorry. I didn't know how I was going to face you today. But it's something I can't help. It's happened. I'm sorry."

"Well, *when* did it happen?" he asked, stupidly.

"Why go into it? Look, yesterday when you were at the CBC I went home in the middle of the day and packed some of my things and sent them to a hotel. I can pick up the rest of my stuff some other time."

"What do you mean? Do you mean you're leaving now?"

"Yes."

"My God."

"I thought the best thing would be if you hold on to the apartment and I'll move my things out to Amagansett. Is that fair? Or would you rather I kept the apartment and you took the beach house?"

"Look, I don't know. It doesn't matter."

"Well, anyway, I made a list of my things that are still there. I left it in the drawer in the hall table. It's just a suggestion of what you could send me. If you disagree with any items, strike them off."

He stared at the mural on the adjoining wall. It was a Dufy sort of pastel of the Eiffel Tower, some flowers, the Madeleine. Last spring they sat in this very bar talking about their trip to Paris. Now she was sleeping with Perry Turnbull. He remembered what he had been doing today. Addressing their Christmas cards.

"Do you know what I did today?" he told her. "I addressed our Christmas cards."

"You mean you've already done them?"

At once he was sorry he'd brought it up.

"Have you sealed the envelopes yet?" she asked.

"Oh, for Christ sake, I just said it ironically."

"But *have* you sealed them?"

"No. I left them open in case you wanted—what's it matter?"

"All right," she said. "I have an idea. I'll have a little notice printed saying we've separated and that from now on my address will be the beach house and that you'll be at the apartment. You could slip the notices in with the cards. It would be a way of letting people know what happened and how they can reach us."

"You mean, reach you."

She ignored that. She looked at her wristwatch. "By the way, I'll be speaking to Sy Weinberg tomorrow. I'll ask him if he can work out some financial settlement, okay? I realize that I'm the guilty party, so to speak. Whatever settlement we decide on, it should take that into account."

"Guilty party. So we're going to end in a cliché."

"Yes," she said. "I suppose so. I'll tell you the truth, I don't feel guilty. I feel sorry for you. But I don't feel guilty. It's happened and I feel happy—happier than I've ever been before."

"Well, that's nice," he said bitterly.

She gave him a look like a slap, then stood up, pulling her camel's-hair coat about her shoulders. From habit, he stood, too. "I'll say goodbye, then," she said. "Will you pay for the drinks? I have to meet someone. Goodbye, Jamie."

She turned and walked past the bar. The bartender smiled and waved to her. "Hi, Miss Abbot."

"Hi, Mike."

Mangan looked at the bar chit and left some money. He waited until she was out of the bar, then followed her. He did not know why he was following her. He did not want her to see him. He came out onto Fifth Avenue just as she crossed the street to the opposite side. She did not look back. He followed her as she walked toward the Metropolitan Museum, and stood watching as she walked up the monumental front steps under a set of huge flapping banners advertising the current show. A man in a camel's-hair coat the color of her own came out of the crowd of people waiting at the museum entrance and ran down, jumping three steps at a time, until he reached her. They embraced. He watched them for a moment as they talked excitedly. He saw her look back toward the Stanhope. But she did not see him. After a few moments, arm in arm, she and Turnbull walked down the steps and Turnbull signaled for a taxi.

Now, three weeks later, lying on the sofa in his father's rented cottage in Quebec, he saw them again, as they were that day, two people walking arm in arm down monumental steps under huge flapping white-and-red banners. It was the last time he had seen her until she showed up at the apartment yesterday afternoon, a stranger, a woman living another life.

Somewhere in the rear of the cottage the outer porch door slapped open. He had heard no car. He went to the kitchen to investigate, but found no one there. Inside the porch door, propping it ajar, was a dog-eared briefcase embossed with the letters ER, souvenir of his father's year of service as a member of a Canadian Royal Commission on the Press. He went outside. In the failing light his father, wearing a fur hat and a heavy Irish sweater, wrestled a wooden box from the trunk of his battered Dodge, and turned, calling out a greeting. With his high color and long gray hair, Pat Mangan, hefting the wooden box, reminded his son of a fish seller in some market.

"Let me help you with that, Dad. What is it, by the way?"

"It's the stuff you asked about. Family records. And the Mangan stuff."

Together they carried the box inside and set it on the kitchen table. Mangan picked a book out, turning its pages.

"Where's Margrethe?" his father said.

"What did you say, Dad?" he asked, still reading.

"Margrethe, is she still out skiing?"

"Yes, I guess so."

"Why don't you look at those later," his father said. "Let's get supper underway. All right?"

"Fine."

His father rummaged through the containers of food, then opened the refrigerator. Reluctantly, Mangan put down the book, a biography of James Clarence Mangan by the Reverend T. R. Drinan, M.A. "Pork chops," his father said. "Potatoes, peas, applesauce. Yes, that should do. So, tell me. What's your plan now? Are you going to get a divorce?"

"Yes. She wants one."

"And you. Do you?"

"Of course. I realize now I never should have married her."

"Do you like Cherries Jubilee?" his father asked. "I see we have tinned cherries and ice cream. All right, we'll have Cherries Jubilee for dessert. Tell me. Why do you think you never should have married her?"

Mangan hesitated. He had come here to talk to his father, but now realized he would not have chosen him as confidant were he in a normal state of mind. But I am not in a normal state, he told himself. And besides, who else will listen to me?

"Well, for one thing," he said, "I have no friends any more. Everyone I know now is Beatrice's friend. Including the people who used to be my friends."

His father sat down at the kitchen table. "Well, Bea's always been very popular. I can understand that." He smiled and gestured. "But surely that's not . . ." He did not finish the sentence.

"Since she left," Mangan said, "something strange has happened to me. It's as if I—the person I was—your son— the person I used to be—it's as if there's nobody there any more. Sometimes I feel as if I'm going mad. Except that there's no me to *go* mad."

"Wait now," his father said. "I'm not sure that makes sense."

"I know it sounds weird. But I mean it. Beatrice and I have been living her career. And to tell you the truth, we've been living on her money. And now that she's walked out on me, it's as if I don't exist any more. Does that make sense?"

His father got up, took Scotch from a cupboard, and poured some neat into two jelly glasses. "Here," he said, handing one over. "It's like any breakup. It's rough. But surely this business of her career and her money is secondary. Surely the important thing is that you were in love with her and she was with you, and now she's left you. The person who's been left always feels badly. Remember your mother."

"But it's not the same thing at all," Mangan said. "After you left, Mother was angry, but she was still in love with you. Still is, perhaps. I'm not in love with Beatrice."

"Are you sure?"

"I saw her yesterday. It was like meeting a stranger."

"You felt nothing at all?"

"I don't know. I know that I don't think about her any more. I think about me. The main thing I feel now isn't anger, it's a sort of panic. I think what those years of being married to her have done to me. The phone never rings now that she's gone. Nobody writes to me. Nothing happens. It's as though I'd ceased to exist."

"Nonsense," his father said. "You broke up, when? Three weeks ago? You'll get over this. You've got your life ahead of you."

"Have I? When you were thirty-four, you were already managing editor of *The Gazette*. At thirty-six I'm nothing. Just an underpaid CBC hack."

His father rose, filled an aluminum pot with water, and put it on the stove. He seemed embarrassed by this turn in the conversation. "Well, most people don't achieve just what they hoped for," his father said. "Not the very ambitious ones. And yours is a special ambition."

"What ambition?"

"Poetry."

"That was a long time ago."

"Was it?" his father said. "I wonder."

"No, no, I'm not a poet. Nobody thinks of me as a poet."

"You still write poetry, don't you?"

"I try."

"You mean," his father said, "that you're a poet, but not a recognized poet."

There was no point in arguing with his father. His father did not understand about poetry.

"As a matter of fact," his father said, "I was very pleased last night when you showed an interest in our ancestor. Asking for these books, and so on."

"I didn't ask for the books, Dad. I asked about family history."

"But you did mention Mangan the poet," his father said. "I remember, years ago, you were excited when you found out your hero, James Joyce, thought highly of him."

"I remember that it didn't seem at all certain that we're really related to him."

"But there must be something in it," his father said. "I mean, my father wasn't interested in poetry, he thought it sissy stuff. But somehow, somewhere, his family believed they were the direct descendants of James Clarence Mangan."

"Based on a rumor in one biography that Mangan had a son. Wasn't that it? An unproven story."

"Well, I suppose," his father said. "Yes, in a way. But I must say, when you showed such a great interest in poetry, I was convinced it was in your blood. I had great hopes once upon a time. I still have, I think . . ." His father did not finish, but finished his drink instead.

"Hopes that what? That I'd follow in his footsteps, and die of malnutrition, penniless, a drunkard and a drug addict?"

"Now, hold on," his father said. "Wasn't it your hero, Joyce, who said that Mangan's addiction to drink and drugs, his dying of neglect, malnutrition, and so on—that that was the sort of life a true artist might be expected to live?"

"I don't agree. I think a life like that obscures the work.

The *poète maudit* is remembered for his drugs, horrors, escapades—for his life itself."

"Well, when *I* visited Ireland," his father said, "I found the opposite. James Clarencé Mangan's poems are in all the schoolbooks. And they're still admired. Listen!" His father held up his hand, and for a moment Mangan thought he was going to recite. But instead he rose and looked through the kitchen window. A car could be heard coming up the back road. "Margrethe," his father said happily, forgetting the discussion, going out of the back door into the cold to open the car door for her. Watching them through the window, seeing Margrethe pull back her yellow parka hood to receive his father's kiss, Mangan felt a flush of embarrassment. How could he expect his father, boisterously kissing his new bride, to take seriously these self-centered fears by his son of a former marriage, fears that must seem as foolish to his father as the long-ago terrors of that little boy who had to be carried piggyback across the lawn because of nonexistent snakes?

"Well, hello, Jamie!" Margrethe's voice suddenly brightened the little kitchen. He received her usual warm embrace and a cold-cheeked kiss. "Is this supper? What are we having?"

"Pork chops and peas," his father said. "Everything's under control. How was the skiing?"

"Fantastic. But we had to wait so long for the lift. It was worth it, though."

"Good. I must try to get up there tomorrow," his father said. "Now, let's clear these books off. Jamie, will you take them into the living room?"

He picked up the wooden box and went in with it, switching on the lamp by the window. He took from the box the family Bible, fingering its scuffed covers, remembering how it used to sit on the top shelf of his father's study. In the flyleaf, a column of lives. He sat in the pool of lamplight, the page open on his knee. The ink had faded to sepia tone on the first entry. A marriage. *Patrick James Mangan, to Kathleen Driscoll, 1862.* Their children's birth-dates followed, then the eldest son's marriage, then the children of that issue. The last entry must have been made by Mangan's grandfather. It recorded his father's birth date: *James Patrick Mangan, 8 August 1917.* The end of the line? Why didn't my father record my birth?

He raised his head to ask the question, but his father and Margrethe had left the kitchen and were laying the table in the dining-room alcove. He put the Bible back in the box and picked up an old photograph album, a book he did not remember ever seeing before. The first half of the album consisted of snapshots, many in sepia tones, positioned on the album's pages by black passe-partout triangles. Some were captioned in a tiny, neat script. Books of photographs had always interested him, and he at once settled himself in his chair, turning the first pages. But, as he did, a number of loose photographs slid out from the back of the book and fell on the living-room floor. Some were in frames. He picked them up, shuffling them together. Ancient tintypes, calotypes, and even daguerreotypes, they were too heavy to be affixed in the book itself. One by one, as though dealing cards, he played them on the opened pages of the album. Against backgrounds of stretched white sheets, or painted canvas, men, women, and children stared at the camera, statue-still, as the unseen photographer, head ostriched under his cloth, prepared to loose his magnesium explosion. Often, the name and address of the photographic studio, scrolled in elaborate curlicues, adorned the bottoms of the photographs, and as Mangan read off the names of Irish cities—Galway, Cork—it came to him that these long-ago kin of his were members of the first generation in human history to see themselves plain, not in a lake's reflection or in the ephemeral shimmer of a looking glass, or distorted by the talents or whim of a portrait painter's brush, but fixed forever as they were in life, awkward in ill-fitting new clothes bought or made for those great occasions of first communions, confirmations, weddings, ordinations. He paused to look at a first-communion portrait of a boy in a white sailor suit with white patent-leather boots, holding in his hand a white prayer book. He turned the portrait over. There was no name on the back. He let it fall on the pages of the album and then saw the next photograph in the deck, a portrait in a scrolled brass frame preserved under glass, a small, shimmering, mirror-bright picture on silver-coated copperplate. It measured about three inches by four and showed a man facing the camera, a head-and-shoulders portrait taken against a plain background. The man wore a silk cravat, a white shirt, and a dark cape tied loosely about his neck by two broad tapes. His longish hair fell to his shoulders and his slight uncertain smile revealed a missing upper tooth. What made Mangan stare as though transfixed by a vision was that the face in the photograph was his own. He turned the daguerreotype over. On the back of the frame, written in a sloping looped script in the top right-hand corner, was the notation: (*J.M. 1847?*)

"Dad?" Mangan said. He felt he could barely trust himself to speak.

His father had come back into the kitchen with Margrethe. "I think I have a little cooking brandy on the lower shelf of the cupboard," Margrethe was saying.

"If not, we can always use whiskey," his father said.

"Dad, come and look at this."

His father turned and walked into the living room. Mangan held out the photograph. His father looked at it, then bent forward into a pool of lamplight and said in a half whisper, "Margrethe, come and see this."

She came and bent over, looking with him. "It's Jamie!"

Mangan's father held the old photograph up near his

son's face. "My God. Whoever this was, he's certainly related to you, Jamie."

"Look at the back."

"J.M. 1847. Funny. I don't remember seeing this before. Was it in that album?"

"Yes, in this loose pile at the back. What year did Mangan die?"

His father handed back the photograph and went to the box of books. He picked up one of the volumes and opened it. "Let's see. There's a chronology here someplace. Yes. 1849. He was born in 1803."

"So this could be him?"

"It could be. Mangan would have been forty-four in 1847."

"The only thing is, his name was James *Clarence* Mangan."

"No, no," his father said. "Clarence wasn't a baptismal name. He adopted it as a *nom de plume*. He used to sign some of his early pieces just 'Clarence.'"

"God," Mangan said. "Imagine if it *is*."

"Wait." His father rummaged in the box again. "There are some frontispieces. Drawings. I don't think there was ever any photograph of him."

His father opened the books and laid them side by side, four frontispieces in all. One was a pencil drawing, showing the head of the poet, his hair long and thinning, his eyes closed. It was attributed as a deathbed sketch. Another was a photograph of a medallion profile. There was also a small volume whose frontispiece was a silhouette of Mangan in 1822, when he would have been nineteen years old. The third book contained a small sketch of an eccentric figure perusing a book at a bookstall. This figure wore a high conical hat like a witch's headgear. A short cape covered his jacket, and beneath the cape a large umbrella was tucked under his arm like a set of bagpipes. The last frontispiece was an amateurish drawing listed as being from the *Freeman's Journal*, a periodical of the day. All these drawings placed side by side differed from each other as would various police artists' renderings of a criminal suspect. On the evidence of the drawings alone, Mangan could see that he bore a faint resemblance to the dead poet. The photograph was something entirely different. It was his face. It could be no other.

"Funny that I didn't notice that photo before now," his father said, picking up one of the books. "Of course, in the days when I was looking into this stuff, Jamie was still a baby. Now, take these two likenesses. The deathbed sketch by—who is it?—Sir Frederick William Burton. And this medallion by George Millbourne. I'd say both of them show some resemblance to you. What do *you* think, Margrethe?"

"The medallion," Margrethe said and laughed. "That's Jamie's nose, all right."

"Is my nose really that big?"

"Come to think of it," his father said, "this would make a nice little page 3 local feature: DESCENDANT'S ASTONISHING LIKENESS TO DEAD POET. All we have to do is photograph you against a plain backdrop in exactly the same pose. The likeness is uncanny."

"Pat! Your pork chops!" Margrethe cried.

His father turned and ran into the kitchen, Margrethe following. Mangan sat down again, looking at the photograph, and then as on an inspiration began to hunt through the pages of the larger of the two biographies, searching for a physical description of the poet. His father and Margrethe were busy with the last stages of preparation of the meal. They called out to ask if he wanted another drink, but he did not answer. A giddy excitement filled him; he forgot himself, forgot Beatrice, was caught up in a search whose object he did not understand. Even when the meal was ready and the dishes were being brought into the dining-room alcove, he did not abandon his book.

"Come on, Jamie," his father said. "Leave that for a while. We're going to have our New Year's dinner."

"Did you find anything?" Margrethe asked.

He turned back the pages of the book. "In 1849, in the year of his death, a friend of Mangan's—a Father Meehan—wrote that Mangan was about five feet seven inches tall, slightly stooped, with a beautifully shaped head. Another description mentions his very bright blue eyes."

"Well, you're taller than that," Margrethe said. "But you certainly have the bright blue eyes."

"Dinner is served," his father reminded them.

"It also mentions his pale and intellectual face. And his silver-white locks."

"*My* hair will be silver-white before I get to eat," his father said.

"Okay. Coming. But listen to this. 'The dress of this spectral-looking man was singularly remarkable, taken down at hazard from some old clothes shop, a baggy pantaloon, a short coat, closely buttoned, a blue cloth cloak still shorter. The hat was in keeping with this habiliment, broad-leaved and steeple-shaped—"

"Jamie!" his father said.

"Sorry." Unwillingly, he put the book aside and went to join them. His father poured wine and, as they sat down to table, held up his glass in toast. "Well, here's to the New Year and to all of us."

"Happy New Year, Pat," Margrethe said, raising her glass. "And a happy New Year to you, Jamie. What a strange feeling it must be for you to find your—what's the word, I forget—it's *Vorfahr* in German."

"Ancestor," Mangan said. "Although, in this case, maybe *Doppelgänger* is a better word."

His father clinked glasses, then erupted in a sneeze of

laughter. "And there I was ten minutes ago saying I once had hopes you'd be a poet like James Clarence. Thank God, you only look like him."

"I don't know. Maybe, after all, I'd be glad to change places with him. I suppose, in his way, he did something with his life."

"What are we going to do with this fellow?" his father said to Margrethe. "He's taking a very, very gloomy view of things these days. He'll get over it, won't he?"

"Of course," Margrethe said, smiling. "Of course he will. That photo *is* amazing, though. What was he, Jamie? Your great-great-grandfather?"

"Yes. Great-great."

"I don't really know anything about your family," Margrethe said. "Except that they come from Ireland. Pat never told me anything. I wonder why."

"You never asked me," his father said.

"Well, tell us now," Mangan said.

"Come on. Why, it would only bore Margrethe. Let's just enjoy this wine. It's a Corton, in case you haven't noticed. And we have two bottles."

"It won't bore me," Margrethe said. "Please, Pat."

"Oh, I suppose in that case," his father said, "why not?" He smiled and sipped his wine. "Actually, we're pretenders to the Mangan crown. I mean, the relative Jamie is interested in, James Clarence Mangan, may not be our relative at all. We have no real proof that we're related. Most of the accounts of Mangan's life state quite definitely that he never married. He was one of four children, three boys and a girl, and according to all of his biographers except one—who I'll come to later—he and his younger brother, William, were bachelors and lived together as drunks and derelicts. So the older brother, John, was the only one to carry on the line. But one biographer—a Father Drinan—insists that Mangan married a widow from a place called Skibbereen in West Cork. She was on a trip to Dublin around 1839 when she met him, and they were married, Father Drinan says, in 1841, and a son was born in that same year. But, apparently, Mangan's drinking and opium taking drove them apart and the widow left him and took the child back to Skibbereen, where she owned two shops. Now what excited me was a family Bible which I found together with Mangan's poems and the Drinan biography and some correspondence from a Father Drinan with the Trinity College Library in Dublin, trying to trace our connection to Mangan the poet. It seems he'd traced back as far as a Patrick James Mangan born in 1841 in Dublin, whom Father Drinan thought to be the son of the poet himself. That Patrick James Mangan was taken by his mother to a village called Drishane in West Cork."

"And you went there yourself once?" Mangan asked.

"Yes. I wrote to Drishane and found there were Mangans still living there. And when your mother and I visited Ireland about fifteen years ago, we got up one morning and drove there from Cork, but your mother came down with food poisoning on the way and we had to turn around and go back without ever meeting those relatives. If they were relatives. To this day, I don't really know if I'm a great-grandson of the poet or not." His father smiled, picked up the wine bottle, and in dumb show asked permission to refill their glasses.

"So Drishane's where Grandfather came from?"

"No. Your grandfather was brought up in Cork and emigrated when he was seventeen."

"Six years younger than I was when I emigrated here from Denmark with my parents," Margrethe said. "I was twenty-three."

"With your hair still in pigtails," his father said fondly. "I wish I could have seen you then. That was when you went to work at Eaton's, wasn't it?"

"Yes," Margrethe said, and laughed. "My first job was at a counter, selling leg warmers."

"Pigtails and leg warmers," his father said, smiling. "When was it I met you? It was about four years after that, wasn't it?"

"Yes," Margrethe said. She turned to Mangan. "I was doing publicity for Air Canada. Your father was in Quebec City on a press junket." She laughed and pointed to Mangan's father. "He asked me to go to a dance."

"Which brings me back to family history," his father said. "*My* father landed in Quebec, seventeen years old, and went on to Toronto, where he got a job as a clerk in the Canadian Pacific Railway and came rapidly up in the world. He was moved to the head office in Montreal and ended up as assistant comptroller of the whole CPR system. Pretty good for a first-generation Irish immigrant."

"And he had two children, right?" Margrethe said. "You and your brother."

"Yes, Jack and I," his father said. He raised his glass and looked at the color of the wine. "Jack never married and I had Jamie. Jamie is the last of our line. Well, of course, not yet. You'll remarry, won't you, Jamie?"

"Never mind Jamie," Margrethe said to his father. "What about us? Did you forget?"

His father smiled, at once complicit and embarrassed. "Well, anyway. Enough history. I'll make the Cherries Jubilee." He rose, took the second wine bottle from the dresser, filled their glasses, then put the bottle on the table. "Let me help you," Margrethe said.

"All right, darling," his father said. "Have some more wine, Jamie."

He watched as his father and Margrethe went into the kitchen, their voices suddenly dropping to whispers. Were they talking about having a baby? Beatrice and I, the stillborn son I never saw. Fetus M., his only name.

He sat, the glass lax in his hand. The voices in the kitchen seemed strange as the sound of dolphins. Dead. As I feel dead. Cast off, cuckolded, dead. He turned and placed his glass on the table, his hand beginning its familiar tremor. And in that moment, oddly gleaming under glass, the photograph stared up at him, dispelling his dread, filling him with that now-familiar sense of giddy elation. For the first time since he had watched Beatrice walk down the museum steps with her lover, he felt cured. He picked up his cure, his antidote, the face of Europe's first *poète maudit*. He stared at that face and the photograph eyes stared back, lit, it seemed, with the same unearthly excitement he now felt.

"Ready?" His father's voice, loud, unexpected, sounded at the kitchen door. His father stood, holding the dish aloft. Margrethe lit a match and ran it over the pool of liquid on the plate. Around the cherries and ice cream, a thin blue flame arose in aureole. His father advanced and laid the dish on the table.

Mangan stared at the bubbling blue flame. The face that was his face seemed to rise before him in its haze, a genie he had summoned to restore his spirit. A genie who had vanquished Beatrice, that robber of his soul. Giddily, he raised his glass. "To Mangan the poet," he cried. "To my resurrection. To my life!"

_____ *The following morning,* when his father and Margrethe set off for the ski slopes, Mangan settled on the living-room sofa, surrounded by books, with a pad for notes and torn slips of newspaper to use as page markers. He did not eat lunch and barely greeted the skiers when they returned at dusk. At six, his father went to the dining-room alcove to write an editorial for the Saturday edition of *The Gazette*, while Margrethe began to prepare dinner. At seven, when Mangan was called to the table, he did not realize what time it was. All day he had been living another man's life. Now, released, he became so garrulous it was noticed. "I don't believe it," Margrethe said to him. "Do you realize that yesterday on the drive out from Montreal you hardly spoke two words to me."

"I'm sorry. I just feel a lot better today."

"I'm glad to hear it," his father said. "All that gloomy talk yesterday about not surviving. It seems what you needed was to find yourself an ancestor. How are you getting on with your reading?"

"Great. It's really astonishing. I've read the Father Drinan biography and also the O'Donoghue one, which seems to be the most complete and official-sounding. But I find the Drinan argument convincing. And the most amazing thing of all is the poems themselves. I remember years ago, when I first looked at them, I didn't like them. But now when I read them, even though I don't like them any more than I did then, I seem to remember them word for word. It's as though they were my own poems. I feel I can recite them to you. It's strange. Even though they're not good. All those cheap tricks and jingles."

"Now, hold on," his father said. "He wrote some good ones. 'My Dark Rosaleen,' for instance."

"My dark *who?*" Margrethe asked.

"Ireland," his father said. "My Dark Rosaleen is Ireland. Wait, I'll read you a verse. Where's the book, Jamie?"

"No need," Mangan said. "I told you. It's uncanny, but I can remember it, after reading it just once. Listen:

> "O, the Erne shall run red,
>   With redundance of blood,
>   The Earth shall rock beneath our tread,
>   And flames wrap hill and wood,
>   And gun-peal and slogan-cry
>   Wake many a glen serene,
>   Ere you shall fade, ere you shall die,
>   My Dark Rosaleen!
>   My own Rosaleen!
>   The Judgement Hour must first be nigh,
>   Ere you can fade, ere you can die,
>   My Dark Rosaleen!"

"I like it," Margrethe said. "It has a great ring."

"Yes, that one's not bad," Mangan agreed. "Corny but powerful."

"Corny or not," his father said, "that's the poem that

made him Ireland's greatest poet. That and a few others he wrote at the time of the famine."

"No, no," Mangan said. "Mangan may be my double, but Yeats is Ireland's greatest poet."

"Believe me," his father said, "for the common people of Ireland, Mangan is still the big man. His poetry was the stuff that sent men out to kill the landlords."

"But Yeats's poetry did that, too. Remember what he wrote about his play, *Cathleen ni Houlihan?*

> "Did that play of mine send out
> Certain men the English shot?"

"For the sake of argument," his father said, "I'll grant you that. But our supposed ancestor is the one who struck a chord in the Irish soul. There's a street and a square named after him in Dublin. And his statue stands in Saint Stephen's Green."

"I wonder, does the statue look like Jamie?" Margrethe said.

"I'll let you know. I'm going to save up and go there this year."

"See what vanity does," his father told Margrethe. "Before he knew he looked like a poet, he had no interest in Ireland."

"But *is* this the poet?" Carefully Mangan unwrapped the photograph from the handkerchief in his pocket. All day he had resisted looking at it. Now, as the eyes stared up at him, he again experienced a giddy sensation of elation. "It's me, all right," he said. "It's an ancestor of mine. But was the Drinan biography right? From everything else I've read about Mangan, women played little or no part in his life. Poetry was his life. Books and booze. Let me read you a description I came across this afternoon. It's by John Mitchel, an Irish patriot and lawyer, and it describes his first sight of Mangan in the library at Trinity College, Dublin."

"My God," his father said. "Are we not to have a meal in this house without readings from the Mangan canon?"

But Margrethe laughed and leaned across the table, touching his father's arm. "Shh, Pat, shh!"

Mangan rose and brought the book to the table. He sat, riffling its unevenly cut pages. "Here we are. This is what Mitchel wrote: 'The first time the present biographer saw Clarence Mangan was in this wise: being in the College library and having occasion for a book in that gloomy apartment of the institution called the "Fagel" library, which is in the innermost recess of the stately building, an acquaintance pointed out to me a man perched on the top of a ladder, with the whispered information that the figure was Clarence Mangan. It was an unearthly and ghostly figure in a brown garment; the same garment, to all appearance, which lasted to the day of his death. The blanched hair was totally unkempt; the corpse-like features still as marble; a large book was in his hands, and all his soul was in that book. I had never heard of Clarence Mangan before, and knew not for what he was celebrated, whether as a magician, a poet, or a murderer; yet took a volume and spread it on a table, not to read, but with a pretence of reading to gaze upon this spectral creature upon the ladder.' That's Mitchel's description. An eyewitness account."

"I like that part," his father said. " 'A large book was in his hands, and all his soul was in that book.' " He smiled and repeated. " 'All his soul was in that book.' "

"Trouble is," Mangan said. "There's a discrepancy between that description and this photograph. I'm thinking of the blanched hair. I'm going a little gray and so is the man in the photograph. But neither one of us has 'blanched' hair."

"Let me see that again," his father said, and took up the

photograph, studying it. "Yes, the hair is only partly gray. But in any case, I suspect, Mitchel's description isn't a factual one. He's out to make an effect. Corpse-like features, et cetera. That's not what I'd call straight reporting."

"There must be other descriptions of Mangan in the biographies that I haven't read yet. Tomorrow I thought I'd read the other two. They're both short. When are we going back to town, by the way?"

"Let's see," his father said. "I'd thought about sometime late tomorrow afternoon."

"We might as well have supper here first," Margrethe said. "If that's all right with you?"

His father considered. "Well, I have to drop in at the paper tomorrow night."

"Look at him, Jamie," Margrethe said. "This year he promised he'd take three days off at New Year's, no newspapers, no television, no radio. And did you see him this evening? Writing an editorial. And the minute he goes back to town, he goes straight to the city room."

"All this peace and quiet makes me nervous," his father said. "But, okay. After supper will be fine. That suit you, Jamie?"

"Good."

"By the way, if you want to hold on to those books for a while, you could take them to New York with you."

"I've been thinking. I may not go back."

He saw his father look at Margrethe, waiting for her reaction. Of course, his father would ask him to stay with them. He thought of his room, just down the corridor from the master bedroom. And Margrethe in his father's bed. He saw Margrethe look at him, warm, smiling, innocent. "Not go back?" she said.

"Well, I can't afford to keep up that New York apartment on my own. I'm moving out. I thought I'd look for some sort of newspaper work here in Montreal. I don't mean on *The Gazette*."

"But why not on *The Gazette?*" his father asked. "We might have a spot for you."

"I'd rather somewhere else, thanks."

"Well, I could have an exploratory word about you with George Harris at the *Star*. Find out the lie of the land."

"That might be good. Or maybe it would be better if I see him myself. Anyway, don't worry. I'm only going to stay with you for a few days. I'll find my own place."

"No problem," his father said.

"We love having you," Margrethe said.

Suddenly a feeling close to tears came upon him and he smiled at Margrethe, smiled at his father, smiled at this old man he had hoped would carry him piggyback over his fears. He had been right to come here. He picked up the daguerreotype, mysterious passport which had enabled him to cross the frontier of those fears, talisman to some future he did not understand. And looking into the eyes of his *Doppelgänger*, that strange elation came over him again, and there and then he resolved that no matter how long it took he would find out if this were really the photograph of the man who was Europe's first *poète maudit*. And if it were, then he must be that man's blood, heir to a talent of which until now he had been an indifferent caretaker. But the wasted years, the marriage years, were over and as he looked into the photograph's eyes, the eyes seemed to glitter, urging him to start again, to pursue his true vocation. Carefully, he wrapped his handkerchief around the frame and placed the photograph in his pocket.

_____ *The next evening,*
after supper, they began to drive back to Montreal. His father and Margrethe set off first in the Volvo, he following
in his father's old Dodge. It had been snowing for much
of the afternoon and as they set out it became a blizzard
which slowed their progress to about thirty miles an hour.
His father had planned to reach the city before eleven, in
time to check the front page of the paper's Ottawa edition
before it went to press. But eleven came and the two cars,
solitary on the snowdrifted highway, had not reached the
city's outskirts. It was after midnight when they crossed
the Champlain Bridge. On the far side of the bridge the
Volvo pulled into the curb. Mangan swung the Dodge in
to park behind it. His father got out of the Volvo and,
pulling a scarf across his nose and mouth to shelter from
the cutting sleet, came back to talk.

"You go on home with Margrethe. I'll take this car and
drop in at the paper. I might just have time to check the
makeup on the Final before they put it to bed."

"Let me come with you," Mangan said.

"Are you sure?"

"Yes, I'd like to have a look at the old place again."

"All right, then. I'll tell Margrethe."

Half an hour later, shaking snow from their rubbers, he and his father entered the newspaper lobby to a familiar atmosphere of flickering fluorescent lights, smells of cleaning fluid, the elevator arrow moving jerkily as though the descending elevator might get stuck between floors. Fourteen years ago, in this same building, Mangan had begun his newspaper life, arriving each day in midmorning, taking this elevator up to the City Room, going to the assignments book to read in Hoffmayer's careless scrawl his assignments for the day.

12 Noon. Rotary Service Luncheon. Mt. Royal Hotel. Mangan.

2–5 Paraplegics Convention, Mt. Royal (ck. feature poss. Phone if Photog required). Mangan.

8 Eddie Cantor Memorial Award Dinner. Speaker Moshe Dayan. Windsor Hotel. Mangan.

Those were his days, a round of endless, dull local stories, at the beck of Hoffmayer, a doltish management lackey who turned out an uninspired set of local pages and who died suddenly at his desk during Mangan's second year on the paper. He remembered Hoffmayer's funeral, reporters and deskmen standing around in Mount Royal Cemetery one hot afternoon, waiting for a minister who did not appear. And how his father, impromptu, managed a graceful eulogy.

The elevator door opened. Three proofreaders got out, their night's work done. One of them, a stout old man in navy overcoat and earmuffs, nodded. "Night, Pat."

"Night, Bill," Mangan's father said.

And now, looking at his father and the proofreader,

Mangan remembered the day old Chief Garvey, the former managing editor, had retired. The staff had chipped in to buy him a matched set of luggage and it was presented in the City Room, after the Final, with speeches and booze. The chief seemed pleased. He made a speech. He said: "Some of us come to *The Gazette* and make it our life. Others pass by." Mangan had passed by after three years, unable to face the continuing tedium of his daily assignments. His father helped him with the move, pulled strings, and got him a job on the Toronto *Globe and Mail*, which was considered the best newspaper in English Canada. I could have made the *Globe* my life, he thought, and retired like the chief with a matched set of luggage.

He let his father go into the elevator before him. They went up to the fourth floor, the building beginning to shake as, below, the sudden rumble of presses began. The Final. So it was after one o'clock. He remembered hanging around the news desk until the first copies came off the presses, then going off with the other juniors to Slats' Tavern for Molson beer and a supper of spaghetti, all of them coming in with their Finals under their arms. The *Gazette* men. The young reporters lived in an enclosed community of their own making. To them, all those outside their trade were civilians, news material to be written up and forgotten. Now, remembering those times, he realized that he had always thought of himself as different from the others. He was Mangan of *The Gazette*, but he was also James Mangan, a poet. He had not, like his father, made the paper his life. Others pass by.

At the fifth floor his father stepped out of the elevator and with a sudden straightening of his shoulders walked briskly down the corridor. His father's private office was partitioned off from the main floor of the City Room, which was almost empty now. A field of steel desks, the aisles strewn with paper detritus as after some rowdy sports event.

At the big table, a frieze of reporters and deskmen waited for the Final to come up, some playing cards, some reading, some lolling and chatting. The entry of Mangan's father was noticed by all, but acknowledged only by the senior few. "Hello, Pat. Hey, Pat," as his father, affable yet distant, waved, then turned into his office.

That morning Mangan had been reading of the entrance of an earlier Mangan into a newspaper. Duffy, editor of *The Nation*, wrote that James Clarence Mangan, one of the most frequent contributors to that journal, "stole into the editor's office once a week to talk about literary projects, but if one of my friends appeared he took flight on the instant. The animal spirits and hopefulness of vigorous young men oppressed him and he fled from the admiration and sympathy of a stranger as others do from reproach and insult."

His father, who had never fled from a stranger, friendly or otherwise, went to his desk, where, ignoring the letters and messages stacked by his secretary, he picked up, one by one, the final editions of the last two days' *Gazettes*, turning to the last page of each to check on the number, then expertly scanning key pages, non-institutional advertisements, sports, stock quotations. Above him, in old-fashioned brown pine frames, immemorialized in the lens wink of old Speed Graphic cameras, were high moments of his younger days: the English press lords Beaverbrook and Rothermere, in white cloth caps and white duck shoes, posing on the shuffleboard deck of the *Empress of Canada*, with his father and old Scott McMurtry, the *Gazette*'s proprietor. His father at a banquet head table with Colonel McCormick of the *Chicago Tribune* on his left and André Malraux on his right. In pride of place in the center of the display, his father's favorite photograph, himself as a young reporter, smartly spiffed out in pinstripe suit, interviewing Roosevelt at the wartime Quebec conference.

A throat clearing sounded at the office door. Mangan turned. Ritchie, black-jowled, looking rough as a bouncer, the usual dead White Owl cigar between his curiously ruby lips. "Hi, Pat. Hi, Jamie."

"Paul," his father said pleasantly, looking up, then lowering his head again to scan a new page of newsprint. "Seems to have been pretty quiet over New Year's."

"Dead," Ritchie said, and then, as though he had committed a gaffe, looked straight at Mangan and, astonishingly, blushed. "Sorry. By the way, Jamie, I tried to get you in New York. Handelman said you'd gone back New Year's Day."

Confused, he stared at Ritchie. "No, I went out to the Townships with Dad."

"You've been there since?"

"Jesus," Ritchie said. "You *did* hear the news?"

"No, what?" his father said. "We didn't even have a radio out there."

"Well"—Ritchie shuffled clumsily toward the desk, picked up one of the newspapers, and opened it at an inside page—"it happened day before yesterday. I'm awful sorry. We thought you'd know." He handed the paper to Mangan.

Mangan's father stood up at once and came around to look. Mid-page, a one-column photograph of Beatrice, a two-column headline.

BEATRICE ABBOT, COMPANION, KILLED IN L.I. EXPRESSWAY TRAGEDY

New York. Jan. 2 (CP) Actress Beatrice Abbot was killed early yesterday morning in a highway accident when a sports car which she was driving crashed and burst into flames. Miss Abbot and a passenger, Perry R. Turnbull, a theatrical producer, are believed to have died instantly.

Larry Caputo, the driver of a trailer truck involved in the accident, told Highway Patrol officers that the small foreign sports car driven by Miss Abbot at "about a hundred miles an hour" ricocheted off his truck, leaped a road divider and crashed into a concrete wall, bursting into flames.

Beatrice Abbot, a two-time Tony Award winner on Broadway and a nominee last year for Motion Picture Academy Award as Best Supporting Actress, was widely known for her starring role in the film "Flight from Orleans" in which she created an unforgettable Joan of Arc, playing opposite Sir John Gielgud. Born to the theatre as the daughter of Delauncey "Del" Abbot, a leading theatrical designer of the forties, she was the star of such long-running Broadway hits as "Spring for Lennie," "The Black Swan," and "Look Homeward." Among her many film roles were—

It went on for two more paragraphs. Then there was a paragraph on Turnbull. At the end there was this announcement.

Miss Abbot is survived by her husband, James Mangan, a freelance writer and broadcaster. Funeral details will be announced later.

He felt his father's hand gripping him about the shoulders. "My God," his father said, then turned to Ritchie. "Anything on the funeral since?"

"We called New York. I thought you'd maybe want to go. There's to be a service on Friday at four."

He sensed his father hesitate. "What do you think, Jamie?"

"It's up to you," he said. "But I don't think you need to, under the circumstances."

"Right," his father said, and then said, in a low voice, "*You'll* go, though?"

"Yes." He was aware now of other faces at the door. Chris Charlton, the telegraph editor, a gray man with failed gray face.

"Very sorry, Jamie," Chris said. "Terrible thing."

And Handelman. "Ah, Jamie, it's terrible. She was a wonderful person." They nodded, touched him, retreated. He could see a copyboy in the corridor, distributing the Final. "Come on," his father said. "Let's go home."

Mute, he accepted a fresh newspaper from the unsuspecting copyboy as they went out into the City Room. Someone had whispered the news and now, with silent tact, men stood around the big desk, nodding to him. The elevator came. Those who had been waiting to take it drifted away. He and his father entered the elevator. No one joined them. The door shut. They went down alone.

_____ *As his taxi*
came through Beekman Place, turning right into the cul-de-sac at the end of East Fifty-first Street, Turnbull's Mercedes sports car ran into his mind. He saw it skid in the snow as she drove it away from the apartment entrance five days ago.

"That'll be sixteen dollars," the taxi driver said. He should have taken the airport bus. His limo days were over.

The doorman was Karl, the one who always got his name wrong. "Morning, Mr. Abbot."

He nodded to Karl.

"You've been away, Mr. Abbot?" Karl said, grabbing his bag, moving crabwise toward the front door.

"Yes. In Canada."

"Yeah, well, I want to offer my sincere, you know, con-dolence. She was a lovely person. Just a lovely person."

"Thank you, Karl. I'll take the bag, thanks."

"Sure? I'll be glad to bring it up for you."

"No, that's all right."

"Okay then, sir." Karl ran ahead to press the button for the elevator. "The staff chipped in for a floral wreath," Karl informed him. "We sent it around to the chapel this morning."

"Thank you, that's very nice," he said to Karl. *What chapel?*

When he unlocked the apartment door, he opened it with difficulty, pushing inward a thick silt of magazines, letters, and messages. Unused, the rooms were heavy with stale air, a hot, dead breath on his face as he entered from the morning chill. He shut the door, and as he did, the telephone began to ring. He reached it at the fourth ring, but whoever it was had hung up. He stood holding the receiver, looking out of the picture window. Huge in the window frame, a rusty tanker passed downriver, decks deserted, prow foaming waves. Who had arranged her funeral? What chapel? Someone must have signed some paper. Weinberg would know. But he did not phone Weinberg. Instead, he dialed the answering service. "This is Mr. Mangan. Any messages for me?"

"Oh, yes, Mr. Mangan. Let's see. Miss Polk called this morning. She called twice yesterday. She said you have her number. And Mr. Weinberg's office called this morning and they also called yesterday and the day before. They said it's urgent. Now, let's see, there was a call from a Mr. Connell, at Gramercy 8-9456, and there was a call from Mr. Leo Davoren, no number. And there was a call from your mother. She didn't leave a number, either. And a call from the Nassau County Police. That's it. Do you want the police number? I didn't give you that."

"No, that's okay. Thank you."

Louise Polk had called three times in three days. That couldn't have been just to offer condolences. She must know about the funeral arrangements. Maybe she had made them. Final representation of her client. He dialed the familiar number and heard it ring, seeing in his mind's eye the somber lobby on Forty-fourth Street, the two elderly desk clerks moving about, slow as earthquake survivors, posting bills in pigeonholes. Under a bright lamp the matronly switchboard operator sat, and now as she pulled the plug he heard her remembered nasal whine: "Good morning, Royalton." On hearing his request she stuck a plug in Louise's switch. Louise had an office in the East Fifties but never went there until after lunch. She would still be in her hotel suite. He imagined it now, those rooms so dark that the light must always be on. She would be lying on her chaise longue in her green silk wrapper, surrounded by icons of her clients, friends, and mentors, from Beatrice all the way back to Gordon Craig. Always, they watched over her from silver frames which were arranged around the apartment in tiers like the balconies of a theater. Everywhere, mementos of that life: set designs, costume sketches, old playbills, and also the special relics of the lonely: stuffed cushions in the shape of cats, Dresden poodles, a real Pekinese named Nanki-Poo, miniature tea sets, toy shoes, a dollhouse, and many dolls, even including a portrait doll of Louise, made for her in childhood at the command of her stepmother, the Contessa Bianchi. And the three white telephones, all with long, coiled cords, which permitted her to walk about expertly flicking the cord away from her feet like a singer manipulating a stage microphone. If she was in, the phone would ring once only, or be busy. She was its faithful attendant.

After one ring, her voice.

"Louise Polk."

"Louise, it's Jamie Mangan."

"Oh, Jamie, I've been calling you. You got my messages?"

"I was in Canada visiting my father. I only heard about it last night."

71

"It's just so awful. So *awful*. If she'd still been with you, it never would have happened. You took such good care of her. I told her that, you know. Did you know I told her that?"

"No, I didn't."

"I told her, I said to her, Bea, you mark my words, Perry Turnbull is not going to look after you like Jamie did. Was I right? God, was I right!"

"I called about the service," he said. "Where's it going to be?"

"At Frank E. Campbell on Eighty-first. You know it?"

"Yes. At four tomorrow?"

"Right. You're going, of course."

"Yes, of course."

"Good. Because E.P. called me and asked. He's going to say a few words and wanted to know if he should mention you. I said, sure. I said, just *don't* mention Turnbull. It's *his* fault, I said. I said, Jamie would never have let her drive in that condition."

"She was drunk?"

"The way I heard it," Louise said, "they'd been drinking since New Year's Eve. New Year's night, they were invited to dinner at Earl and Cissie's. Cissie told me that when they arrived Turnbull was drunk and Bea was high, but she was still okay. Well, anyway, they had dinner and about eleven o'clock they told Earl they were going to drive out to the Island. To the beach house, you know? Well, Turnbull was so falling-down drunk by then that Bea had to drive. And she was pretty high herself. Oh, my God, Jamie, I still can't bear to think about it."

He hesitated. "What about the body?"

"Oh, it's—ah—cremation, I believe. Sy Weinberg had to go over to Long Island to identify the body. His office is taking care of the arrangements. You better call him, I guess."

72

"I will. I'll call him now."

"Right. Oh, Jamie, what can I say. I'll see you tomorrow, then. Take care."

The phone receiver made a loud sound as he replaced it. Cremation. Last night, alone in the bedroom of his father's house in Montreal, suddenly he had begun to weep. He had wept, remembering the stories Beatrice had told him of her life, wept for the waste of her death, for the years they had spent together, for that time when they were in love. It was a harsh, painful weeping which wore itself out, then started up again, lasting for about an hour, after which, like someone eased of a fever, he fell into a heavy sleep. Ashes to ashes, dust to dust. Her only human remains some ashes in an urn, the only evidence that she had walked on this earth some photographs, a heap of newspaper clippings, a few reels of film. No child, no continuance. From now on, she would live fitfully in the minds of those who had seen her act and of those who had known her. He would remember her most. Yet already he had begun to forget her.

The telephone rang.

"Is Mr. Mangan there?" a girl's voice asked.

"Speaking."

"Oh, Mr. Mangan, will you hold one moment? This is Mr. Weinberg's office. We've been trying to reach you."

Weinberg's voice. "Jamie, how are you? You've been out of town?"

"I was in Montreal visiting my father. I only heard the news last night."

"I see. I thought you might be out on the Island someplace. We did our best to reach you."

"I'm sorry. We were at a lake. There was no phone or even a radio."

"No?" Weinberg said in the way he had, a way which implied he might or might not believe what was said. "You know about the service, of course?"

"Yes."

"Good. Look, maybe if you have a minute you could drop by the office sometime today. I'd like to go over the arrangements with you. Can you make it?"

Friendly, correct, the manner one uses to deal with a client's wife. "All right, Sy, I'll come over. Say in half an hour. Would that be okay?"

"That would be good. See you then."

No mention of her death, no condolences as yet. Weinberg, the orchestrator of many a divorce settlement, knowing how quickly love becomes its obverse, would wait for a sign of sentiment before offering his regrets. Officially, he acted for both of them, but his fee was computed on Beatrice's earnings alone. And now Mangan thought of the morning six years ago when he and Beatrice stood in Weinberg's office while three junior lawyers witnessed their new and separate wills. Each was to be the other's sole heir. And Beatrice, an only child, had inherited all of her father's estate. Suddenly he felt tense in that hot, airless room. Unless she had changed her will in the past three weeks, he would be her heir. He would get all her money. He might even have enough to forget about the CBC job, go away somewhere, and do nothing but write poetry. Again he felt that strange surge of excitement which came over him when he looked at the photograph of his double. He took the photograph from his pocket, unwrapping the handkerchief which protected it. The eyes of the photograph stared into his, glittering, complicit. Of course, she could have changed her will in the past three weeks. She might have made a new will in favor of Turnbull, or someone else. Weinberg would know. He stared at the photograph. Should I call him back? But the photograph's eyes seemed to mock his anxiety. You're going to see him now, aren't you? You'll know within the hour. The photograph eyes seemed brutally triumphant. You know the answer already, they said. You know it. You've won.

In the offices of Weinberg, Greenfeld, Kurtz and Norris, a warren of narrow corridors led past rooms lined with shelves of leather-bound law volumes, rooms in which in seeming incongruity modern copying machines hummed in constant activity. The offices of the senior partners were large; Weinberg's particularly so, with a corner view of the Lower Manhattan skyline. His desk was also large, and on it were piled legal documents of varying sizes. However, Weinberg rarely consulted print in the presence of clients. His phone rang constantly: his counsel was continually sought. Interrupted after an initial "Hello, Jamie" by one of these phone calls, Mangan sat down facing Weinberg, trying to simulate deafness as Weinberg counseled a worried author. He stared across the room at the view of Manhattan, then at a small table placed against the wall, an altar to Weinberg's private life. Color photographs displayed his wife, Abby (pretty), and his two small sons (much orthodontal work in evidence). There was also a portrait of Weinberg himself, younger, but wearing a gray wig and beard, playing the role of Duncan in a Columbia Law School presentation of *Macbeth*.

On the telephone, Weinberg clarified for his client something which he had already explained. "No, no. Twenty percent is the European. That's split fifty-fifty between your agent here and the subagent in Germany. The fifteen percent is just for England. That's a special arrangement. Just for England. Right. The split? You mean of the fifteen? Yes, well, it's sometimes split fifty-fifty, sometimes seventy-thirty. Okay? All straight now? Good. How's Marisia? Great. Give her my love. Talk to you soon."

Weinberg put down the receiver and shook his head in silent comment on the inevitability of telephone interruption. He was a tall man, tanned winter and summer, with a profile his actor clients might have envied. He dressed conservatively in well-cut pinstripe suits, rarely removed his jacket in the office, and now, as he stood up and came around the desk to offer a belated handshake, revealed only one minor incongruity of dress, Italian vicuña loafers, gold-snaffled, which seemed out of place on his feet.

"Jamie, how are you? I'm terribly sorry." He waited, watching for Mangan's reaction.

"It was an awful business," Mangan said. "Such a shock."

"Yes, terrible. Abby's been in a state ever since she heard. She was so fond of Bea. As we all were. I've been trying to reach you, you know. I'd no way of finding out where you were."

"Yes, I'm sorry. I was in Canada, as I said."

"Well, as I couldn't reach you, I'm afraid we had to sort of take over. I went down to identify her."

"Oh."

"The cremation was, frankly, because of the condition of the body."

"I meant to ask you," Mangan said. "What about Turn-bull? Is he being buried—I mean, he's not being buried with her?"

"His funeral is today, I believe," Weinberg said. "At his family burial place in upstate New York."

"Oh."

Weinberg opened a folder. "As for the arrangements for Bea," he said, "we'll have music, two musicians who will play backstage. I have the program here, Mozart, Telemann, Couperin. Julie Harris was going to read one of Bea's favorite poems, but she's come down with flu. So E.P. will read it instead."

"What favorite poem?" Mangan said. "I don't remember her having one. You don't mean one of mine?"

"She did it in a play. I have it here someplace, a note from E.P. Where is it?"

"She did a play about Christina Rossetti," Mangan said.

"That's right. And she recited some poem, right?"

" 'When I Am Dead, My Dearest.' Is that it?"

Weinberg was at his desk. "Wait. Yes, that's it. And after that, Leo Davoren will say a few words. It will be very short. Very simple. What do you think? Does that sound all right? You don't object to the poem, do you?"

"No, no."

"Have you anything you'd like to see added?"

"No."

"I forgot to mention that there'll be a special seating section, the first two rows. Next of kin and some of the more prominent people."

Next of kin. But Beatrice had no living kin except for an aunt, remote in Tennessee. Her father, Delauncey "Del" Abbot, was himself an only child, son of a thrice-married Florentine principessa, née Hanson of Philadelphia. From her father, a thirties aesthete, forties theatrical designer, Beatrice had inherited her expensive tastes and an estate which she told Mangan was worth a hundred and fifty thousand dollars at the time of the will's reading but wasn't worth half of that today. And for as long as Mangan had known her she had always decorated her dressing rooms with a vita of photographs depicting her father's life: a photograph of the ball his mother gave in the Hotel Crillon in 1925, five hundred guests all in white. A Cecil Beaton photograph of Del at twenty with Harold Acton and Virginia Woolf in the Tuscan landscape of his mother's estate at Fiesole. A theatrical sketch of his first set design, *The Sea Gull*, at Yale, and a larger sketch of his Broadway success, *A Palace in Siam*. There was a snapshot of him on the Riviera with Cole Porter, in Paris with Bricktop, and one of him braving the waves at Nantucket carrying his one and only baby daughter in his arms. At dinner, night after night, that daughter reran the serial of his life, his amours and escapades, his theatrical triumphs. He was her flamboyant father, she his one and only. Her mother, *tipa antipatica*, had divorced Del and remarried a great deal of money, dying rich and lonely in Brazil, leaving Beatrice with only one living blood relative, the forbidding Aunt Edna Abbot of Oak Ridge, Tennessee, who had sent best wishes and a Georgian silver cream jug at the time of their wedding but had remained silent ever since.

"She had an aunt in Tennessee," said Weinberg, the mind reader. "But I believe there's been no contact there for some years."

"Yes, that's right."

"So the funeral arrangements are up to you. And you're satisfied, are you?"

"Yes, of course. And thanks very much for all your trouble, Sy."

"No trouble," Weinberg said. "By the way, I'll charge your disbursements to the estate. You realize, of course, that you're her sole heir."

Shameful excitement filled him, but he had planned beforehand to make some token protest. Her sole heir! He said: "She'd probably have changed her will if she'd lived."

Weinberg shrugged. "The point is, she didn't. And, as a matter of fact, only a few days before she died she was telling me she wanted to be generous with you about the divorce settlement. I'm sure she'd have wanted you to have the money. And as you know, there's no one else."

The phone rang. "Sorry," Weinberg said and picked it up. "Hello? Oh, Howard, I'm in a meeting right now. Let me get back to you in about fifteen minutes, okay? Thanks."

He replaced the receiver. "About the estate," he said. "Beatrice told me you have about two hundred thousand in joint savings and C.D.'s and so on. Right?"

"Yes. So I believe. She handled our money. As you know, it was mostly hers."

Weinberg ignored this. "And then there's her father's estate. That's the major item." He paused and looked at Mangan.

"Well, I don't know anything about that," Mangan said. "Beatrice sort of looked after it."

"Well, it's—let's see—" Weinberg opened a file, consulted a note. "Well, I'd say the portfolio is worth somewhere in the region of three hundred thousand."

"Is it? That much." Seventy-five thousand, she had given him to believe. Not more. He was shocked. Why had she lied to him? What else had she lied about?

"Then there's the apartment. And the house on the Island. And that's about it."

Three hundred thousand, plus two hundred thousand, plus the beach house, which was worth, say, a hundred thousand in today's market. And their equity in the apartment. He was rich.

The phone again. Weinberg grimaced, then pressed a button, saying, "Sally, no calls. Not now. What? Well, tell him I'll call him in a minute."

Rich. Mangan thought of the photograph in his pocket. He could go to Ireland. He could track down that forebear. Weinberg wanted to take a call, didn't he? Mangan stood up. "Look, I'll be running along now, Sy, I know you're busy."

"That's all right," Weinberg said. "Damn phone. Is there anything else? Any other questions?" But as he said this, he rose, coming around the desk to shake hands again. "Well, in any case, we'll be in touch. And I'll see you at the service tomorrow."

"Yes, see you tomorrow. And thanks, Sy."

As he went into the corridor, he passed the office used by Weinberg's secretaries. One of them, a middle-aged woman, nodded and smiled at him. As he passed, he heard her whispered voice.

"That's the husband."

Shortly after three o'clock on the day of the funeral service, Mangan, wearing his dark suit and a specially purchased black tie, put on his overcoat and left the apartment. His intention was to kill time by walking all the way to Eighty-first and Madison. He estimated that he would arrive at the funeral chapel about ten minutes before the service was scheduled to begin. When he set off, the weather was cold and blustery, with skies so dark it seemed like late afternoon. He walked up Second Avenue to Sixty-third Street, where he turned, going west. He was on Sixty-third between Lexington and Park Avenue when the skies broke, sending down a sleeting, freezing rain which cleansed the street of people. Mangan, hatless and without umbrella, ran for shelter under the awning of an apartment house halfway down the block. But as he stood huddling, pulling his overcoat collar up to his cheeks, the sleety rain attacked him, striking at an angle under the awning. A doorman, standing inside the double doors of the apartment, noticed his plight and opened the outer door. "Come on in, sir."

Mangan, grateful, nodded and said, "Thanks," as the doorman, letting him in, went on to open the inner door, admitting him to an elegant lobby furnished with imitation Louis XIV furniture and lit by large shaded table lamps. An elderly man was waiting inside, dressed for the street in a black homburg hat and British Warm overcoat. He came forward as Mangan entered, moving past him, narrowing his eyes shortsightedly as he peered out at the street. Decided, he stepped back and drew off his leather gloves, stuffing them dandyishly into the breast pocket of his overcoat. "That's going to last," he said, and produced a tortoiseshell cigarette case and gold-plated lighter. "There's no chance of a cab, I suppose."

"I could ring the rank, Mr. Halperin," the doorman offered.

"Yes, thanks. Will you? For all the good it will do," the elderly man said. He lit his cigarette. The doorman went to a wall telephone and dialed a number. Mangan heard the elevator come to a stop behind him and, turning, saw an old lady, frail, wearing a fur coat, a corsage, and a plastic hat to protect her hair, being assisted carefully over the elevator step by a middle-aged black woman companion dressed in nurse's cloak, white dress, stockings, and shoes. The old lady smiled vaguely in Mangan's direction, then nodded to the elderly man in sudden recognition.

"Hello, how are *you* today?"

"It's raining," the elderly man said.

"Oh, is it? Oh, dear. Did you hear that, Mary?" the old lady said, turning to her companion. "It's raining."

"Well, maybe we wait a bit, Mrs. Kemp," the black woman said. "Maybe you'd like to go back up?"

"Oh, *no*," the old lady said, pettishly. "I'm dressed now. I'm all ready."

The doorman, telephoning, turned to the elderly man. "No answer, sir." He replaced the receiver. "Want me to go out and try?"

"No, no," the elderly man said. "Too wet. I'll wait awhile."

The doorman nodded, then smiled at the old lady. "Hello there, Mrs. Kemp."

"Hello, Rudi. How are you today?"

"Just fine, just fine." The doorman bobbed his head deferentially, then went again to the glass doors, peering out. Mangan also stared at the street, seeing a sheeting rain which filmed and blurred all visibility. He looked at his watch. It was already three-thirty. He was aware of a small tension in the lobby: people kept inside against their will. He heard the nurse-companion murmur something insistent, indistinguishable. "All *right*," the old lady said and allowed herself to be led to one of the lobby chairs. She seated herself. Her companion stood on her right, readjusting the ties of her cloak. "I usually know when it's going to rain," the old lady said. "I can feel it. I'm a barometer," she said, and laughed nervously as though afraid that no one was paying any attention. And, indeed, the three men in the lobby, unsure of the particularity of her remarks, stared about them, avoiding her eye.

Three-forty. Even if it weren't raining, Mangan doubted if he would be able to get there on foot by four. "Any chance of a taxi on Park?" he asked the doorman.

"Park's the worst," the doorman said. "Every one of the doormen there will be out on the street with a whistle."

Which was true.

"Look at it," the elderly man said, staring out through the doors. "Look at it come down."

Mangan looked at it. Anxiety gripped him. He saw himself coming in late, dripping wet, everybody staring as he was ushered up to those front seats reserved for next of kin. Imagine being late for your wife's funeral. Maybe even coming in while E.P. read the poem or Leo Davoren said his few words. "What about Madison?" he asked the doorman. "Better chance there, I guess."

"You've got to get there first," the doorman said. "You'd be soaking wet."

Which was true. Maybe he should stand outside in case a cab went by in front of the door. He looked again at his watch. It was a quarter to four. "Well, I'll have to do something," he said to the doorman. "Thanks."

The doorman obligingly opened both sets of doors for him and he found himself outside under the awning on Sixty-third Street. Two cars passed, sheeting up waves of water, forcing him to move back from the pavement's edge. He fidgeted, dodging gusts of rain which squalled under the awning. Surely he would find a taxi within the next ten minutes. But after further minutes of hopeless waiting, he decided to strike out in the downpour and make for Madison Avenue. As he stepped from the awning's protection, rain hosed him, soaking his hair, fanning waves of wetness against his knees and calves. He ran to the junction of Sixty-third and Park Avenue and, as the doorman had predicted, saw uniformed figures with huge umbrellas blowing piercing whistles, scanning the lurching wagon trail of traffic as it splashed uptown. Cabs passed, all taken. He stood under an awning until the light changed, then plunged across Park going toward Madison. He held the points of his overcoat collar pulled up about his face, but his shirt collar was already damp. His cheeks streamed water, his hair was plastered to his skull, his trousers from knee to ankle were soggy wet. When he reached Madison Avenue, he turned uptown, moving intermittently, stopping to check on the traffic. Occasionally he thought he saw a cab with its roof light lit and in excitement would run out among the oncoming cars. On one of these sorties he stepped into a large puddle, soaking his shoes and socks. This taxi hunt slowed his pace so much that it was nearly four by the time he reached Seventieth Street. There were still no cabs. He moved on toward Seventy-second, a two-way street, but there, at the traffic lights, entered into a hopeless contest with others and in a six-minute struggle lost three cabs to more ruseful strivers. Then, in sudden panic, he decided to forget about a taxi and push on, on foot. The rain seemed to acquiesce in this decision, for as he started off again, it slackened to a sleety drizzle. But, still walking, he kept turning around to look for taxis, although by the time he reached Seventy-ninth Street he had not seen one empty cab. Up to this point he had remained in a state of tension, but when he consulted his watch and saw that it was already past four o'clock, he trudged on, squelching water from his shoes with each step, his momentum slowed, his movements automatic. He would be late. He would refuse to let them put him at the front of the chapel. Other people would be late as well. It was not his fault. He would stand at the back of the chapel. He was late. Not his fault.

However, as he approached Eighty-first Street, his anxiety quickened again. The funeral chapel was a four-story brownstone building on the northwest corner. Over the main entrance a huge, rain-draggled American flag flew at half mast, and as he came closer he noticed six or seven chauffeured limousines parked illegally on the block. No one was going inside. He looked at his watch and saw that it was four-fifteen. And so, out of breath, soaking wet from hair to shoes, he went into the entrance hall, its muted chandelier and warm lighted student lamps on adjacent side tables giving the visitor the impression of entering a private house. Two ushers, both in dark suits, turned to look at him. One of them came over, solicitously.

"The Mangan funeral?" Mangan said.

"Ah—is that—ah—Beatrice Abbot?" the usher asked.

"Yes."

"This way, sir," the usher said. "By the way, are you a relative? There are some special seats."

"I want to be at the back. The very last row."

"Yes, sir. This way, please. The service has just started."

He fell in behind the usher, his eyes on the usher's back as though he were taking part in a school procession. The usher opened doors and music was heard. The usher turned to him and, beckoning, led him to the rear row of chairs, which were not occupied, then left, silently closing the doors again. Mangan sat, unbuttoning his overcoat, glancing at his soggy trouser legs. Timidly, as though afraid of what he might find, he lifted his gaze and looked at the room.

There was no altar. Instead, he faced a sort of stage with banks of greenery and flame-red poinsettias in what looked to be a permanent arrangement. In front of these were many funeral wreaths and floral sprays, some with silk ribands and little white cards identifying the donors. The music came from behind the greenery. The musicians were not visible. At the right-hand side of the stage was a microphone and a small lectern. The chapel was not filled, although almost all the rows of chairs were at least three-quarters occupied. At the front, slightly set apart from the other chairs, were two rows, filled with people. In the very front row he identified Louise Polk in a black veil, with Weinberg beside her. In the front row also were three Broadway producers, four film stars, and two stage directors. In the second row he identified five of Broadway's leading players. Less celebrated actors and actresses were sprinkled among the mourners in the mid-section of the chapel, and there were dozens of other people he knew, all of them Beatrice's friends, some of them rich theatrical backers. There were also people he had not expected, a girl who had once acted as Beatrice's understudy, a waiter from Sardi's, two elderly women who owned a costume business, and a madwoman who had created a disturbance on the opening night of Beatrice's last show.

As he stared around, identifying these people, the musicians came to the end of their piece. When the music stopped, the mourners seemed to relax and moved their heads about, noticing and identifying some of their neighbors. At once Mangan ducked his head down and pulled up his overcoat collar to screen his face. Estranged or not, he was Beatrice's husband and should not be at the rear of the chapel. But even as he ducked to avoid being seen, he became aware that the room's attention had suddenly shifted and that heads were craning forward to someone who had got up from the front row and now approached the lectern. In a moment, Mangan saw E. P. Brittain's handsome silvery head moving above the crowd. E.P. was wearing a beautifully cut, dark, double-breasted suit, and as he reached the lectern he laid a small sheaf of notes under the reading lamp. He could have been a banker, a leading surgeon, or a senior State Department official preparing to make an important announcement. Indeed, he had played all these roles successfully on stage and screen, and now as he lifted his great head to look out over the assembly, it was hard to credit that he was not acting but speaking as a private citizen at a real funeral service.

"Friends," said E.P. "And all of us *were* her friends. But we who are gathered here this afternoon are only a fraction. For Beatrice Abbot numbered her friends in the hundreds of thousands. People who never knew her, people she would never know. People who met her in a darkened theater and who in that moment became something more than those we speak of as admirers, as fans. People, ordinary people all over the world, who felt about this vibrant young woman as they would feel about their best friend. That was her gift, Bea's special gift that transcended even her great skills as a performer. It was art, but it was something more than art. It was real. I am not here today to speak of Bea's art. Others will tell you of that. I am here, as we all are, to remember Bea our friend. Some of you, many of you, will remember a few years ago when she played the part of Christina Rossetti in that moving and beautiful play, *The Terrace in the Garden*. She had a great, great admiration for the poetry of Christina Rossetti. You will remember the Rossetti poem which Bea spoke so beautifully just before the final curtain of the play. It happened to be her own favorite poem of Christina Rossetti's. Perhaps, today, it can serve as her epitaph—that perfect epitaph she would have wished us to hear this afternoon."

E. P. Brittain paused and looked out at the house. All was silence, expectation. Some seemed near to tears. He glanced down at his notes, and then, lifting his great head, began to declaim.

> "When I am dead, my dearest,
>   Sing no sad songs for me;
> Plant thou no roses at my head,
>   Nor shady cypress tree:
> Be the green grass above me

With showers and dewdrops wet;
And if thou wilt, remember.
And if thou wilt, forget."

The speaker paused. A woman directly in front of Mangan caught her breath as though stemming tears. But in the main the audience seemed uplifted, as by a great performance. And again, raising his head, E.P. spoke.

"I shall not see the shadows,
I shall not feel the rain;
I shall not hear the nightingale
Sing on, as if in pain;
And dreaming through the twilight
That doth not rise nor set,
Haply I may remember,
And haply may forget."

E.P. bowed his head as though he had come to the end of a prayer. Then, clear-eyed, he looked out at the room. "We will remember her," he declared. "We will not forget her. And we will remember her as she would have wished us to remember her. With no sad songs." He paused. "Thank you," he said. He took up his small sheaf of notes and stepped down from the lectern. Mangan waited for applause. Applause seemed proper to this performance. But instead, as E.P. took his seat in the front row, the unseen musicians began to play, a violin and piano beginning a Mozart sonata. The audience shifted in its chairs as though waiting for the next item on the program.

Mangan had not been to a funeral since his schooldays. The last time had been his grandfather's in the Church of the Ascension in Montreal, a big, dignified funeral befitting a senior figure in the Canadian Pacific Railway hierarchy. His grandfather's coffin, oak with brass fittings, lay on a high, draped catafalque athwart the center aisle of the church like the hull of a Viking ship. Loud organ tones pealed as old heavy men in dark suits came forward to view through the open panel the face of one they had known for forty years. The dead man's widow, frail, in black muslin veil and deep mourning weeds, was led to the casket, looked at the dead face, then covered her eyes with black gloved hands as though to hide the sight. It was a solemn requiem, the Host raised in hushed solemnity, the tinkling Sanctus bell heard by all save his grandfather, who lay in the open coffin beneath the church's vaulted ceiling, his dead face lit by a stained-glass window of his benefaction on the right-hand side of the nave. There in the church to which, long years ago, he had brought his children to be baptized, a parish priest climbed the winding pulpit stairs to speak of him in a way which brought his family, sitting in the front pew, unashamedly to tears.

His grandfather had died in his community. His death was a part of his life. But here, in a room which she had never seen, a room filled with flowers and greenery, with music whose tone was joyful and light, an actor had read a poem which had no significance for the dead woman it was supposed to commemorate. Here, there was no body. No hearse waited outside to bring the mourners to a cemetery, to spaded earth at the rim of a grave. Here an audience waited for a Broadway producer to eulogize an actress and praise her gift for aping people she was not. It was the actress who was commemorated here today, not the woman. For who among this audience really knew the woman who had walked out on her marriage, who had died drunk, roasted with her lover in a wall of flame.

That was her funeral pyre. That was the time for weeping, for rending of garments, for gnashing of teeth. But who among this audience was capable of such grief? Certainly not he. For, of all here present, wasn't his attendance the most ludicrous, he who, far from mourning her, had sat in Montreal filled with hatred for her on the very night she died, who sat here now unweeping, the unworthy inheritor of all her wealth.

Leo Davoren, portly and assured, rose from his seat, nodding and smiling greetings to the film stars in the front row as he made his way toward the lectern. Now he would take out a speech, written for him by some writer he had hired two days ago and ordered to produce something suitable, sentimental, and sincere. Davoren! Davoren, who knew her only as an element in the successful deals he had put together, who saw her socially only at business lunches and dinners, who had fought with her many times, haggling over dollars and perquisites. Davoren! The waiter from Sardi's should come forward and deliver the eulogy. He knew her just as well.

But why *not* Davoren? He was the sort of person Beatrice might have chosen herself. He was a Caesar in her world. For her, that was what mattered.

Davoren put his notes on the lectern, then fitted a pair of half spectacles over his ears. Watching him do this, Mangan foresaw Davoren coming up to him after the service, wrapping an arm around his shoulder, telling him of his sorrow. Foresaw others, many others, who would come to him and perform the same empty rite. A charade, another performance, a disgusting fraud! Why should he go through with it? What did it matter to anyone whether he was here or not? By next week, none of these people would care whether he lived or died. He thought of the Christmas cards and rose in sudden panic, trying not to make a noise, but clumsily scraping the floor with the legs of his chair as he pushed it back and stepped into the aisle. Those in front of him raised their heads, acknowledging the interruption, but no one looked directly at the leaver. Turning his back on the room, Mangan made his way in heavy tiptoe toward the exit doors, opening them as Davoren spoke his first words: "One day, about ten years ago, my secretary informed me that I had an appointment with a young actress. I had not made the appointment myself. I was not pleased."

He shut the doors on that voice. The ushers waiting in the outer hall turned and looked at him inquiringly. "Are you all right, sir?" one asked. He nodded and went past them, buttoning his soaking overcoat. As he reached the doorway, three young men loitering just inside looked up. They held cameras and strobes and were familiar to him from the past; paparazzi, freelances who earned a living by picking up shots of the famous at social events. Their eyes found his face and dismissed it; a *tabula rasa*. They went back to their conversation.

The rain had stopped. The chauffeurs standing in a knot by one of the parked limousines looked at him, wondering if the service was already over. Avoiding their gaze, he turned into Eighty-first Street, passing by a side entrance to the funeral chapel, a place where coffins would be taken in and out. At once, he had the sensation of being followed. He was sure that someone had seen him leave and was coming around the corner to ask him to go back. Head down, he quickened his pace, pretending a brisk walk to a firm destination, but he panicked, the walk became a half run, his trouser legs wrapping themselves wetly around his calves as he shambled down the block. He did not risk a look behind him until he came to Fifth Avenue, but when he did there was no one on the street. Of course not. None of those people gave a damn if he attended the service or not. Most of them wouldn't care if they never saw him again. Most of them never would see him again. His life as Beatrice Abbot's husband was over.

He looked across Fifth Avenue. Facing him was the Metropolitan Museum, huge, gray, and monumental, like some Soviet Palace of the People. Over the main entrance an outsize red-and-white banner advertised an exhibition of Russian paintings. Three weeks ago, under that same banner, he had seen Beatrice kiss her lover, then run down those steps with him, going off to her new life. Ignoring the traffic, he stepped out blindly, crossing Fifth Avenue. On the far pavement he turned toward the museum's main entrance, drawn on as though the building were a terminal from which he would depart on a journey. He climbed the monumental steps. Already, daylight was fading over New York and myriad lights began to be switched on as though in tabulation of the millions of lives in this city. He went into the huge entrance hall: the guards, seeing that he carried nothing, waved him on. In front of him people swarmed to and fro, going to the information desk, queueing at the entrances to exhibits, clustering around the gift shops. After a moment's indecision he went and sat on one of the octagonal banquettes in the middle of the hall. He shut his eyes. The voices of the crowd echoed in the high vaulted ceilings above him like the cry of birds in some great cave.

She was dead. The anger he had felt against her, the self-doubt he had tormented himself with in the past weeks, all that was over. She was dead. All that was left of her now was her money, money she might not have given him had she been able to prevent it. The great, the noble thing to do now would be to renounce that inheritance. But he knew he had no intention of doing the noble thing.

The museum was closing. People came down the great staircase and emptied out of the ground-floor galleries. Time to go. Back on Madison Avenue, the funeral service would be over. Some of those who attended it would speculate on his absence and assume he had stayed away from a cuckold's spite. But it no longer mattered what those people thought. He was no longer Beatrice Abbot's husband, an involuntary hanger-on in her world. Nor was he James Mangan, the nineteen-year-old student whose poem had been published in *The New Yorker*. In the years between, he had been like Scott Fitzgerald, an indifferent caretaker of his talent, but, unlike Fitzgerald, at thirty-six he had been given a second chance.

A museum guard passed by. "Closing," the guard warned. "We're closing."

All about him voices, footsteps, the sounds of leaving. As he rose to go, he felt, heavy in his side pocket, the daguerreotype in its brass frame. He touched it through the cloth of his jacket. I will go to Ireland.

PART TWO

_____ *As he drove into*
the town of Bantry, he passed a high stone wall which ran
for more than a mile enclosing a huge estate, once the seat
of English earls, now a museum to a vanished way of life.
Ahead, as he came around the elbow of Bantry Bay, small
fishing boats were moored at stone quays, and behind them
the edge of the town spilled down to the water in a cluster
of gray, severe buildings: convent, warehouse, church. He
drove into the main square, which opened on the quays. A
fair was in progress. All around were neighing mares, colts,
bellowing calves separated from their mothers, dull heifers
lifting their tails to drop gobbets of hot turd on the concrete. Wild-looking, poorly dressed people walked about,
raw boys and girls, women in mourning black, red-faced
farmers in cloth caps. He parked his little red rented Ford
in front of a row of plain public houses, whose dark rooms
were loud with talk and heavy with the stench of urine and
yeast. Buyers and sellers of animals spilled from pub to
pavement and back again in the course of constant barter.

Farther up the town, Mangan saw a maze of streets and shops. He walked three blocks before he came to what he sought, a kiosk marked with the word *Telefōn* in the Irish manner. The phone system was old-fashioned. He put in coins as instructed and asked the operator to get him the Sceptre Hotel in Drishane.

He had arrived in Ireland that morning, flying from New York to land at Shannon at 8:00 a.m. local time. For Mangan, still on New York time, it was the middle of the night. A heavy-looking man in a worn tweed suit waited for him outside the airport customs area.

"Mr. Mangan? I'm from Collins and O'Brien. I have your car for you, that you booked in New York."

They went to a car-rental counter, where Mangan signed some papers. Afterward, the heavy man, pushing an airport cart filled with Mangan's baggage, preceded him out into the cold morning light. "Is this your first visit, then?"

"Yes."

"You will get rain, I'd say. It is not the best time of year for a holiday. Here is your car, so."

His car was alone in the parking lot. The heavy man took out a road map and spread it across the car roof. "Drishane, was it? Well, you'll take the road here to Limerick, then on to Cork City, do you see? And then to Brandon and so to Bantry. It's a good road all the way. When you get to Bantry, you turn down in the direction of Mizen Head. That's the very end of the country, down there. The very end of the land, as you might say."

"How long should it take me?"

"I'd say six hours would see you nicely."

And so he had set off, driving somewhat uncertainly on the left-hand side of the road. At noon he reached Cork, the city in which his great-grandfather had lived in British Army married quarters after service in India. From Cork, his seventeen-year-old grandfather had sailed to Canada to seek his fortune. He stopped the car and walked along what seemed to be a main thoroughfare, a wide, winding street with statues in it, filled with a clamor of pedestrians hurrying in and out of old-fashioned department stores and cheap-looking cafés. In one of these cafés he had a sandwich and a pot of tea, then drove on to a town called Brandon. Now, six and a half hours after leaving Shannon, he was in Bantry, and still not at his destination.

In New York, in the Irish Tourist Office on Fifth Avenue, he had asked if there was a hotel in Drishane. The girl consulted a book. "There's a little place called the Sceptre," she said. "Small, you know. But you should have no trouble getting a room at this time of year. Give them a ring when you're on the road, just to be sure they're open."

In the telephone kiosk in Bantry, the phone rang and rang, but there was no answer from Drishane. After a time the operator came on the line. "No answer, sir," she said.

"Could the number be out of order?"

"I wouldn't say so."

"Well, would the hotel be closed?"

"I don't know, sir. You could try later."

He came out of the kiosk. It was beginning to rain. By the map, Drishane couldn't be more than half an hour's drive. He went back to his car. He had not slept on the plane and now had trouble with drowsiness as he drove out of Bantry and came to a sign which said: TO MIZEN HEAD. He turned in at the sign onto a road narrower than any he had traveled, a dangerous winding road with hedgerows like blindfolds. That sense of a familiar unfamiliar which he had felt earlier now deserted him. Here his readings of Joyce and Yeats and O'Casey were no help. He felt he did not know Ireland at all. The very end of the country, the heavy man had said. The very end of the land, down here.

After driving for about fifteen minutes, having passed

through a village called Durrus, he again saw the sea; this time a great lough, a long, wild inland reach of ocean, far below on his right. On the perimeter of this lough were small patchwork-quilt fields, poorer than any he had passed to date. Cottages built lonely in the lee of hillocks overlooked these fields, their windows facing away from the cold sea winds. In the next ten minutes of driving he saw no other car or no living thing, except for some gulls circling a bog. Again the road forked inland and he drove alongside the rim of a deserted stone quarry. On a hill above him were the ruins of three old roofless cottages, abandoned perhaps a hundred years ago. He passed a crossroads, with a tiny grocery shop and placards out front advertising *The Irish Times* and *The Irish Press*. At the crossroads, a sign: DRISHANE 5.

His eyes felt heavy. As soon as he reached the hotel he must get a few hours' sleep. The sea came up again on the horizon and he saw what seemed a rock far, far out, with a lighthouse on it. The car went over a hump of road. In the distance, a huddle of slate rooftops, and thrusting above them the gray spire of a church. He came to a road sign: DRISHANE and drove into the village street, which intersected with a small cross street, which led up to the church, the presbytery, and the school. In the main street were five small shops, three public houses, a bank, a garage, a post office in a tobacconist's shop, and a two-story building painted a surprising mauve, with a sign over the door: THE SCEPTRE HOTEL. He parked at the hotel doorway and got out.

There were two people on the street, a woman coming out of a food store and a man sitting idle on a small tractor. Both were looking at him, without seeming to do so. The front door of the hotel was shut. There was a brass bell socket, with a bell, which he pressed. He heard it ring inside. The woman went back into the food store and a moment later reappeared with another woman, both looking at him. The man on the tractor lit his pipe. Mangan rang again. After what seemed a long moment, he heard slouching footsteps. A bolt was drawn behind the door. It opened to reveal an old woman in black cardigan and gray woolen dress, who seemed to be having trouble with her lower set of false teeth.

"I'm looking for a room," Mangan said.

"I'm sorry. We're shut."

"Shut?"

"Mr. and Mrs. Fallon that owns the hotel have gone on their holidays to Majorca. They'll be away till next week. I'm sorry, now."

"Is there another hotel somewhere in this area?"

"There's a hotel at Crookhaven, but it's shut as well."

Behind the old woman, a plain girl came up the corridor, wiping her hands on a dish towel. "*Wachair*, tell them to ask at Feeley's. Go and ask at Feeley's, sir, it's just across the street. Seamus Feeley would know if there's any place open. You might find a bed-and-breakfast place."

The old woman nodded in agreement, her dim eyes not seeming to focus on him. "Yes, sir, just across the street there," she said, pointing past him. "D'you see the sign?"

"Thank you," he said. The girl nodded. The old woman gave him a wandering smile and a bob of her head as she shut the heavy door. He turned back to the street. A cold wind blew up. Black clouds slid overhead, casting a running shadow on the pavements. He went across the street, watched by the man on the tractor and the woman at the doorway of the food store.

The door to S. Feeley's office was shut. In the glazed window was a legend: S. P. FEELEY, AUCTIONEER & REAL ESTATE. Under it a cardboard notice: CLOSED. But next door in the same building was a small general store which also bore the sign: S. FEELEY. He went into the store, which was like the front room of a cottage, jammed with tiny aisles, lined with grocery items, a cold-meats section, hardware, sweets, fishing tackle, Irish sweaters, rubber boots, and a bakery counter. The shop seemed empty. As he went up to the cash register, a voice from the rear called "Shop!" and a fat, fair woman came in from what seemed to be a kitchen in the back of the premises, holding a large black cat in her arms. She let the cat down and looked up, seeming startled. Then, swiftly, she masked her startled look with a shopkeeper's half smile. "Afternoon, sir. You'd be wanting?"

"I was told to ask for Mr. Feeley. It's about a room. The hotel is shut and they sent me over here."

"It would be a room for yourself, then? Bed and breakfast?"

"Well, yes. Or just a room?"

"Just a minute, please."

With a conciliatory smile the fat woman turned away and went to the rear of the premises. After a moment she came back, beckoning. "If you'll just step this way, sir, please."

The shop was in the front part of the Feeley home. Behind it was a big modern kitchen, and there was a passageway with a new figured carpet which led under a colored oleograph of the Sacred Heart to a parlor with a suite of matched furniture. Passing through the parlor, they entered a room which from the reversed sign in the glazed window was the office to which he had been directed in the first place. It was a small crowded place with a turf fire burning in the grate. On the mantelpiece above the fire was a colored plaster statue of the Virgin Mary, a bottle of Paddy whiskey, two glasses, and a recumbent gray cat. There were two old stuffed armchairs before the fire and all around the room a jumbled profusion of steel filing cabinets and tables spilling over with loose folders. At a wall desk under a large-scale Ordnance Survey map sat a small, stout man of about Mangan's age, dressed in a tweed jacket, an Aran turtleneck sweater, corduroy trousers, and battered suede boots. He was totally bald, and when he turned toward them, his thick rubbery lips curving in a smile, his bulbous eyes set back in the sides of his head like the eyes of an animal, he reminded Mangan at once of that intelligent, amiable mammal, the dolphin.

"This is my husband," the fair woman said. "Seamus, this is the gentleman." She nodded to Mangan and withdrew.

"It was about a room, was it?" the stout man asked.

"Yes. The hotel sent me over. They said you might know of some place."

Feeley smiled his curving smile. "The Fallons do be off to Spain. Isn't that the height of it? The Irish running off to the Continent for their holidays while the Continentals come here for theirs. Oh, the world is a funny place, all right."

His hand flipped toward an armchair. "Have a seat, will you? What was the name again?"

"Mangan. James Mangan."

"Mangan? We have that name here in this very parish."

"I know. That's why I came. I think some of them might be my relatives."

Feeley's sideways eyes slid around in his head. "Be damn and you have the look of a Mangan, so you have. I'd say you might be related all right to some of them around here. My wife is related to Mangans. My wife, Una. That lady you just saw."

"Is that so?"

"It is. Now, you're looking for a B and B, is that it?"

"Sorry?"

"Bed and breakfast. How long would you be thinking of staying?"

"Well, it depends. A few weeks?"

Feeley reached up and carefully removed a folder from the seemingly inextricable mass of papers on the top of his desk. "Bad time of year," he mused to himself, his thick fingers flipping through sheets. "Most of the B-and-B trade is in the summer, of course, but there's still one or two. No, that one's closed and let's see, there's just Mrs. . . . Mullin . . . Mrs. Mullin . . . Mrs. Mullin . . . here we are. No. Closed in December and January. Well, now." He stared at the folder, then slapped his hand down on it. His dolphin head craned up as though someone were about to throw him a fish. "A possibility!" he said. "There is a house up beyond in Duntally, a two-story house, three bedrooms, a parlor, a kitchen and sun porch. It belongs to a Mangan, as a matter of fact. Dinny Mangan. He let it for the holidays this year. Be damn and I have the key here someplace. There is linen and blankets—the lot. There's a Mrs. Kane that lives down the road. I'd say she'd be glad to come in and clean up for you. Can you cook a bit yourself?"

"Yes. But it sounds big for one person."

"It is big. Yes, it is big. But sure that's all the better. Now, I'm the agent in this matter and I'd say we can arrange terms that will suit you." Feeley opened a bottom drawer in his desk and took out a circle of keys, all with tags on them. He spun it like a prayer wheel and stopped it with his index finger. "Ah! Here tis. Duntally."

He rose up. "This house is only ten minutes by car from Drishane. A bit over half an hour on foot. Will we go and have a look, so?"

They went out into the street. As at a signal, the man on the tractor started his machine. "Will we go in my car or in yours?" Feeley asked. "We'll take mine," he decided, without waiting for Mangan's answer. And so they set off.

Feeley's car was more powerful than Mangan's and was painted a strange metallic green. The interior smelled of sheep, and the back seat, like an extension of his office, was strewn with folders, briefcases, Ordnance Survey maps, and old newspapers. They passed through the village and turned up a narrow side road. As they entered this road, a man came down it, standing upright on a tiny donkey cart, reining in his donkey. Scything into the high grass of the ditch, Feeley managed to avoid this obstacle without slackening his speed and at the same time raised his hand from the wheel to wave cordially at his near-victim. Past high fuchsia hedges they climbed at reckless speed until the car reached a crossroads and turned right onto a bare, narrow, lonely road which ran along a ridge of mountainside. Far below, like a postcard view, was Drishane and its church spire, and beyond it, distantly, the great bay curving out to a headland, and on the horizon, rising like a sword from the gray sea, the lighthouse rock. "What is that rock?" Mangan asked, pointing. Feeley looked, then cast his dolphin grin on his passenger. "Fastnet," he cried. "Fastnet lighthouse," then pointed ahead. "See that house?" It was the first house they had come to in minutes of driving, a newly built bungalow by the roadside, its yard still strewn with building debris. "That's Mrs. Kane's place. She's the woman who'll do for you. Ah, she's a grand person."

Past Mrs. Kane's the road forked. Feeley took the smaller fork, which was simply a rough track, so narrow that the car could barely move within its limits. Ahead in a hollow just off the road, fenced in by a shield of ragged hedges, was an old two-story house with faded pink walls and a high slate roof. Its glassed-in front porch faced the road and a small neglected front garden. At the rear of the house were very old outhouses, thatched, and with the irregular stone walls of Irish peasant cottages of the last century. The outhouses seemed abandoned, their roofs sagging. "Here we are, then," Feeley said, as his car whipped through a gateless back gateway and came to a halt on a rocky promontory in the yard outside the farmhouse's back door.

There were no hens in the yard. The house had the look of being abandoned, yet when Feeley unlocked the kitchen door there was no shut-up smell inside. All was clean, as though it had been swept and dusted that morning. The kitchen was furnished with four wooden armchairs with faded green seat cushions. Its wooden table was grooved in the service of countless meals. The stove was an old-fashioned gas cooker and there was a large open hearth with a fire set in it and turf stacked nearby ready for burning. Mangan saw cutlery, glasses, and china in the glass front cupboard, and someone had built an unpainted bookcase into the far wall and filled it with Penguin paperbacks, a dictionary and encyclopedia, and other, older volumes. Over the mantelpiece there was a large photograph of Pope John and a colored oleograph of Our Lady hung at the kitchen door, intertwined with a crucifix made of palm leaves. The house was not cold or damp. There was a bathroom next to the kitchen, and Feeley pointed out the water heater beside it. "It's a good house," Feeley said, as he preceded Mangan into the parlor. "Last summer's tenants were well satisfied with it."

The parlor faced the glassed-in sun porch, which gave on a view of the neglected front garden and, beyond it, the bay and the lighthouse on the rock. "Will we go upstairs?" Feeley asked and led Mangan up a narrow flight, past a statue of the Virgin Mary in a landing alcove, to three bedrooms on the upper floor. In the largest of these bedrooms, which they now entered, there was a picture and a scroll dedicating the house to the Sacred Heart, and under it, burning bright, a small lamp in the shape of a heart.

"I thought the house was empty," Mangan said, pointing to the lamp.

"Oh, that never goes out," Feeley informed him. "It runs on the gas. *In perpetua*, as you might say. And look here, sir. Plenty of blankets and sheets. You could move right in, make up your bed, and have a sleep after your long journey. Will you be wanting the house?"

"Yes."

"Grand. Will we go downstairs, then? Is there something else you'd like to see?"

"No."

"Then, tell you what. I'll run you back to the village and we'll get some stuff for your breakfast. Come back here and have a good sleep and then stop in to see me sometime tomorrow. How would that suit you?"

"Fine. Do you want a deposit?"

"Ah, not at all. Not at all. And the price will be reasonable. I can assure you. Tis nice and quiet, isn't it? Very quiet. A grand place for a rest."

And then they drove back to the village. An hour later, having collected his car and retraced his route up the narrow, lonely roads, Mangan reentered the empty house called Duntally. As he went in, putting down two paper bags of groceries on the kitchen table, daylight was beginning to die outside, and as he entered the parlor, with its sun-porch view of bay and headlands, the evening sky was filled with an almost supernatural light. The lighthouse flashed suddenly like a signal from some secret source. As he looked down at the fields surrounding the bay, it seemed to him that he had gone back in time: there was a stillness in this scene as in a painting of medieval times. The distant vista of fields, the church spire and the slate rooftops far below, all of it was like a world long gone, still as a Poussin landscape, unchanged and unchanging. There was no sound at all, not even an insect's hum or a bird's cry. Caught in that stillness, he stood unmoving. It was as though his life had stopped.

Loud, sudden, the rain came down. Loud because it was the only sound. The sky darkened. The rain beat on the slates, wept against the windows, made the ragged hedgerows in the deserted front garden writhe and twist. He felt alone: never so alone as now. Turning from the rain, he went back into the corridor and climbed up the stairs. In the largest bedroom the little heart-shaped lamp burned like a wound. Awkwardly, he put sheets and blankets on the double bed then, stripping off his clothes, lay down on an old, lumpy mattress hollowed from the bodies of other sleepers. The rain beat on the roof but he no longer heard it.

He woke in darkness and slid into panic, not knowing who or where he was until he saw the bright-lit little red lamp above his bed. Much later, at dawn, a cock crowed, wakening him again, and he lay for an hour, warm in the bed, looking at the windowpane lashed with rain, at the little red lamp and, above it, at Christ exposing his Sacred Heart. He slept again for an hour and at eight in the morning rose up in the damp cold room, dressed, and went down to the kitchen, where he put a match to the stacked turf fire in the grate and lit the gas stove to boil water for coffee. The rain had stopped. He went through the parlor to stand in the glass-walled porch, where again he could see that landscape, still as a medieval painting, unchanged and unchanging, the fields, the sea, the great headlands circling the bay like outstretched arms. Far off on the horizon the Fastnet lighthouse flashed its secret message. It came to him that he was looking toward America from a point of land which was the most westerly part of Europe.

He heard the water boil. He went back into the kitchen, where he made coffee and began to fry the bacon slices which Feeley had cut for him yesterday in his shop. As he stood by the kitchen window turning the frying bacon with a fork, he became aware that he was being watched. For a moment he did not trust this instinct. Then, as he carried the frying pan to the sink to pour off the bacon fat, on the periphery of his vision he saw a woman in the yard outside.

She was deliberately not looking at him but instead looked up as though searching for something on the worn green flanks of mountain which rose behind the house. The woman was old and stout and wore a man's gray tweed jacket, under it a raveled cardigan. Her black skirt hung askew, its placket unhooked; her brown lisle stockings were twisted, and she wore a pair of man's boots. As she stood there he thought of her as a female derelict. Yet, a moment later, turning away from the mountainside which she had pretended to study, she lifted her head and it seemed to him that her gray hair stood out in aureole against the sky's light like some crown of grace.

He watched her cross the yard and climb a hillock, disappearing from view behind one of the decaying stone outhouses. He knew that she knew he had seen her. He put down his frying pan, unbolted the kitchen door, and stepped out into the morning chill. There was no car or bicycle in sight. Could she have walked up here? Could she be the cleaning woman Feeley had talked about? He remembered the neat new bungalow which had been pointed out as the cleaning woman's house. Surely that new bungalow didn't belong to this old tramp.

He crossed the yard. The long grass wet his shoes as he climbed the hillock to see where she had gone. But when he reached the top, she was nowhere in sight. Ahead, in the landscape in which she had disappeared, he saw an unused potato patch and a wild hedge, behind which he heard a noisy brook. He went forward to the hedge and peered through it, but could see no place where she might have hidden herself. Mystified, he went back down the hillock and into the house. As he picked up his frying pan again, suddenly she came into sight in the kitchen window going down through the yard into a little rough lane at the end of it, a lane he had not noticed before. Where had she disappeared to up there when he looked for her? Not wanting to seem to pursue her out of doors, he ran upstairs and peered out of a bedroom window. Now he saw her again. She was still in the lane, that lane which he had not noticed before but which connected his house with a small old cottage farther down the hillside. White smoke came from its chimney. He saw the old woman enter her yard, scattering a few chickens and ducks, which flocked to her as she went toward her door, which was open. She went in.

So he was not alone up here. He went downstairs, cut bread, and ate his breakfast. Afterward he unpacked his bags and laid out all the Mangan books he had brought from Montreal, together with the notes he had made on them in the past several days in New York. By that time it was after nine. Dressed in his raincoat and a hat, he went out into the rain. He looked down the lane in the direction of the cottage, but from the yard the cottage was invisible. Yet when he got into his car he felt sure that someone was watching him. Uneasy, he drove away.

In Drishane the village street was deserted and all the shops seemed shut. He parked outside Feeley's store and walked across the broad pavement to look in the shop window. At that moment the tobacconist's shop across the street, which doubled as the post office, opened its doors. A young girl came out, placed two newspaper placards advertising *The Irish Times* and *The Irish Press* on the pavement in front of the shop, then went in again. Mangan turned back to look through Feeley's window, but there was no sign of life among the clutter of merchandise. He heard a grating sound above his head and, looking up, saw Feeley's rubbery white face grinning down at him.

"Mr. Mangan. You're bright and early. Did you sleep all right?"

"Yes. Sorry, I thought you'd be open. I'll come back later."

"Don't stir. I'll be down directly," said Feeley, withdrawing his head. Mangan heard the upper window shut and footsteps on the stairs, yet when the shop door was unlocked and opened, the person behind it was not Feeley but his wife, the fat, fair woman he had seen yesterday. "Good morning, Mr. Mangan," said she, smiling her anxious smile. "Come in, please. Seamus will be down directly. You're early, so."

"Is my watch wrong? I thought it was ten o'clock."

"It is, it is. Ah, we don't get up at the crack of dawn in Drishane. Come this way, sir. Did you sleep well?"

And so, talking, she led him into the kitchen behind the store and sat him down at a table covered with a formica top. The kitchen was very modern, with a large refrigerator and a bacon-slicing machine, a freezer and aluminum sink fittings. "I was just wetting some tea," Mrs. Feeley said. "You'll join us in a cup?"

"Oh, no, that's all right."

"No, no, you will. Milk and sugar?"

As she spoke, her husband entered the kitchen, wearing his turtleneck sweater and corduroy trousers, smiling, his thick curved lips curiously immobile, so that his smile became a mask, hiding rather than revealing his mood. "Rashers, I will have," said he loudly. "And how were those rashers I cut for you yesterday, Mr. Mangan, sir?"

"Rashers?"

"Rashers of bacon. This bacon," Feeley said, lifting a side of bacon, placing it on the machine, and cutting off three thick slices, which he immediately handed over to his wife, who put them in an electric frying pan. "It comes from West Cork pigs. And that is the best of bacon, I say. But maybe you're not a man who's interested in material things, Mr. Mangan. May I ask what line of work are you in?"

"I'm a writer."

"Ah! A newspaper writer?"

"No."

"No? I thought, being interested in the Mangans . . ."
Feeley broke off. His wife at the frying pan had given him
a warning look.

"Why is that?" Mangan asked.

"Why is what, sir?"

"Why would a newspaperman be specially interested in
the Mangans?"

"Oh, no reason. I just meant that you coming here in the
dead of winter, looking for your family tree, so to speak,
that's a bit of a detective story, isn't it?"

"Is it?" Mangan said. He watched Mrs. Feeley ladle a
fried egg on her husband's plate. "Well, I am a newspaper
writer, as it happens. And I sometimes write for documen-
tary films. But this is strictly a vacation. A personal thing."

"So you are a film man."

"No, not really. I sometimes write film commentaries.
On the United Nations and so on. For television."

Feeley bent to his plate and, carefully picking up the
whole fried egg on his fork, swallowed it in one bite. "And
you were wanting to know about the Mangans," he said.
"Well, there are two families of Mangans in this district.
There is Daniel Mangan, they call him Dinny. He lives
with his mother up your way at Duntally. They are con-
nections of my wife, through marriage, you might say."

"They are not," said Mrs. Feeley. "Seamus, will you give
over with that. He's always saying I'm related to Mrs.
Mangan. I am not."

"Well, anyway," Feeley said, "there's Dinny Mangan
and then there's his first cousins, Con and Kathleen. They
live up your way, too. Farther up the road on the top of
the mountain, a house called Gorteen."

"Are they still up there?" Mrs. Feeley asked. "I heard
he'd moved over by Skull now that the house is sold."

"No, he's still up there. The furniture is still in the house
and I let him stay on till the man comes. Oh, they're still

around. I saw the girl coming out of King's the other morning with half a dozen of stout."

Mrs. Feeley turned off the electric frying pan and stood over the kitchen table, staring at her husband. "You never told me about meeting the sister."

"Oh, hold your whist, woman. I didn't meet her. I just saw her in the street."

"Did she speak to you?"

"She did not. Now, Mr. Mangan, about your inquiries. The best thing for you would be to start with Father Burke, our parish priest. He does often be asked about parish records and so on. If you have relations here, he's the man will track them down. You'll find him at the presbytery just up the street."

"Did you speak to her?" Mrs. Feeley asked in a thunderous voice, ignoring this talk about the priest.

"I did not."

"Did she see you? If she saw you she spoke to you."

Feeley sighed and rose, wiping his mouth with the back of his hand. "Una, will you allow me one minute?" He turned to Mangan. "Father Burke does be in the presbytery all morning, barring an emergency. Why don't you go up there now?"

Mangan, realizing he was being dismissed, rose and said his thanks. "Not at all." Feeley gave his dolphin grin. "And after you've finished with the priest, if you stop in here I could run you out to see Dinny Mangan."

"Dinny won't be at home," Mrs. Feeley snapped. "And you're going nowhere, do you hear me, Seamus?"

Her husband shrugged. Quickly, he ushered Mangan out of the kitchen and through the shop. "Sorry about that." He winked his dolphin eye. "It's her time of life. Hot flushes—the lot." He unlocked the shop door. "Now, you go straight up the street, first right at the cross, and it's the first house past the church. Good luck, Mr. Mangan."

The village was beginning to stir. As Mangan walked out, a small cart came up the street noisily hauling a rubber-wheeled milk cart loaded with empty clattering milk churns. The driver, a middle-aged man in a cap, tipped a wave to Mangan as he passed. A fat boy came out of an alley beside one of the pubs with a dolly on which he had stacked two yellow metal containers of propane gas. He lowered the dolly and nodded to Mangan. "Nice day."

"Nice day," Mangan echoed. He started up his car and drove to the cross street, where, as instructed, he turned right. Ahead, the high spire of the church seemed to reel in the sky, so swiftly did the clouds scud past behind it. The church, like most others he had seen in Ireland, appeared unconscionably large for the village which surrounded it. Enclosed by a graveyard full of Celtic crosses, it was a grim gray fieldstone building with, beyond it, a house in the same stone, surrounded by a low stucco wall. A small iron gate led up a graveled walk to the gate of this presbytery. There was an old-fashioned bell, which he grasped and pulled. Within the house he heard it ring.

Footsteps. An old woman in carpet slippers, gray work apron, and faded flowered dress opened the door.

"Yes?"

"Father Burke?"

"Who is it calling?"

"My name is Mangan."

"Come in, please."

The hall smelled institutional, an acrid stink of cleaning fluid and carbolic soap. The floor was shining wood, and as she moved ahead of him she shuffled her slippers as though by her action she gave an extra polish to its surface. "Nice day," she said, opening a parlor door to the right of her hall. He went in and she closed the door behind him. The parlor was large, with a bay window which gave on the front garden and the street beyond it. The pictures on its walls were holy and palm leaves were twisted in cruciform shape over the door. On the mahogany dining table in the center of the room were copies of Catholic Truth Society pamphlets and African Missionary Society magazines. Six dining chairs were spaced around the table, in neat unuse, but in the bay-window alcove were two much-worn green leatherette armchairs and a small round table bearing an ashtray. Mangan went to the window and sat in one of the armchairs. At once, the door opened. He stood, as though caught in the commission of a theft. "Don't get up," a soft voice advised.

The priest who entered the room was not at all what he had expected. He had envisaged an older man. But this priest was younger than he, a thin, pale-faced youth, his clerical suit one size too big for him, its stiff black serge trousers already shiny with wear in the knees and seat. His cheap celluloid Roman collar was attached to an ill-fitting black dickey. His hand, which he held out to Mangan, was rough as a farmer's, its middle and index fingers painted brown by nicotine stains.

"I'm Denis Burke," he said. "And you must be Mr. Mangan."

"How do you do," Mangan said. "I hope I'm not disturbing you."

"Not at all. Delighted to meet you," the priest said, his smile revealing a mouthful of decaying teeth. "I hear you've come in search of your ancestors."

"How did you know that?"

"There is nothing a person does not know in a place like this. That is the drawback of living here. You know too much about everybody, but it is not enough to keep your brain in rapid circulation. Sit down, won't you?"

Outside the window the stormy skies had muted to an obedient gray. A soft rain began to fall. The priest proffered cigarettes, then lit one himself. "Well, let's see. You came to Drishane yesterday looking for a room in the Sceptre. Seamus Feeley fixed you up in the old Mangan house at Duntally." The priest laughed. "That was a start, wasn't it? And he tells me that you were born in Canada and you live in New York. Am I right so far?"

"Yes."

"Well, now. Tell me, what do you know of your family history?"

So Mangan told him about the family Bible, which he had brought from Canada. He told about Drishane in the Bible's record of births and deaths. He told about his grandfather sailing from Cork to Quebec, about his father's abortive visit to Drishane many years ago, and, finally, that he was trying to find out if the family was related to James Clarence Mangan, the poet. He told of the Drinan biography with its theory that Mangan had not died celibate but had married a West Cork woman who left him and went back to Skibbereen. And that the son of that marriage had moved from Skibbereen in later years and settled in Drishane.

"Mangan the poet?" Father Burke said. "Now, that's interesting! Hundreds of lines of his I read when I was a boy in school. And his son lived here, did he?"

"Yes. At least, according to one of his biographers. The other biographies contend that he never married at all. But it seems very odd that we in Canada would have books by and about him, and this tradition that we're related to him, if it was just an invention of that one biographer, who, incidentally, was a priest. A Father Drinan."

"James Clarence Mangan," Father Burke said. "I'm sure I have his poems someplace. When did he die?"

"Eighteen forty-nine." Mangan reached in his inside pocket and produced the daguerreotype. "This may be a photograph of him."

"But it's a photograph of you!" the priest said. He turned

the daguerreotype over. "J.M. 1847. Isn't that interesting. I didn't know they had photographs that far back."

"Those were among the first."

As the priest stared again at the photograph, a man pedaled up to the presbytery on a bicycle. He put the bicycle against the garden wall and opened the gate and hurried up the path. Now he rang the presbytery bell with several urgent peals. The priest rose, went to the bay window, knocked on it with his knuckles, and when he had secured the man's attention, nodded to him. He then turned back to Mangan.

"His wife must be sick again," he said. "I will have to go with him. I'll not be long. Look—would you like to come with me? We could talk in the car."

And so they went out into the soft rain. The heavily built man nodded to the priest. "It's Molly," he said. "Sorry now, Father."

"That's all right, Kieran. Is she bad?"

"She's bad," the man said. "The doctor is with her."

"I'll be with you directly," the priest said. He went down the hall and returned in a well-worn black raincoat and black hat. He carried a small bag. "My car is round the side," he said. "Do you want to follow on the bike, Kieran?"

"I'll do that, Father. I'll be there shortly," the man said. He got on his bicycle and pedaled off. Mangan and the priest walked around to the rear of the house, where the priest's battered little car was parked in an alley. "I may have to give her the last sacrament," the priest said. "But it won't take very long. Where did you come across that photograph? I've been thinking about that. Would there be any other photographs of Mangan around?"

"Apparently not," Mangan said. "Before I left New York I cabled the National Library in Dublin. They cabled back that there is no known photograph of him in existence. There are sketches and pen-and-pencil portraits, but all of them differ. And none of them is just like this daguerreo-type."

"So it could be a photograph of someone who wasn't the poet?"

"It could. But it's certainly someone who's related to me. And it looks a bit like the deathbed drawing of Mangan done in a Dublin hospital."

By now the little car was out of the village, and as it went along the small high-hedgerowed road, it slowed to a stop behind six swaying cows, which a small boy had let out of one field and was herding toward another field. The boy looked back, nodding respectfully to the priest. The cows were shunted to one side and the priest drove on and, far-ther up the road, turned into a narrow rough driveway, which led over rocky grazing foreland to a cottage under a spur of hill, sheltered from a sweep of strand and the rain-drenched, foaming sea. A child in a yellow slicker waited for them there, holding open an iron gate. The priest drove through the gateway, and the boy shut the gate behind them and ran on ahead into the cottage. There was another car in the farmyard. "That's Dr. Murphy's car," the priest said. He took his small bag and got out, saying again that he would not be long, and went hurrying toward the door of the cottage, leaving Mangan alone in this unfamiliar land-scape. The rain had turned to squall; the wind picked it up and lashed it in gusts across the yard, blurring the car's windshield, blinding out the view. Rain, heavy as the rain on that day of her funeral, himself soaked and floundering on Madison Avenue on that last day of his life as her hus-band. It was as though on that funeral day they had ended together, she and he, and now, one week later, reborn but not renamed, searching a new identity, he had crossed the frontier of this land, carrying in his pocket like a passport a photograph of himself as a man long dead. To sit here in this priest's car while the priest administered extreme unction to a dying Irish woman seemed a dream which like all true dreams moved at its own mysterious pace, without logic, toward a purpose he did not understand. To have spent his first night in Ireland, not in a hotel, but in that old farmhouse, in a room filled with holy pictures and a lamp in the shape of Christ's heart—all of it seemed a dream which might lead him not toward the ancestor he hoped to find, the first *poète maudit* whose statue stood in parks, whose name was known to Irish history, but to humble relatives in this strange backward place, to people he might even be ashamed to claim as kin. Like the daguerreotype in his pocket, he was the bearer of a face to which no certain identity had yet been attached. Like the man in that photograph, he had once been someone, was now no one, and might here, in this small wild country on the edge of Europe, discover who and what he would become.

The rain, beating and squalling, isolated him in the car so that he did not see the two figures leave the cottage. The car door opened. The priest looked in, smiling. "This is Dr. Murphy," he said. "And this is Mr. Mangan from America," moving aside to let the second man see Mangan. The doctor was a ruddy person with an inquisitive eye. "How do you do," he said and peered again, closely. "Your name is Mangan? Are you by chance a relation of the Mangans hereabouts?"

"Yes, I think so."

"You look like . . ." the doctor said, and stopped. He turned to the priest. "How long is it you've been here, Father?"

"Three years."

"Ah, you wouldn't remember the man I'm thinking of, then. Good day to you, Mr. Mangan. Goodbye, Father."

He moved off in the rain. The priest got into the car and banged the door, which shut improperly. "I wonder what man he's talking about," Mangan said.

"I don't know," the priest said. "As I said, I'm not that long in Drishane." He started the engine and drove to the gate. The child in the yellow slicker stood in the pelting rain holding it open. The priest waved to him as they passed.

When they returned to the presbytery, Mangan went to his own car and brought the family Bible into the priest's parlor. Father Burke sat down and read the flyleaf, then closed the Bible and asked: "Can you leave this with me?"

"Of course."

"That way I can compare it with the parish records. But I'm afraid that will take a bit of time and I have to go out again. I have word of a death up by Dunmanway. I'll have to leave you now."

"That's all right. When will I get in touch with you?"

"Come back in the morning," the priest said. "Between ten and eleven. I'll be here, please God."

The priest's old housekeeper let him out. It was no longer raining, and in the rapid and dramatic changes which seemed normal here, the sky was now clear and cold, with high fleecy clouds. He drove down into the village and stopped outside Feeley's store. At once Feeley's head popped up behind the auctioneer's sign in his window, and a moment later, smiling his strange dolphin grin, Feeley bounded out of the shop door and came to join him. "How did it go with Father Burke?"

"Oh, fine."

"He's a grand young man, isn't he?" Feeley said. "And I have other news for you. Dinny Mangan will be around to see you at six this evening. He'll come to your house himself."

"Thank you. And what about the other Mangan family? Con Mangan?"

"Well, yes, there's them, of course," Feeley said. "But I have a feeling, just a notion mind you, that 'tis the Dinny Mangan connection that you'll be closest to. He's a grand chap, Dinny, a grand chap."

"But perhaps, as I won't be seeing Dinny till this evening, I could go and see the other Mangans now."

Feeley put his head on one side as though to ponder. His white rubbery skin glistened as though it were wet. "You *could*," he said, slowly. "Yes, you could. But you don't know where they live, do you?"

"I could follow directions."

"You could, you could. It's up your way, so it is."

"Perhaps you could tell me the way?"

"I would run you up, but I am desperate busy," Feeley said.

"No need. Where would it be in relation to where I'm living now?"

"Where would it be?" Feeley wagged his head as though considering the merits of this question and, suddenly, seemed to come to a decision. "Why not?" he said, as though to himself. "Yes, it's not hard to find, not hard at all. Look, the road you are on, the road that goes up to your house, you don't turn down to your house, do you see, but you continue on up. The road becomes a boreen a bit further up the mountain."

"A boreen?"

"A little road. Just a track, do you see. But the car will manage it. Oh, yes. You go right up to the top of the mountain. Go to the very top of the road. Over the top you'll see the sea. But, before you get to the very top, you pass a house. It's off behind some whin bushes. That's Gorteen, the old Mangan house. That house is two hundred years old, so it is. But don't go to the house. Continue on up the road and right at the top there's a bit of a field on the left and there's a caravan there. That's where Con hangs out, when he's home. Do you follow me, now?"

"Yes, thanks. Just go up to the top of the mountain."

"That's it. And remember that Dinny Mangan will come by to your place at six. And by the way, sir, I'd not mention to Con that you're seeing Dinny. Or vice versa, as they say." Feeley smiled and wagged his head. "Mind you, if anyone asks, I said nothing."

"Thanks again."

"Pop in and see me in the morning on your way back from the priest's. Let me know how you get on."

"All right, I will," Mangan said, but as he drove off he wondered how Feeley could have known he was going to see the priest tomorrow. Surely in the few minutes it took to drive from the presbytery to the store the priest had not phoned Feeley with the news? And as he turned up the road toward Duntally, it came to him that life in Drishane was the obverse of his life in New York. There, in the last weeks, he had discovered that nobody knew or cared whether he lived or died; no neighbors saw his comings and goings; there was no community. Here, even though he had arrived only twenty-four hours earlier, every one of his movements was known, every step he took was noted and commented on by one of the inhabitants. Irrationally, this pleased him. Here he was of interest for himself; his name had a familiar ring on these tongues. Here, for the first time in years, no one knew him as Beatrice Abbot's husband.

At the outskirts of the village he turned up the side road toward Duntally. There were few houses on this road, and by the time he reached the crossroad higher up, there was no house in sight in any direction. Turning at the crossroads, he drove along a bare narrow road which circled the mountainside, past grazing lands whose only inhabitants were black-faced sheep which cropped indolently on grassy knolls by the roadside, indifferent to the car's passing. He passed the new bungalow surrounded by the rubble of its building and then, coming to the gateway to Duntally, drove on up the road, which began to climb more steeply, narrowing to two ruts where the wheels of cars and carts had passed before him. Purple patches of heather and large isolated rocks broke the gray-green monotony on either side. He was forced to shift down to second gear to ascend the last steep incline that led to the mountaintop. On his left he saw the whin bushes Feeley had spoken of, which even in their present wild state evidenced a man-made regularity at odds with the untouched wilderness here at the mountaintop. The house they sheltered was concealed from view, but as he passed it he saw the ridge of its buckled slate roof. At the very top of the incline the car almost stalled, then ground forward to rest on the ridge. Ahead was blue sky, and as he looked down he saw the little track of road fall precipitously down the other side, going toward a ribbon of intersecting road, far below, a road which ran among cultivated fields, around the sweep of a sea bay enclosed by wild headlands. This splendid panorama was marred by a dirty yellow-colored caravan trailer, up on wooden blocks in a field on his right. From the trailer on a clothesline which extended to a rock on the hillside, sheets and miscellaneous garments flapped like the flags of poverty. A quiff of smoke rose toward the sky from a dirty exhaust vent. Someone was at home.

Mangan drove his car into the mouth of the small field. At once, a sheepdog with foxy face and black-and-white piebald colors jumped down from its perch on the makeshift stone wall surrounding the field, to come at the car yowling and snapping. Mangan feared dogs. He did not open the car door but stared at the animal, which bared its teeth, then jumped up, bracing its forefeet on the door. He made a menacing gesture, safe behind the door, and the dog dropped back on four feet and, yowling, began to edge away. He looked toward the trailer, where the door was opening. A young woman stepped down. "Spot! Come in out of that!"

The dog, still barking, ran feverishly back toward the young woman, then ran forward again, feinting at the car. Mangan could no longer remain under cover. Reluctantly, he got out.

"Spot!" the young woman cried again, and the dog with a few halfhearted barks abandoned the field, retreating under the trailer. Mangan advanced, ashamed yet irritated by the dog and his own cowardice. The young woman, narrowing her eyes, peered at him as though she could not see him properly. Then, when he was close, he saw that there came on her face a look of astonishment. She was tall, younger than he had first imagined; about twenty, he supposed. She wore dirty blue jeans, tightly sculpted to her legs, and a baby-blue cardigan, unbuttoned in front, tucked into the jeans. Her reddish-blond hair fell to below her waist. Her eyes were a bright blue, her features pretty but insipid, her skin pale and unhealthy, a slum pallor at odds with this wild, lonely place.

"Hello," Mangan said. "I'm looking for Conor Mangan."

But the girl did not seem to hear him. She stood staring, as though he had come to arrest her.

"Is he at home?" Mangan said awkwardly.

"What's your name?"

"My name is Mangan, too. I'm from Montreal, originally. I think we might be relatives."

"Then you're the man that's staying at Duntally?"

"That's right."

"You're the one who's a fillim star from America."

Where on earth had she got hold of that story? Feeley? "No, I'm not."

"But you have to do with the fillims. Isn't that right, now?"

He was going to say it was his wife who was mixed up in films, but decided not to get into that. "No, absolutely not."

"Too bad," she said, and smiled. Her features, which had made him think of the vapid beauties of female saints in modern Catholic Church sculpture, were transformed by that smile. At once, despite her dirty clothes and slum pallor, he felt an overwhelming attraction toward her.

"I'm mad for the fillims," she said and laughed. "I'm Kathleen, Con's sister. He's gone up to Bantry, but he should be back soon. Do you want to come in and wait for him?"

"All right. Thank you."

He followed her up the steps, eying the moving arcs of her thighs. Underneath the caravan the dog set up a grumbling bark, then subsided. When the girl opened the door, Mangan noticed two bunk beds, one atop the other, partitioned off at the far end. So she slept in the same room with her brother. The sitting area was crowded and sleazy, with two velveteen armchairs and a small sofa with stuffing coming out of rips in its arms. There was also a rickety card table on which sat teacups and a jar of jam; a kerosene table lamp, a four-burner butane-gas ring, and, beside it, a counter containing a disarray of food cartons, dirty dishes, and a sink filled with wet clothes. In the center was a tin stove with a funnel which poked through an opening in the caravan's roof. The pleasant smell of burning turf in the stove was offset by a stale body odor from the girl. On three of the living-area walls were, variously, lithographs of Pope Paul, John F. Kennedy, and Our Lady appearing to Saint Thérèse at Lisieux.

"Do you want a cup of tea? I have it wet already. Are you here on your holidays?"

"In a way. I'm trying to trace someone who might be a relative of mine. Did you ever hear of James Clarence Mangan?"

Her face was blank.

"He was a poet," he said.

"A poet?" she said. Did she seem to flinch, or did he just imagine it. "What relation would he be to you, then?"

"Well, he could be my great-great-grandfather."

"*That* far back," she said. "Sure, who knows that far back?" She lifted the kettle off the ring and poured boiling water into the teapot. She smiled at him and again he felt that overwhelming attraction. But then she walked past him to pour the tea and the acrid smell of her body came into his nostrils, filling him with distaste. So these were the Irish Mangans, dirty, semiliterate gypsies. And yet, despite his distaste, the attraction remained.

"Milk and sugar?" she asked.

"Thanks. Whose is the big house back there?"

"Gorteen? It's ours. But the roof is damaged. That's why we're living in this caravan. I like it, the caravan. It suits me rightly. I suppose Mrs. Feeley's told you a few yarns about me?"

"No."

"Did she not, now? Has the cat got her tongue, then?" She laughed and sat down on the torn sofa, leaning forward, handing him his teacup. The half-buttoned baby-blue cardigan showed her young breasts. "That ould fool," she said. "Sitting there in her shop like a hen on eggs."

He sat opposite her. He now had an erection. She reminded him, not of women he had known in his adult life, but of the pubescent temptresses of his boyhood, those first forbidden fruits of sexual encounter, which remained the most erotic memories of his life. He felt his face hot and avoided her eye, afraid that she might guess the cause of his perturbation.

"Do you know, I think you're shy," she said and laughed.

He shook his head.

"How could a person be shy and them in the fillims?"

"I'm not in the films."

"I wish *I* was in the fillims," she said. "Ah, I suppose I'm too ugly." As though posing for a photograph, she paraded her profile for his inspection. "There's a pal of mine, a girl from Dublin that used to come here on her holidays, she's in the telly now in England. She was in a Kung Fu. Ah, but anyway, she had bosoms out to here." She gestured, then hooked her fingers into the unbuttoned cardigan, pulling it open wider so that her breasts were almost completely exposed. She smiled at him. "Too small?"

"No. I mean, I don't think it matters," he said, staring in excited dismay at her rounded childish breasts.

"You're just saying that." She lifted the teapot, offering him a second cup. "What's your first name, again?"

"James."

"Do you not get Jim or Jimmy?"

"Jamie. But I don't like it."

"And are you married?"

"I was. My wife died."

"I'm sorry, now. Do you have children?"

"No."

"It must be lonely for you, so. Was she sick long?"

"No. She died in a car accident."

She leaned forward, pouring the tea, her reddish-blond hair falling about her cheeks. "More milk?"

"Thanks."

She rose and went to the counter to fetch a milk bottle. When she turned away from him, he stared like a voyeur at her long, straight back and girlish buttocks. "How old are you?" he said. "Or do you mind my asking?"

"How old do you think I am?"

"I don't know. Twenty-two?"

"Get away out of that! Do I look that ancient?"

A sadness filled him. For the first time in his life he felt he had crossed the bar: had become a widower sailing out on a sea of no return. This girl could be his daughter. "I'm sorry," he said. "I'm bad at people's ages. How old would you say I am?"

It was a mistake, a desperate attempt to tack back, to return to that innocent harbor where, in his own mind, he was young enough for any girl. "Would forty be about right?" she asked.

"Younger."

"Well, you're over thirty, I'd say." She put back her head and laughed. Below the floor, Spot growled, then began to bark. She got up and went toward the caravan window, saying: "That'll be Con."

Mangan stood up, putting down his teacup. He saw, coming in at the caravan door, what at first seemed to be a little boy in a torn sports coat with dirty flannel trousers tucked into rubber fishing boots. The newcomer looked at the girl, then looked up at Mangan. He was not a boy but a small man, almost a midget. His skin had the flayed redness of the Irish countryman, and on his chin was a heavy blue undergrowth of beard. "So you're the Mangan from the United States, am I right?" he said at once.

"That's right."

The little man looked at him again, then turned and looked at his sister. "Amazing."

"Yes. I nearly dropped dead," she said.

The little man turned back to Mangan. "You look like a relative of ours. Did you know that?"

"The doctor, Dr. Murphy, told me I look like someone who used to live here. Would that be the same man?"

"I'd say it would," the little man said. "An uncle of mine who's dead now. You're the spit of him."

"And what was his name?"

But the little man simply laughed and shrugged and said to his sister, "Well, he wasn't a fillim star, our uncle, was he, Kath?"

"This man says he's not a fillim star, either."

"Is that a fact? So Feeley was wrong-shipped, as per usual," the little man said sourly. "I'm not surprised. Ah, you had no luck, running into the same Feeley the first minute you landed up in Drishane. Putting you into Duntally."

"The hotel was shut."

"I know. But you could have stayed with us. We'd be glad to have you, wouldn't we, Kath?"

Mangan looked at the girl, then looked at the partition beyond the two single bunk beds.

"Not in the caravan," the little man said, as though he understood the look. "But there's beds and plenty at the old house down the road. Will you take a bottle of stout?" He reached under the tattered sofa and brought out a cardboard carton containing black bottles of Guinness. He took two of these to the sink and opened them, pouring the heavy stout into glasses. "Kath, do you want a glass?"

"I do, surely."

"So you're on your holidays?" the little man asked Mangan.

"He's here looking for his great-great-grandfather," the girl said, and laughed.

"This uncle of yours," Mangan asked, "the one you say looked like me. Do you have a photograph of him?"

"Down at the other house, maybe." The little man handed him a glass of stout. At that moment Mangan thought of the daguerreotype in his pocket, but something warned him not to take it out. Let them show him a photograph of their uncle first.

"Your health now," the little man said.

He sipped the heavy stout. It was not to his liking, but he imitated his host and Kathleen and drank a long, deep swallow. "When was it your people emigrated to America?" the little man asked.

"Sit down," the girl urged, and so he sat and took out the notebook he had compiled in the past week in New York, giving the birthdates of his father, grandfather, and great-grandfather. In the next half hour he went over his family history, going back to the family Bible listing births in Drishane. In that time, they drank two more bottles of stout and Conor Mangan pored over Mangan's notebook as though it were a racing form. Suddenly he stabbed a finger at a page. "India!" he said. "It says here that your great-grandfather went to India. I have a photo down at the house of a soldier on a draft to India. Now that could be the very man. Your great-grandfather. Patrick James Mangan, it says here. That was his name, was it?"

"Yes."

"Will we go down to the house and have a look?"

Mangan stood at once. The stout had made him light-headed. India, the army, a photograph of a soldier. It seemed his quest was on track. "Right, then," he said. He turned to the girl, uneager to leave her behind. "Will you come, too?"

"Of course I will." And so the three of them went down the caravan steps out to a blustery, overcast afternoon, fast-flying clouds coming at them, slicing into the mountaintop. The dog, after a preliminary growl, came from under the caravan and fell in at Conor Mangan's heels. Through the wet grass of the field they went to the road, where, parked at an angle to prevent its rolling downhill, was a small, battered pickup truck. "We'll take the lorry," the little man said.

"You take it on your own, then," the girl said. She reached for Mangan's arm. "The two of us will walk, won't we, Jim?"

"Right, then. Stretch your legs," the little man said, and hopped into his truck, the dog after him. The girl stood, smiling, still holding Mangan's arm as the truck moved out and went past them in low gear down the incline of the road. And so, arm-linked, Mangan and the girl followed, leaning back to counteract the steep slope. She shifted her grip, putting her arm around his body, and he in turn slipped his arm about her waist, feeling the soft warmth of her under her cardigan. The fast-moving clouds came on them, enveloping them in a mountain mist. He looked at her and smiled, and she smiled that smile he could not resist, then leaned against him provocatively in the mock-innocent way of little girls he remembered from long ago when sex was all delicious frustrated anticipation. Her red tresses blew about, obscuring her features, and she removed her hand from his waist to brush her hair back out of her eyes. At that moment, without thinking, Mangan pulled her to a standstill on the steep incline and took her in his arms, kissing her, feeling her soft mouth open to his.

He felt elated, guilty, and surprised at his boldness, then, remembering her youth, turned in sudden fear, peering ahead in the mist, worried that the manikin her brother might be watching. But the little truck was invisible in the mist. He looked at her again with an uneasy grin and she took his arm, urging him down the steep road, both of them breaking into an involuntary run which continued until they reached the high ragged hedgerows surrounding and concealing the house. Opening to the yard was a rusted, unhinged gate, revealing a cobblestone driveway green with weeds. Beyond, in the cloud mist, they saw the truck sitting in the yard and Conor Mangan, the dog at his heels, hurrying toward the front door.

Despite the girl's arm entwined in his, despite the evidence of his eyes that there was a car, a man, and a dog in the yard, Mangan felt utterly alone in this place. The house, a tall two-story building of gray stone, faced him as though it were somehow aware of his intrusion into its territory. Its aspect was at once minatory and compelling, as though it willed him to approach, yet intended to destroy him. As he came toward it, the faded green front door seemed false as a *trompe l'oeil* painting, giving no hint of how he might penetrate this façade. It was not, as he had expected, an old farmhouse, but rather the sort of minor manse which might have been built for a minister, not here on the top of a mountain, but on the outskirts of a small town. Behind the house was an inner yard with abandoned stables, a cow byre, and a barn in which stood a high old jaunting cart, its wheels buckled, its leather seats rotted and soaked by rain. In the yard also was an old plow turned on its side, sticking up like a whale's fin. And as he stood gazing on this scene, he felt that he was looking, not at a real house in a real yard, but at a photograph of such a house, caught in the wink of a shutter on some day long ago.

And then the dog began to bark, running around the front steps as the little man lifted a heavy iron key from under the doormat, put it in the door, turned it twice in the lock; then, grasping the iron doorknob, which was high as his chest, pulled the door toward him with a loud clatter of its wooden footboard on the stone step. He looked back, a gnomelike figure holding the door open on an interior darkness, and with his free hand beckoned Mangan to enter.

And so Mangan went forward, the girl following after him, and as the little man saw them approach he preceded them into the house. It was dark because the corridor doors were shut, and the little man moved ahead through a field of bowls and tin cans placed to catch ceiling drips, opening the doors of the ground-floor rooms to let light fall into the hallway. The first door he opened revealed a large dining room with a table and chairs in dark brown rosewood. However, the room seemed to be used as a storeroom and the dining table was covered with jumbled heaps of old sweaters, undergarments, and cardboard cartons containing sheepskin rugs. Empty stout bottles sat in boxes on the floor and there was a large sack of meal in one corner and an old canvas-and-leather trunk in another. They passed on, the little man opening the door on the right of the corridor, which gave on a rectangular sitting room. Mangan hesitated at the threshold, held by what he saw there.

"Go in, go in," the little man said. "That's the right room for former history. We don't use it now. I suppose they never did use it much. It's the parlor, the place where you'd put your visitors in the old days. The photo we're looking for should be in here someplace."

Mangan went in. Through the cracked and dusty windowpanes a blear northern light beat down on the objects in the room, highlighting them in the manner of an old-fashioned time exposure, seeming further to bleach the flowered wallpaper and cretonne furniture covers, which were already faded by age and wear. This strong light fell impartially on two armchairs, a chaise longue, a painted firescreen, and an occasional table, leaving shadowed around them the many pictures, photographs, and drawings which adorned walls, tables, and mantelpiece. Only one of these pictures was familiar to Mangan: a framed lithograph of Veronese's "Madonna and Child." The many others were all of real people, ranging from ill-executed portraits in oils to silhouettes, daguerreotypes, and group photographs in sepia tones. As Mangan hesitated in the way of someone entering a picture gallery, uncertain where to start his inspection, the little man skipped ahead of him in a proprietorial manner. "This is the room, do you see. All the Mangans are here, even the skeletons in the closet. Over there now, those old fellas, those were all original oil paintings done by one family of painters that still lives in Bantry. Harrington is the painter's name and it's a trade that's handed down from father to son, and one of that family, Teig Harrington, was down here a few years back and he told me this picture, the first one here in the corner, was done by his great-grandfather. And they're all of Mangans or women married into the Mangan family, the people in these paintings. Would you credit that, now?"

He would, and he did. The oil portraits were mostly oval in shape, the work of artists who aimed at a likeness but who were weak on anatomical details and lacked the skill to depict the folds of garments. Each portrait had some obvious defect which gave it a naïve quality, an ill-formed hand, an awkward pose, a wooden pleat of dress. The clothes of the subjects labeled the sitters within their particular era. Thus, the earliest was of an elderly man who wore a high hat and knee breeches with a fob sticking out from under his cutaway coat in the style of the late eighteenth century. The portrait next to it was of a stout person wearing a Vandyke beard and mustache, with a black cravat wound around his high collar in the nineteenth-century manner. There was also a woman in a wasp waist and leg-of-mutton sleeves, a matriarch of Victorian times. A man in black string tie and fustian suit seemed from a later period. At least, Mangan thought, if all of them are Mangans, we were not peasants. Nor gypsies hiding in the bogs. But it was the framed photographs, the daguerreotypes, calotypes, and tintypes which most attracted his interest. He moved about, peering, searching for a face which might be his own.

Suddenly the girl behind him said, "It stinks in here. There must be a dead rat someplace." Her diminutive brother had already seated himself at a writing desk and now took from the bottom drawer a large photograph album, which he hunched over like a child, turning the pages of a book too big for him to handle. "This is the old album," he said. "It's here someplace, that photo. What did you say your great-grandfather's first name was, again?"

"Patrick James."

"It's someplace," the little man repeated.

The girl walked to the window and stood, hands on hips, leaning forward to peer through the cracked, dusty panes at something in the yard. Seen thus, silhouetted against the blear, bright light, she seemed curiously childish, out of place among the dead heavy portraits in this room. He felt like one of those lecherous older men who stand outside schoolyards watching schoolgirls in their gym dresses. She had allowed him to kiss her. She might allow him to do more.

"Hah!" The little man rose, beckoning. "Come and look at this."

The girl turned around. Mangan went over to the desk. On a page of the big album which contained several other snapshots stuck in by passe-partout edgings was a sepia studio photograph of a British soldier standing by a packed kit bag, to which was tied an old-fashioned solar topee. Underneath the portrait was a notation in faded violet ink.

PAT. Portobello Barracks, Dublin. 1863.
On draft for India. 1st Batt. Old Bombays
(Now Royal Dublin Fusiliers).

"This lad here," said the little man, putting his nicotine-stained forefinger on the photograph face. Patrick James Mangan. It is my guess and I am right, I will wager, that this lad is your great-grandfather. And the same man is my grandfather Conor Mangan's father. So we are the same family, do you see? From the selfsame man. Your man here. And I will tell you that this man is buried now in the graveyard down by Dunmanus Coos. And that he came home from service in India and died in British Army Married Quarters in Cork City."

"How did *you* know all that?" the girl asked.

"There's a lot of things I know and a lot more I make it my business to find out, my girl." The little man turned and looked up at Mangan. "I have the same interest as our friend Jim. I want to know who are the people who made me what I am today."

"They could have made you a bit bigger," the girl said.

"Good goods go in small parcels. Do you know, Jim, there were no small people before me on either side of the family. Were there some small people in your own family?"

"Not that I know of."

"Ah, don't heed this fellow," the girl said to Mangan, and laughed. "Sure he's not my brother at all. The Wee People left him under a cabbage in our yard."

"Don't make fun of what you know nothing about," the

little man snapped. "Those that makes fun of the Wee People, their teeth will drop out."

"Tell that to your granny," she said. "You'll have Jim here thinking we're a lot of ignorant culchies. Wee People, how are you!"

"Ah, shut your mouth," the little man shouted. He turned to Mangan. "As I was saying, Jim, if this photo is right, and I'd say it is, then you and me would be cousins."

Again, Mangan bent over the album. The sepia-toned photograph revealed the young soldier, awkward and lumpish in his ill-fitting tunic and regimental cap. He had a mustache which drooped doggily about his mouth, giving him an apologetic look. Pat for Patrick. Was that the Patrick for whom Mangan's father had been named? He bore no facial resemblance to Mangan's father. His face seemed stupid, his body graceless. He was a victim, a poor Irish peasant who had taken the English Queen's shilling to sweat for five years on the barracks square in Bombay, the raw, Regular Soldier of a Kipling tale.

He looked up from the photograph. The girl is right, he thought. There is a smell of decay in this room. Could this young private be a descendant of the poet Mangan? Was this dull face, content to end its days in British Army Married Quarters in Cork, Ireland, the same face that sired my grandfather, who sat at ease in rooms designed by Stanford White in the Mount Royal Club, comptroller of all the millions in the Canadian Pacific Railway's purse? And did my father, the managing editor, spring from this dolt's family tree? He peered closer at the photograph face, little bigger than a postage stamp. But the bland young features gave back no secrets.

The girl, pretending to examine the photograph, leaned into him from behind. At once, like the flick of a whip, the touch of her body brought him to heel. "A soldier," she said. "I hate soldiers. Taking orders and drilling and evicting people from their houses."

"You're soldier stock yourself," her diminutive brother snapped.

"I'd rather be a tinker."

The little man shook his head, as though to brush away this remark. "Come here, Jim," he said. "Look, this is my grandfather, and my grandmother with him."

The photograph now held out for his inspection showed a family grouped together in a photographer's studio, wearing the Sunday best of seventy years ago: a man and his wife staring into the camera with wild, wind-burned faces, and about them their life's harvest, two little girls in pinafores, three boys in short trousers. "This boyo here is my da," said the little man, pointing to one of the children. "He has the look of me, they say."

He had. But he did not look like Mangan, who turned from the book and continued his inspection of the photographs on the mantelpiece and on the walls. The girl rose and went out of the room, saying she was cold and it stank.

"Light the stove in the kitchen, then," the little man said. "We'll be in directly. Do you want to look some more at this album, Jim? Is there somebody you're looking for in particular?"

"Did you ever hear of James Clarence Mangan?"

"Clarence," the little man said. "That's a queer sort of a name."

"A poet."

"We had an uncle who was a bit of a poet. And I think there was one before that. I heard my daddy talk about that lad."

"But you never heard of James Clarence Mangan? He was a famous poet. His poems are still taught in the schools."

"I'm not much of a scholar," the little man said. He shut the album and put it back in the drawer. "Come in the kitchen, we'll have a drink. My uncle that's dead, now, he was a poet. He had his writing published in the newspapers in Dublin and Cork."

"What was his name?"

"Michael," the little man said, mysteriously dropping his voice to a whisper. "Michael Mangan." He stood and nodded his head toward the kitchen. "He's a bit of a sore subject in this family. Especially with her nabs there, Kathy. So mum's the word, if you follow me." He ushered Mangan into the hallway and shut the parlor door carefully behind him. "Rats," he explained. "I try to keep them out of the parlor. That's one of the good rooms that's not too spoiled by drips and drabs from the bloody roof. There's a very few leaks in that room."

He turned and led Mangan into the kitchen, a narrow, high-ceilinged place which ran the length of the back of the house and was not, as it would be in an Irish farmhouse, the hub of daily living. For one thing, there were no pictures on its gray damp walls, and the fireplace, hung with cooking pots, had a look of disuse. It was a cold room with dripping taps and cracked sinks, its only furniture a long wooden table and rough kitchen chairs. Heat came from a butane heater camped in the center of the room, with three of the wooden chairs around it. The girl, already in place, stood straddled over this heater, warming her slim buttocks as the little man led Mangan through a maze of buckets and tin cans, into each of which, from time to time, a slow drip fell.

Mangan was all eyes for the girl, and as she watched him approach, he was again struck by her resemblance to a statue, the slum pallor accentuated by the gray tones of this dismal room. "Are youse two going to drink?" she asked suddenly.

"Of course we're going to drink, Kathleen mavourneen," the little man said. "It's your cousin from America that's here. If that's not an occasion for drinks and jollification, I don't know what is."

"Then where *is* it?" the girl asked.

The little man laughed. "Get us glasses," he said. He himself went out of the kitchen, leaving Mangan and the girl looking at each other in the complicit stormy manner of people between whom some physical contact is imminent.

"He's a cute one," she said. "He always keeps it hid. Have you drunk poteen before?"

"No."

"Con has good stuff. You're safe with his stuff. 'Tis one of his sidelines." She smiled at him, filling him with illicit hope. "You're a gas man," she said suddenly. "Imagine dropping in out of the sky like this to someplace you've never been."

"A *what* man?"

"A gas man. Do you not have that saying in America?"

"No."

"A gas man, did she say?" Conor Mangan came quickly back into the room, carrying two Coca-Cola bottles filled with what looked like plain water. He winked at Mangan. "A gas man is a man who is good gas. A man you can joke with. A man who can make you laugh."

"I see."

"Dinny Mangan, now, my sainted cousin down Duntally way, is no gas man. Did you say you were going to meet him this evening?"

Mangan had no memory of saying any such thing, but he nodded. "Yes. After six. He's coming over to Duntally."

"Have you seen the mother yet?" the girl asked.

"I haven't met any of his family."

"God help you, then." The little man poured the watery fluid into their glasses.

"Not too much, now," the girl warned.

"Listen to her," said the little man, laughing, pouring generously, then raising his own glass in a toast. "*Sláinte!*"

"*Sláinte!*" Mangan said, clinking glasses. The liquid did taste like whiskey and was not harsh as he had feared. He drank it as they did, swallowing it down, and almost immediately felt it go to his head. He smiled at the girl, whose slovenly beauty was so different from Beatrice's American girl-next-door good looks.

"Grand stuff," the little man said, pouring again.

"No, no," Mangan said. "Easy there."

But he was gone. He knew it. The stout and now the poteen, the intoxication of the girl's presence, all of it filled him with a sensation close to tears, not of sorrow, but of release. And forming as in a turning kaleidoscope, fragmenting, forming again, there came before him a series of images from his former life; the Place Vendôme, when he and Beatrice stayed at the Ritz; a hundred invited guests milling on the lawn in Amagansett at a summer cocktail party; Beatrice's name in lights on the marquee of a Forty-sixth Street theater; the bank of red poinsettias and greenery in the Frank E. Campbell Funeral Chapel. These images collided, fell away, like images in a film already fading in his memory. Here, in a dank kitchen sitting with this slovenly Irish pair drinking illicitly distilled spirits, he felt at home as he had never felt at home in New York or Montreal.

"Oh, he's a gas man, all right," the girl said, laughing, putting her arm around Mangan's neck. "Sure, I think he was only codding us when he said he wasn't in the fillims. He *is* in the fillims, I tell you. Tell us, Jim, what fillim stars do you know? I mean to chat to."

"Dozens."

"Do you, now?" The little man rose up, clapped his hands together above his head, and began a merry little jig. "How would I be for the fillims?" he cried. "Would I be a Fred Astaire or even a Mickey Rooney? I'll have you know you are watching a semifinalist in the Three County Junior Ballroom and Tap Dancing Contest held four years ago this summer at the Empress Ballroom in Cork City."

Jigging and heel-clicking, the little man weaved in and out among the buckets and tin cans, as the girl, releasing her hold on Mangan, began to clap her hands; Mangan then followed suit, handclapping in a bout of hilarity which ended with the little man coming to a heel-stomping finale in front of the heater. The girl, laughing, turned to Mangan, putting her arms around him in a hug, throwing her head back at the same time as she pressed her soft thigh against his genitals.

"Let's have another wee jorum, the lot of us," cried the little man, taking up the second Coke bottle and pouring three stiff pegs of poteen. "And, by the holy, there's a picture I forgot to show you. It's right at the beginning of the album. It was a famous picture in its time. Wait now and I'll get it." He poured poteen into the glasses, then skipped out of the room, leaving Mangan with the girl, her arms still around him, her soft thigh nudging his prick, which swelled and grew erect. In all the years he had been married to Beatrice he had not slept with another girl. He had even felt ashamed of his lustful feelings for his father's young wife. But here he was, contemplating sleeping with a girl just out of her teens, carousing with her ne'er-do-well, midget brother in the manner of that opium-taking, drunken eccentric, the first *poète maudit* of Europe, before Baudelaire, before the term itself was invented. Perhaps that was why Jamie Mangan had never written great poetry. He had not lived a poet's life; he had lived as a conventional student, a conventional newspaper reporter, and a conventional husband and dogsbody to a famous wife. He had not sought the life of his ancestor, a life of poetry induced by stimulants, by a deliberate derangement of the senses, by wandering the streets like a mendicant, sitting all evening in stinking taverns, everything in excess, even the poetry itself:

O, the Erne shall run red,
With redundance of blood . . .
And gun-peal and slogan-cry . . .
Ere you shall fade, ere you shall die,
My Dark Rosaleen!
My own Rosaleen!

Life lived in a heightened, hallucinatory state, eroding one's health, hastening death. And from the sacrificed flesh, a few phoenix verses which would last.

And now the little man skipped back into the room, winking complicitly as he saw Mangan with his arms around his sister. "I have it here," the little man cried. "It's a postcard, do you see. This is the oldest photo you'll find in this part of Ireland. That's my great-great-grandmother, that woman there. Would you credit that, now?"

"What year is it?"

"I'll tell you the year. It's marked here on the back. 1880. Do you see it there in the corner? Now this is what is called one of the Lawrence Views. A Dublin man called Lawrence that went up and down the country—he was the very first to do it—taking views for picture postcards. He asked my great-great-grandmother to come out on the road and stand for him. And afterward he sent her this copy. It was a picture postcard that was sold in the shops, the same as they are today."

It was, indeed. Printed across the bottom of the card in white lettering was GORTEEN, WEST CORK. A lonely winding road ascended to a ridge of mountain, the same road Mangan had come up earlier, the road outside this house. On that road a woman stood as though commanded to stop by the photographer. She was old, her long, black dress draggled at the hem, a dark wool cloak about her shoulders, a high black bonnet on her head, its laces tied under her chin. Her face weathered by sun and wind, she stared at the strange contraption that was the camera.

"It was her that lived in the house that was here before this one was built. She was an O'Keefe from Skibbereen. First she married a grocer, a man called Boylan who had two shops in Skib. He died when she was only twenty-five, and she went up to Dublin and met and married a man called Mangan. And they had a child, a little boy, and the story is she fell out with Mangan and came back here without him."

"But that must be him!" Mangan cried. "James Clarence Mangan, the poet. The dates are right, Skibbereen. It's the same story I heard in Montreal."

"Anyway," the little man said. "She came back here with the little boy and that little boy grew up and built this house. And had three boys himself. And one was my grandfather and the other was murdered, they say. I don't know about the third one, but that could be your connection."

"It must be," Mangan said. "The third son would be James Patrick Mangan, my grandfather. One of the three grandsons of the poet himself."

"Well, there were poets in our family, all right," the little man said. "My uncle and his uncle are the ones I heard tell of. But, d'you know, I think that the name James Clarence Mangan rings a bell, after all. I heard of it someplace. At least I think I did."

"Did you ever hear of 'My Dark Rosaleen'?"

"The Rose of Tralee," the girl suddenly sang out. "That's the one I like." She began to sing.

"Oh, the pale moon was rising above the green mountain,
   The sun was declining beneath the blue sea,
   When I strayed with my love to the pure crystal
      fountain—"

"That's not the right one at all," the little man snapped. " 'My Dark Rosaleen,' I have heard that one. It's a different one entirely."

"*That made me love Mary, the Rose of Tralee*," the girl sang, ignoring him.

"Ah, will you give over with that," the little man shouted. "I told you, it's the wrong one."

"But you've heard of 'My Dark Rosaleen,'" Mangan said to the little man.

"I think my uncle used to recite that one," the little man said. "I remember now. Wait. Stay here, the pair of you. Don't stir." He turned and hurried out of the room again. The girl turned to Mangan, smiling the smile that transfixed him. "You could stay with us," she said. "There's beds upstairs. You'd be quite comfortable." Smiling, she came toward him and daringly put out her hand, her delicate fingers cradling the bump of his genitals, gauging his stiffening. Gently, she felt for and squeezed his penis.

"But you don't use the house yourselves," he said, in a choked voice, trying to make conversation, unwilling that this unexpected pleasure should cease.

"I like the caravan," she said. Her delicate fingers spread and with the palm of her hand she began rubbing up and down on his penis. Poteen fuming in his head, he stared at her as though hypnotized and at that moment heard the loud heel taps on the stone of the corridor outside, signaling the little man's return. At once, she took her hand away. The little man came in, holding aloft yet a third Coca-Cola bottle of the colorless liquid. "One for the road, now," he cried.

"For what road?" the girl said. "We're not going anyplace, are we?"

"Jim is," the little man said. "It's five now and he has to be back in Duntally to meet his nabs, Dinny. He will blame myself if you come late."

"Sure what do we care what he says?" the girl asked. "Why doesn't Jim move up here and to hell with your man Dinny? What do we care?"

"We'll not anger him, so," the little man said. "Jim will meet him on time tonight. And you could tell him that you're moving up here. How would that be, Jim?"

Mangan looked at the girl. Desire suffused him. "Yes, well, yes, that would be nice. If you're sure it's no trouble?"

"No trouble at all," the girl said. "I'll be expecting you first thing in the morning."

And now the little man was pouring again, and he was saying no, no, telling him to go easy. But he did not mean it. He felt high. He felt happy.

"*Sláinte* and *sláinte* again," the little man cried, raising his glass. "Here's to us, the blood of the poet, as the saying goes."

"Ah, give over with that," Kathleen said. "Look at him, pretending he cares about poetry. He couldn't recite you a poem to save his life."

"Well, I don't know Mangan's verses," the little man said. "But I know others."

"*I* know them," Mangan announced drunkenly. "It's amazing, but I just read them once, some weeks ago, and it was as if I'd written them myself. Without even trying, I know them by heart."

"You're joking me," the little man cried merrily. "Let's have that one you said, then. 'My Dark Rosaleen.' Do you know that one?"

"Of course."

> "O my Dark Rosaleen,
>   Do not sigh, do not weep!
> The priests are on the ocean green,
>   They march along the deep.
> There's wine from the royal Pope,
>   Upon the ocean green;
> And Spanish ale shall give you hope,
>   My Dark Rosaleen!
>   My own Rosaleen!

> Shall glad your heart, shall give you hope,
> Shall give you health, and help, and hope."

He paused, catching his breath, ready for the next stanza. They smiled at him, happy, hanging on his words. He smiled at their smiling faces, happy in his turn, at home as he had never been at home.

_____ *At ten minutes to six*
he drove his rented car into the yard at Duntally and got
out, pleased that he was still early for his meeting with
Dinny Mangan. Mist mingled with the dusk, swelling up
in fat clouds from the valleys below. Far out on its solitary
ocean rock the Fastnet light winked its bright minuscule
warning. All else was still, gray-green, lonely. He could
see no other light, no other house. For a moment he stood,
taking deep breaths in an effort to clear his head from the
muzzy, inebriated feeling produced by the poteen, and
then went to the kitchen door, lifting the doormat under
which he had hidden the door key. A strange voice moaned
behind him and he turned to see five cows coming in off
the road, their leader, a heifer, emitting a loud moo at sight
of his car in its path. The cattle paused and then, lumber-
ing, moved around the car with infinite slowness, coming
on down the path, passing him with insolent bovine stares
as they moved through the yard into the little rough lane

which led to the house hidden below his. And at that moment, looking back toward the road, he saw the same stout old female he had seen that morning, her gray hair disheveled, wearing her man's tweed jacket and male boots, carrying a long switch to herd the animals. She had not seen him, but now, as she did, her face changed and he saw a look of unease come over it. She lowered her head, as though afraid to look at him further, and blundered on past him.

"Good evening," he called lamely, but no answer came. Ahead of her, the cows had stopped again. Urgently she raised her switch and struck the rear animal on its bony crupper. The cow lurched forward, almost colliding with another as the old woman called, "Hi! Hi!" striking out in haste at their rumps, hurrying them down the lane and out of sight.

Mangan unlocked the kitchen door and switched on the electric light. He realized that he had forgotten to buy any food for his evening meal. He lit the gas stove and made himself a cup of instant coffee. Outside, dusk began to obscure the yard and roadway. The house was so quiet he could hear the gas pilot in the kitchen stove and the ticking of the grandfather clock in the adjacent parlor. There was no need to stay on in this house, cooking solitary meals, sleeping above in that room beneath the red votive lamp. Up there in Gorteen he would be with Kathleen. And wasn't it Kathleen and her brother who had led him to the point in his researches where it looked pretty certain that his father's story was true? He and these Mangans in Drishane were indeed descendants of the poet. The priest, with his parish registers, would confirm it all tomorrow.

Suddenly, policeman-loud, startling him, someone pounded on the kitchen door. He went to open. A rush of mist met his face like damp smoke. Standing in this mist was a stout man of about his own age, wearing an ill-fitting gray pinstripe suit with waistcoat, a stiff white collar, and a cheap silk tie. He was shod in large black boots like an off-duty policeman. "Am I disturbing you?" he asked in a high, loud voice.

"No, no. Come in, please."

The boots advanced with a parade-ground clump. Mangan shut the door. The newcomer wore round, old-fashioned spectacles, the right lens of which magnified the eye, giving it the look of an opened oyster. He stared at Mangan, coming up close to peer into his face a second time. "Mr. Mangan, am I right?" he asked in his high voice.

"Yes. And you're Dinny Mangan, I assume."

"That is correct." The newcomer looked around the room, as though searching for something. "You have a window open?" he accused.

"No, I don't think so."

"There is a draft. There does be a very catching cold going around Drishane. Do you not have a fire?"

"I'm not good at setting fires."

"Nothing to it. Let me do it for you."

The newcomer got down on his knees after first placing a piece of newspaper on the floor to protect his trousers. He took turf from a wooden box on one side of the hearth and from the other some turf briquettes and cubes of a white sugarlike substance. All of these he arranged in a pyramid as he spoke. "Yes, there is a very catching cold in Drishane and in Crookhaven, too. I was in Crookhaven this morning, there were four people down with it. And one woman, Mrs. Boyle, they are afraid she has pneumonia. And do you know what I'm going to tell you? Pneumonia is very catching, particularly for the visitor."

He produced a kitchen match from his waistcoat pocket, struck it on the heel of his boot, which was cleated with steel sole protectors. He put the lit match to the white sugarlike substance, which he had inserted at the base of the pyramid of turf and turf briquettes. It blazed at once.

"Paraffin," said he. "That is what is in those little white fellows. Paraffin is your man for this job."

He rose, dusting his kneecaps, and replaced the newspaper beside the hearth. "Thanks very much," Mangan said. "Would you like a cup of coffee? I'm afraid I don't have a drink to offer you."

"Not to worry on my account." The newcomer pointed to his lapel. There was a tiny pin in it, in the shape of a heart surrounded by a white border. "I am a Pioneer, you see."

"A Pioneer," Mangan said. "What is that, exactly."

"You are joking me, surely?"

"No."

"Do you mean to tell me that in America they have never heard of the Pioneer Total Abstinence Association, founded by Father Matthew and spread the length and breadth of Ireland! Sure and when you passed through Cork—you were in Cork City, weren't you?"

"Yes. Yesterday."

"When you passed down Royal Parade in Cork City, there was Father Matthew's statue, facing the River Lee. Father Matthew. A Cork man born and bred."

"I'm sorry. I missed it."

"Well, and do you know what I'm going to tell you? I never miss it. The drink, I mean. I took the pledge five years ago. Stout, sherry, whiskey, the lot. I never miss it. So a cup of coffee would be most acceptable, thank you."

As Mangan went to the stove to prepare the coffee, he became aware that his visitor kept staring at him. "So your name is Mangan, is it?" the visitor asked.

"It is. It's on my passport."

"And I hear tell you've come looking for relations, is that right?"

"Yes. I'm trying to find out if there's any connection between my family and the poet James Clarence Mangan. Have you ever heard of a connection?"

"And why would you be interested in that?"

"Why not?" Mangan poured the coffee and handed it to his visitor, who took it and put it down on the table, untasted.

"I hear you are a journalist by trade," he said.

"That's right."

"Are you quite sure it's the poet James Clarence Mangan that you're interested in?"

"What else would I be interested in? I'm sorry, I don't quite understand."

"Well, now, perhaps I was a bit hasty," the visitor said. "Perhaps there has been a bit of a misunderstanding on my part. I will tell you straight that I was annoyed with Seamus Feeley for putting you in here without consulting me. I have no intention of letting this house to you. I have my own reasons for that. I cannot tell them to you, but they are good ones. No fault of yours, I hasten to add. I must say, though, that if your name is Mangan and you are trying to establish some connection with the poet James Clarence Mangan, there is nobody hereabouts who can help you. I have heard tell someplace that we *might* be some relation to that poet, but I don't honestly think that there is anyone here who could tell you for sure one way or the other. And if you are digging around in our family history there are certain things that neither me nor my mammy want to discuss. I will be straight with you. I do not want you in this house. I do not want you asking questions. I bear you no ill will, but I would like to see the back of you. Did you pay Seamus Feeley a deposit on the rent?"

"No. He said he would speak to you about it."

"All right, then," the visitor said. "No money has changed hands. You can stay here tonight, but I will be obliged if you leave in the morning. I am sorry now, if that does not suit you."

"Oh, it suits me fine," Mangan said, "Your cousin Conor has invited me to stay with him."

"Well, that is up to you, of course. I would not advise it, but that is another matter. I came up here tonight to tell you to leave and I have done that. I apologize to you for any inconvenience you may have been caused."

"That's all right," Mangan said. Suddenly he had a vision of his visitor below in his little cottage, dressing up in his Sunday best to walk up the lane and evict him, the unwanted tenant. And at that moment he realized that he felt ashamed of his possible kinship to this maladroit, pompous fool. "By the way," he said. "Let me pay you for the two nights here."

"That will not be necessary, thank you very much," the visitor said. He rose with a scraping of his heavy, cleated boots. "I will leave you now. Put the key under the door when you lock up in the morning. Good night to you."

And shut the kitchen door with a dismissing slam. Mangan heard the ring of his boots on the cobbles outside and thought of him in his formal suit, marching down the lane to report to the old woman, that female tramp who herded the cows. He rose and took the visitor's untasted coffee to the kitchen sink, remembering again that he had bought no food for his evening meal. Going to the cupboard, he found some bread and two slices of uncooked bacon left over from his breakfast. It would have to do. Again he became aware of the unearthly quiet of this place. He could hear the drip of raindrops on the windowpane and the faint sound of a tree branch creaking in the wind outside. He was on the end of a peninsula on the tip of this island country, alone in the Atlantic Ocean, cut off completely from the world he knew. Everything that was happening to him seemed as different and distant from the events of that other world as is a fairy tale from the evening news. And as he stood listening to the tiny sounds outside in the still Irish night, he seemed to hear a doorbell ring, a familiar ring, the sound of the doorbell in the apartment on East Fifty-first Street in New York. He turned around and saw Beatrice come in out of the mist, just as he had seen her the day before her death, booted and furred, her opulent new clothes like costly vestments donned in preparation for her funeral pyre.

It was not a hallucination. He knew that he was imagining her; that she was not really here. Yet he willed her to pirouette on her expensive cognac-colored boots and stare quizzically at the portraits of Pope Paul and the Virgin Mary on the wall. He willed her to sit down on the uncomfortable wooden armchair across the hearth, letting her beautiful dark mink coat fall away from her body, stretching out her legs as she had that day, like some youthful Regency buck.

"So this is how the world ends," she said. "Not with a bang, but a whimper."

"What do you mean?"

"Ambition should be made of sterner stuff."

"Stop quoting lines," he said. "Don't you have any original thoughts?"

She seemed about to cry. "When I am dead, my dearest, sing no sad songs for me."

"I'm sorry about that," he said. "It wasn't my choice, that poem. E.P. just picked it because you'd used it in that play."

She shut her eyes as though memorizing:

> "I shall not see the shadows,
> I shall not feel the rain;
> I shall not hear the nightingale
> Sing on, as if in pain."

"I know," he said. "I'm sorry. But if you'd been with me, I wouldn't have let you drive."

She shook her head.

"The Moving Finger writes; and having writ,
Moves on: nor all your Piety nor Wit
Shall lure it back to cancel half a Line,
Nor all your Tears wash out a Word of it."

"Yes," he said. "It's too late. But I did try to look after you when we were together. I loved you. I used to blame you for my career, or lack of it. But maybe it wasn't your fault."

She smiled.

"How vainly men themselves amaze
To win the palm, the oak, or bays."

"But *you* won them," he said. "You were a victor. You worked harder than I did. I think my trouble was, and is, that I don't have a real ambition. I wanted to be a poet, but I didn't work at it. I didn't work at anything."

She stared at the fire.

"It must
Be the finding of a satisfaction, and may
Be of a man skating, a woman dancing, a woman
Combing. The poem of the act of the mind."

"That's it," he said. "Oh, I've thought that many times. Perhaps I'm not capable of the act of the mind. Yet, you know, I had an odd thing happen today. I began to recite some verses of Mangan the poet to some Irish relatives of mine. And when I said those verses aloud, I felt the way I've never felt about any of my own poems. I was excited —exhilarated. It was as though I'd made up those verses myself. And my cousins were excited, too. It was an amazing sight. This little fellow, almost a midget, and his sister, applauding like crazy."

She smiled.

"A sweet disorder in the dress
Kindles in clothes a wantonness."

"Oh, come on," he said. "The girl's almost young enough to be my daughter. Besides, we're probably close cousins. Did you see that other cousin of mine, by the way, that pompous ass who was just in here with his suit and his big boots?"

Again she smiled.

> "One of the low on whom assurance sits
> As a silk hat on a Bradford millionaire."

"Exactly. But it's funny I felt at home with the other two, the little fellow and his sister. At home as we never were at home."

She turned her gaze on the fire and said in a low, bitter tone:

> "And from my neck so free
> The Albatross fell off, and sank
> Like lead into the sea."

"Okay, I'm sorry. I was wrong. That summer in Amagansett, we were happy, the time I built the deck and the walkway. And anyway, don't misunderstand me. I'm worried about feeling at home here—they may be my relatives, but they're very different from me. They're dirty and wild, they prefer to live in a stinking trailer rather than in a house. They're the sort of people if *they* inherited your money they'd never do a tap of work until they'd spent every penny of it. I said they're different from me, but supposing they're not? When I got your money I told myself this was my chance to try again, to really work at poetry, 'to win the palm, the oak, or bays.' And I came here because I found a photograph—this one—" He drew the photograph from his pocket and began to unwrap the handkerchief. "I mean, it looks as though I'm really descended from the Irish poet Mangan. Remember, I mentioned him to you a few times? But this photograph is of a man who lived one hundred and thirty years ago, a man who might be Mangan himself. And as you'll see, it's my face." But as he spoke he looked at his face in the photograph and at once experienced the familiar giddy sensation, held by those glittering eyes which were his eyes. And when he looked up from the photograph he could no longer maintain the illusion that Beatrice was in the room with him. The chair by the fire was empty and he could not summon her image again in his mind's eye. The room was cold.

"Come this way,"
Father Burke said, leading him out of a back door of the presbytery, through a yard which connected with a side door of the church. The priest opened the door and went into a corridor, Mangan following. The corridor led into the vestry, a room with two large oak wardrobes, some processional banners furled and stacked in a corner, a row of cupboards on top of which were a censer, a platen, and three statues in states of disrepair. On the cupboard drawers were handwritten file cards, variously marked: *altar linens, surplices, tapers, Catholic Truth Society.* There was also a desk and a chair, and on the shelf behind the desk were rows of notebooks and files. On the desk was Mangan's family Bible, surrounded by several old, legal-size ledgers, their pages marked with paper slips. One was open, with a pad on top of it. The pad was filled with notations in a small, clerkly hand. The priest turned to Mangan, his boyish features lit by a smile. "As you'll see, I did my homework last night. Sit down there and I'll show you."

There was only one chair. "No, you," Mangan said, deferentially.

"Sit," said Father Burke, and it was an order. He took up the pad and turned back the page.

"We did pretty well," he said. "We've followed the fish upstream almost to the source. Now, look here." He leaned over the ledger, his finger tracing its way along lines in faded violet ink. "The earliest record of your family in our Drishane parish registers would be this one—the year is 1862—the marriage of Patrick James Mangan to Kathleen Driscoll. I can trace down from this to the present time. But who was Patrick James Mangan? Well, my record shows he was baptized in Holy Cross Church, Dublin, and he was the child of a James Mangan of Dublin and Ellen O'Keefe, the widow Boylan of Skibbereen. Now, that man, James Mangan of Dublin, that might be your man, the poet. But you'd have to check the baptismal records in Holy Cross Parish in Dublin. That way you might find out where that James Mangan was baptized. And that could tell you if he's Mangan the poet."

"I'll do that," Mangan said. "I'm planning to go on to Dublin when I finish here." He took out his notebook and wrote down the dates and names from the register, while the priest got up and produced two further registers, which he opened at marked pages.

"Now, coming down the years from that beginning in 1862, the records are all here," the priest said. "Whether you're related to Mangan the poet or not, you are certainly related to the Mangans who live here in Drishane. I've compared the dates in the family Bible you left with me with our records here and they tally out.

"As you can see here, the Patrick James Mangan who was married in 1862 had three sons, one born in 1872, one in 1874, and the youngest in 1875. The ten-year gap between marriage and children seems to have been because he

156

was off serving in India. The youngest of those sons, James Patrick Mangan, would be your grandfather. There's no record here of *his* marriage, of course, because he emigrated to Montreal, as your family Bible shows. And he lived until 1952, wasn't it?"

"Yes," Mangan said. "I was ten when he died. I remember his funeral."

"And the Mangans who stayed on here in Drishane were the descendants of Patrick James Mangan's oldest son, Conor James. Now, there are only two male Mangans left here, Dinny and Conor. And neither of them has married as yet."

"So what relation would I be to Conor and Kathleen?"

"Kathleen?" the priest said.

"His sister, Conor's sister."

"Ah, yes." The priest bent over his ledger. "Let's see, I'm very weak on these consanguinity things. I'll have to work it out, it will take a minute. Anyway, it's not that close."

"That's all right," Mangan said. "Don't bother. I'm afraid I've put you to a lot of trouble already."

"No, no, I found it interesting," the priest said. "Especially the possibility that the James Mangan of Dublin mentioned here *could* be the poet himself. The dates are more or less the same. But, as I said before, you'd have to go to Holy Cross Parish in Dublin to continue the trail." He rose and stacked the ledgers in a pile, removing the markers. "By the way," he said, "maybe you'd like to see where most of these relations of yours are buried. They're not in the churchyard here, it's too new. The old graveyard for this parish was at Dunmanus Coos. A beautiful spot. Two of the Fenian leaders, killed in '98, are buried there, by the way. O'Bofey and Sean Rahilly. Which reminds me, I'm going down that way now on a sick call. I could drop you off there and pick you up on the way back."

"Dunmanus Coos?" Mangan said. "Isn't that down by the sea on the other side of the mountain?"

"It is, surely."

"Well then, I'm driving in that direction myself. I'm going to stay with Conor Mangan and his sister."

"Are you, so?" The priest put his head on one side, as though digesting this information. "You were staying at a house belonging to Dinny Mangan, were you not?"

"Yes. But I have to move. I have my bag in the car. I thought if you were driving past the graveyard I could follow you."

"Grand," the priest said. He took out a key chain and, as they left the vestry, locked the door. In the yard a drizzle had started. Father Burke went back into the presbytery for his overcoat, and a few minutes later Mangan was following the priest's little car up a road outside the village, a road which intersected with a narrower road that climbed steeply up the mountainside. The rain, in the astonishing way of the country, stopped as quickly as it started and now the sky was blue as on a summer's day, the sun's heat warming the wet road in front of his car, sending up a small fog of heat mist from the road's gravel surface.

On his left, surrounded by low walls of heaped stones long overgrown with grass and broken down by trespassing cattle, was an abandoned farmhouse, its thatched roof collapsed, its cow byre lichened with weeds. And as he followed the priest's car up to the summit ridge of mountain and came to the fall of the road down the other side, he saw, below, desolate on a headland facing the sea, an older ruin, a Norman tower.

The little car ahead of him picked up speed on the descent, puttering along gaily until they reached the coastal road, which wound below the presence of mountain between a brilliant flowering of wild red fuchsia hedges. They passed a farm where a dog ran out barking, making foolhardy feints at the car wheels. An old man and then an old woman emerged from the farmhouse kitchen door, waving to the priest's car, peering in bewildered curiosity at Mangan's car, which followed. The old man wore a dark serge suit and the old woman a gray blouse, a gray apron, and a knitted black wool shawl. They were the clothes these people's parents might have worn a hundred years ago. As he passed, Mangan waved. The old man waved back.

The priest's car turned down toward the sea. As Mangan followed, he saw on a bluff just overlooking the rocky headland and the spume of wave an enclosed field of crosses and plinths, the graves overgrown and untended, the grave-yard's iron gate padlocked with a rusting iron chain. The priest's car stopped outside the gate and the priest got out, his angular black-suited figure outlined like a scarecrow against the sky and the blustery wind which whipped his clothes against his body. When Mangan parked, the priest pointed to the gate. "There's a step over there," he said, indicating a stone ledge that jutted out of the wall to the right of the gate. "A footstep. You can climb over. The graves of your family are down there on the right, near the sea. Just look in that general area."

"Thanks. And thanks for all your help."

"Not at all." The priest's face grinned at him, eyes narrowed against the wind. "And if you find out for sure that you're Mangan's descendant, send me a postcard, will you?"

"I will."

"Good man, then," the priest said, holding out his hand. "And good luck to you."

"Good luck," Mangan echoed, and the priest got back into his car, waving as he drove on down the road. Within a minute he was quite alone, the other car gone as if it had never been. He looked back up at the mountain and with a start of recognition saw a small yellow speck, high up. Kathleen's caravan. Below, on lower slopes of the mountainside, were small cottages, little farms boxed in by fields surrounded by low stone walls, narrow roads intersecting, linking the dwellings with each other. But the road up to Kathleen's caravan on the mountaintop passed no other houses. The yellow speck was all alone on the summit. Mangan turned and mounted the stepping-stones on the cemetery wall, coming down on the other side, inside consecrated ground. He moved through shin-high wet grass, past gray stone plinths and lichened Celtic crosses. There was a path and he made for it, but it was long unused, its stony track infested with stinging nettles and rank yellow dandelion. He turned to the right as the priest had indicated. Above him, a shifting sky of darkening clouds came around the headland, throwing a great shadow on the graves. He stepped off the path, approaching the far corner of the graveyard, scanning names on the plinths and headstones. Almost at once, a greening stone loomed before him and he saw his name writ large.

MANGAN

PATRICK JAMES MANGAN
Departed this life
1 January 1899

There in the cloud-darkened field Mangan took out his notebook and compared the dates he had written down from the family Bible and the parish register. This was the grave of his great-grandfather. He saw again the dull young face in Conor Mangan's photograph album, the boy who had taken the Queen's shilling, served in India, and sired a Canadian Pacific Railway comptroller, at home in the drawing rooms of Montreal and New York. My great-grandfather lies here.

Light rain fell like spittle on the names of the dead. He moved on to a nearby grave and read the headstone.

FERGUS MANGAN
Erected by his loving family
1919–1972

He consulted his notebook. Fergus Mangan was the father of Conor and Kathleen. The rain, growing heavier, began to spatter his page, blurring the names and dates he had copied from the priest's ledger. He shut the notebook and put it in his pocket, moving on, searching the gravestones. But now he was down at the edge of the cemetery, the oldest part, it seemed, where most of the graves were unmarked, or recorded only by simple grassy mounds of earth. Beyond this point the graveyard sloped steeply toward the sea, so that the great sweep of Dunmanus Bay, the rocky cliffs, and the ruined Norman tower far out on the headland were visible from where he stood.

He looked at the tower and thought of the broken-roofed cottage he had seen earlier, relic of emigration or famine. Abandoned, castle and cottage were co-equal in neglect, testament to the way in which this country, more than any other he had known, seemed to master time and history, rejecting men's efforts to make their presence last. Ashes to ashes. He saw Beatrice walk away from him that day, her camel's-hair coat draped like a cape about her shoulders as she hurried out to meet her new lover. The rain chilled him, wept on his face. He turned back from the sea to the graves and, retracing his route along the weed-choked paths, reached the cemetery gates and climbed the stepping-stones in the wall. As he reached the top of the wall and prepared to descend, a small truck came down the road, passing his parked car. There were four workmen standing up in the truck, wild-looking fellows with red, windblown complexions, dressed in old suit jackets and trousers in the Irish manner. They looked at him and he noticed that one of them at once turned away as though to hide his face. He nodded to the passing men and two of them acknowledged his greeting. Mangan stared at the one who had turned away, or the back of his serge jacket once part of a Sunday-best suit, now wetted by rains, worn with age. A stoutish fellow, he seemed, with ears which stuck out. Why is he avoiding me? Mangan wondered, and as the truck rattled on down the road, diminishing in perspective, the stance of the workman's back suddenly reminded him of Dinny Mangan, his visitor of last evening. It was an illusion, surely, for these men with their shovels and scythes were the County Council workmen he had seen on the roads the other day weeding ditches and trimming hedges.

The little truck rounded a bend and disappeared from sight. Within seconds, all was still again. Mangan looked up to the mountain, his eyes drawn to the yellow speck on its summit. He turned his car around and drove along the shore road until he came to one of the small intersecting roads that led toward the mountaintop. He went up this road, driving hesitantly as though he had entered a maze, his eyes searching among the jigsaw of stone walls and winding roads for the route toward that yellow speck.

He made a wrong turn. The car climbed past two small farms and ended up in the yard of a third farm, halfway up the mountainside. He backed out, pursued by barking dogs, and retraced his way to a crossroads, turning up again, always searching for the yellow speck. After another false turn he at last found himself on a lonely little road, the sort the priest, yesterday, had called a boreen. There were no farms ahead, and as he climbed ever upward, the yellow speck became the outline of the caravan, perched on the side of the road at the very ridge of summit. As he shifted down into second gear for the last climb to the top, his heart began to beat in an irregular, excited manner. Conor Mangan's little truck was not parked on the road ahead. A wisp of smoke rose from the trailer's chimney. On the clothesline, a peach-colored slip and a cotton dress danced demented in the high wind. He parked the car on the ridge of the road, opposite the opening to the field where the trailer was. He felt his hands tremble as he switched off the ignition. When he got out, he could see the small road falling away on either side of him, back toward the sea whence he had come, and on the other side toward Drishane. He went in at the entrance to the field, expecting the dog to run out at him from underneath the caravan. But no dog came. All was silent and still, with gray clouds drifting into the mountain face, swirling mistily about him as he crossed the field. The clouds moved on, clearing, and he saw that the caravan door was shut. He climbed the steps and knocked. Perhaps she had gone down to the village with her brother? He knocked again, his tension beginning to abate as he considered the chance that he might have to wait up here, alone, until someone returned. No one answered. He came down the steps and went around to the back. Here the field tilted up toward the mountain rock face, so that when he stood on tiptoe he could peer into the caravan's kitchen window. He heard a radio playing inside, very faint, a fiddle and pipe, an Irish air. "Kathleen?" he called loudly.

But no one answered. He peered in and saw the untidy kitchen counter littered with food cartons and dirty dishes. He moved along the bank to a curtained window, and through its parted folds saw the caravan's sleeping space with two bunk beds. They were empty. He walked around the caravan, coming back to the front entrance. At that point he noticed a bicycle leaning against the low stone wall of the field in which the caravan stood. It was a large, old-fashioned man's bicycle, with a bell, a pump, a lamp, and a chain guard. The second thing Mangan noticed about this bicycle was that its owner must be a very tall man, for the distance from seat to pedal was very great. So the bicycle probably did not belong to Conor Mangan.

As he stood looking at the bicycle he heard a small growl

in its vicinity and suddenly a dog which had been concealed behind the wall leaped up on top of the stones and stood, its head thrust forward, showing its teeth. It was not the dog he had seen yesterday, although all the dogs in this district seemed of the same type, piebald mongrel sheepdogs, much given to barking and menace at sight of a stranger. This dog was larger than the one which had hidden under the caravan, and watching, he realized that it would not attack him if he did not advance any farther. It saw itself as the guardian of the bicycle. "All right, boy," he said conciliatingly, and backed away.

The dog ceased its barking, but continued to watch him narrowly until he had retreated to the door of the caravan. It then sat down on the wall, ears pricked, studying him as though he were some errant sheep. He turned and walked out on the small road and there on the ridge summit looked down at the splendid panorama of sea, the wide sweep of bay, the headlands, like the forelegs of some enormous Sphinx, stretching out into the sea, pointing toward America. Below, on the other side of the road, he could see the rooftop of Gorteen, the Mangans' strange house, and faraway in a valley the spire of Drishane church, the village rooftops clustered around it like spilled playing cards. As he stood, lulled by the beauty of the views on either side of the mountain summit, undecided whether to wait or not, he heard the dog behind him bark once. He looked back and saw the dog standing on the low stone wall, tail wagging, looking across the field to the rocky promontory behind the trailer. From the shelter of this rock came a tall old man in a shabby black serge suit, a stained old uniform cap of some sort on his head. His trouser legs were tucked tight by bicycle clips and he carried a large old leather satchel strung by a strap over his right shoulder. He was collarless and unshaven, gray-grizzled, with a high, purplish complexion. As he approached, Mangan heard his heavy boots squelch on the boggy grass of the field. He touched his forefinger to his cap in salute. "Nice day, sir."

"Yes, isn't it."

"Grand, yes, grand," the tall old man said, proceeding past Mangan, going toward the dog who stood on the wall, tail wagging frantically. Mangan looked back toward the rock face and at that moment saw Kathleen come around it, brushing mud from her jean-covered bottom. She saw him, smiled, and waved to him. "Hello there, Jim. How are you today?"

"Fine," he called. He looked back at the tall old man, who had picked up his bicycle and was wheeling it out onto the road. The dog, tail wagging, frisked about him in great excitement, but was ignored. The tall old man threw his leg over the crossbar and, giving himself a push, mounted the bicycle and turned down the precipitous incline toward Drishane, his fingers gripping the hand brakes to slow his progress. The dog, running ahead, scooted in a bounding gallop across the grassy ditch, keeping pace with the bicycle's rushing progress. Mangan watched it go down into a hollow, saw the old man pedal up a small rise, then disappear over another hump of road. He turned to Kathleen. "So, you're back to see us," she said, and smiled as though she were happy at this news. He stared at her young rounded breasts, half revealed in the unbuttoned baby-blue cardigan. What had she been doing around the other side of the mountain with that old man? "Who was *that?*" he said, pointing off down the road where the cyclist had gone.

"Oh, that's Pat the Post," she said. "He had a letter for me."

She held up a letter with an English stamp on it. "It's from a boy I met last summer. He was here on his holidays."

But why had they gone around the rock face, the two of them? "Where's Con?" he asked.

"Ah, he's gone to Cork. He forgot to tell you yesterday,

but he's arranged with another man to pick up a load of scrap iron down there."

"I'm sorry I missed him."

"Is there anything I could do?" she said.

He looked at her. "I was wondering. I mean, you said something yesterday about being able to put me up in the house."

"We can, surely. You're very welcome. I'm sorry you missed Con, but he should be back tomorrow night. Did you bring your case with you?"

"Case?"

"Your suitcase."

"It's in the car."

"Then we can go down to the house directly."

"Whatever you say."

"We'll go down now and I'll show you your room, and you can leave your case in it. After that, we can come back here and get something to eat. The kitchen in the house is no good at all. The chimney has something wrong with it."

As she spoke she began to walk him toward the car. "Where's your dog?" he asked.

"Spot?" She looked around. "I don't know. Out after rabbits, I'd say."

In the car's front seat, sitting beside him, she leaned back, locking her hands behind her head, revealing to him the lift of her young breasts. The car went gingerly down the steep narrow road, turning in at the rusted unhinged gate. Again, he saw the tall two-story house of gray stone, that house which would have seemed at home on the outskirts of a town as it was not here at the top of a mountain. Again, as he got out of the car, it was as though the house seemed aware of his penetration into its territory, and as he removed his bag from the back seat and walked toward the front door, he was seized with a feeling that the place willed him to approach, yet intended to harm him. He stood waiting at the faded green door as she found the large iron key, unlocked and pushed inward, the wooden footboard clattering on the stone step.

Together they entered the dark hall. To his left was the large dining room cluttered with boxes and cartons and the shut door of the parlor containing photographs and paintings. She negotiated their way among the maze of tin cans on the floor, and they climbed a flight of uncarpeted stairs and crossed the first-floor landing, its aged, uneven boards groaning under their tread. The landing opened into a corridor similar to the one on the floor below it, on either side of which were three shut doors. Kathleen opened the first one. On entering, he was surprised at the size of the bedroom. There was a large three-sided bay window. The room was uncurtained, so that the morning entered in a gray cloudy light which glossed the furniture with a ghostly patina, turning chairs, bed, and tables into artifacts resembling sculpture. The bed was the thing he noticed, for it was very old and large, so high off the ground that it reminded him of beds he had seen in museums. The walls were unadorned with pictures, save for an oval lithograph of the Virgin Mary over the chimneypiece. There was also a large oak wardrobe, a dressing table with standing mirror, a white enamel washbasin on a marble stand, a white enamel chamber pot underneath it. The floorboards were bare. The only ugly note in the room was a modern propane heater, which sat in the unused fireplace. He put down his bag. Kathleen went to the bed and undid the counterpane, pulling it back to show clean white sheets and pillows. "I made it up for you last night," she said. "Con said you'd come." She laughed. "He ran into Dinny at Deegans after supper and heard that Dinny had given you the order of the boot. Is that right?"

"It is."

"If you want hot water to shave," she said, "you'll have to put that little tin yoke on top of the heater. Will I leave you here now, or do you want to come back to the caravan with me?"

He turned to her. She was smiling; she stood in a mocking, provocative pose, her rich, reddish hair falling below her waist. What if he were to kiss her, as he did yesterday?

But yesterday when he had kissed her he had acted unthinkingly. Now, as he started toward her, he saw her mocking posture. Would she laugh at him? Confused, he came to a standstill.

"Well," she said, "are you coming or staying?"

"What?" He did not understand her.

"Are you coming up to the caravan with me or do you want to have a lie-down here and come up later?"

"I want a kiss," he said thickly, and reached for her, taking her into his arms, his mouth blundering toward her face. Her soft lips found his, opening to his kiss, and at once her left hand slid down to his crotch, fondling his genitals. Lust clouded his mind and in an urgent clumsy lurch he pushed her back onto the high old bed. She laughed and rolled away from him, and as she did, he saw her unzip her jeans, dragging off a pair of pink bikini briefs in the process. He stared at white thighs, rounded buttocks. Her cardigan was now open all the way, so that her young breasts were exposed to him. He knelt clumsily on the bed beside her, and as he did she expertly unzipped his fly, pulled down his trousers, and, taking his member in her childish fingers, brought it to stiffness with the grasp of an expert.

He held her shoulders, beginning to slide his hands down over her breasts. Naked, she seemed even younger than in her jeans and cardigan, and now as his hands explored her, cupping her breasts, sliding down to fondle her belly and bottom, it came to him that she might be even younger than twenty. Maybe she was underage? But this prospect, while it produced in him a qualm of alarm, also elicited a shiver of illicit pleasure. As his mouth went hungrily down on her small round breast, guilt was transformed into the impure delight of the forbidden. In his fantasy he became her master, her body his to do with as he wished. But in reality he was quickly made aware that this near-child was infinitely more skilled in venery than Beatrice or any other woman he had known. It was she who—abandoned, naked, trembling yet cajoling—brought him again and again to the point of ejaculation, yet managed to prolong his pleasure. Roiling around in the bed, rearing up over her buttocks, which somehow seemed to tremble beneath him, he became aware that, without a word being said, she had divined his dream and was acting it out, playing the part of the young girl as victim, assigning to him the role of lustful tutor, older lover, occasion of her sin.

And so he spent in her and lay, breathing heavily, and she put her hand on his belly, her reddish locks spread over his thigh. She smiled up at him, her eyes so childish and innocent that he was inflamed once again to fondle her, to caress those long, slender thighs, to glut himself with kisses on her youthful breasts. And all the time, like a child doing what she had been told to do, her delicate fingers slowly kneaded his penis to full size. His face flushed, he asked her to kiss his cock, and submissively lowering her head until all he could see below him were masses of red hair, she brought him deliciously to a second climax, an event rare enough in recent years for him to experience a sense of triumph. He laughed. He felt insatiable. He held her head against his chest and, staring out of the large window at the morning light on the cold mountain face, felt a rush of joy, and almost without thinking, as though he had composed it for the occasion, cried out one of Mangan's stanzas.

> "Over dews, over sands
> Will I fly, for your weal:
> Your holy delicate white hands

Shall girdle me with steel.
At home, in your emerald bowers,
From morning's dawn till e'en,
You'll pray for me, my flower of flowers,
My Dark Rosaleen!
My fond Rosaleen!
You'll think of me through daylight hours,
My virgin flower, my flower of flowers,
My Dark Rosaleen!"

She raised her head from his chest, tossing back her red mane of hair, smiling that smile which entranced him. "Are you at the poetry again?" she said. "Oh, you *are* a fillim actor, you must be."

"No, I'm not.

> "Oh, my red Rosaleen.
> And one beamy smile from you
> Would float like light between
> My toils and me, my own, my true,
> My Dark Rosaleen!
> My fond Rosaleen!
> Would give me life and soul anew,
> A second life, a soul anew,
> My Dark Rosaleen!"

"You're a gas man," she said, twisting about in sudden girlish merriment.

"No, it's true. That's what you've given me."

"*What* did I give you?" she asked.

He struck a pose.

> "A second life, a soul anew,
> My Dark Rosaleen!"

"Go on with you. Or, tell us, then, what will you give *me*? Will you give me twenty pounds? Con would kill me for telling you, but we're flat broke, the pair of us. His fault. He's spent the dole and the assistance, the lot. Is it true you're rich?"

"It's true!" he shouted, his voice mad loud in the quiet room. "I'll give you twenty pounds. I'll give you a hundred, a thousand. Come here, my red Kathleen."

"That will be the drink talking. A thousand quid? I've never *seen* a thousand quid, let alone held it in my hand. It must be the vodka you're on, for I smell nothing."

"I'm not drunk on drink, I'm drunk on you." He pulled her up onto his chest, his hands sliding down along her smooth thighs. To his astonishment, his penis was again rising to the occasion. To go on fooling around with her in this high old bed seemed to him the summa of everything he wished for, and now as if she perfectly perceived each nuance of his fantasy, she turned away from him and knelt, touching her forehead to the mattress as though making obeisance to some god at the foot of the bed. In this posture her luxuriant red tresses fell away to reveal a defenseless white nape of neck as she presented her long, straight back and upraised trembling young bottom. He knelt, reaching out to caress and fondle the soft white buttocks. If happiness was this, then he wanted it never to end, unholy though it be, this joy. For she must be almost young enough to be his daughter.

"How old are you, Kathleen?" he whispered, as he handled her soft thighs.

"Nineteen," she whispered back, submissively. "At least I'll be nineteen at the beginning of next month. Will you still be here for my birthday?"

Eighteen. Half his age. With a moan of pleasure he penetrated her. "I will. Of course, I will."

_____ *A pebble struck the wall* outside the bedroom and fell back into the yard. Boots crunched on gravel. A second pebble lobbed up and struck the windowpane as Kathleen raised herself on her arm, her red hair obscuring her face. She brushed aside her tresses and put her finger to her lips, cautioning silence. The footsteps walked about in the graveled yard. "Kat'leen?" a man's voice shouted up.

Mangan, aroused from post-coital slumber, looked at her face, which in the misty early-afternoon light was the color of rose-tinted marble. Again, she warned him to silence.

"Kat'leen, are you there at all? Have you somebody wit' you?" Coarse laughter followed this. The footsteps crunched around on the gravel. "Are you there?"

She smiled at Mangan, that smile which undid him. They heard the footsteps retreat. She rose up naked, slight, graceful as a naïad, and ran to the bedroom window. Curious, he followed her. Below the window, going off down the steep mountain track bent low over the handles of a racing bicycle, was a dark-haired youth wearing a raincoat over a footballer's striped jersey and white shorts. He wore bright stockings and football boots, and from the way he wiggled the handlebars and ran the bicycle up on the ditch, he seemed to be drunk. Kathleen giggled as the bicycle skidded on the bank. Its rider fell off, got up, grabbed the handlebars, and vaulted on again to career precipitously toward the turn of the road. "That's Denis Dolan," she said. "They must have won the match."

Mangan stared at the boy's dark head of hair, watched it disappear around the bend. "Who is he?" he asked. Jealousy seeped into him. "What did he want?"

"Ah, he's a butty of Con's. He was looking for a drink, if you ask me. Listen, Jim. Talking about drink, do you have any money on you?"

"Of course."

"Well, could we go and get a feed of stuff, rashers and bread and eggs? And whiskey and stout? I haven't a thing left up above in the caravan."

"Of course," he said, and watched her run to the middle of the room, pulling on her clothes as though she were in a race. "We'll drive to Skull," she said. "That way we won't have them gawking at us in Drishane. In Skull you can get Fuller's cakes, and grand sausages—the lot. Will you buy me a chocolate cake? Will you, Jim?"

"Anything you want."

"Do you like me, then?"

"I think you're fantastic."

"Go on with you. You that's worked in the fillims, you must have had your fill of girls. Did you ever go out with a fillim star?"

"Yes."

"Who? Go on, tell us."

"You might not know her," he said, wishing he hadn't got into this.

"I'll bet I do. Is it in fillims or the telly, she is? Tell us her name?"

"Beatrice Abbot."

As soon as he had said Beatrice's name, he felt he had betrayed her. But Kathleen's face merely registered puzzlement. "Beatrice Abbot? Wait a minute. What was she in?"

"You probably wouldn't know her," he said. "Doesn't matter."

"Is she gorgeous?"

"Not like you."

"Ah, go on with you." She laughed, obviously pleased. She put on her cardigan. "Will we go?" she said. "I love shopping. I think we'll get a walnut cake as well as a chocolate one. I like walnut cake with white icing."

"Fine."

Dressing hurriedly, he followed her downstairs, the loose floorboards protesting under his tread as he went along the front hall. It was, he realized, the house itself and not its ghosts which disturbed him. It had about it the ominous air of frailty of a bomb-damaged building, and so it was with a sense of coming out of danger that he stepped into the misty light of the yard. Letting him pass in front of her, Kathleen reached back and pulled the heavy front door shut with a slam like gunshot.

"Were you born in this house?"

She seemed disconcerted by the question. Pulling her cardigan about her throat, she moved off without answering, going quickly toward the car. A stiff wind whipped across the yard, and at that moment he heard a dog nearby utter a small, piteous yelp. He turned toward the abandoned coach house at the end of the yard and saw, inside, anxiously tail-wagging, Kathleen's dog, Spot, tied to the axle of a broken-down jaunting car. The dog seemed afraid of him and eased away as though he might strike it. He looked back and saw Kathleen sitting in the front seat of his car waiting for him. He went to her. "Spot is back there," he said. "Tied up."

"Spot?" she said. "He's all right. Are you coming?"

He got in the car and they drove out of the yard. "But who tied Spot up?" he asked.

"I did."

"I thought you said you didn't know where he was."

"I forgot. I tied him up earlier because Pat the Post was coming."

"The postman? But they must be used to dogs."

"Pat has his own dog that runs along with him when he's on the bike. He fights with Spot."

But how did she know the postman would come up here today? Or did he come up every morning? He looked at her: her face was serene. Her profile now seemed to him the most beautiful he had ever seen. Why had she lied earlier about the dog? But it was better to forget it: let sleeping dogs lie. It did not bear to think of ugly old postmen, drunken footballers, the bicycle brigade which pedaled up these roads to see her.

"Did you go with her long?" Kathleen asked.

"Who?"

"The fillim star. The one you were telling me about."

"I was married to her."

She stared at him, incredulous, then delighted. "You're joking me?"

"No, I'm not."

"You were married to a fillim star? Wait now. Tell us again, what pictures she was in?"

"Did you ever see *Springtime?* That was a big one. She played the sister."

"Oh, God, I *know* her. She was Deborah, the one he didn't marry. The nice one."

"Yes, that's her."

"And you were married to her. Are you not still?"

"No."

"Is she your wife that died, then?"

"Yes."

Ahead he could see the high slate roofs of Duntally, where he had slept last night, and as they came around the screen of hedge he saw the old derelict woman in the yard, scattering to the chickens scraps from a bucket. She looked up at the car, peering, too far away to see them.

"Do you know that old woman back there?"

"That's my Aunt Eileen. Dinny's mother."

"I'll tell you the truth," Mangan said. "There's something about her that gives me the creeps."

Kathleen laughed. "It will be you that gives *her* the creeps."

"What do you mean?"

"Never mind. Turn left now, at the cross. It's about twenty miles on to Skull. Are you hungry?"

"A bit."

"They have grand toasted sandwiches in Cullen's Lounge in Skull. We can get a drink there, too." She put her hand on his thigh and mischievously slid her long, delicate, slightly dirty fingers into the crook of his crotch. "Do you like me, Jim?"

"Like you?" he said. "You'll never know how much."

She smiled at him. "Well, I like you. And that's a miracle."

"Why, a miracle?"

She laughed. "Ah, it's a long story. I'll tell you someday when I'm more inclined."

Inside the door of the lounge bar at Cullen's Hotel in Skull, a circular wire rack of picture-postcard views, retired from its summer position as tourist bait in the hotel's front lobby, sat by the wall, gathering dust. Mangan, in an adjacent booth, finishing his second gin-and-tonic and, eating a toasted ham sandwich, inspected these postcards as he waited for Kathleen to come back from the washroom. Skull Harbor, Roaring Water Bay, Dunmanus Bay, Mizen Head, and Crookhaven, summer views in bright sunlight which the tourists would buy and inscribe "Wish you were here," small boasts of holiday privilege to those they had left behind in Belfast or Birmingham, Dublin or Dulwich.

But now it was winter in Skull. Only locals moved in the town's wet, narrow streets. Cullen's Lounge Bar was empty. The boy who had served them drinks and toasted the sandwiches in an infrared oven stood behind the bar, pretending to listen to a football match on the radio, but in reality with his ears tuned to their conversation. There was, as Mangan had already divined, a special winter boredom in this place, the young gone to work in England, the old abandoned, living on their untilled farms, dependent on assistance and pension checks. The few young who remained seemed very young indeed, subteens pretending adolescence in jeans and T-shirts, their half-finished faces ill at ease in this fancy dress of a larger world. Among them, in these streets of shops which opened late and shut early, in this silence of empty roads and the certainty of rain, Kathleen's beauty and wild high spirits were as odd as a clown's costume. And later, as he walked through the streets of Skull with her, helping carry the myriad paper and plastic bags she heaped on him, he became aware that the men who remained eyed her with sad lust, while the women shopkeepers, though avid for the pounds she spent so liberally, greeted her with the painful condescension of those who have denied themselves all sinful pleasures for the sake of a higher good.

One of their last shopping stops was the off-license. She had him bring the car up to the entrance. "We'll get two dozen of stout," she decided. "Con's a great one for stout. And we'll get a bottle of Cork gin. Will we make it two? You like gin better than whiskey, don't you?"

"I'm easy."

"And two bottles of Power's whiskey, just for insurance. We'll be needing minerals. Will that do us now?" She turned to him trustfully, as though she were a child and he the responsible adult.

"I'd say it would." He handed two twenty-pound notes to the thin man who had prepared their order. As the man made change, Mangan saw him look up from his till, staring into Kathleen's cardigan. A fourteen-year-old boy appeared, eyed Kathleen, then awkwardly hefted the carton of bottles, following them out to the street.

"The butcher's now is our last stop," she said. "And then we're done. Tell us, Jim, would you fancy a bit of roast beef? It's very dear, I know."

"Roast beef," he said. "Best they've got. And a big one."

She put her arm into his and hugged him to her. "Oh, you suit me fine. You're what I've been looking for. The men around here are mice compared with you."

The butcher's shop was off the main street, a bare, brutal place, with worn wooden counters, carcasses hanging from steel hooks, and a window full of chops, liver, oxtail, and stewing meat. The butcher, a strong fellow in a bloodstained white apron, went into the back room to bring out his best roast. As they waited, an untidy elderly woman stopped in the street outside the shop window, peered at the cuts of meat, then came in at the front door. She looked first at Kathleen and gave a small, startled smile. "Hello, there," she said. "Are you back, so?"

Then, almost without interest, her eyes went to Mangan, the stranger, and on looking at his face she started, as in fright. She remained staring: her mouth open, her eyes glazed, as though she had suffered some sort of attack. Kathleen, who at once noticed, came forward, put her hand on the woman's arm, and said, "It's all right, May. He's from America. He's a relative of ours from America."

The butcher had returned and was holding up a large

piece of meat. "This is a lovely one," he said to Kathleen. "How many ribs would you be wanting?"

"Would that one be all right, Jim?" Kathleen asked. "Will we get a big one?"

"I have another here I can show you," the butcher said, and while Kathleen busied herself with the roast, Mangan looked at the woman called May. She was small and gray-haired and wore an old purple cloth overcoat, short and out of style. Her legs were thick and knots of varicose veins stood out under her stockings. As the sound of the butcher's hacksaw filled the shop, Kathleen returned and introduced them. "This is my cousin May who lives up by Ballymore. This is our cousin Jim Mangan from New York."

The woman stared, her mouth open. "God, I wouldn't credit it," she said under her breath, and looked significantly at Kathleen.

"How's John?" Kathleen asked.

But the woman seemed not to hear. "You're from America, you said?" she asked Mangan. "And a cousin of ours?"

"Yes. My grandfather James Patrick Mangan emigrated to Canada from Cork back in the eighteen-nineties. I wonder, would you ever have heard of him?"

"James Patrick is a family name, all right," the woman said. "Isn't it, Kathleen? But I don't know. I'm not well up on the Mangans. I'm sorry, now." She turned to Kathleen. "I have to be getting along. I've a lot of shopping to do and I'm getting a lift up home in half an hour." She smiled weakly at Mangan. "Nice meeting you. Enjoy your holidays."

"That will be seven pounds and forty pence," the butcher said to Mangan.

They paid and went out, with more goodbyes.

"She looked at me as if she'd seen a ghost," Mangan said. "It's this uncle of yours—Michael Mangan—that's the one I look like. Right?"

"Ah, you have look-alike on the brain," Kathleen said. "Anyway, thanks be to God she was in a hurry. She'd wear you, that one. She's married to a man who's paralyzed from the waist down these fourteen years and cannot be left alone in the house. So she never gets out. That's the first time I've run into her in two years."

"This person I look like, this Uncle Michael who died, Con said you didn't like him. At least I think that's what he meant. Is that true?"

He was putting the roast into the trunk of the car when he asked this and at first he imagined she had not heard him. He looked up, thinking to repeat the question. "I said . . ." he began.

"I heard you." She turned away and got into the car. He got in beside her and started the engine.

"What's wrong?"

"Nothing."

"Why are you so interested in who you look like?" she said crossly.

He looked at her. He did not know why she was angry, but he feared her anger and, suddenly, decided to tell her what he had not told her or her brother until now. "Actually, it was a likeness that brought me to Ireland," he said. "An old photograph I found among my father's papers in Montreal. Actually, it looks just like me. It could be a photograph of me."

He was driving through the main street as he said this and for a while she did not answer him. Then: "Do you have the photo with you now?"

"As a matter of fact, I do."

"Show it to me."

"Wait," he said. He drove through the village and, when he reached a clear stretch of road, pulled the car off into the grass beside the ditch. He took the photograph from his breast pocket, unwrapped it from the handkerchief, and handed it to her, watching her as she stared at it, then stared at him, comparing him with the photograph. Without saying anything, she turned it over, looked at the inscription.

"Who's J.M.?"

"I'm not sure. I think it's James Mangan, the poet. He died in 1849. That would be two years after this photograph was taken. He's the one whose poetry I've been reciting to you. If I'm right, he's my great-great-grandfather."

"Are you sure this photo is that old?"

"Yes. It's a daguerreotype. They were the first photos ever taken and they can't be reproduced. Each one is an original. So this must be at least a hundred years old. More, I'd say."

"Then it's not him," she said.

"Not who?"

"It's not Uncle Michael. I thought it was."

"So I look exactly like him, do I?"

"Yes. But you don't have a missing tooth. The photo has a tooth missing just like he had. That's why I thought it was him."

"A missing tooth?" he said, studying the photograph again. And saw what he had forgotten, the gap in the upper front teeth. "That's fascinating."

"Is it? Are we going to sit in this ditch all day?"

"Sorry." He started the car and drove back along the road in the direction of Drishane. The rain had stopped and a strong wind buffeted against the side of the car. So he looked like her uncle Michael, the one Con said she hated. Was that why she had told him it was a miracle she'd gone to bed with him? He looked sideways at her. Now was the time to ask her again about this uncle. She had slipped down in the seat so that her head rested on the headrest and at the moment he looked at her she began to sing in a soft, haunting voice.

> "Oft in the stilly night,
> Ere slumber's chain has bound me,
> Fond memory brings the light
> Of other days around me."

He was surprised at the beauty of her voice and by the simple unself-conscious way she sang. It was as though she had forgotten him and imagined herself to be alone in the car. The questions he had meant to ask her went from his mind. He drove on, listening as though in a trance.

> "I feel like one
> Who treads alone
> Some banquet hall deserted,
> Whose lights are fled,
> Whose garlands dead,
> And all but he departed.
> Oft in the stilly night,
> Ere slumber's chain has bound me
> Fond memory brings the light
> Of other days around me."

Her voice, small and pure, the words of the song, nostalgic and sad, echoed in Mangan's head as he stared ahead down the bare empty ribbon of road. On either side was a landscape which seemed to fit her song, for they were driving in a turf bog, a lonely deserted place with layers of earth spaded up like brown loaves and, at intervals, rectangular turf stacks like funerary monuments to some forgotten tribe. In this landscape he listened to her clear young voice and felt a strange emotion, close to elation, close to tears.

> "And other friends, long parted . . ."

In his mind he saw her naked as she was this morning, in the high old bed of the mountaintop house, her red hair falling away from the nape of her white neck, her back bowed down as if in sacrifice to him. He remembered her laughter as he urged her to buy more sweets and cakes, saw her run ahead of him into the shops, heard her sing beside him now as they drove on through the bog, the light fading to darkness in the sky above them. And as he did, he experienced a happiness which differed from anything he had known in his former life. The person he had been no longer seemed to be present with him in this car as he drove through the wild, darkening Irish countryside. That person would have made guilty judgments on this girl, whose past was dubious, whose conversation was banal, who was no novice in the ways of love and perhaps pretended affection simply to get money from him, who now sang in her beautiful soprano voice, only to distract him from asking awkward questions about a dead uncle. The person he had been, the person who would make these judgments, had faded from his mind. It seemed to him that he could no longer clearly remember his own past, and were he now to speak of his boyhood in Montreal, his student years at McGill, his days as a young poet, newspaper reporter, husband of Beatrice Abbot, he would recite the facts only as he would a story he had memorized, a life told to him by someone else. Now he was a man who, improbably, was the lover of a very young girl, who felt excited and alive when he recited the poems of a poet long dead, a man who carried in his pocket an old photograph of a mysterious double, a man who knew nothing of his true past save that his ancestors were poets like himself. And so, as Kathleen ended her song and leaned close to him, he felt exultant and free and increased the car speed until they were flying along the lonely ribbon of road. He turned right at the sign before Drishane, going helter-skelter up the narrow mountain road, turning onto the even narrower track which led past Duntally. There, in the darkness, he saw the silhouette of the house in which he had slept for the past two nights. No lights shone, nor was there any light from the cottage hidden behind it where Dinny Mangan lived with his strange mother. Downshifting to second gear, he went up to the high ground, to the mountaintop, the lights of Drishane glimmering far beneath as they came around the curve and started the last steep ascent past the minatory façade of the house called Gorteen. As the car passed by the front yard, he heard the dog bark. He drove on up the last rise to the yellow caravan, where he parked on the ridge, turning his wheels in at right angles to the ditch.

"What about your dog?"

"I'll get him later," she said. "First we'll light up inside."

She went up into the caravan and lit the kerosene lamp. He followed her in, making three trips to carry up the various parcels of food and drink. When all the things had been deposited on the counter by the stove, he heard the dog again.

"I'll go and get him," he said.

"Let him be, he's all right."

"But he's been tied up all day."

"All right, then," she said. "Go, if you want. Will you be able to see your way?"

"Sure. It's not really dark yet."

"I'll pour us a drink while you're gone. Will you have gin or whiskey?"

"Gin-and-tonic."

"And will a lamb chop with sausages and egg be all right for your supper?"

"Great."

He went out, down the steps, and walked across the wet grass of the field. There was no moon but here, high on the mountaintop, the night sky was a light faded color as on a long summer's night. All around was a stillness so total that there were no faraway sound waves of traffic or airplanes, or indeed of any noise at all. Even the dog was silent. He reached the road and went down its precipitous incline, his footsteps grating loud on the small stones of the roadbed, going toward the house, which presented to him its gray stone façade, its windows like dead eyes as always seeming to repel him. And now as he turned into the yard he heard a strange piteous cry as of some bird or small animal. He stopped. The cry seemed to come from the house. He listened, but it did not repeat itself.

In the blackness of the coach house the dog rose up with a flurry of paws and a growl of alarm, then, recognizing him, came to greet him with a craven tail wagging and went down on its forelegs, fawning. He untied it and it skeltered past him, bounding across the crackling gravel of the yard. Now, as he grew more accustomed to the strange twilight, he could see the house almost as plainly as in daytime. Again, he heard that small piteous cry, somewhere up there under the roof. Light rain wet his face, increasing as he went out of the yard and back up the steep road to the caravan. By the time he reached its shelter, the rain was thick and drenching. He climbed the steps, his face and hair wet, blinded by the light from the propane lamp as he entered, not seeing her until she came from the small bedroom area, a different girl. For she had changed from her jeans and cardigan to a long white cotton dress like a nightdress, crumpled, almost translucent, and as she stood against the light of the lamp, the delicate erotic lines of her slender body came up like a photographic print in a developing tray. He stared, transfixed, and felt his penis stiffen in his trousers.

"When will your brother be coming home?" he asked, and she laughed as though she understood the hidden intent of his question.

"I was thinking about that. He told me he might stay over in Cork. But his nose might tell him there's food and drink here. I'd say we'll see him home before the night is out."

She came forward and handed him a very large gin-and-tonic. "Here," she said. "That will stand to you, as they say. Drink it up."

But he put the glass aside on the rickety center table and caught her, kissing her, his hands sliding down her back. "Wait," she said. "I'm cooking the supper, now. Don't worry. Time enough for that."

"But when?"

"Later on. When you go back to the house, I'll come to you."

"Promise?"

"I promise. Now let's have a few drinks and maybe a few laughs." She went to the radio and turned it on. Tinny Irish country music filled the caravan. She switched to another station and the loud crash of rock. He hated rock, hated radios, but he smiled at her and raised his glass in toast. This was his new life. He had better get used to it.

Later, as they were finishing the greasy mixed grill she had cooked up, the dog barked in alarm, the caravan door slammed open, and her diminutive brother walked in. He seemed about to loose some complaint, but at that moment spied an unopened whiskey bottle on the counter. Refusing her offer of food, he opened the bottle and poured himself half a tumbler of whiskey. "Get the dishes cleared away," he said. "Get a drink in your hands, will you, the pair of you. Drink! God, isn't it great to have it. Your health, Jim. Wasn't it lucky, now, we found each other."

Three hours later they were all of them drunk. Mangan sprawled on the sofa with Kathleen by his side, while Conor, looking like a schoolboy in torn flannel trousers and Irish sweater, sat propped up on the kitchen counter. Suddenly, with an eldritch speech, Conor raised the whiskey bottle. "One dead man!" he cried, and poured the dregs of the bottle into his glass. Mangan, watching this performance, suddenly became aware that because he and Kathleen were drinking gin, the tiny man had finished the entire whiskey bottle on his own. This rapid consumption, coupled with the fact that he had not eaten, had produced in the last hour a heavy slurring of Conor's speech and a change from his initial high good humor to a cantankerous argumentativeness which now seemed on the edge of erupting into an open fight with Mangan or Kathleen, or both.

In that moment of perception, Mangan's mind delivered to him an answer to this problem. He arose and, walking with the care of a man whose own equilibrium is no longer under his complete jurisdiction, went to the counter and, reaching down behind it, produced the second full whiskey bottle. Smiling at Kathleen's tiny brother, like a teacher rewarding an apt pupil, he unscrewed the cork and put the bottle down near its empty twin. "Your health, Conor," he said.

"Right. Kill the bloody dead man!" Conor screeched, grabbing up the empty whiskey bottle and flinging it to smash in a splintering mess against the wall. "On to the second man, my lads!"

"For crying out loud," Kathleen protested. "It's me that will have to sweep that up."

"Well, sweep it up, then," Conor screeched. "You bloody tinker, you! What do you know about keeping a place decent, you tinker's hoor. Sure, look at this caravan. Filthy dirty, it is." He turned to Mangan, pointing a declamatory finger. "Did you know that, Jim? Hey, Jimmy, did you know that this one was off for two years traveling the length and breadth of Ireland with a tinker that already had a wife? Did she tell you that now? I'll bet she didn't."

"Ah, will you give over, you drunken scut," Kathleen cried. "Sure, that's all former history. Jim is my lad now." She put her arm around Mangan's neck and kissed him, missing his cheek, her lips landing on the tip of his nose. "You like me, don't you, Jim?"

"You're lovely," he said and kissed her back. *A tinker's whore?*

"This girl here is in *my* charge," Conor said, slurring, lifting his glass and drinking down the whiskey so fast it made him cough. "This wee girl here, d'you know what I mean? I'm her brother. Yes, I'm her brother, and when she came back from hooring around with that tinker in his caravan, with a sick wife and a child in it, too—I said when she came back from that carry-on and no decent person would speak to her—our parish priest Father Collins, God rest his soul, gave her into my charge. Do you follow me, Jim? She's in my care. Q.E.D. *Quod erat demonstrandum.* Signed, sealed, and delivered. Inquire here at the office. Do you follow me, now?"

"Oh, for crying out loud," Kathleen said. She got up, went into the kitchen area, and came back with two slices of an almond-icing cake which she had purchased that afternoon in Skull. "Here, Jim. Have a bit of this. It's good stuff. Fuller's cake. I love it. Do you want another gin?"

"Of course he wants another gin," Conor screeched. "Give the fuckin' man a fuckin' gin. Give him a fuckin' gin!"

"All right, all *right*," Kathleen said. She looked at Mangan, who made a furtive signal to her, refusing the drink. She went to the gin bottle, took Mangan's glass, poured a little gin into it, and filled it up with tonic. "One for the road, love."

"One for the road, my arse!" Conor Mangan screeched irritably. "It's the shank of the evening, am I right, Jim? Am I right there, Yank? Tell us now. Have you ever met Telly Savalas, the Kojak man?"

"No, I haven't," Mangan said. "Have a drink."

"Ah, go and fuck yourself!" The tiny man suddenly leaped off the counter, missing his balance and falling face down on the floor. Mangan rose unsteadily to help him, but Kathleen, like a mother going to a child, expertly picked up her tiny brother and set him back on his feet. "Now mind your tongue, Con," she said to him. "Come on with me. I want a word with you." "

"Fuck off!"

"Come on."

She was both taller and stronger than her inebriated brother. She put her arm around him and led him into the bedroom area, pulling the dirty curtain shut behind them. Mangan heard her voice, whispering in some tongue he did not understand, Irish, he supposed.

"I know *your* fuckin' game," the little man shouted suddenly.

Again, Mangan heard her low, urgent whisper. The little man replied in the strange tongue. She whispered again and he bellowed in English: "Where's the fuckin' whiskey? Bring us a drink, for Jaysus' sake."

Kathleen pulled aside the curtain and beckoned to Mangan. "Bring him the whiskey, will you, love?"

Mangan, bottle and glass in hand, went into the sleeping alcove. The small man lay spread-eagled on the bed, his features turkey-red, his eyes glassy and loose in his head, the left one wandering. Kathleen took the bottle and poured whiskey in the glass. "I'll leave the bottle on the dresser," she said. "Do you hear me, Con? I'll put it on the dresser with the cork in it. Don't spill it, will you, like a good lad? Do you hear me, Con?"

"I heard you. I heard you," the little drunkard said, sucking on his whiskey. "Sure, I had a bloody awful day, so I had. Packy took off with my lorry and left me stranded. I had to get lifts all the way back from Cork. And walk up here from Drishane."

"You never told me that about the lorry," Kathleen said. "Where is it now?"

"I tell you, Packy took it."

"But what about the scrap you were to pick up?"

"The scrap thing is banjaxed," the little man said in his slurred, contentious voice. "'Twas all Packy's fault. He never found the fella. Packy went off with the truck and left me. I got a lift back as far as Bandon and then I had to walk four miles before I got another. And then in Timoleague I was a whole bloody hour waiting for a fuckin' lorry driver to come out of the pub. Never asked me if I had a fuckin' mouth on me. I tell you, I had a hard row to hoe, so I had, while you were gallivantin' around Skull with your Yank, here." He reached out, trying to find the chair seat to put his glass on. She took the glass and put it on the floor where he could reach it.

"Have a nap now, Con," she said. She bent down and gently brushed the little man's hair clear from his sweating brow.

"I don't want a fuckin' nap. I had a hard row . . ." the little man muttered. But his eyes were closed, and as they watched, his nostrils trembled in a snore.

"He's away with it now," Kathleen said. "I'd say he'll sleep awhile."

"I should think so," Mangan said. "A whole bottle of whiskey."

"Oh, that's only an appetizer. When he wakes up he'll polish off the other one as well. We'll hide the gin, or he'd have that, too."

She pulled the dirty curtain shut as they came out of the sleeping alcove. She went to the kerosene lamp and turned it down. "Are you sleepy yourself?" she asked, smiling.

In the dimmed light he saw her move among the cluttered furniture of the caravan, picking up the gin bottle and glasses. Her long white cotton dress swirled round her ankles, and again he thought of some Madonna statue in a poor village church, the hair painted red, the white gown, the alabaster purity of the features. Her feet were bare, and looking at them, he felt a rush of erotic attraction. He moved toward her.

"Wait," she said, putting up her hand to stop him, although she had not seemed to see him move. "I'll give you the gin to take down to the house. And here's a torch." She brought him a flashlight. "Go on down, now," she said. "You'll find the key under the doormat. Turn it twice to the right. I'll be down later."

"When?" he asked. He tried to embrace her, but she moved off easily, in a way that was designed not to anger him.

"Soon," she said. "I want to tidy up that glass before he walks on it. Go on, now. Do you want me to bring down some sweets or cake, or something?"

"No, no." She was waiting, willing him to go, so he took the two gin bottles in the plastic bag which she handed to him and, switching on the flashlight, stepped outside, feeling the rush of cold night air brace him as he negotiated the steps of the caravan. Underneath the steps, the dog growled. He felt wet drizzle on his face as he crossed the squelching boggy grass of the field, but the cold night air was tonic and his muzzy, drunken heaviness began to leave him. He reached the road and stood on the ridge of mountain. The night sky was still pale and cloudless, and he saw before him the great sweep of bay, the jutting promontories of the headlands standing out to sea, and, in the distance, the tiny, winking, deceitful light of Fastnet Rock. The wind buffeted his face as he turned his back on the sea and went down the steep narrow road to the old house.

Tinkers. Kathleen had spent two years on the roads with a tinker family. On his first day in Ireland, when Mangan stopped for gas outside Cork, he saw ahead of him off the highway two shabby motor trailers, a small truck, and two old painted horse caravans, drawn up like settlers' wagons on the shabby grass. Around a campfire in the rain squatted a fat woman, a middle-aged man, and two scruffy youths. Their cur dogs snuffled for scraps in a nearby trash receptacle. When Mangan asked the gas-station attendant if these people were gypsies, the man paused in his work and said, with a shake of his head, "Not at all, sir, they're not gypsies. Those are Irish people—tinkers, we call them. They wander up and down the country, itinerants, as you might say. Mind you, the County Council has houses provided for them, but they will not bide in them. Always in trouble, that lot. You'd have to watch your belongings if some of them are around." And then, as though relenting, the gas-station attendant spat on the ground. "God help them, there's some say the tinkers is people left over from another time, from the famine days when half of Ireland walked the roads without a home."

"But how do they earn a living?"

"They don't. They used to repair pots and pans, sir, but sure everything is plastic now. There's no call for their services. They'd be on some form of public assistance, the most of them. That and what they can beg, borrow, or steal."

Tinkers. But come to think of it, what difference was there in that life and the life she now lived in a caravan with her drunken, ne'er-do-well brother? Did the postman pay her for favors rendered? Or the drunken footballer who threw a stone up at the window this morning? Kathleen Mangan, my love. Are she and her brother, and Dinny and his derelict mother, descendants of the poet, or simply people left over from another time, their speech debased, their lives mean and pointless as that of cur dogs snuffling around a trash heap? And don't I fit in, too? Walking down a road now, carrying two bottles of gin in a plastic bag, waiting for an eighteen-year-old tinker's whore to come to my bed. A cur dog engaged in a pointless sniffing out of unknown ancestors, living off the scraps of his dead wife's fortune.

And then, as that melancholy thought filled his mind, a dog barked in the night far below in the valley, and up the road Kathleen's dog barked back. The dismal yapping continued as he walked on, suddenly eerily certain that in the surrounding dark fields someone was watching him. The moon, which had been invisible all evening, slid out from behind a brow of mountain, round and bright and ghostly full, and in its light he stopped and looked about, trying to see some hidden watcher. Ahead, the long windows of the house reflected the moon's ghostly orb as it slid across their glassy surfaces. He turned in off the road, his footsteps scrunching on the gravel of the yard as he went up, pulled aside the doormat, and found the key. He turned the key twice in the door, as Kathleen had instructed, and pushed. With a loud clatter of its wooden footboard, the door opened into blackness.

His flashlight beam picking out the litter of pots and pans on the floor, he made his way cautiously down the front hallway. To his left was the closed door of the parlor containing the portraits and paintings, and as his light slid across that door, he stopped, feeling a twinge of the same excitement he had experienced when he looked at the daguerreotype of the man who was his double. As though compelled, he reached out and opened the parlor door. Moonlight flowed through the long parlor windows, shadowing the cretonne-covered furniture. He raised his flashlight to the picture-covered walls and set it searching among the painted and photographed faces.

And then, loud as a shot, a tin can was kicked over·in the corridor outside. At once he switched off his light and stood silent. Heavy boots sounded on the flagstones and another flashlight beam moved in a jumping circle on the corridor wall. The circle of light came in at the parlor door and hit him in the face. He switched on his own light, raising its beam like a sword to intersect the stranger's. It came to rest on a man's dirty tweed jacket and gray cardigan. He raised it farther and there, facing him, was not a man but the strange, gray-haired old woman he had seen herding cows at Duntally, Dinny Mangan's mother. She moved her head out of range of the flashlight's beam and, turning, ran back down the corridor, knocking over tin cans in her blundering progress back to the front door. He ran after her and caught up with her outside in the yard as she reached the wall and her old bicycle, which was propped against it. He caught hold of her by the arm. "Just a minute," he called. "What are you doing here?"

The flashlight she held was her bicycle lamp. Trembling under his grip, she fitted it back on the handlebars. "I might be asking you the same thing, sir," she said in a soft, uncertain voice.

"I live here. I was just going to bed."

"Dinny said you were living with them up in the caravan. I just saw you come from there."

"So you were watching me." Her trembling increased. He released her arm. "Don't worry," he said. "I'm not going to hurt you." As he spoke, the moon slid off into cloud, and suddenly the only lights in the yard were the circles of their flashlights.

"I didn't mean to follow you," she said. "I took you for someone else."

"For your dead husband? I look like him, don't I?"

He felt her start. She lifted her bicycle from the wall. "I must be getting home," she said. "I'm sorry I bothered you."

"Please. Stop saying you're sorry. Just tell me why you followed me into the house."

"I've not been well," she said. "I was in the hospital for a while. I'm sorry. I made a mistake. You're an American. Now that I hear you speak, I can hear that. And you are a young man. I made a mistake, that was all."

"It's all right," he reassured her. "No harm done. Look, why don't you come in and have a drink with me? There are candles in the kitchen. Just one drink before you go down home."

Looking down at her, at her unkempt gray hair, her hunched shoulders, her veined and liver-spotted hands, he felt a sudden rush of tenderness. Somehow her weeping reminded him of his own mother, who had wept so much that day his father told her their marriage was over. He went to the sink, mixed gin and bitter lemon, and brought it to her. "Drink that up," he said. "It will do you good."

She raised her head and wiped her eyes with a large linen handkerchief which she took from a pocket of her jacket. "Thanks, now," she said. "I shouldn't be having this."

"It will do you good," he repeated.

"Well, I haven't slept well this past while," she said, and drank. "Dinny said the doctors say drink makes it worse. But I don't know. Dinny's a Pioneer. He never touches drink." She began to weep again.

"Is there anything I can do? Did I upset you, is that why you followed me? Isn't it because I remind you of your husband?"

She stared at him with tear-swollen eyes. "Why did you come into this house tonight?" she asked.

"I'm sleeping here."

"Sleeping here? Where?"

"Upstairs."

"Oh, my God," she said, and wept.

"Why? What's wrong with that?"

"Was it Seamus Feeley who put you in here?"

"No. It was Conor who invited me."

"But how can he do that?" she said. "It's not his house any more."

"Whose house is it, then?"

"It belongs to some Englishman. It was sold last year."

"But the pictures and the furniture are Conor's."

"The Englishman hasn't moved in yet," she said. "I

suppose Con is the caretaker. He'll have to move his things out when the Englishman comes next summer."

"But it *was* Conor's house?"

She drank at the gin, taking a long swallow as though it were medicine. "It was, surely," she said. "But he drank it all away when his father died."

"When was that?"

"His father? It's some years back."

"Your husband and Conor's father were brothers?"

"They were, yes." Again, she began to weep.

"I'm sorry," he said. "I didn't mean to upset you. There's just one thing I want to ask. I have a photograph here, a photograph of someone a long time ago who looks like me. I wonder, would you look at it? Maybe you'd know who it is?"

"I don't know the Mangans well at all," she said. "Where's the picture?"

He took out the daguerreotype and unwrapped it. As he put it down on the table beside her, his *Doppelgänger*'s eyes seemed to gleam in secret collusion. She picked the photograph up and looked at it, holding it close to her eyes. "You say it's old?" she asked, wiping away her tears.

"Yes, very old. It's one of the first photographs ever taken. At least a hundred years old."

"It has the look of my husband," she said. "And of yourself. But it can't be either of you, can it? I was going to say it might be my husband's uncle Dan. They say he was the living image of Michael."

"You never met him?"

"Oh, he was before my time."

"And what did he do, this uncle?"

She looked at him in an unfocused way, as though she had not heard him. He poured more gin into her glass and she looked down at it, then picked it up and drank it. When she put the glass down again, she turned her head and stared at him in a way which for the first time made him suspect that she might not be sane. "He was killed, that uncle. He died a terrible death," she said. "He was a schoolteacher once. And a poet, the same as Michael."

"A poet. Your husband was a poet, was he?"

"He was. He had poems published in many's the place. Part of his trouble was, he didn't get the recognition, you know? Not enough. Anyway, he used to say poetry was all that mattered to him." She seemed about to weep. "But that wasn't the truth."

"What do you mean?"

She looked at him; then, as though caught in an indiscretion, stood up to leave. "I have to go," she said. "Dinny will be worried stiff about me. I should have been home ages ago."

"No, no, please wait, just a minute," Mangan said. "I've come a long, long way to find this out. You say that both your husband and his uncle were poets. And that they looked alike, they looked like me. Do you have any of your husband's poems, by chance?"

But she looked at him as though she had not heard him. "I have to go," she said desperately. "I must go now." And turning, blundered out of the kitchen into the dark corridor, her heavy boots loud on the flagstones. He hurried after her, lighting her way with his flashlight. "It's all right," he said. "Maybe I can come and talk to you tomorrow. This is all very important to me. Tell me, was it only your husband and his uncle who looked alike, or were there others in the family?"

"Just those two that I know of," she said, and went out ahead of him into the dark yard. "I'm sorry now for disturbing you. Drink is not good for me, the doctor said. When I have drink taken I'd not know what I'd be saying. So, you're not to mind me, sir. I'm sorry, now."

The moon slid out from behind a cloud. There was no

longer need of his flashlight. She went to her bicycle, switched on the headlamp, and began to wheel the bicycle out of the yard. "Tell me," he said, coming after her. "Did your husband ever speak of James Clarence Mangan, the poet?"

But she ignored his question. She wheeled the bicycle through the gate. "James Clarence Mangan," he said. "He was a very well-known Irish poet."

"I don't know, sir," she said, in a voice which made him think she was lying. She put her foot on the pedal of the bicycle, preparatory to mounting.

"Wait," he said. "Could I come and talk to you tomorrow?"

"Talk to me about what?"

"I'm interested in trying to trace that photograph I showed you."

"Why do so many Americans come here to look at graves?" she said. "Do they not have graves enough in their own place?"

"We want to know where we came from. That's normal, after all."

"But it's what you *do* that matters," she said with great seriousness. "If you keep looking over your shoulder, sir, you'll find things you don't want to find. Pray to God, that's my advice to you. God will help you, no matter who you are or what has happened to you. I must go home now. Goodnight and thanks for the drink."

"What about tomorrow? Couldn't I come and talk to you some more?"

But she had mounted the bicycle and now, pedaling uncertainly, she turned it down the precipitous road. At once the bicycle gathered speed and he saw her grip the handbrake to slow its momentum. The bicycle's headlamp shone on a double row of fuchsia hedges and then the bicycle disappeared from sight behind the hedgerows. A cloud covvered the moon. In the blackness he shone his own flashlight down the road. But now the road was empty.

He turned back, going toward the house. Strange old woman on a bicycle, living link to that man who had looked the image of him, link, too, to an older, look-alike uncle of her husband, an uncle who was also a poet, who "died a terrible death." Poets like me, their legacy a pile of published clippings yellowing in some farmhouse dresser drawer, feuilletons on the editorial page, a sonnet beneath the weekly book reviews, a slim book printed by some minor press. And all of us may be linked to that older, greater poet, the first *poète maudit*. We inherit his face, his genes, and things we don't want to look back on. What was it she said? "If you look over your shoulder, you'll find things you don't want to find." Beatrice's funeral, the massed flowers on the leafy green stage, the duo playing Mozart, the speeches, the absence of her body. Do they not have graves in America? No, we do not.

He went into the house and made his way toward the flight of stairs leading to the second floor. He went up on loud-creaking floorboards and entered the high, old-fashioned, bay-windowed bedroom. His flashlight found the kerosene lamp on the table and he turned the little wheel which brought the wick up, lit the lamp, then replaced its glass funnel. In the lamplit room, shadows danced off the walls. So Conor Mangan does not own this house. I am here illegally, a squatter in some English absentee landlord's bed. He looked at the high old bed, rumpled from the morning's delights. Weary, heavy with all the gin he had drunk, he stripped off his clothes and lay naked on the tousled sheets, watching the shadows cast by the lamp on the high ceiling above him. He had heard light rain on the windowpane and then, just as his weariness brought him to the edge of sleep, saw a circle of light strike against the ceiling, shining up from the yard below. He jumped up and ran to the window and, as he did, heard someone enter the house, a light step coming quickly along the hall. Expectant—it must be Kathleen—he stood facing the bedroom door. The footsteps came up the stairs, and suddenly wary, he bent over, his hands protecting his genitals.

It was in this strange half crouch that he met Kathleen as she came in at the door, a torn tweed overcoat over her long cotton dress, her hair wet from the rain.

"Were you not asleep?" was the first thing she said.

"No. I had a visitor."

She had begun to take off her overcoat and paused to stare at him as he said the word "visitor." "Who?"

"Dinny's mother."

"What did she want?"

"She came up here to take a look at me. To make sure I'm not her dead husband returned to life."

Kathleen threw the overcoat on a chair. She seemed annoyed. "Did she tell you that?"

"Tell me what?"

"About her husband. About Uncle Michael?"

"No, not exactly."

"Did she say anything about me?"

"No."

"Are you sure?"

"Of course I'm sure. What would she have said about you?"

"Ah, Jesus." Kathleen shook her wet hair out. "How do I know? Where's the gin?"

"In the kitchen."

"*Where* in the kitchen?"

"On the table."

"I'll get it," she said. "I need a drink. I had to clear all that bloody mess, bottle and glass and muck."

"I'll get it for you," he offered, but she was out of the room and down the stairs at a run. He sat on the bed until she returned with the plastic bag and two glasses.

"So you gave her a drink," she accused.

"Yes."

"If Dinny finds that out, he'll knock her block off. I bet she hasn't had a drink in years. She was in the loony bin, did you know that?"

"She said she had been sick."

"Sick? She was two years in Our Lady's—it's the Cork asylum. Straitjacket and all the rest of it."

"When was that?" Mangan asked.

"What do you want to bother your head with all that for?" Kathleen said. She poured gin in two glasses and handed him one of them. "Don't you want to go to bed?"

"I'm just curious. What happened that put her in the madhouse? Was it something her husband did?"

Kathleen looked at him, then began to unhook her dress. Suddenly she smiled, and as she did she pulled down the bodice to reveal her bare breasts. Smiling, she eased the dress down over her hips, letting it billow out and fall in a deflated heap about her feet. Her smile left her. She shook out her long red hair and looked at him in that downcast, submissive, almost frightened manner which had so entranced him earlier. He stood, staring at her high small breasts, the delicate lines of her long legs, the down on her lower belly, the undulant thighs. It was as though she had decided to silence his questions by invoking the ukase of her body, and as he looked he felt his penis rise, his inquisition forgotten. At once, as though under hypnosis, he assumed the personality of his fantasy, he the master, she his servant, afraid of him, eager to do his bidding.

"Are you going to do dirty things to me again?" she said, in that soft, fearful voice.

"I am." He went to her, took her in his arms, felt her soft flesh tremble against his bare body.

"Will you beat me?" she asked. "Don't beat me. I'll do what you want."

"Did the tinker beat you?" he said, easing her back toward the high old bed.

"He did."

"He beat you to make you do dirty things?"

"He did."

"And who else beat you?" he asked, excited and at the same time ashamed of his inquiries.

"Many's the one. I'm afraid of you. I'll do what you want."

"Kneel up on the bed," he commanded her. "Kneel with your back to me the way you did this morning."

Submissive, she climbed up on the mattress. As though making obeisance to the foot of the bed, she turned away from him and knelt. She lowered her forehead to touch the sheets, presenting to him her upraised young bottom. He knelt on the bed, his mind tumbling in a spin dryer of inchoate desires. The questions he wanted to ask her, the link to those dead poets, the line of men who bore his face, all these enigmas were forgotten in the siren enchantment of this youthful body stretched out before him. With a moan of pleasure he reached forward to fondle her tender Circean bum.

_____*Light, and a sound in silence,*
woke him to the drinker's instant guilt. He opened his eyes
on a ceiling, then closed them as though that one blink were
enough to tell him all. He felt her stir beside him as the
sound grew louder, a car in low gear coming uphill, passing
the house. He heard her start up and jump out of bed. He
opened his eyes again and lifted a heavy head to face the
day. She stood by the window, naked, bent over, peering
out. The car sound diminished as the vehicle went on up
the mountain. Then it stopped. Her reddish-gold mane of
hair swung in a quick graceful parabola as she jerked her
head around to see if he was awake. She raised her hand,
warning him to silence.

He stared, gloating miserly at her naked body. Ill with
the gin and weak from the night's repeated sexual awaken-
ings, he felt an instant avaricious lust to possess her again.
She was beckoning him. He got off the bed and went
toward her, but as he did he saw that she was alarmed. She
had moved to the side of the window, as though afraid that

someone outside might shoot at her, and now she signaled him to do the same, indicating that he should look out but with caution.

At first he saw nothing. The sky above erupted black smoking clouds as though a forest fire burned on the other side of the mountain. Rain lashed the ground, sheeting and squalling across the bare rocks and mossy bogland. And then, as though some invisible hand had refocused the lens of his eye, this blurred picture showed clear detail: the yellow caravan up above on the ridge; his red rental car parked off the road. And in the field beside the caravan a small official-looking blue car, its violet roof signal turning and blinking.

"Who is it?" he asked.

"The Guards."

"Who?"

"The *Garda*. The police."

He looked at her and saw, with shock, the state of panic she was in. She turned and ran to the chair, fumbling with her dress as she pulled it up over her hips. "Jesus God," she said under her breath. She turned to him. "Hook me up, quick."

He went to obey her. In a panicky voice she told him to get his own clothes on and stay away from the window. "If we're lucky," she said, "they'll not come in here."

"But what's wrong? What do they want?"

"How do I know?" She was close to tears. "It must be Con they're wanting."

When he finished hooking up her bodice, she ran to the window again and knelt on one knee, peering out over the top of the sill. "Oh, Jesus, lookit, will you!"

He joined her at the window and she dragged him down beside her. Together, they peered over the top of the windowsill and saw two uniformed policemen coming down the caravan steps. Between them was the diminutive figure of Conor Mangan holding a yellow slicker over his head as protection against the sheeting rain. The three men walked across the wet field to the waiting police car.

"He doesn't seem drunk," he told her.

"Thank God for that. He must have slept through. Jesus, when they see the whiskey and food in there, they'll be sure he lifted something." She was hunkered down like a child as she spoke, her face drawn with fright. She was shivering. He went to the chair and got her overcoat, which he put around her shoulders. But she did not notice. "What are they doing now?" she asked, huddling down below the windowsill. "But don't let them see you."

Cautiously, he approached the window. The police car backed out of the field, its violet flasher still turning. With a lurch it reversed onto the road, then came slowly down the steep incline. "Have they gone past?" she whispered.

The police car came on. When it reached them, it swung in at the gate and drove across the yard. He did not need to answer her. As soon as she heard the engine stop, she leaped away from the window like a wild animal and ran, bent over, to the big old wardrobe which stood in the corner of the bedroom. She turned, her hand on the wardrobe door. "Tell them you never saw me. Tell them you slept here on your own. Tell them we were in Skull all day yesterday, just you and me, and be sure and tell them all that stuff was bought with your money. Oh, Jesus!"

She started in fear as someone hammered on the front door. She jumped up into the wardrobe, pushing her way past the clothes he had hung inside it. She pulled the wardrobe shut, whispering, "Go on down. Go and open!"

As he left the bedroom and began to descend the stairs, the police again hammered on the front door. "I'm coming, I'm coming," he said, under his breath. "What's the rush?" But as he approached the door, his irritation no longer sustained him. What if he told them there was no one here and they searched and discovered Kathleen hidden in the ward-robe? He had not shaved, had a hangover, and smelled of liquor. Kathleen was only eighteen. He had no legal right to be staying in this house. As he opened the front door, he had veered toward guilt.

The policeman, duck-wet, wearing slicker and leggings, was red-faced, with bright-blue eyes. "Morning," he said, then shook himself like a dog. "It's coming down heavy. Mind if I stop in for a minute?"

Without waiting for an answer, he advanced into the hallway, stamping his boots on the doormat. "Is that your car up there beyond? The Ford Escort?"

"Yes."

"It's a hire car, then?"

"It is."

"You are here on your holidays?"

"Yes."

"Do you have papers on you? A passport?"

"Yes, of course," Mangan said, but as he pulled out his passport he brought out, with it, the handkerchief-wrapped daguerreotype. Clumsily he pushed the photograph back into his pocket, anxious, although he did not know why, that the policeman should not see it.

"So your name is Mangan," the policeman said, inspecting the passport, then handing it back with a nod. He pointed out into the rainy yard. "Do you see the car there? Do you see the lad in it?"

In the rain, the car, its violet flasher turning, Conor Mangan's face like a wet biscuit pressed up against the rear window. "Yes, I do."

"That lad says he's a cousin of yours. Would that be correct, now?"

"Yes, I think we may be related. But I just met him the other day."

"Then you are not sure that you are his cousin?"

"No."

"I see," the policeman said. "Well, now, he claims that the pair of you spent the day together, yesterday. That you were here and that you went on to Skull. And that his sister was with you, also."

Mangan looked at the policeman, who looked at him as though waiting for him to make a false move. "Well, yes. Yes, he was with us."

"Will you be prepared to make a statement to that effect if called upon?"

Glum, he nodded. The policeman took out a thick black-backed notebook and wrote in it. He replaced the notebook in his hip pocket. "His sister, now, I believe she is here in the house with you."

"No. No, she's not here now."

"She *was* here, then?"

"Yes, but she's not here now."

The policeman pointed out to the car in the yard again. "The lad out there has got the wrong end of the stick, has he?"

"I believe he has, yes."

"Where is his sister now, could you tell me?"

"I'm afraid I don't know."

"But she does live here, I take it?"

"She lives up in the caravan with her brother, I believe."

"And you are living here? In this house?"

"Well, it's just temporary. I was staying in a house farther down the road. I've just spent one night here."

The policeman rubbed his hand over his wet red face, wiping away a drop of rain which had gathered on the end of his nose. "I believe it's an Englishman who owns this house. A Mr. Harmon. Are you a friend of his?"

"No. I was asked to stay here." Mangan pointed uneasily at the white face behind the window of the police car. "He asked me."

"Him?" the policeman said. "I understand he's just the caretaker now."

"It was his house until recently."

"It was," the policeman said. "That's right. But it's not now. His sister is not in the house, you say?"

Miserably, Mangan nodded.

"Well." The policeman appeared to consider. "If you see her, will you tell her we are taking her brother to Bantry to make a statement? And that herself and yourself may be called as witness."

"A statement?" Mangan said.

"In connection with the theft of a lorryload of scrap metal," the policeman said. "You will be staying on in this area for a few more days, I take it?"

"I think so."

"What is the license number of your car? I forgot to put it down," the policeman said, pulling out his notebook again.

Mangan felt for his wallet, found the rental receipt and read off the license number.

The policeman wrote it down. He turned and looked up at the sky. "I hope this weather will clear for you," he said. "Of course, we do normally have rain at this time of year. But we don't get many tourists in January."

"Yes. That's why I can't get a hotel room."

"Is that a fact?" the policeman said disbelievingly. "Well, now, enjoy your holidays."

He tramped back across the yard and got into the driver's seat of the car. The overhead violet flasher was switched off. The police car's tires spun on the wet cobbles as it accelerated out of the yard and down the steep road. Mangan reached for the front door, its wooden footboard making a clattering sound on the stone as he drew it shut. At once, as though she had been waiting for the sound, Kathleen appeared at the head of the stairs, huddling against the cold, her worn tweed overcoat pulled tight about her neck. "What did those boyos want?" she asked.

"They're taking your brother to Bantry to make a statement."

"About what?"

"Something to do with stealing a load of scrap metal."

"Oh, God, wouldn't you know it. He has nothing but bad luck when he teams up with Packy Deane."

"Well, there's something else I'm not crazy about," he said. "Your brother told the police he was with us yesterday. Here and in Skull. I had to lie to that cop to back him up. We may be called as witnesses."

"But what's wrong with that?" she said. "What else would you tell the police?"

"Well, it makes me an accomplice, or something. And you, too. If it's a robbery, we're guilty of collusion, or perjury, or something. You could be put in jail for that."

"You're a Yank. You'll be all right. You're not going to turn informer on your own cousin, are you? Anyway, it's not you has to worry, it's Con that has to worry. Listen, the thing now is for us to go up to the caravan and get some breakfast in us. Then we'll drive to Bantry and inquire for him at the Guards station. He'll be needing a lift back when they let him out. Here—will you do that for me, now?" And then, as though to seal her power to make him do what she wanted, she came up to him and kissed him on the lips, a Judas kiss, bonding him as her accomplice. "Come on, then," she said, and led him to the front door, smartly shooting up the tent of her big old umbrella as they stepped out under the pouring heavens. She slipped her arm in his and led him across the yard and up the steep road. Rain reverberated on the umbrella top, and on either side of the road the ditches were fast-flowing rivulets of water and broken reeds. The rain sealed them in under the umbrella, and as he leaned forward into the road's incline, he thought of his present world, tiny, enclosed by Kathleen. And he thought then of his father and his mother, neither of whom had the slightest idea of what was happening to him. He wondered if, indeed, they ever thought of him these days.

He imagined his father in his newspaper office, initialing some proof pages, then calling out to his secretary to place a call to California. He imagined his mother picking up the phone in her Naugahyde armchair in her office facing the Pacific Ocean at Santa Monica. In the dayroom behind her, waiting for their art-therapy class, mad people in playclothes. "Have you heard from Jamie?" he imagined his father asking, and his mother, pleased at the novelty of this call, but still confused by her old angers over his father's betrayal, saying plaintively how would she have heard, she was so far away now, and then his father telling his mother that Jamie had gone to Ireland to track down his ancestors. They would gossip briefly about the irony of Beatrice's leaving all that money to him, thus enabling him to indulge these whims, and would end by promising each other to be in touch in case they heard from him.

But they had not heard from him. Nor would they hear from him. And now, as Kathleen tightened her grip on his arm, urging him up the steep incline in the driving rain, it came to him that, unbeknown to his parents or to anyone else who knew him, he was again a woman's prisoner.

Three hours later he drove with her up the narrow peninsula from the land's end of Ireland to the town of Bantry, coming in along the seafront to the great open square where a fair day of horse selling was taking place against a backdrop resembling a Norman seaport, the cluster of gray, severe buildings, a jumble of narrow streets in which poorly dressed people milled about, raw boys and girls, women in black dresses, red-faced farmers in flat cloth caps. There, on Kathleen's instructions, he parked the car outside a pub facing the Civic Guards station. "All right now," she said to him, "I'll wait in the pub. You go in and ask about him. They'll heed you, you being a Yank and a tourist. Just find out what's up and, if you can, tell Con we're waiting over here in Glendon's Lounge. Will you do that for me, love?"

He would. But first he took her into the pub and settled her with a drink in the nearly empty lounge bar, behind the noisy male clamor of the public bar out front. "I won't be long," he promised.

In the outer room of the Civic Guards station a woman was sitting on a bench trying to quiet a large barking dog. There were four old bicycles stacked against a wall, and a row of black raincoats hung on hooks along another. At a desk a young policeman, his tunic unbuttoned, was laboriously filling out a document. He looked up when Mangan entered, relieved at this break in his penman labors.

"You were wanting?" he asked.

"I came to see if you have a man called Conor Mangan here."

"And why did you come to ask that?"

The dog began to bark.

"Shuush, now," said the woman. She slapped the dog on its back, causing it to cringe beneath her feet. Then it rose and barked again.

"Well, he was brought here from Drishane to make a statement," Mangan said. "I wanted to give him a lift home when he's finished."

"Is that a fact?" the young policeman said. "Well, nothing has happened yet. We're waiting for the sergeant."

"I see. Well, I'll be over in Glendon's Lounge. If you'd tell him that?"

"Ah, will you stoppit, you bad dog," the woman cried, striking the beast across its muzzle.

"I will tell him, then," the young policeman promised. "As I said, he is here and we are expecting the sergeant. But when he has made his statement, it will have to be typed up and signed. You'd better be prepared to wait awhile, if you're going to wait."

"Fine," Mangan said. The dog suddenly lunged at him, pulling the woman from her seat as she held on to its collar, dragging it up short, its forelegs in the air. He waited until the barking subsided, the woman again striking the dog across its muzzle. Then, with a nod to the policeman, he left the station. He cut across the busy street and re-entered Glendon's Lounge. Earlier, when he had left Kathleen in the lounge, the only other customers had been an elderly man and his wife, who sat on high bar stools, looking through the opening into the public bar, bored with each other, envious of the life in that larger room. But now, when he reentered, the couple had gone. Instead, there were two young men sitting in the booth on either side of Kathleen. No one else was in the lounge, and neither they nor Kathleen noticed his arrival. He stood stock-still, filled with jealousy until he realized that she had not invited them to sit with her. They were here to bait her.

The taller of the youths wore a darned navy fisherman's jersey and rubber Wellington boots. His raw face split in a loose grin as he tried to put his hand down the front of Kathleen's cardigan. His companion, a chubby youth in a greasy blue suit, pushed *his* fingers down the waistband at the front of her jeans. She struggled, pushing and slapping at both of them. "Quit it, will you! Get away, now. I'll tell my fella on you. He'll be back in a minute."

"Go on with you," said the tall one. "You have nobody. Where's his drink if there's two of you?"

"Will you *stop* that!" Kathleen said, as she dragged the chubby one's hand out of her jeans. Enraged, Mangan stepped forward. At once, the taller youth swung around and gave him a hard stare.

"What do you think you're doing?" Mangan said in a thick angry voice.

Both louts at once slid out of the booth, wary, facing him in a wrestler's crouch, their hands held low. "Enjoying your holidays?" the tall one said. His chubby mate gurgled in appreciative laughter. Mangan struck out at the tall one, who deflected his blow with skilled ease.

"Easy there, Yank," the tall one said. "I'd say you're a bit past taking on the pair of us at once."

"Say you're sorry, now," said the chubby one.

"Yes, say you're sorry," said the tall one. "What call have you going around hitting people who never did you harm?"

In answer, Mangan swung again, but again the tall one deflected his blow, then, smiling, raised his fist to menace Mangan, who at once ducked back, falling into a boxing stance. Both louts laughed. "Lookit," the tall one said. "Mohammed Ali himself." Then turned his back contemptuously. "Come on, Mickey, we'd better go and see to that mare of yours."

And they went out, banging open the glass-paneled door to the public bar, the door swinging shut behind them as they were swallowed up in the move and shouting and press of the all-male crowd in the larger room.

"Sorry about that," Kathleen said. "Come and sit down, love." She patted the seat beside her. "What happened with the Guards?"

"Who are those bastards?" Mangan said, ignoring this. "Do you know them?"

"I don't. I met the big one at Crookhaven at a dance last summer, and when he came in the bar, he remembered me."

"Why didn't you get up and leave?"

A white-aproned barman came around the bar from the public side. "Will you be wanting anything?"

"Yes, a gin-and-tonic," Mangan said. "Kathleen?"

She nodded. "Two, then," Mangan told the barman, who

began to make the drinks while Mangan explained to Kathleen what had happened in the police station.

The barman put the drinks on the counter. "Now, sir," he said.

Mangan went to the bar, paid, and picked up the drinks. "By the way, where's the men's room?" he asked.

"The gents is through the public there, down at the end of the corridor."

"Thanks."

As he went back to the booth, he glanced through the glass-paneled swinging door, but there was no sign of the louts in the public bar. He put the drinks down by Kathleen. "I have to go to the toilet," he said.

"Are those lads still out there?"

"No, I checked."

"Well, be careful, so."

He went through the glass-paneled door into the public bar. A roar of talk and the heavy smell of draught porter met him as he moved among the farmers, horse dealers, and fishermen at the bar. Again he took inventory, but his adversaries were nowhere in sight. At the end of the room a passageway led to the rear of the premises. On the right at the end of this passageway was a door marked *Fir* in Irish script. It was a cold, concrete-floored room like an out-house. There was no toilet. The floor was wet, and an over-powering smell of urine, vomit, and porter pervaded the place. A primitive, chest-high flush pipe spilled greenish jets of water down the urinal walls. An old man passed him, buttoning as he went out.

Fastidiously trying to breathe through his mouth to lessen the stench, Mangan stood up to the wall and began to urinate from a full bladder. As he did, the door opened behind him. Vulnerable, his back to the intruder, he felt a momentary flicker of alarm.

Suddenly a hand grabbed at the seat of his pants, taking

a firm grip on the slack of material. Simultaneously, a second hand gripped his collar. Still urinating, he was jerked away from the wall. He let go of his penis and peed down the leg of his pants. He was whirled around, like a drunk about to be thrown out of a saloon, and in that brutal trajectory saw the face of the smaller, chubby lout grinning as, efficiently, the lout kicked him on his right shin, then kneed him in the groin. The hands which held him from behind released him as, choking, he fell on his knees on the wet, stinking concrete floor. The tall lout loomed over him, dragging him to his feet, then jerked him forward to smash the flat top of his head into Mangan's face. At once, Mangan's nose bled, and he felt as if his teeth were loose. Again, that ramming head struck him full clout. Hands released him. He fell on the floor and rolled over into the gutter of the urinal, full of yellow piss and vomit. No word had been spoken. He heard the sound of footsteps behind him, and suddenly he was kicked in the small of his back. The kick made a noise like a woman beating carpets on a line. The chubby one was now above him and his foot was raised to stamp down on Mangan's ribs. Mangan, gagging and moaning, felt a new and terrible pain in his chest. He fainted. He came awake as a kick landed on his rump, then heard them grunt as they went on making a football of him, kicking him as he rolled slowly across the foul floor. And then one of them kicked him in the head. Pain shot up behind his ear. A sheet of white light filled his shut eyes. He did not hear them leave.

He woke, looking up, seeing unknown faces peering down at him. He gagged. "Easy now," a man said, cradling an arm behind his shoulders and raising his head. He felt a severe pain in his chest and again lost consciousness. When next he opened his eyes he was being carried down a back alley, among a double row of peering faces. Two men were waiting and lifted him up into a panel truck. "Easy now. Steady there." He was laid on blankets and it was then that he saw Kathleen scramble in and hunker down beside him. The panel door shut. The truck engine started up. "Where are we going?" he asked thickly. His mouth hurt.

"The hospital. Now, you're all right. You'll be all right."

"Yes, you'll be all right," one of the men said, holding him steady in the moving truck.

"How many was it come at him?" the driver asked.

"Who knows," Kathleen said.

The truck's motions jarred his spine. He felt like vomiting but held it in. After a while the truck stopped and he was lifted down onto a stretcher trolley and wheeled into a hall with marbled walls and a salmon-pink ceiling. "I want to throw up," he told Kathleen, who walked beside him, her hand on his shoulder. A nurse came with a kidney dish and he vomited, then spat blood. His chest hurt. He told this to the nurse. He remembered little after that, until a doctor examined him, asking him where he hurt.

"Were you kicked?" the doctor asked, and then said to the nurse that he had better go to X-ray. In the X-ray room they took pictures of his chest, then rolled him over on his stomach for more pictures. He had a vague memory of being wheeled into a small ward. A young doctor in a white coat taped his ribs and questioned him about the fight. "Did you give as good as you got?" the doctor asked, then turned to a nurse and said: "Wash him. There's a terrible niff."

He slept and was wakened often so that they could take his blood pressure and his temperature. He woke on his own in the middle of the night and heard a man beside him in the ward calling for the nurse. In the morning, an old woman in a blue coverall came by and swept up under the beds. A young girl in a white coat brought him a tray with a cup of tea and a boiled egg and a piece of toast. After a while, Kathleen came in. She bent over him and kissed him on the cheek. "Ah, poor love," she said. "Anyway, you're all right. The doctor says you can go home today."

A nurse came in with his clothes. "You have a couple of broken ribs," Kathleen said. "They gave you a right hammering, whoever they were. I told the Guards you didn't know them and you never saw them before." She narrowed her eyes at him, warning him to say nothing in front of the nurse. "They're a right scourge, those Guards. They say they want to speak to you before you go." She turned to the nurse. "You'd think when a visitor to this country gets hurt, they'd have the decency to take his word for it that he didn't know the fellas that did it."

The nurse said nothing. She looked at Kathleen in a way that spelled disapproval. "You'll have to wait outside now, until I get him dressed," the nurse said. Kathleen went out. The nurse pulled a curtain around his bed. While the nurse was helping him to dress, an older doctor in a white coat came in with two young doctors who seemed to be Indians. The old doctor looked at the chart on his bed.

"Any respiratory problems?" he said to no one in particular. "No, sair," one of the Indian doctors said. The old doctor then looked at Mangan. "Bad luck a thing like this happening on your holidays," he said. "Did you have a lot to drink?"

"No, not at all."

"They just set on you, did they? Well, anyway, I want you to take things very easy for a week or two. Will you do that now, like a good man?"

Mangan said he would.

"He can go home any time," the old doctor said to the nurse.

"Before he leaves, the pliss are asking to speak with him," one of the Indian doctors said.

The old doctor nodded. "Goodbye, then," he said to Mangan. "You're lucky it wasn't worse."

The three doctors left the ward. The nurse gave him his

jacket. "You can put it on later when you sit up," she said. She went to pull open the curtain surrounding his bed, but at that moment two Civic Guards came through the curtain.

"Just let it be, will you?" one of them said. "Thanks very much." The nurse went away. This Civic Guard was the same man who had spoken to Mangan the other morning at the house on the mountaintop. "Hello again," the Guard said and Mangan noted a new, half-contemptuous familiarity in his manner. "You've been to the wars, I see."

"I'm afraid so."

The second policeman sat down on a chair by the bed, took out a black-backed notebook, and licked the point of his pencil with the tip of his tongue.

"Can you tell us how this happened?" the first policeman said.

"We were in the lounge bar," Mangan began. He found it hurt his chest when he spoke and so kept his voice at a whisper. "I came back and found these two guys annoying the girl I was with."

"Can you speak up a bit?" the second policeman said.

"What girl was that?" the first policeman asked.

"She's outside. She's a cousin of mine."

"Ah yes. That would be Kathleen Mangan. It was the brother we had in custody," the policeman told the other policeman. "And what happened then?"

"Well, I told them to leave her alone. And then later on, when I went to the john—"

"The gents?" the second policeman interjected.

"Yes, the gents. I was having a leak when they grabbed me from behind, knocked me down, and kicked me. The same two characters."

"How do you know they were the same?"

"I saw them."

"You could identify them, then?"

"Yes, I could."

"Did he say yes?" asked the second policeman, writing in his notebook.

"He did, yes," the first policeman said. "Do you know their names, or who they are, by any chance?"

"I heard one call the other Colum, and he called the other bastard Mickey."

"Colum and Mickey," said the second policeman, writing it down. "No surnames?"

"No."

"And why would they lay about you in that fashion?" the first policeman wondered.

"I told you. They were trying to annoy this girl and I threatened to hit them unless they left her alone. They left, and later on they came after me in the gents."

"That was very severe action, surely, for a little argument of that sort?" the first policeman said.

"Yes, it was."

"I was wondering, though," the first policeman said, "whether this affair could have any connection with that matter I spoke to you about yesterday morning?"

"What matter?"

"The theft of a load of scrap from Kerrigan's yard in Cork City."

"What are you talking about?" Mangan's chest hurt because he was shouting. "I'm a visitor here. I'm not some local crook. I have no need to steal any scrap."

"Of course not. Of course not," the policeman said. "But the people you are staying with, now, that could be another matter. And you said yourself you're prepared to make a statement saying that one of the suspects in this case was not in Cork City but was with you on the day of the robbery."

"But that's something else," Mangan said, furious. "This is something totally different."

"Sorry, now," the first policeman said. "Maybe you're right." He looked at the second policeman. "All right, Kevin, I think that will do us for the moment." Both rose and buttoned their slickers. "You're going back to Drishane, are you?"

"I suppose so."

"Well, keep in touch with us, will you? The sergeant said to be sure and tell you to let us know if you are thinking of leaving this district. It's because of your statement, you understand."

"I see," Mangan said. He had been lying down, dressed, on the hospital bed and now he tried to sit up, expecting the policeman to depart. But when he sat up he at once felt nauseated.

"That is a bad rap they hit you there in your mouth," the second policeman said. "You've lost your right incisor, so you have. That's a good biting tooth. You will be missing it." He smiled, revealing a gap in his own front teeth. "I lost mine a couple of years back. Kicked by a horse, I was."

Mangan put his hand up to his hugely swollen lip, felt a hole where the tooth had been. His mouth was so sore that he had not noticed the space until now. "We'll say goodbye, then," the first policeman said.

"Goodbye to you," echoed the second.

"Goodbye," Mangan said. They went out, and through a gap in the curtain he saw them in the hospital corridor, speaking in a low voice to Kathleen, who was sitting on a bench. He strained to hear what was said but could not catch it. The police then went away down the corridor and Kathleen came into the ward. She was holding a small plastic bag containing his wallet, traveler's checks, the daguerreotype, his car keys, and some change. "Here's your stuff," she said. "I just looked in your wallet there. I see you're a bit low on cash. Could you change some of these yokes before we go?" She held up the traveler's checks.

"What happened to Con?" he asked.

She gestured hopelessly. "The Guards are taking him to Cork. They say he's assisting them in their inquiries and he's to be held until further notice."

"In jail?"

"Yes. You see, it was his lorry that was found with the scrap in it. That makes it bad for him."

"Would you like me to drive you to Cork?"

"Ah, what's the use?" she said. "We'll go on back to the caravan, the pair of us. You're not fit to be running around chasing the likes of Con. And it's his own bloody fault. You'll have a nice rest now in the caravan."

The caravan. The sleazy sofa, the narrow bunk beds, the remembrance, his first day in Ireland, of the tinkers huddled by a fire off the main road, the cur dogs sniffing garbage. He felt himself shiver, as though he had a temperature. He thought of the high-ceilinged bedroom in that strange house, the bedroom where he had first possessed her. "I prefer the house," he said with a giddy laugh. "Can't we go there?"

"We can, surely," she said. "I know you. You like that big bed, don't you?"

"Yes, I do."

"Well, will we go, then?" she asked.

He nodded. When he stood up, his head spun. He let her take his arm and she led him down corridors, through doorways, and out into a yard at the rear entrance to the hospital. She put him on a bench in the sun. There were two other people on the bench, a woman with a bandaged head and a man with metal crutches. "I can drive, you know," Kathleen said. "If you sit nice and easy, I'll go down the town and bring your car back. Are you all right, now?"

He said he was. The weak morning sunlight washed over him as he leaned his throbbing head against the rough bricks of the wall. His tongue sucked at the hole where his tooth had been. Where could you get a tooth replaced in a place like this? A pain nagged under his rib cage each time he breathed. He put his hand there. It was on the opposite side from his heart and as he touched himself he felt the frame of the daguerreotype in his pocket. The *poète maudit*. Life lived in the gutter. Drunken brawls in pubs. But now he was too ill to think about that. He wanted to lie down. He looked up toward the hospital's rear entrance to see if Kathleen was coming with the car. There was no sign of her, but as he turned his head in the direction of the entrance, he saw a large traffic mirror positioned over it to show drivers whether the way was clear. In this mirror, distorted by magnification, he saw his head and shoulders as in a fun house glass, a sight which so startled him that he rose from the bench and approached the mirror for a closer self-scrutiny. Standing beneath it, looking up, he saw for the first time the extent of his facial injuries. His nose was swollen and bruised. Around one of his eyes was a bluish-red color, bulging over the eyebrow, with a Band-Aid covering a cut. His upper lip, very swollen, was drawn back over his teeth, revealing, as the policeman had said, a missing upper incisor on the right side. It was a face a person would turn from, the sort of face he used to see mornings on Eighth Avenue when he lived in Chelsea, drunk since daylight, begging a quarter, arrogant and vicious beyond all help.

But I am not that man. And yet, now it made sense: the Civic Guards' new, half-contemptuous air of familiarity, the old doctor's inquiring as a matter of course whether he had a lot to drink yesterday. He looked like a drunkard; he looked like a vagrant who might be mixed up in the theft of a load of scrap metal from a junkyard. He glanced at the two other discharged patients sitting on the bench, the woman with her bandaged head, the man with metal crutches. They had fallen into a desultory conversation of the sort strangers make when waiting for a bus. They had not spoken to him. They looked as though they had been in hospital. He looked as though he had been drunk. If only they knew: he thought of Weinberg in that impressive office overlooking Manhattan, his elegant suit, his Italian vicuña loafers, the voice detailing the two hundred thousand in savings accounts and a portfolio worth somewhere in the region of three hundred thousand. And, of course, the apartment and the summer house on the Island. He was rich: he had more money now than that Irishwoman with her bandaged head or that Irishman with his metal crutches would earn in several lifetimes. And then, as he began to smile at the irony, the thought came to him that perhaps, after all, his fellow patients were not wrong. For here, coming in at the gate, was Kathleen in the rental car. The woman with the bandaged head and the man with the metal crutches watched as Kathleen got out of the car and came toward him in her torn blue jeans and soiled baby-blue cardigan, her beauty whorishly pallid in the cold morning sunlight, a fit companion for the man he had just seen in the mirror. He looked again at his fellow patients, seeing Kathleen with their eyes. At that point the bandaged woman caught his eye and nodded to him in a kindly fashion. "Good luck, now," she said. "And safe home to you."

"Thank you," he said. He got up and went to join Kathleen, his joints stiff, his gait unsteady. She took his arm, grinning at him as though amused by his new disreputation. "Ready, love?"

"Ready," he said.

_____ *"What about money?"*

They had long left Bantry and were driving down the peninsula, approaching Drishane along the rim of bay above small patchwork-quilt fields and lonely cottages overlooking the ocean. Kathleen, turning from her driving, made an O with her mouth. "I forgot," she said. "I meant to take you to the bank. Wait. There's a bank at Drishane. I *think* it's open."

And so, some minutes later, they drove into the sleepy street of Drishane and Kathleen parked the car outside a building of concrete and tin which looked more like a storage shed than a place of business. A sign over it said ALLIED IRISH BANK. Leaving Kathleen, who said she had to buy milk, he entered these premises and spoke to the solitary clerk, arranging to change two hundred dollars in traveler's checks into Irish pounds.

"Are you on your holidays?" the clerk asked, as he paid the pound notes over.

"I am, yes."

"I'd say you've had poor weather. But I heard on the wireless this morning that there's a high-pressure area coming this way tonight. It should be nice tomorrow, please God. There you are, one hundred pounds ten pence. Thank you very much, now."

He went out. Whatever the bank clerk had thought of his appearance, he had been properly polite when he saw the wallet of traveler's checks. When I am shaved and changed and tidied up, I will look like someone who has been in an accident, that's all. But what about my missing tooth?

The main street of Drishane was deserted. Kathleen was nowhere in sight. Some of the shops had their front doors shut, as though they were closed for lunch. Walking stiffly, feeling the pain in his chest, he came down the steps from the bank building and regained the street. He saw that the door of Feeley's shop was open and went toward it, thinking perhaps to find Kathleen there. But when he looked up, there was only Mrs. Feeley at the cash register, making up accounts. She looked at him in alarm.

"Mr. Mangan. How are you? Oh, God help you, we heard you were hurted. Are you all right?"

"Yes, thanks."

"Can I get you something?"

"I was just looking for someone."

"Young Kathleen, is it?" She gave him a shrewd look. "I saw her go into Kelly's a while back."

"That's farther up the street, is it?"

"Fourth shop on your right, across the street."

"Thank you."

She smiled minimally and turned back to her accounts, but as he went out into the street he heard a furious tapping on the windowpane. It was not her windowpane, he realized, but the adjoining one, the window which bore the legend s. p. feeley, auctioneer & real estate. And behind the window, urgently beckoning him to enter, was Feeley himself, looking just as he had on the first day of Mangan's arrival here, his rubbery lips, pale glistening skin, and bulbous eyes again reminding Mangan of the head of a dolphin.

But now, as Feeley moved to the adjoining street door, which admitted to his office, and opened it, there was about him something peremptory, less amiable than on their former meetings. "Come in, will you," he ordered. "I've been looking to have a word with you."

The crowded office smelled of whiskey, and indeed on the mantelpiece there was, as before, a bottle of Paddy and two glasses. Feeley's large cat sat in one of the armchairs by the fire and her master dusted her off to the floor as he indicated that Mangan should sit down. "Well, now," he said, peering at Mangan's bruises. "They gave you a real hammering up in Bantry. And I hear tell you didn't even know the fellas that did it?"

"That's right."

"Were you—I mean, did you have a few jars in you? There's a certain crowd that goes around looking to take advantage of a man who has drink taken."

"I wasn't drunk. Not in the least."

But Feeley winked as though he did not believe this, then composed his rubbery features into a look which dismissed all levity. "I hear you are squatting in my house at Gorteen."

"*Your* house?"

"I am responsible for that property. I am acting for Mr. Harmon, the new owner. I believe the police were up to see you the other day and they mentioned it to you."

Mangan nodded uneasily, shuffled his feet like a claimant, and looked out of the window to see if Kathleen was in sight. "I'm sorry," he said. "It was a misunderstanding on my part. Con gave me to believe it was his family home.

There were even family pictures in the parlor. I had no idea the house belonged to someone else."

"Well, I am telling you now that it is not his house and that he had no right to be putting you in there," Feeley said. "I was the agent in the transaction, and when he sold the house, it was agreed he could keep his stuff in it until next June. But he had no right to put anyone in there. If it hadn't been for the Guards tipping me off, I'd have had no notion of what the pair of you were up to."

"I wasn't up to anything," Mangan said. This is what comes of hanging around with low-lifes, he thought. I look like a tinker now and this bastard is treating me like one. "I'm sorry for the mistake," he said. "And it *was* a mistake. I'll move out at once. And if it's a question of my paying rent for my stay there, I'll be glad to do it. Money is no object."

But did Feeley believe him that money was no object? He smiled in an unbelieving manner. "Now, hold your horses. I know the trouble you've had in finding a bed here. And no one knows better than me what a right twister your pal Con Mangan is. Now, I don't want you to take me up wrong on this, but I'll say something to you now, if you'll let me. Can I say it to you, man to man?"

"Yes, of course, what is it?"

Feeley leaned forward, his bulbous eyes fishily intent. "Mark my words, you're not in good company there. These two, Kathleen and her brother, are not the sort of relations any decent man would want to own up to. If they *are* your relations. The police are keeping a very strict eye on the pair of them, and not just because of that business in Cork City. And there is something else I might as well mention. The longer you stay around here, the harder it's going to be on poor Dinny's mother. That poor woman is not right in the head, and it would be an awful thing to have on your conscience that the sight of you drove her back to the asylum. I'm just telling you all this now in a friendly spirit, mind you. If I were you, I'd go home to America. This place is bad luck for you. Go on up to Dublin and finish your holidays there. Look at you. Sure you might have been killed."

"I'm not on holiday," Mangan said. "I came here to trace my relatives and in particular to find out if there's a link between my family and the poet James Clarence Mangan. I'm here to do research on that. I'll move out of that house up on the mountain right away. That's what you called me in here for, isn't it? I'm sorry about the mistake. But apart from that, what I do is my business."

"Ah, quite so. Of course you're very right, so you are," Feeley said in a new conciliatory manner. "Believe me, I was just trying to be of help. And as far as the house is concerned, there is no hurry. Stay a few days there, by all means. The Fallons, the people that run the Sceptre Hotel, are due back from Spain at the end of the week. You could probably move into the Sceptre then. But what I was saying about bad company was only for your own good. Ah!" Suddenly Feeley turned away from Mangan, his face opening in a false smile. Someone had tapped on the office windowpane. Mangan, looking up, saw Kathleen in the street, peering in.

"There she is," Feeley said maliciously. "A little girl that has seen a lot. Hello there, lovey," he called through the windowpane, smiling and blowing a kiss at Kathleen. He laughed and turned back to Mangan. "I hope the wife doesn't see me," he said with a knowing wink. "I'll let you out, so." Bustling ahead, unlocking his office door.

"So there you are, Jim," Kathleen said. "Hello, Seamus."

"Where is your brother today?" Feeley said to her.

"He's in Cork City, I think."

"And what is he doing in Cork City?"

"Well, you know his truck was stolen," Kathleen said

innocently. "Somebody took it and tried to make off with a load of scrap metal from Kerrigan's yard in Cork. The Guards found the truck and today they're giving Con a lift down to Cork to reclaim it."

"Oh, so that's the story," Feeley said, gurgling with a laugh that was all disbelief. "Is that what he told you, then?"

"It's the truth," Kathleen said.

"Not the way I heard it, but never mind," Feeley said. "As I was telling your American friend here, the Guards were in to see me in connection with your brother letting people sleep in Mr. Harmon's house."

"Sure, what harm was there in that?" Kathleen said, smiling at Feeley as though to win him. "Anyway, Jim here has all sorts of money. He'll be glad to pay you a few quid for rent if that's what's worrying you. Wouldn't you, Jim?"

"I already offered."

"And I already refused," Feeley said, smiling. "Off with you now, the pair of you. And mind what I told you, Mr. Mangan. For your own good."

"What was he telling you?" Kathleen asked as they walked back to the car. Mangan looked about him. Although there was no one on the street, he had a distinct impression of being under surveillance from every window.

"Nothing. Just some stuff about him being responsible for the house."

"The stupid ould git," she said and laughed. "Are you tired? Do you want me to drive the car?"

"No, I'm fine."

"Still, I think you'd better go to bed the minute we get to the house."

He looked at her. "So we're going to the house, are we?"

"Too right, we are."

"Will you stay with me, then?"

"Are you up to it?"

He laughed and started the car. They drove off, laughing, down the street of invisible eyes.

A few hours later something frightening happened. They were in bed. She had, as usual, brought gin and cake to their lovemaking and afterward fell into a restless sleep. He did not sleep. His head ached, his ribs hurt at each breath, his swollen upper lip throbbed like a pulse. The gin had left him light-headed but did not lift him into drunkenness, and now he lay in a pain-filled daze, listening to the mutter of rain on the bedroom window, watching cloud shadows drift across the room. Shadows made him think of the places which were now, officially, his homes: the cottage on Bluff Road in Amagansett, its windows shuttered against the winter gales; the apartment on Beekman Place, its venetian blinds like closed visors, slatting the furniture in the dusty rooms.

Homes no longer. Here he was the sailor home from the sea, the hunter home from the hill. He turned his head to look at the rumpled heap of bedclothes under which she slept, the sheet fallen away to reveal her naked back down to the cleft of buttocks. Gently, he ran his fingers down her spine to catch and fondle the soft swell of her bottom. At once, she shuddered like a foal, and sat bolt upright in the bed, as though he had electrocuted her. She screamed, deafeningly loud. Her head twisted around to stare at him, her eyes wide open, her face screwed in a rictus of terror. Her hands went up to ward him off as she continued to shriek, making a sound so loud that it filled the room, echoing off the mountaintop, away to the distant sea.

"Kathleen!" he yelled. "Stop it, Kathleen! It's me."

She stopped screaming and stared at him, as though she recognized him, but suddenly, in new terror, retreated back across the bed. Then, drawn by some awful curiosity, she came back, crawling on all fours across the coverlet to pull

the blanket off him and reveal his nakedness. She stared at
his genitals. "Oh, my Jesus!" she wailed. "Oh, Jesus!"

"What's wrong? Kathleen, what's wrong?"

But she screamed again, jumped off the bed, and cowered
in a corner of the room. "What did you do?" she wailed.
"Take it away. Take it away from me. Oh, God, are you
going to die?"

"Kathleen, wake up. What are you talking about?"

She approached him uncertainly, staring at him in terror.
"We'll have to get a doctor," she moaned. "We'll have to
have a doctor."

"Look, it's me, Jim."

But she did not seem to understand. "You'll have to get
a doctor. You'll bleed to death. Oh, God!" And she turned
from him, huddled down in the corner, her red hair falling
over her face.

He got off the bed, pulled on his underpants and trousers, and, careful not to frighten her, went toward her
slowly, his hand raised in a gesture of conciliation. "Kathleen, wake up. It's just a bad dream. This is Jim. Jim."

But she rocked, keening, not looking at him.

"It's all right," he said. "Wake up. You're just dreaming."

But she was not dreaming. He realized that he was afraid
of her. She looked up at him, her mad eyes seeing him, yet
not seeing him. "Aunt Eileen," she said. "I'll have to get
Aunt Eileen." She turned from him and went distractedly
to the window. "What will I tell her? What will I tell
her?" She turned from the window and stared at him, her
hand smoothing her hair back over her brow. As she stared
at him, she seemed to see something she had not seen before and now, slowly, wonderingly, she came back toward
him. He said nothing. She was mad. She did not know him.

But then, as she peered at him, she seemed to take hold
of herself. "I'm just dreaming," she said, and ran back to

the window. She pulled up the sash and he went to her, thinking she was about to throw herself out. But instead she leaned over the sill and retched. He came up behind her. She retched. Rain wet her face and hair. He did not touch her. She leaned out, the retching over, panting, rain drenching her face. She pulled back, then closed the window. Her face was no longer haunted. She turned to him with a weak, shamefaced smile. "Did I have one of my turns?"

"Yes."

"I'm sorry," she said. She went to the table, took up the gin bottle, poured herself a gin, and held up the almost empty bottle. "We'll be needing more."

"I've had enough."

"I haven't," she said. "I thought you had plenty of money."

"Of course I have."

"Then we'll drive down to Crookhaven. Anyway, we have to pick up food for our supper. I said Crookhaven because I'm not going to Drishane to have them all staring at us." She bent and put on her cotton panties. She then pulled the long white dress up over her hips. "Or maybe you just want to lie here and rest. I can drive the car and do the messages. Just give me the money. I'll not be long."

She turned her back and he began to hook up the bodice of her dress. "No, that's all right," he said. "I'll come with you." He finished hooking up her dress and as he did she swiveled around and kissed him on the lips. "My own fillim star," she said. "Did I give you a fright with that turn?"

"A bit."

"Old nightmares about nothing," she said and kissed him again. He kissed her. Better not to think. Better to drive her to Crookhaven and buy her all the gin she wanted.

He did not want to lose her. He could not bear to lose her. It was only a nightmare, forget it.

"That's right," he said. "An old nightmare."

And so he drove her to Crookhaven, at the end of a long inlet, a deep-water harbor, and a cluster of buildings along the quay. Rain squalls sent long, rippling shivers down the waters of the inlet, rocking the few fishing boats at anchor. The entire vista—village, church, and boats—seemed empty as a picture postcard, and so it was with a sense of surprise that they rounded a bend outside the village and came upon a truck parked at the side of the road, a small truck which Mangan recognized as being the same one which had rattled past him the other morning when he visited the old cemetery by the sea. And the same four laborers were down in the ditch now, scything and shearing the hedgerows, wearing old suits of clothes, rubber boots but no overcoats, as though they held the rain in contempt. As Mangan drove past they looked up, and at that moment he remembered the day at the cemetery when one of them had hidden his face and he had believed the man was Dinny Mangan. And now as he searched the upturned faces, one of the workmen blundered up out of the ditch waving at the car as though to flag it down. The man, seen plain, was indeed Dinny. But as he waved to stop the car, Mangan ignored him and drove on, aware of Kathleen half drunk beside him, unwilling to have words with this disputatious relative. The other workmen, seeing him drive on, also began to wave. "Stop! Wait a minute!" their voices yelled after him.

Kathleen, rousing herself from a doze, looked back at the shouting men. "That's Dinny. What's he want?"

"Shall I drive on?"

"No, better not."

Unwillingly, he brought the car to a stop and heard the

sound of Dinny's boots as the man pounded up the road behind him. "Does he work on the roads, then?" he asked Kathleen. "I thought he worked in some office."

"And isn't that just what he'd want you to think," she said scornfully. "Sure he hides from you if you meet him with his mates. And would you believe it, every night he goes home and puts on his good suit and a tie before he goes out to the church for devotions. He used to—" But she stopped her sentence, for Dinny had now arrived at the car window, panting, his glasses misted, his old suit and collarless shirt giving him the look of a down-and-out begging on the street. He looked briefly at Kathleen as though gauging her intoxication. But then his gaze settled on Mangan, and at once he assumed an expression of awe as though he had just been vouchsafed a miraculous vision. "What happened?" he said. "Who did that to you?"

"Somebody hit him in a pub in Bantry," Kathleen said. "Look, Dinny, we're in a desperate hurry. We have to get to the shops before they close."

"I declare to God," Dinny said, still staring at Mangan. "Kathleen, do you remember the time my daddy was hurt after the football match?"

"Is that what you stopped us for?" Kathleen said crossly. "Come on, Jim, let's go."

Mangan put the car in gear, uneasy about offending her, yet uneasy at pulling away. But Dinny stepped forward and gripped the sash of the car window. "Hold on now," he said. "I just wanted to ask you a question. Was my mammy up your way today?"

"She was not," Kathleen said. "Is she on the loose again, then?"

"God forgive you for those words," Dinny said. "And maybe He will not, after all my mammy did for you." He looked at Mangan and Mangan was touched by the sudden humility of his look. "I'm sorry I was short with you the other day, sir. It's not your fault that the sight of you upsets my mother. She spoke to you about it, didn't she?"

"Yes, she did."

"Well, she is missing again since this morning and it is my guess that it is yourself she is looking for. As long as you are in these parts, she will not be easy in her mind. If she does come to you, let me know and I will come and fetch her home."

Kathleen leaned over and tried to disengage Dinny's grip on the window. "All right now, you have said your bit. Will you let us go?"

But Dinny did not let go. "Listen, sir," he said. "If you are on holidays, how long will you stay?" The distorted lens of his spectacles made his eyes swim as though he wept. "I am not asking out of curiosity, I am asking for the sake of my mother."

"I don't know how long I'll be here," Mangan said. "But I promise I'll let you know as soon as I can."

"Father Burke says you are interested in the poet Mangan?"

"Yes. Don't you remember I asked you about him when we first met?"

"Oh, come on," Kathleen said tipsily. "I'll break your bloody knuckles if you don't let go."

"I was not helpful when you asked me," Dinny said, his hands still gripping the window. "But listen to me now, sir. I will make a bargain with you. I will be able to assist you with those inquiries if you will promise me to leave here as soon as you find what you are looking for. Would that sort of bargain interest you?"

"It might," Mangan said. He put the car in gear, aware that Kathleen's impatience had turned to rage. "I'll speak to you about it later. Maybe I could come up to see you at your house one evening."

"All right, then," Dinny said, at last releasing his grip on the car window. "And if you see my mammy, you'll let me know."

"Yes," Kathleen shouted angrily. "Go on, Jim."

The car leaped forward, but as Mangan looked back through his rear-view mirror, he felt strangely moved at the sight of that poorly dressed figure standing supplicant on the crown of that narrow, lonely road, worried for his mother, who had lost her mind. And as he drove on, he watched Dinny's figure become smaller in the mirror until, at last, it was a tiny black silhouette, which turned and went back down the ditch.

"When did Dinny's father die?" he asked, but Kathleen turned from him and stared in angry silence at the gray, shut village houses up ahead.

"I'll need money for the food store. And I want you to go into Shea's and get us two bottles of gin and a bottle of whiskey for Con if he comes back from Cork. And wait for me there in the pub."

"Okay. But when you join me, will you tell me about Dinny's father?"

"Oh, Jesus, Jesus!" she shouted. "Will you give over with that. I need a drink, I tell you. I'm leppin' out of my skin with nerves. God, you're like a bloody detective. Is that all you care about?"

He said he was sorry. He said of course he cared about her. He said he hadn't meant to upset her. He said he loved her. By that time they had reached the food store and she took the twenty-pound note he gave her and got out, directing him to the pub up ahead. When he went into the pub the room was so dark that at first he could not see if there were any other customers. Gradually he discerned two heavy old men in cloth caps and the inevitable black greasy serge suits, sitting glum over huge glasses of porter. They eyed him, then gave him a tentative nod of greeting. There was no one behind the bar. He cleared his throat loudly and shuffled his feet, and at last a young girl came out from the back. She stared at him with distrust. "Yes?"

"Two bottles of gin, please, and a bottle of Irish whiskey."

Silently, she went to fetch the bottles. His bruised face and swollen lip had again acted as his passport into that tinker world, stamping him as dangerous, drunken, a man you would not cross. The two old men at the bar exchanged the most minimal of glances when they heard his drink order, then dutifully addressed themselves to their pints as though engaging in a ritual of devotion which could not be interrupted by speech. He went to the pub window and, looking out through the glass lettered with the sign JOHN JAMESON LTD DISTILLERS, saw Kathleen, not in the food store but in the green telephone kiosk down at the end of the street. She was speaking to someone, and as he watched she hung up and came out of the kiosk, turning in his direction, the hem of her long white dress swinging crookedly behind her. She pulled the lapels of her cheap cloth overcoat tight across her bosom as though she was cold, then stood swaying, looking about her as though lost. Uncertainly, she turned in the direction of the quay, wandered forward a few steps, and sat on a wet iron bollard, from which a big gray gull arose and flew away. He watched her as she sat there, saw her head sway as she began to rock in the same way he had seen her rock earlier when she had her "turn."

"Will I put it in a bag?" the girl's voice asked from behind the bar.

"Yes," he said, still peering through the glass. He saw Kathleen get up and wander toward the quayside. She sat down on the wet quay, letting her legs hang down over the water. In haste he paid for the bottles and ran outside, aware that the girl had come after him to see what was wrong. He ran across the street, reaching the edge of the quay just as Kathleen leaned forward dangerously, as though she were about to ease herself off and drop down to the greenish waters below. "Kathleen?" he called.

She looked up at the sky, as though listening to her name shouted from far off. He put down the bottles on the quay and knelt behind her, gently taking her by the shoulders. "It's me, it's Jim," he said. "I've got the bottles. Shall we get some food now?"

"We have food at home," she said dully. "I want to go home." It was a sudden wail as though she would break into tears, and so, gently, he raised her up. "We'll go home," he said. "We'll go now." The white seat of her dress was wet and stained by the slime of the quay. It stuck to her bottom, but she did not seem aware of it. As he led her toward the car, he saw the girl and the two old men watching from the pub, and other watchers too, their faces pressed to the window of the food store. The wind whipped, blowing the front of Kathleen's skirt up into her face. He smoothed it down again and, gentle as a nurse, brought her to the car and seated her in the front passenger seat.

"The bottles," she said, without turning her head. "You forgot the bottles."

He ran back to the quay. The plastic bag which he had placed upright on the ground had fallen over on its side, but the bottles were not broken. He clutched the bag to him clumsily, aware of the village faces, seeing himself as they must see him, a shambling figure with a bruised face, companion to a dazed, drunken girl. He got into the car and turned it around, driving back the way they had come. "Are you all right?" he asked, but she did not hear him. Farther up the road he saw the little truck and the men working in the ditch. Again they turned around, and this time three of them waved. Dinny did not wave but stood in the ditch staring at the car, the rain wetting the circles of his spectacles, giving him the look of a blind man. Mangan glanced at Kathleen. "Are you all right?" he said again.

"The Guards are holding Con."

"What?"

"They told me to ring up the court in Cork before five o'clock. I just got through to them now," she said. "Con and Packy Deane were arraigned this afternoon and charged with stealing a lorryload of scrap iron. Someone informed on them. They're to come up for trial on the fifteenth of next month."

"Who told you this?"

"One of the clerks at the courthouse. That's why I had to ring up before five. The courthouse shuts at five."

"Why didn't you tell me you had to phone?"

"Con said I wasn't to tell you. He said the police would never charge him." She began to rock again, violently, and as the car rounded a bend her forehead struck the windshield.

"Be careful," he said. "Did you hurt yourself?"

But she did not seem to hear. She rocked and rocked. "The clerk said he could get five years," she said, as if to herself. "The caravan is only rented. And I get nothing. I have no assistance, nothing."

The road ahead came to the crook of the long sea inlet, and the car crossed a narrow bridge and turned up toward Drishane, the mountain, and the yellow, dirty caravan on top of it. He looked at her as she rocked beside him, her blue eyes staring ahead, the glory of her long red hair framing the altar of her perfect features. Impossible to think of so desirable a girl as a waif. But in the last two hours all that had changed. As he watched her rocking to and fro, isolated in her worry and misery, her very youth and beauty seemed an added handicap. What shopkeeper's wife would allow this girl to work close to her husband? And for that matter, what work could she do? She seemed to have no skills and little education. England? Wasn't that the Irish answer? She could always emigrate, he supposed.

"What about England? There are jobs there."

"I was going there last winter. Two fellows I know promised to pay my fare. But Con said if I got a bad turn there, there'd be nobody to help me. They'd put me away like they did Aunt Eileen. And there's no work here. That's the God's truth, I'm telling you. I've looked for work. I wrote away to Dublin for a job in nursing. But I never got my School Leaving. You need your School Leaving. I'd do anything to get away from here. But there's no one wants me."

I want you. God, how I want you. Never mind the nightmares, the bad turns. You're so young, you could learn to forget the past. In New York in our big bedroom overlooking Beekman Place you could sleep in peace.

A cyclist lurched suddenly into his line of vision and he had to pull the wheel over sharply to avoid a collision. Looking back, he saw the cyclist waving frantically, as though to stop him. It was the old postman he had seen the other day behind the mountain with Kathleen. Through his side-view mirror he saw him hop off his bike, still waving. Mangan stopped the car and backed up the road.

"It's Pat the Post," Kathleen said, rousing herself from her miserable rocking.

The postman undid his satchel. "Nice soft day," he said, gesturing up at the drizzling rain. "I waved to you, sir, because I have a letter for you that was sent in error to the Sceptre Hotel. Wasn't it the lucky thing now that I saw you, for I'd have had to head up the mountain tomorrow to give it to you."

He handed over a large envelope which Mangan recognized instantly by the engraved notation of Weinberg, Greenfeld, Kurtz and Norris. "It's a Special Delivery, sir. Maybe you'd better read it directly, in case you'd be wanting to make some answer."

As Mangan tore open the envelope, he heard the old post-man say to Kathleen, "I hear Con's in a bit of trouble."

She looked up at him sullenly. He smiled, displaying a mouth naked of all but three long yellow teeth. "I hear that he and Packy Deane are assisting the police with their inquiries, as the saying goes. From Cork City jail, no less."

"So you think that's funny, do you?"

"Ah, now no offense, Kath. Go on with you. Sure, and it will take better men than the Guards to nail anything on the same Packy. And he and Con are best butties."

"They are that, I hope," said Kathleen, as though swearing an oath.

"And what about your letter, sir?" the postman asked. "Not bad news, is it?"

Mangan had not looked at the letter. Now he fingered its several sheets, first glancing at one labeled *Disbursements: Funeral*, amazed at the size of the total; then going on to sheets of figures mostly to do with Beatrice's father's portfolio of investments. He turned quickly to Weinberg's letter and skimmed its official yet chatty prose. The will would be probated on the twenty-fifth of the coming month. "In the meantime," Weinberg wrote, "to answer your question, I'd make a rough estimate of the value of the entire estate, including real estate, as being in the region of $800,000."

"No, not bad news," he told the toothless postman.

"No answer, then?"

"No, thanks."

"Well, I'll be on my way then, sir, as soon as you sign this receipt for the letter."

Mangan took the form and a pen and signed. The post-man turned to Kathleen. "Now, don't you worry your head. Con will be all right. He'll be all right."

Mangan started the engine. He noticed she had begun to rock again. Eight hundred thousand. A hell of a lot of money. A great fortune in Ireland. He waved to the postman as they drove off. She rocked. She is in misery because she thinks she will not be able to manage her life if her drunkard brother goes to jail. But I can manage her life. I can take her away from here. I can show her London and New York. I can get her doctors and sedatives for her "bad turns." Beatrice never needed me. This girl needs me.

And so he took her home, through Drishane and up the winding road past Duntally, where Dinny lived with his half-mad mother, and on up to the very top of the mountain and the dirty yellow caravan on the topmost ridge. And as he parked the car there, her mood seemed suddenly to change. Her dog ran toward her, barking, and she went to it and in the way of a little girl picked it up, fondling it as though it were a doll, running across the wet grass to the caravan steps, her gloom gone, swift as childish tears. Again he thought of her as a child, his troubled child to whom he would be father and lover and fairy prince. But as he picked up the liquor bottles and followed her toward the caravan a less flattering simile came to mind, not fairy prince but Sugar Daddy, thirty-six and eighteen. Crabbed age and youth cannot live together.

But thirty-six wasn't old, was it? Never mind what they said in his youth about not trusting anyone over thirty. He watched her skip up the steps of the caravan after pushing the dog back into its lair beneath the chassis. Pygmalion replaced the Sugar Daddy image: he would bring her to New York, buy her clothes, teach her table manners, send her to college, Professor Higgins to her Eliza. But he remembered that Professor Higgins did not sleep with Eliza. Not bloody likely. A truer model was probably the professor in *The Blue Angel*, the stout Emil Jannings playing the love-besotted academic, standing in the wings in some run-down cabaret crowing like a cock on the orders of Marlene Dietrich, his imperious young tart of a mistress. *Co-co-ri-co! Co-co-ri-co!*

"What are you screwing up your face like that for?" she

asked as he came in, ducking his head at the low caravan door.

"Co-co-rico-co!" he crowed. "I was imitating a cock."

"That doesn't sound like a cock," she said. "Not an Irish cock. But then you don't have an Irish cock, do you?" She laughed smuttily and went to the sink. "Gin," she said. "That's your only man. Let's have a bit of gin, now. Are you hungry? Do you want me to fry you up some rashers and sausage?"

"No, I'm not hungry."

"You need looking after," she said, opening one of the fresh gin bottles and pouring lavishly into two half-washed tumblers. She added a splash of bitter lemon. "You poor old soldier," she said. "I keep forgetting you're just out of the hospital. Are you tired? Do you want to lie down on the sofa for a while?"

He looked at the dirty green plush sofa, its pelt rubbed bare along the back and armrests. "I wish we could go down to the other house," he said.

She took her drink and sat on the sofa. "Come here a minute," she said. "Sit by me. Tell me. Do you like me at all?"

He looked at her saint's profile. It seemed almost sacrilegious to answer with a simple yes. "Kathleen," he said, "do you know I never met anyone as beautiful as you?"

"But do you like me?"

"I'm mad about you. I'd do anything in the world for you."

"Ah, you're joking me." She drank more gin. "You were married to a fillim star," she said, as though reminding herself.

"You're much more beautiful than she was."

"I'll bet at your age you've said that to a lot of girls."

"At my age?" He was wounded. "How old do you think I am, then?"

"You must be thirty, at least."

"Does thirty seem old to you?"

She stared at the soiled chenille rug. "I was thinking," she said. "Con will be over thirty by the time he gets out of jail."

"But he hasn't even been tried yet."

"He did it," she said. "And I know in my bones that they'll get him for it." She looked at him. "You said you'd do anything for me. Would you lend me my fare to America?"

He went to her and sat beside her on the dirty sofa. He put his arms around her and kissed her plaster-cold cheek. "I'll do more than that. I'll take you myself."

"I don't want you to take me. We have an aunt in Pittsburgh on my mother's side. She'd write a letter for me so that they'd let me in. But I couldn't be asking her for the fare, for her husband is just a lift man that runs the lift in some office there. Anyway, they'd write the letter for me saying they'd look after me. What sort of place is Pittsburgh?"

"It's no place," he said. "Listen, I have a big apartment in New York City. And I have a very nice summer house right on the sea out in Long Island." He kissed her again. He sang:

> "Oh, I will take you home, Kathleen,
> To where you heart has never been,
> Way across the ocean wide,
> I will take you to my home, Kathleen."

She looked at him. "Did you just make that up?"

"No, it's an American song. Don't you know it?"

She shook her head. "Don't be singing or saying any more poems, will you?"

"Why not?"

"I don't like it. And with that face on you and saying poems, you're like somebody's ghost."

"Your uncle Michael?"

"Ah, let me alone." She disengaged herself from his arm, got up, and went to the sink, where she poured herself more gin.

"Careful with that," he said.

"It's your only man, gin." She laughed. "It's right for what ails you." She drank and, drink in hand, went to the caravan's dirty window and, pulling aside the faded curtains, looked at the dark bluff of mountain outside. "I could manage in America," she said. "At least I'd be away from all of this. Last summer I worked in a hotel up in Ennis. It's called the Old Ground Hotel, did you ever hear tell of it?"

"No."

"Oh, it's very grand. I made the beds. I could do that in America."

"You wouldn't have to. I'd be your sponsor."

But she continued to look out of the dirty window. "I met an English fella the time I was in Ennis. He was like yourself, over on his holidays. I met him at a dance, and when I told him I was at the Old Ground, he didn't know that I meant I was working there. He wanted me to go to England with him. He said he was mad for me. Just like yourself. And do you know? When he found out it was as a maid I was working in the hotel, he was ashamed to sit in the lounge bar of the hotel with me. It would be no different with you. You're only with me now because you're on your holidays."

"That's not true. I'll prove it."

"Oh, there's no need for that." She turned from the window and looked at him. "I'll tell you what. You lend me my fare to Pittsburgh and a few quid to get me started and I'll go down to the house with you tonight and stay with you and look after you and do whatever you want for as long as you're here in Ireland." She made a mock gesture of spitting in the palm of her hand and held her hand out, palm upward, in the same gesture he had seen the cattle dealers use in Bantry when they struck a bargain. "Put your hand on it," she said. "It's a fair bargain. You'll not regret it."

He took her hand in his. "But I mean it," he said. "We'll go to America together."

"I don't want that. I made you an offer. You lend me the fare and give me, say, fifty quid as a thank-you present. That's what I want. No more and no less."

He laughed and kissed her. "Whatever you want," he said. "I told you I'll do whatever you want."

"Right, then." She went to the sink, put bread, butter, gin, and a chocolate cake into a cardboard carton. "Do you want a fry before we go down to the house?"

"No, I'm not hungry."

"All right, I'm ready, so," she said. She switched on the flashlight and blew out the kerosene lamp. "Come on," she said.

In the flashlight's cold beam he looked at her. She was trembling. "Look, we don't have to go down there. I mean, if it upsets you."

"No, I'll be all right." She ran down the steps. "Come on," she called. "And close that door."

He came out and shut the caravan door. The dog had run out from under the steps and was frisking about his mistress, a moving blur of excitement in and out of the circle of her flashlight. Gradually, as his eyes became accustomed to the night, he saw that the sky was a shifting chiaroscuro of grays and blacks, backlit by a cold theatrical moon. The clouds, running as before a storm, sundered as they struck the mountain face, bringing with them a light drizzling curtain of rain. Ahead of him she walked swiftly across the field and onto the precipitous narrow road, the dog padding along on her left, her flashlight searching out the ground in an erratic sweep. He heard the clink of bottles in one of the plastic bags slung over her arm and the gravelly sound of her footsteps as she started down the steep road toward the gray sinister house, its rooftop and east wall now visible above the fuchsia hedge which hid its yard.

And then, suddenly, the dog ran ahead of her, yelping as though it had been kicked. Her flashlight searched for it and found it, fur flat on its skull, snarling in a mixture of rage and fear as it stood in front of an opening in the ditch. The flashlight leaped about like a will-o'-the-wisp but discovered nothing. The hedge was low and sparse, the hole in the ditch revealing only a green slope which culminated in the gray stone of the mountain bluff. But the terrified dog continued its ear-offending yelps until Kathleen, shouting, bent, picked up a stone from the road, and threw it, striking the dog in the hindquarters. "Gerroutofthat, Spot! Go on home. Go on!" She lifted a second stone and threw it, missed the dog, who turned tail and went larruping up the narrow road, barking, turning its head back as though it were pursued.

"What caused that?" Mangan asked.

"It might be a cat."

She turned away from the gap in the ditch and went on down toward the house, he following a pace behind her. His swollen lip throbbed constantly; the gin he had drunk on and off since afternoon had failed to deaden the pain of his many bruises. He felt dull and brutish, a stumbling bull led on by the nose ring of his lust. He looked at his keeper as she hurried ahead, leading him into the yard of the old house. He thought of the cattle drover's gesture she had made just now when she proposed her bargain, the mock spit on her palm before she led away her prize, a prize worth, perhaps, a passage to America and a few pounds for services rendered, but old, unsuitable to accompany her on her journey to a new life. Co-co-ri-co!

And now, having entered the yard, he looked up at the

high sloping roof, visible in the light of that cold theatrical moon which appeared over the top of the mountain ridge, and as Kathleen hurried forward and bent down, her flashlight finding the rug and the key hidden under it, the house gave out that piteous cry he had heard before, as though some small animal were trapped in its roof. "Did you hear that?" he said to Kathleen, but she had found the key and wrenched it around in the lock, dragging the door open with a harsh clatter of its wooden floorboard on the stone. As always, he experienced the minatory presence of the building which faced him, but as the small cry echoed in his ears, he felt a new and strange sensation. It was as though the house feared *him*, feared his approach, feared his penetration of its secrets. And so, with Kathleen's impatient light to guide him, he made his way down the hall mined with tin pots and cans, aware of her increasing nervousness but losing his own unease.

"There's two lamps in the kitchen, we'll get them and bring them upstairs. That way we'll have plenty of light in the room."

He obeyed her, lighting matches in the dank kitchen as he took the glass cones off the kerosene lamps and turned up the wicks. Then, each holding a lamp, they made their way out again and started the ascent of the stairs. "Do you want to go to the toilet?" she said. "Well, go then, because once we're up, I don't want you up and down the stairs in the night."

"All right." He left her and went down the back passage to the narrow lavatory with its ball-and-chain tank and cut newspapers stacked in the toilet-paper box attached to the door. He saw her light going up the flight of stairs and then, his own lamp filling the lavatory's narrow space, urinated and went to wash his hands in the little sink in the adjacent bathroom. It was as he came out of the bathroom that he heard the cry again, and this time it was close, so close that he started and his hand holding the lamp shook in alarm. It was just ahead, wasn't it? Slowly, he went forward into the hall corridor. He could hear her footsteps on the floorboards of the bedroom above and, looking up, could see the light streaming onto the first-floor landing from the opened bedroom door. Could it be a rat or a bat which uttered that small, piteous cry, not quite animal, yet not quite human, either? Let it be. He should go up. She was alone, she was afraid, and she was waiting for him. But as he went toward the staircase, he noticed to his surprise that the door of the sitting room was open. He had always been careful to close it. And Kathleen had not opened it. Slow, aware of the sound of his own footsteps, he went down the hall and into the room. His kerosene lamp filled the shadowy parlor with a warm golden light, bringing furniture, photography, portraits, and bric-a-brac into focus as though a stage were suddenly lit. He stood staring at the Victorian clutter, seeing for the first time the heavy green plush curtains drawn back from the bay windows. It seemed that at any moment he might hear the sound of voices in the hall as dinner guests returned for an evening of conversation here in the parlor with music perhaps and maybe a song or two.

But there were no voices. The room was still. The portraits of these unknowns who might be his forebears looked down at him in dead indifference and in the photographs the subjects seemed fixed in a moment of play-acting, their poses designed to hide, not reveal, the truth of their lives. And then again he heard the tiny cry, and this time it seemed to come from the valance of the curtains above the window. He put the lamp down on a nearby table and reached in his pocket for his flashlight, thinking to turn its beam on the crannies up there. As he did, he strained forward, listening for the tiny cry. But the cry was not repeated, and as he stood waiting to flash his light, he had the conviction that whatever had cried was no longer in the room. Cautiously, he stepped into the alcove of the bay window, then looked at a face which moved to the left of him. He stared in terror at the face: a narrow old mirror framed in a gold-scrolled leaf and in it, glaring at him, ghostly pale, eyes glittering with the steely hysteria of an insane person, the features frighteningly bruised, lip swollen, missing front tooth: himself. And in that moment he knew why this house resisted him. *I am the ghost that haunts it.* I am come back to these rooms where whatever bloody deed that frightened Kathleen once took place. He stared at his ghostly mirror face, an image which, seen now in the gold-scrolled frame, rang in his mind like the bell around the neck of some lost animal high on a mountainside drifting toward its death. And then he put his hand in his pocket and for the first time in days drew out that other face in a frame, that face which confronted him now, eyes glittering with the steely hysteria of the insane. As he looked, he saw what he had forgotten. The photograph also had a gap in the upper right front teeth. From framed photograph to framed mirror he consulted these identical images, and as he did, the elation which had filled him in the past when he looked at his unknown *Doppelgänger* changed to fear. It was as though the daguerreotype was now a document sentencing him to some future doom. And at that moment Kathleen cried down to him. "Jim, where are you? Are you coming up? What's keeping you down there?"

He took the lamp and went out, shutting the door tight as he left the room. He went up the flight of stairs, calling out to reassure her. "It's me, Kathleen." When he went into the bedroom he found her, naked except for an old blue coverlet which she had wrapped around her, sitting cross-legged on the bed, drinking gin and eating a slice of yellow pound cake with chocolate icing. "Where were you?" she asked, with her mouth full. "You were long enough."

"Did you hear somebody crying?"

"That's just mice," she said. "Shut that door. That's another reason we'd be better off in the caravan. It's freezing in this house."

He shut the door and, standing close to the heater, stripped himself to his underpants and socks. His rib cage was bound around with a pink bandage.

"God, you're a sketch," she said. "Do you want a drink?"

He shook his head and removed his socks before getting under the covers. "Get in with me," he commanded her. "The bed's cold." At once obedient, she let slip the coverlet and, naked, slipped in beside him. She reached out to retrieve the gin bottle and her glass. She took a drink, then lay down. Her hand under the sheets took hold of his penis, which jerked to semistiffness.

"How big a place is Pittsburgh?" she asked. "Bigger than Dublin?"

"About the same size."

"The winters are desperate in America. I saw them on the telly."

"If you come to America with me, I'll take you south for the winters. You can lie in the sun."

But she did not seem to hear him. She began to pull on his penis, a shade dutifully, he thought, and this surmise was confirmed when she reached out her other hand for her glass and took a pull on her gin. "Can I make this man stand and deliver?" she whispered, and with practiced assiduity plunged her head under the bedclothes, and her warm moist lips found the head of his prick. Then, while he lay staring in troubled ecstasy at the high shadows of the ceiling, she skillfully worked her passage to America, bringing him to the point of climax with her mouth and then throwing back the bedclothes to reveal herself as a prize for the taking: young, pointed, quivering breasts, small rounded belly, long limber legs, assuming again like an accomplished actress her role as his trembling, compliant victim.

And so, weary though he was and aching from his recent beating, he rose over her, led blindly back to lust by his youthful governess. There, in the one bright room in that dark house, he again came to climax, rearing over her tender buttocks. And at the precise moment when he began to come inside her, loud footsteps sounded on the stairs outside. In panic, his orgasm spending in a dead rush, he crouched over her body as though to protect her. He felt her stiffen below him in silent terror. The footsteps approached the door. Someone knocked. "Kathleen?" a woman's voice cried out.

Kathleen squirmed below him, staring at the door, which slowly opened inward. "Maeve, no!" she screamed, and flung herself out from under Mangan, scrambling off the bed, crouching down on the far side of it. At that, the woman outside the door seemed to start and then came forward boldly into the room, the derelict old woman wearing a man's tweed jacket, Dinny's mother.

"It's not Maeve, Kathy," she said in a gentling voice, a voice one might use to quiet a frightened child. "It's only me, only Aunt Eileen." But Kathleen cowered away, going on her hands and knees to a corner of the room, hunkering there, her long naked legs drawn up to her shoulders, her face averted from the visitor, her glorious hair spilling down over her back, uttering a senseless keening, which erupted suddenly into a high nightmare shriek as the old woman stretched out a hand as though to touch her. "Kathleen, Kathy, listen now, it's Aunt Eileen, it's only me, Kathy love, it's your Aunt Eileen, everything's all right. Maeve is not here now, she's far away."

Ignored by the two women as though he were not in

the room, Mangan got off the bed and shamefacedly pulled on his clothes. The old woman knelt on one knee in front of Kathleen and touched her on the forehead with her fingers. Kathleen shrieked, then subsided into a dull trance as the old woman began to stroke her brow.

Mangan approached them. "Kathleen," he said, but the old woman held up her hand, cautioning him to silence. "She'd not know you just now. Just let her be." She resumed her caresses. Kathleen began to tremble and stare about the room as though searching for something dangerous. "There is nobody," the old woman said softly. "It was only me. I'm sorry, now, that I disturbed you, Kathy." She inched herself closer until she knelt beside the girl, and gradually, very gently, took her in her arms, rocking her as she would a small child. "It's all right now, it's all right, Kathleen. It's only me. Only Aunt Eileen."

Gradually the strange tension left the girl. She turned and looked up at the old woman who held her in her arms. "What are you doing here?" she asked in a nearly normal voice.

"I woke up this morning feeling poorly. I went out, thinking a walk would do me good. But I couldn't tell you where I've been." The old woman smiled distractedly. "I was wandering out there on the boreen. I thought I was on the road for Skull, but I couldn't for the life of me tell you why I was wanting to go there. And then it was dark and I saw the light in this house and knew where I was. I felt better then. So I came in, thinking to ask you how is Con getting on? Poor Con, I hear the Guards are after lifting him in Cork."

"Him and Packy Deane," Kathleen said. She looked over at Mangan. "Jim, will you pass my clothes?"

He went to the foot of the bed, where her clothes lay. "Excuse me a minute, Aunt Eileen," she said and, disengaging herself, got up and went to dress, modestly turning her back on her aunt. But as she put on her dress a change came over her again. "They say he'll get five years," she said, as though to herself. "Five years. I'll be all alone." She began to rock to and fro where she stood. The old woman, watching, got up and signaled Mangan to follow her out of the room. As he went toward the door, he looked back at Kathleen. The rocking had stopped. She stood completely still, her eyes dead as a statue's. She did not see them go.

On the dark landing the old woman moved close to him. He could smell milking cattle and peat fires on her old tweed jacket. He was expecting a shocked lecture on his behavior, but there was no rebuke. Her voice was light and gentle. "It's this house that's the cause," she said. "It has a bad memory for her, do you see. She should not be here. She needs taking care of, but I cannot stay up at the caravan when I'm needed down at home. So I'd suggest, sir, that you let me take her home with me tonight."

"But she may come out of it. She did, this morning."

"Well, I don't know about this morning," the old woman said, and for the first time he detected a note of reproach in her voice. "My guess would be that she didn't rightly come out of it. Anyway, she should not be here in this house with you. Not in the state she's in."

"Does she get these attacks often?"

"Now and then. Do you have your car outside?"

"It's up at the caravan."

"Maybe you'd go and bring it down here. I'll meet you at the front door with Kathleen. Will that be all right?"

"Yes. But will she come with you?"

"She will. She'll be glad to get out of this house. Do you have a torch?"

"It's all right," he said. "I can find my way."

"We'll meet you downstairs, then." The old woman turned and went back into the bedroom. He went down the back stairs into the hallway, past the closed door of the parlor, and out into the moonlit yard. Somewhere in the field above, Kathleen's dog began to yelp, and from far off a second dog answered, then a third, like inept buglers attempting to sound his retreat. He reached the road. A soft rain met his face, thickening as he hurried stiffly, painfully, uphill toward the car. Once inside the car with the engine roaring to life, he had an impulse to drive on down past the house and, traveling through the night, reach Shannon at dawn, hurrying out to the great planes which waited like remote-control toys to lift off for America. But then remembered her crouching in a corner of the bedroom, her long naked legs hunkered up, and felt again that curious mixture of tenderness and lust which had held him since the first day he followed her up the steps into her caravan.

He released the hand brake and drove down in a rush toward the old house. As his headlights blazed on the road ahead, he saw the light in the upper window go out. He swerved into the yard. Ahead of him a flashlight pointed to the cobblestones by the door, and as he parked, it circled back and he heard the heavy front door slam. They were waiting for him, the shabby old woman holding an umbrella over the girl, bedraggled and dazed in her long white dress, clutching to her breast as if it were a baby the white plastic shopping bag containing the gin bottles. He opened both front and back doors and the women got in together into the back of the car. "There now, darling, there now," the old woman kept murmuring as she helped Kathleen to seat herself. And then, in the car, having managed to separate Kathleen from the gin, she leaned forward and placed the plastic bag on the front seat beside Mangan. "It will be all right here, Kathy darling. If you're wanting it, I will get it for you."

Down they went, the rain heavy, blinding the windshield despite his busy wipers, down the narrow track of the boreen until they reached the slightly broader road below. And now, ahead, far out, he could see the deceitful winking eye of the Fastnet lighthouse and, soon on his left, the slate roof of Duntally. He drove into the farmyard, his headlights blazing on the house's faded pink walls, the abandoned outhouses, their thatched roofs sagging. "Slow now, sir," said the old woman, leaning forward and pointing. "Just down here, down in the back."

As he entered the narrow lane between untended hedges, it came to him that both the house he had left and Duntally were empty, their owners, or former owners, living in smaller, more primitive dwellings behind them. One of those dwellings was now in range of his lights, the old cottage half hidden under the lee of the hill. A cat ran across the yard and he heard a clucking of wakened chickens in the henhouse. The cottage was dark. The old woman got out, murmuring, "We're home, Kathy, we're safe home." She put up the umbrella against the rain and led the girl across the yard toward the cottage door. "Will you be all right yourself, sir?" she called back. "Hurry on in, now. The rain's not too bad."

He followed them into the cottage. In the big open hearth the remains of a turf fire cast reddish shadows on the low-roofed interior. He was surprised when the old woman switched on the light and he saw an electric light bulb under the shade which hung over the kitchen table. Lit, the room was a sort of kitchen–sitting room with low wooden and rush-matting chairs grouped around the big open hearth, on which, in the red remains of burning turf, the old woman placed an ancient iron kettle full of water, which she drew from a sink in the adjacent scullery.

There was a plaited rush crucifix hanging over the fireplace, and in a corner the inevitable tiny perpetual lamp burned under a picture of the Sacred Heart. Now, as Dinny's mother settled Kathleen in an armchair under this votive lamp, Dinny entered, scraping his muddy boots on the stone step before he crossed the threshold. His old felt hat was soaked and tiny rivulets of water dripped from the hem of his heavy overcoat. "So you brought Mammy back," he said. "I'm much obliged."

"No, it was your mother who brought us here," Mangan said.

"Mammy?" Dinny advanced to peer at his mother, who was efficiently setting out teacups and saucers from a large mahogany cabinet ranged against the wall.

"I'm all right, son," the old woman said as, drawing him aside, she whispered with him in a corner. Are they talking about finding Kathleen in bed with me? Mangan wondered.

"What are you whispering about?" Kathleen cried suddenly. "Are you talking about me?"

"Nothing, love, nothing," the old woman said. "I was just asking Dinny to get milk."

"You want milk," Dinny said. "Right, then." He turned to Mangan and for the first time in their meetings smiled at him in welcome. "Sit down, Mr. Mangan," he said. "Take that chair, it's better than the other one. You'll have a cup of tea with us? Of course you will."

Mangan sat in the rush-bottomed chair which had been set aside for him. The room had a pleasant smell of burning turf and also a smell of freshly baked bread. As he looked about, he noticed that this cottage, small and crowded with furniture which was a little too large for the room, was nevertheless clean and swept and scrubbed, in direct contrast to the caravan inhabited by the other branch of the Mangan family. There was a glassed-in bookcase with leather-bound books on its shelves, the Waverley novels of Sir Walter Scott, two books on accountancy, the stories of Maupassant, sets of Dickens and Shakespeare, and a Latin grammar. And now, as she set out the tea things, Dinny's mother put sugar in a sugar bowl and laid teaspoons and a small pitcher of milk carefully by her good teacups on the kitchen table. He noticed for the first time that, despite her disheveled appearance and her strange habit of wearing a man's jacket and boots, she was very clean in her person—again, in direct contrast to Kathleen, who sat staring at the fire in her soiled white dress, her fingernails dirty, smelling of gin and body sweat. And as he watched the old woman meticulously rinse out the teapot with hot water, preparing their tea, he sensed the nature of the difference between Dinny and Con Mangan and their respective dwelling places. Dinny had come down in the world and was desperately trying to maintain his dignity. Con, on the other hand, though he had also come down in his fortunes from that gray two-story house to his present squalid caravan lodging, embraced his new status and gloried in it.

"Give us a gin," Kathleen said suddenly, turning to Mangan.

Dinny, coming in from the scullery with a shining tin pail of fresh milk, stopped and said, "It is partly the drink that has you in this bad way. We're going to have a cup of tea, now."

But she ignored him. She pointed to Mangan. "Get the gin out of the car."

"Now, wait, love," Dinny's mother said, coming forward and putting her arm around Kathleen, leaning forward to whisper, "What if I give you one of my pills? That'll do you better than gin."

"Give it to me, then."

The old woman put the teapot on the hob, went into the bedroom, and returned, holding out a red-and-white capsule.

"Are they the same lads you gave me last time?" Kathleen asked.

"The same. You'll be sound asleep before you know it."

Kathleen took the pill and popped it into her mouth. "Did you know that I'm going to America?" she said.

Both Dinny and his mother looked at Mangan, as if for confirmation. "Not with him," Kathleen said. "I'm going to stay with my aunt Bridget in Pittsburgh. He's just lending me the fare."

"And what do you hear about Con?" Dinny asked her. "How is he getting on in this trouble of his?"

"The clerk in the courthouse in Cork says he'll likely get five years."

Dinny and his mother exchanged a look. "But that's terrible," Dinny said. "Don't they have a solicitor?"

"I don't know, nor do I care," Kathleen said. She stared glassily at Mangan. "God, isn't it like a ghost story, him sitting there by the fire with his face bashed up."

"Milk and sugar, sir?" the old woman asked.

"And it was in Bantry that it happened," Kathleen said, and laughed in a shaky manner. "Bashed in Bantry, the both of them."

The old woman offered milk and sugar to Dinny.

"Did he lose a tooth?" Mangan asked.

They all three looked at him.

"This tooth, was your father missing this tooth?" Mangan said, pointing to the gap in his own mouth.

"That's the thing of it," Dinny said. "He lost it just the same way you did, one time he got in trouble in Bantry when he had drink taken, making remarks to some fellows in a pub that were coming home from a football match."

"Ah, will you give over with that ould yarn," Kathleen said, suddenly beginning to rock and stare into the fire.

"It was yourself that started it."

"Never mind, Dinny," the old woman whispered. "Kathleen is right. Are you sleepy, love? Those pills work very quick."

Kathleen nodded, staring into the fire, her eyes glazed

as though she were drunk. The old woman put down her teacup and went over to her. "I'd say you'd be better lying down, love."

Obediently, Kathleen nodded and stood up. "I feel it," she said thickly.

"You can sleep in with me," the old woman said. "And, Dinny, if Mr. Mangan doesn't want to go back up to Gorteen tonight, you could put him in the house beyond. The bed he had is still made up with his sheets on it. Would you like to stay down here, sir?"

"Oh, that's all right," Mangan said, but was grateful for the offer. The thought of going back alone to that dark house disquieted him and so he was pleased when Dinny joined in, nodding agreement. "Good idea, so."

"But it would be a trouble for you."

"No trouble," Dinny said.

Kathleen, her eyes glazed, her gait unsteady, allowed the old woman to take her by the arm and turn her in the direction of the bedroom. As they moved slowly past the kitchen table, she seemed to remember something and turned to Mangan. "You're staying the night?" she said, her voice suddenly anxious.

"Yes, he is," the old woman reassured her.

"I'll see you in the morning, then?"

"Yes, of course," Mangan said. "Just have a good sleep, now. You'll be all right in the morning."

She looked at him as though she waited for an answer to some question. Then a placating half smile came over her features. Her glazed eyes tried to focus on him. "It's promised now, for my fare, isn't it?"

"It is."

"The fillim star's husband." She smiled vacantly. "Did I give you a fright back there?"

"No, no."

"Just old nightmares. Aunt Eileen has them, too, don't you, Aunt Eileen?"

"I do, love, I do. Come on, now, it's past your bedtime. Good night, Mr. Mangan."

"Good night," Mangan said, but Kathleen, breaking away from the old woman, caught at his hand. "Only nightmares," she said in an anxious tone. "I'll be all right in America. I'm sure of that."

"Of course you will." He watched the old woman lead her into the bedroom. It was not just nightmares. He could not bear the thought of losing her, but he would lose her. She was mad. It would never be the same again.

When they had gone, he became aware of the loud ticking of a clock. He looked up and saw Dinny Mangan sitting across the hearth, sipping his tea and staring at him over the rim of his teacup. Caught, Dinny blushed until his florid complexion went dark red, and lowered his eyes to contemplate his large workman's boots. "She'll be all right," he said, as if to himself.

"Kathleen?"

"Yes, she'll be all right. It's that brother of hers, feeding her drink all the time. Drink is bad for her in her condition."

"Has she had mental troubles before?"

Dinny looked up as though he had discovered something interesting on the low-roofed ceiling of the cottage, his neck straining, his complexion deepening again. "Did you say mental troubles?" he asked in a high, uncertain voice. "No, I wouldn't say so. Though she does get these bad dreams from time to time that do leave her very low in herself. My mammy has had to nurse her a few times. But she's a young girl. With God's help, all that will pass."

He paused. Again, his face darkened, approaching the color of wine. Finally, almost stifling with embarrassment, he said, "That is, if she is let alone."

For a moment they sat in a dreadful silence. Then Mangan said, "You mean, by me."

"Yourself and others, yes."

"I know you probably won't believe this," Mangan said,

"but I don't normally go around picking up eighteen-year-old girls."

Dinny took up the poker and rattled it furiously among the red turf embers. "What you do or don't do back in America is none of my concern. And I will tell you straight out what Kathleen does is not my concern, either. It should be, but it is not. What does concern me is my own mother, who is very fond of Kathleen. And what she saw tonight was enough to break her heart. My mammy is a saint, Mr. Mangan. She has no bitterness in her for any soul living or dead. But she has suffered more than I can tell you, and seeing you like she did tonight with Kathleen is more than she can be expected to bear. She has had mental troubles of her own, as you know, and I don't want to see her back in Our Lady's Hospital, God forbid. So I am asking you now, man to man, here in my own house. What is it you want in Drishane? And is there any way I can persuade you to leave us in peace?"

Mangan looked at the fire. He did not speak. *Go away and stop molesting a young mad girl. That is what is being asked of me.*

"The other day I saw you looking around in the cemetery," Dinny said. "I was with the other lads in the truck that passed by. What is it you want, exactly?"

Mangan touched his pocket. The daguerreotype was there. He drew it out and handed it to Dinny. "This was found together with some books by and about James Clarence Mangan in my grandfather's papers in Montreal. Look at that picture. It's me, isn't it?"

Dinny picked up the photograph by the edges of its frame as though it were explosive. He adjusted his round spectacles and peered nearsightedly at it.

"Hmm," he said noncommittally.

"I understand it's also very like your father."

"It is not my father."

"I know that. It's a daguerreotype, they were the earliest sort of photographs. Look on the back of the frame. See the date."

"Eighteen forty-seven," Dinny said. "That would be Mangan's time, all right."

"Do you think it's his photograph?"

The distorting lenses of Dinny's spectacles effectively visored his glance. "Let me ask you a question," he said. "Is that what you came to Ireland to find out?"

"Yes."

"And you expect me to believe that's why you came all this way?"

"It's a strange time in my life," Mangan said. "My wife died unexpectedly. I didn't know what to do with myself."

"I am sorry."

"No, it's just that I—well, dammit, I was excited when I found this photograph. There's something about seeing your double who lived a hundred and thirty years ago in another country. And who might have been the famous poet. I've always had a special interest in poetry. I've published poems of my own."

"That is interesting. It fits."

"How does it fit?"

"It's not up to me to tell you," Dinny said. "I am trying to make a bargain with you. If I put you in touch with a certain person who can give you the answer to these questions of yours, will you give me your solemn promise to go home to America once you have them?"

"But why?"

"For my mother's peace of mind. And for Kathy's as well. You will know why once you get your answers."

When I get my answers. He sat in the silence which followed, hearing the loud, ticking clock. The excitement he had first felt when he picked up the daguerreotype in his father's cottage in Quebec surged back like the rush of a drug, and again he sensed himself to be on the verge of revelation of a mystery, the mystery of his double who had lived a hundred and thirty years ago. Someone was alive who knew these answers. Someone here in Ireland knew.

"Where do I find this person?"

"First I need your promise. Your promise that you will leave Ireland."

A promise that he would leave Ireland. Not a promise that he would leave Kathleen. He could make that promise and be waiting for her in America when she came to join him on the money he provided. For now, when it was time to promise, he could not think of losing her. Maybe he would not lose her. Maybe she could be cured. "A promise?"

"Your solemn word of honor. And I will hold you to it."

"That I leave Ireland when I know these answers, as you call them."

"And that you never come back," Dinny said. "And let me tell you now that I am the only one who can tell you the name of this person and where to find them. I promise you you cannot find out from anyone else. I am the only person in the world who knows."

"All right," Mangan said. He felt at the same time ashamed of his duplicity and yet like a man who watches a roulette ball fall into a pocket on the wheel, winning him a great sum.

"It is a promise, then?" Dinny asked.

"Yes, I said *yes*."

"One more condition. You will not tell anyone, not my mother or Kathleen or anyone, the name of this person and that you have met him."

So the person is a man. "All right, I promise."

At that, Dinny rose up and went to the scullery door, where several garments hung on coat hooks. He took down his wet overcoat and buttoned himself into it. "Right," he said. "I will take you up to the house now. I have to write a long letter tonight explaining who you are and telling this man why he must help you. In the morning I'll come for you and give you breakfast and put you on your road. But tomorrow, before you start, you had better go back up the mountain to the other house and take your luggage. For I doubt you'll be wanting to come back this way once you get to where I'm sending you."

"Why is that?"

"You'll see," Dinny said cryptically. "This place is a fair journey from here, and once you are there you would be on the road to Shannon airport. You could go straight home when you have finished your business."

"But I promised to give Kathleen her fare to America. I think I'd like to come back and speak to her and make sure she's over this attack."

There was a long pause. Dinny studied the fire. "Well, that is your prerogative," he said. "But I'd say she might be better in the morning. You could speak to her before you go."

"I still would like to come back and see her. To say goodbye."

"I think you will not be wanting to come back. But never mind. Suit yourself. Are you ready, now?"

"Ready." He rose, going out into the rainy night after his host, hurrying up the little lane behind Dinny's flashlight to the rocky back yard and the shut kitchen door of the Duntally house. Once inside, Dinny switched on the light and laid the door key on the scullery table. "You know your way. It is the big bedroom upstairs. The bed is made up. I will give you a shout at seven, for I have to be at my work by eight. You could save me time if you will give me a lift down to the crossroads for Drishane."

"Okay. At seven."

"Good night to you, Jim."

"Good night, Dinny."

The door shut. Here, back in the first house he had slept

in, he looked at the familiar furniture, the stove on which he had cooked his first breakfast. He turned off the light and went upstairs to the big bedroom, undressing under the scroll dedicating this house to the Sacred Heart, the red lamp in the shape of a heart burning small and bright over the bed. Tomorrow he would begin to know what it was that had happened in this house and in the house on the mountain. Tomorrow he would meet a man who would tell him if his double was Mangan the poet. Tomorrow.

He took the daguerreotype from his pocket before hanging his jacket on a chair and looked once again at that face which was his, at those eyes which now seemed to mirror his own with their look of steely, controlled hysteria, at the gap in the teeth on the right side of the mouth. He no longer felt elation at sight of this, his mysterious self. Instead, he again felt fear, the same fear he had felt that night in the shadowed parlor of the house at Gorteen. Was this photograph a document which would one day pronounce judgment on his own life? Tomorrow he might know. As he pulled the bedclothes over his naked body he thought of Kathleen lying drugged and asleep in that little cottage and of the old woman lying beside her in the bed, wakeful, her mind filled with what mad memories, with what tale of blood and wounds and shrieks in the night. And as he switched off the lamp and lay in the shadowed red glow from the votive lamp above the bed he tried to imagine what sort of man he would meet tomorrow, this man who could link him with his forebears, with Dinny's dead father, also a poet, and the father's uncle, a poet who had died a terrible death. And who might name the man in the daguerreotype, the man with his face who had walked this earth one hundred and thirty years ago, perhaps the poet Mangan himself. And so, excited, fearful, anticipating morning, he fell into a fitful and exhausted sleep.

_____ *Hens, their orange feathers glistening,* their vermilion head wattles jerking around like fools' caps, their diamond eyes nervously darting to and fro, stalked through the soft morning light in and out of the threshold of the cottage, rushing forward to peck at what might be crumbs of food. The old woman raised her arm, banishing them. "Chu-chuck!" she cried. "Chu-chuck!" The hens fled outdoors and a heavy shadow replaced them on the bright floor as Dinny came in from the yard with three brown eggs in his hand.

"Would you like yours soft-boiled?" the old woman asked Mangan.

He nodded. "How's Kathleen this morning?"

"Sleeping the sleep of the dead," the old woman said. "Those pills are the lads, all right. She'll not stir before noon."

"I was hoping to speak to her before I go."

"Ah, I wouldn't wake her," the old woman said. "That's the best medicine for what ails her. Sleep and plenty of it."

Dinny had gone back to the wall desk in the corner and now folded several handwritten sheets and put them in a long brown envelope which he carefully licked and pressed shut. He took out a fountain pen and wrote something on the envelope. The old woman, meantime, sat down at the table, took a large loaf of soda bread, and cut three slices off it with a sharp knife.

"How far away is this place?" Mangan asked Dinny. "Would I have to spend the night?"

"What place is that?" the old woman asked, and Dinny gave Mangan a disapproving look. "It's a place he's going to get his car seen to," he said. "It's about thirty miles out of Bantry. You *could* be back tonight. Depends on the garage. As I told you last night, I'd say you'd be better to take your luggage with you."

"But as I told you, I still want to come back and see Kathleen."

"Suit yourself," Dinny said after a pause.

The old woman put butter on the table and poured three cups of strong tea. The eggs jiggled in the iron pot as the water boiled.

"Well, if Kathleen is still asleep when I go," Mangan told the old woman, "will you please tell her that I'll be back tonight, or tomorrow at the latest?" He turned to Dinny. "There's another reason why I have to come back. The police may want me for a statement."

"What statement?"

"Kathleen told them Con was with us the day that stuff was stolen. We're supposed to make a deposition or something."

"And was he?" the old woman asked, ladling out the eggs.

Mangan shook his head.

"They should not be putting you in that position," Dinny said severely. He put the brown envelope in his jacket pocket. "Jim is giving me a lift down to the cross," he told his mother.

"I was wondering why you were so late getting started. What's that you're writing? You were up very late last night. Was it writing, you were?"

"I have a letter I want Jim to post," Dinny said. "It is about my insurance. I wrote it last night."

The old woman served the boiled eggs, and all three sat into the table. The hens again began their forays into the kitchen. "Chu-chuck!" the old woman called. The hens fled.

"This garage," Dinny said to Mangan. "Do you have a map in the car?"

"Yes."

"Well, I will show you on the map the road you must take to get there. We will talk about it on the way down. We will have to hurry. I'm going to be late for my work."

They ate swiftly, in silence. "Do you want more tea, either of you?" the old woman asked.

Dinny looked at Mangan. "No thanks," Mangan said.

"Are we ready, then?"

"Yes."

"Safe journey, Mr. Mangan," the old woman said as Dinny headed for the door. But at the last moment Mangan hung back. "Is she in here?" he asked, and went to the bedroom door. "Don't worry, I won't wake her."

The old woman came after him, looking her disapproval. Mangan turned the doorknob and in the dark, small bedroom in an old brass double bed saw Kathleen, her lovely young face still as marble, her long red hair tumbled over the pillows. She slept like a child, all peace and innocence. It could not be over, could it? "Tell her I'll be back," he said to the old woman. "Don't forget to tell her. It's important for her that she know I'll be back."

"That's Dinny calling," the old woman said. "You'd better be going."

"You'll tell her?"

She nodded and gently shut the bedroom door on the figure of the sleeping girl. In the yard Dinny waited, wearing his old serge suit jacket, worn trousers, and workman's boots. As Mangan drove past the door, the old woman came out and waved to them. Up the winding lane, through the back yard of Duntally and out onto the road. Then Dinny adjusted his spectacles and consulted the road map, marking it with a stub of pencil. "You will go through Bantry and take the road south. Halfway down the peninsula you will see a sign that says Butler and Castle Head. You will turn there and go on straight down to the end of the peninsula. The road is not good. When you reach the town of Butler, you turn right—I am marking it here on the map. You will go on two miles and you will see another sign for Castle Head. You will come to the end of the road facing the sea. Leave your car there. You will see a fence to your right. You will climb over that fence and go up a track toward a farmhouse that you will see on the headland overlooking the sea. There is a bad-looking dog there, but he won't bite you if you are not afraid of him. The farmhouse is not a farm any more, but was all done up by a rich German man that comes for his holidays in the summertime. He has a caretaker there, a German lad. If you see him you will ask for Johnny—remember that, *Johnny*—and he will direct you. If not, you continue on past the farm—it is all the German's land—and climb the mountain behind. On the top you will see a second head standing out to sea and on it some old ruins of a castle. Go down there and you will find the man you are looking for. If he is not there, wait in the castle keep until he comes. He will not be long, for he will see you making tracks toward his place."

"And who is he?"

"I will let himself tell you that. Here is my letter to him. And here is your map all marked up. Can you remember the rest of it?"

Mangan reached his hand across the gearbox and was handed the brown envelope. He read what was written on it:

IMPORTANT   TO M.J.M.   FROM DINNY

"So, I ask for Johnny," he said. "M.J.M. Are those his initials?"

"They are. He goes under the name of Johnny in those parts, but Johnny is not his right name. You will have all that explained by himself. I have told him that you write poems." Dinny permitted himself a small smile. "That will stand to you with him."

"Is he a poet, then?"

But Dinny did not answer. They drove on down the mountain, seeing Drishane below them like a miniature in the morning light, its church steeple, the purple wall of the Sceptre Hotel, the huddle of gray slate roofs. As they came down to the crossroads connecting their road with the main road from Drishane to Skull, Mangan noticed a now-familiar truck at the side of the ditch. Sitting on its tailboard were three workmen in their serge suits, their scythes and shovels stacked against the cab of the truck. The driver, a large man with a pipe turned upside down in his mouth, sat at the wheel. He and the three workmen looked back in curiosity as Mangan pulled in behind the truck. Dinny turned and put out his hand, horned with calluses, the nails ditch-digger thick but clean and trimmed. "I'll say goodbye, Jim," he said. "You'll be back this way before you go, then?"

"Maybe tonight."

"You'll be welcome to spend the night at Duntally. But, remember now, not a word of what you see or hear to my mammy or Kathleen."

"Okay."

He watched as Dinny walked up to the truck ahead, the workmen on the tailgate saluting him. "How's the boys?"

"Morning, Dinny."

"Sorry I'm late, lads."

Mangan pulled out, passing them. All waved to him as he went by.

Two hours later he reached the end of the peninsula. In the last hour, as Dinny had predicted, the road was not good. The town of Butler was on a steep downhill street which ended at a quay facing a sweep of bay and the Atlantic Ocean. Although it was after 10 a.m., the shops had not yet opened, and there were no vehicles in the street. He drove down almost to the quay before he saw the road to the right, a road so narrow that if two cars met on it one would have to back up until it could pull in at a gap in the hedge. He went two miles up this road and did not see a single house or meet any vehicle. The hedges disappeared, leaving a view of the land on the other side, bare, barren, all rock and bog and moss. Ahead, lonely as a crucifix marking a highway death, was a signpost at the junction of the road. It pointed to Castle Head. He followed it, the car jolting on the rough surface, his speed down to ten miles an hour as he moved out onto a high headland with cliffs falling on either side toward strands far below. As he went on, the road dipped down until it came to an end at an abandoned stone jetty, its sides slimed with sea moss, the waters beneath swirling in a heavy bed of kelp. He left the car there and, looking to his right as Dinny had instructed, saw a barbed-wire fence on top of a low stone wall. A set of stepping-stones was cut into the wall, and above them was a new, printed sign: NO TRESPASSING. He ignored the sign and used the stepping-stones, carefully parting the barbed wire.

On the other side of the wall was a footpath, a narrow,

little-used track in the long rush grasses, leading back up the headland to a white, two-story farmhouse overlooking the sea. It seemed to be about half a mile away, and as he settled down to the uphill walk, the intermittent rain through which he had driven all morning was hurried off by strong, gusty winds coming in from the sea. High cumulus clouds sailed over the blue dome of sky. Below, to his left, the sea fielded a platoon of angry whitecaps to race on top of its blue-marine depths. The bare green head-land, the white house, the azure sky, all of it reminded him of a painting harshly etched, lonely as a Hopper landscape. He felt alive with expectation, as though, like someone in an old tale, he at last approached the sacred place to meet the oracle who knew all secrets. He put his hand in his pocket and touched the daguerreotype as though it were a charm. And at that moment, running down toward him, silent, at great speed, he saw a huge black dog.

At once his fear of dogs came upon him. In the car com-ing here he had uneasily remembered Dinny's warning and wondered if before approaching this place he should find a stick to protect himself. But he had done nothing and now, more menacing in its silence than any howling wolf, the dog came at him, straight as a train track. He stopped. The black dog ran right up to him, then skidded back on its hind legs and stared at him, its lips curled back over long fangs, emitting now a low continuous snarl. *He won't bite you if you are not afraid of him.* Remembering Dinny's advice, but with no confidence in it, Mangan made a step forward, then another, until the dog was inches from his knees. Suddenly the animal slunk aside, letting him pass, and, as he quickened his step, followed him, snarling, snap-ping its teeth at his heels. Resisting the urge to run, he went up toward the house at a measured pace.

He saw chickens behind a wire run, pigs in a yard, and smoke coming from the chimney. The dog suddenly ran wide from behind him as though circling to attack, rushing through the long wild grass, passing him, going toward the house ahead, and as it did, it began to bark, its angry sound caught and half lost in the gusty Atlantic winds. Mangan saw that his route led through the farmyard, past the front door of the house, and that he must open the yard gate to go on. The gate was not locked. The dog had reached the front door and stood there, barking, as though to alert the occupants that an intruder was on the way. As Mangan opened the gate and closed it behind him, a young man came out from the front door. He wore jeans and an Irish sweater, and with his fair hair and tanned face he seemed like a tourist. "Morning," he said.

"I'm looking for Johnny. I have a letter for him."

"A letter for Johnny?" the young man said. He spoke with a slight European accent. "For Johnny," he said again, and smiled. "Do you want to leave it here? I can give it to him when I see him."

"No, I have to deliver it," Mangan said. "It's a letter of introduction."

"To Johnny?" The young man smiled again. "Very well, then. Go on up this path, up the hill there—right up to the top. Once you are up there, you can see the other side of the headland and a second headland. On it, right at the end, looking out to the ocean, there is the ruin of a castle. Go down to the castle and see if you can find him. If not, you will have to come back here and leave your letter. Good luck. You're an American, aren't you?"

"Yes."

"I worked once in Santa Rosa, California. Semiconductors," the young man said. "Good luck with Johnny."

And waved and went back inside the house. The dog, which had stood guard beside him, turned and, ignoring Mangan completely, went down the yard and crawled under the half door of what seemed to be a stable. Mangan went on, climbing uphill, the track now little more than a rabbit run, sinking up to his knees in heavy gorse and long grasses, then scrambling over rock and climbing up rock face to the higher ground. He was out of breath by the time he reached the top of the headland and looked back down at the farm and its outbuildings.

Apart from his car, which he could see far away as a tiny red speck on the road where it ended at the sea, the farm and its outbuildings were the only sign of man in that entire vista of land and ocean. And then, turning, he looked over to the other side of the headland on which he stood, and saw a twin headland jutting out into the ocean. Both headlands rose hundreds of feet above the sea, and as he looked over at the far one, he could see, at its lip, a stone ruin like a Norman keep, overlooking sheer cliffs and, far below, small sandy beach coves. All this, Dinny had said, was the German's land. And as the German's neat white compound was the only human habitation on this headland, so, on the far headland, the ruined stone castle was the only man-made thing. All about was land used only as lookout point and stronghold by long-ago Norman conquerors and since abandoned to seabirds, rabbits, and, here and there, high on the rocky ground a few black-faced sheep.

He began the long trek down the far side of the headland into a grassy gully, wet with rivulets, and up the slope of the second headland, moving out toward the castle at its tip. White and yellow heather, yellow gorse, and tiny beautiful wild flowers met his grasping hands as he climbed the steep incline and again reached high ground. From here he could see that the headland sloped down as it went out to sea. As he started down toward the ruined castle, he could see ahead of him a splendor of white-capped waves and high, scudding clouds. As he continued his descent, he began to notice narrow tracks, sheep paths with sheep droppings everywhere. He even disturbed a few sheep, large and fat in their thick woolly coats, with black faces and curious amber eyes. They looked at him with no fear and, indeed, refused to interrupt their grazing to let him pass. The headland was vast. It took him almost an hour to reach the land surrounding the castle or keep. Here, long ago, men had laid out a green, grassy meadow enclosed by an ancient broken stone wall. The castle was Norman, as he had surmised, a square keep three stories high, with, around it, the ruins of attendant buildings. An interior wall enclosed what had once been a courtyard or jousting field. Ivy and weeds grew in and out of all these ancient habitations, and when he looked up he saw that the ruin was roofless. Sheep grazed in the interior court, ewes and lambs settling comfortably in the shelter of these ancient walls. Perhaps the shepherd, Johnny, also lived in the ruins. Mangan climbed through a gap in the courtyard wall and went toward the looming rectangular shape of the keep. He went in at an archway, a door opening which gave into a lower chamber. Inside were sheep droppings, thistles, nettles, and a stagnant smell of damp. He could discern in the shadows the shape of the lower chamber, the ten-foot-high fireplace, the narrow slitted Norman windows. The stone ceiling was still intact. The upper stories must be reached by a stairway, but he walked around the lower chamber and did not find one. He went out again and peered up at the top of the keep. The upper stories appeared to have collapsed and there was no way to climb to the top of the tower. "Go down to the castle and see if you can find him," the German had said. But there was no sign of anyone.

He thought of calling out "Johnny?" but felt foolish. There was no one here. He looked at his watch and saw that it was already past noon. He went out of the courtyard and walked down to the tip of the headland, which was less than a hundred yards from the castle. Here the headland split into two fingers, a narrow fjord hundreds of feet deep. Far below, wild seas crashed on rocks and curled on a small sandy strand. Seagulls coasted upon the air currents above the chasm, delicate as paper airplanes, ignoring him as though he were a ghost.

He turned back toward the keep. In another country this ruined castle on its splendid promontory of land would be a tourist sight, a national treasure ringed by guards and regulations and opening and closing hours. Here in Ireland it was a sheep pen. He looked back up the headland, remembering that the young man had said that Johnny might not come and that he could leave his letter at the farm. Why hadn't Dinny mentioned this possibility? He sat in a tumbled-in gap in the courtyard wall, feeling hungry, tricked, on a fool's errand, alone here at land's end in an empty ruin. He rose and walked the length of the grassy courtyard. The sheep, dozing in the shelter of the walls, looked at him with amber, contemptuous eyes. And then at the end of the courtyard he saw a wooden box, like a mailbox, jammed on top of the loose heavy stones in the wall. He went toward it and saw that it had been daubed with red paint. JOHNNY. MESSAGES. The box was open. Inside, in a plastic folder, was a child's notebook and a pencil. Through the plastic he saw, written on a sheet of child's ruled paper in a handsome italic hand:

> Leave note stating your business.
> It will be picked up soon.
>
> Johnny

Was this where he should put his letter? And if so, how long must he wait? Angry at Dinny for not explaining this rigmarole, he took out the thick brown letter and placed it in the box, then turned and looked up the mountain slopes. There was no one in sight. He walked back across the courtyard and, as he did, two huge black crows came in to land before him, flapping their awkward wings. They settled on the grassy court, waddled a few steps forward, then shut their wings and looked at him, heads sideways, reminding him of judges in an old French cartoon. "Kaah!" one of them cried, and the other, as though alarmed, opened its wings again and followed by its mate, flew up to the top of the tower. He turned to see what had disturbed them and it was then that he noticed the dog. It was coming down the mountainside, and when he turned toward it, it at once sat down, watching him, then rose stealthily and came on, a black-and-white border collie stalking him as though he were a runaway sheep. It ran quickly now and, reaching the courtyard wall, jumped up on it, watching him. Then, as though satisfied that he would not move, it jumped down, ran down the yard, and vaulted up on the wall beside the message box, poking its nose expertly inside to seize the letter in its jaws. It turned, looked at him, then jumped down the other side of the wall and ran up the mountain slope, lifting its head high and making clever small detours when it encountered high grasses. He watched it go up until it became a speck on the mountainside and disappeared in a hidden gully.

Above him, a gull cried in anger and wheeled out toward the ocean. He sat facing inland, watching and waiting. The cold wind whipped his face, and behind him, far below, he heard the repeated rush and break of the waves. He was watching for the dog to reappear, but it did not, and as he sat there on the wall like a target he felt he was being watched. He searched the rising slope behind the ruined castle, but the only movement back there was of the three sheep he had passed on his way down. He waited. Time passed. His watch said ten past one. The blue sky began to cloud over and within minutes was gray, the sun screened behind a milky haze. The wind increased.

Behind him he heard the sheep bleat and, turning, saw

two ewes hunch to their feet, spilling their sleeping lambs out from the shelter of their legs. He looked behind them and saw two sheepdogs leap upon the wall, the small black-and-white collie which had delivered his note and its twin, but with brown-and-black markings. The dogs looked at him, then jumped into the grassy courtyard and sat, as on guard, facing him. He heard a step somewhere behind the wall. It was in the ruined keep. He turned toward the keep, sure that he was being watched, and as he did, a voice called out above him.

"Look up this way. Look up at the tower. I want to see your face." It was a man's voice, pleasant, musical, and at ease. It spoke in the local accent.

Irritated and a little afraid, Mangan turned, jumped down off the wall, and walked to the center of the court-yard. He faced the tower. As he did, he saw a shadow move in the slitted Norman window on the second floor of the keep. How did the man get up there? There was no stair. He peered at the narrow window, a long slit in the stone, designed for a bowman to slip his longbow in and release an arrow. He could see in silhouette a head with a hat on it. The second floor of the keep must have some sort of roof, for it was not open to the sky as was the roofless uppermost story.

"Stand still there, will you?" asked the voice.

He stood, showing his face.

"My God," said the voice. "Stay where you are. I'm coming."

He listened for footsteps in the tower, but heard none. The crashing waves, the high wind, caused his ears to play tricks on him. But the dogs, with their keener hearing, ran across the yard to the ruined entrance to the keep. A man appeared in the doorway, a man of about Mangan's height. He wore an old felt hat, turned down all around, and a fisherman's black slicker, stiff as a tarpaulin, which had the collar turned up, visoring his face. He wore stained old tweed trousers and rubber Wellington boots.

Now as he came closer the man reached up to the collar of his slicker and opened it, letting it fall back to reveal his windburned face, which was partly hidden by a few weeks' growth of beard. But even with the beard, even in the shadow cast by the low-brimmed hat, Mangan saw it clear. *It was his face.*

He stood and stared, filled with the giddy feeling he had first experienced when he looked at the daguerreotype in his father's cottage in Quebec. But this giddiness contained a sensation of fear, not elation. For the image in front of him moved and was alive and came toward him, smiling his own smile. This image of himself as an old man put out a hand. He took that hand, feeling the hardness of a workman's palm. *But it was his hand,* the fingers and nails and palm the exact size and formation of his own.

"So you are Jim Mangan," the stranger said.

"Yes."

"My name is Michael Mangan," the stranger said, and stared at Mangan, seeming surprised by his surprise. "Dinny told you nothing, then?"

"Nothing."

"He's close, all right, that lad. It's a good thing, I suppose."

"I thought you were dead," Mangan said. "In fact, I was told you were dead."

"I am dead," the stranger said. "Dead to the world."

As he spoke, he laughed, and Mangan saw that there was a gap in his mouth in the same place where he had lost his own tooth. "I have been dead now, for the past six years." He shook his head, as though marveling at what he saw.

"You're the first," he said. "The first to know I'm alive. And isn't that poetic justice? My spitting image. Come on." He put his arm around Mangan's shoulder. "Let's go up."

The two sheep dogs, obedient to their master's every move, rose and followed them into the keep. In the dank lower chamber amid the nettles, thistles, and sheep droppings the stranger, loosing his fraternal grip on Mangan, went to a weed-filled opening in the wall and, firmly grasping a bunch of nettles, pulled them aside. "Through here," he said. "Mind the nettles. They discourage any wee boys who might come this way."

The opening, as Mangan climbed through it, revealed itself as the doorway to a stairway which wound round up stone steps. The dogs followed them up the stairs until they came into the second-floor chamber by a narrow door opening similar to the one on the ground floor.

Here, the first thing Mangan noticed was that there was no proper roof, but a large green tarpaulin, very worn and stained, was stretched tight over the place where the original roof had collapsed. This tarpaulin produced a sail-like flapping sound which, heard against the crash of waves below the tower, gave the impression that they were not on land but at sea. The room itself was a medieval shell, with its great fireplace still intact. The stranger cooked his meals in it, as evidenced by the burning turf fire, with two iron pots and an old kettle suspended over it by an iron bar and chains. There was little furniture in the room: a large, homemade table piled with books and sheets of paper. There was also a chair made from wooden crates, and on the floor a boxlike bed, like a low coffin, in which there rested incongruously a bright-orange nylon sleeping bag. The walls carried no picture or ornament but were lined with orange crates converted to bookcases, containing mostly paperback books. "My home and my castle," the stranger said. "I wish to God I'd known you were coming, for I'd have borrowed, begged, or stole to get you a drink to mark this occasion. Our meeting is a cause for celebration. I will tell you why later on."

"I have drink in my car," Mangan said, remembering. "Pity I left it there."

"No pity," the stranger said. "It will not take me long to fetch it up for us."

"But I left the car down by the jetty at the end of the road. That's about an hour's walk."

"For you, my lad, not for me. I have shortcuts. Are you hungry? There is bread there and cold lamb. And eggs in the bowl. Is your car locked?"

"No."

"Where is the drink?"

"It's in a plastic bag on the front seat. Shall I come with you?"

"No, no, you'd only slow me up." The stranger beckoned his dogs. "I'll not be long. Eat something, now. I'll be back directly."

And suddenly, like a magician, his double disappeared through the dark opening, the dogs at his heels, leaving Mangan alone in the chamber. He turned and walked to the slitted window and looked down at the grassy courtyard, seeing the man emerge from the keep, buckling his slicker about his neck, the dogs vaulting the wall, using the stepping-stone. Is that the way I move? Is that my walk? He saw his older self go swiftly up the steep path and watched his walk until he disappeared from view from the narrow window.

Above, drops of rain pelted the taut surface of the tarpaulin, making a loud tattoo in the dark chamber. Mangan, moving about, found a stack of children's exercise books on the table and beside them a dictionary and some old books in Gaelic. He moved to the makeshift bookcases and read name after name with rising pleasure: Marvell, Donne, Hopkins, Yeats, Eliot; there were also several poetry anthologies, including the *Faber Book of Modern Verse*. There were paperbacks of Dostoevsky, Gogol, Tolstoy, Turgenev. There were histories of Ireland, books on the

Irish language, Joyce's *Portrait*, Camus's *The Plague*. There were novels by Lawrence and Hardy and the collected essays of Swift, all of them titles he would be pleased to see on his own shelves. To find them in this remote place, the makeshift library of his mysterious double, filled him with sudden, enormous pride. This was the true relative he had come three thousand miles to find. He went to the table and picked up an exercise book off the neat stack piled there. He opened it and saw the handsome script. He realized that the script was not italic as he had thought, but closer to uncial, and that the book contained verses in Latin.

He put the book down and picked up another, which was not in Latin but in the Irish language. This was obviously a workbook, with verses scratched out and written anew. Above, the rain thundered on the tarpaulin roof. He shut the books and rearranged them neatly, so that his host would not know they had been disturbed. Perhaps his double wrote in the Irish language and therefore was not widely known? To have opened his book without his permission now seemed a base act. Better to let him introduce his poems himself.

Mangan went back and sat by the dying fire, putting fresh pieces of turf on the embers. Here at land's end, a man amid his books in a ruined Norman tower, living like a hermit writing his verse. He felt elated as though he had stumbled on a treasure. There was a loaf of brown bread, and suddenly ravenous, he cut two slices, stuffing the bread into his mouth, crumbs spilling onto the dirty stone floor. He sat, watching the turf catch and burn, its brown hairy fibers singeing like an animal's hide. The rain ceased as swiftly as it had begun and the slatted window filled with sunlight. He went to look out. In the kaleidoscope of Irish weather, the sky was now free of clouds. Gulls flew in lazy parabolas over the white cliffs. Who was Michael Mangan, and why was he hiding here under a false name?

And then, startling, as though he had asked the question

aloud, a voice called up, "Are you still there? I'm back." And he heard footsteps in the winding stone stair. His older double entered the room, holding the plastic bag with its gin bottles, the dogs slinking at his heels and going almost furtively to lie near the fire. "That wasn't long, was it?" his double said as he hung his black slicker on a stick stuck between the stones of the wall, and pulled off, at last, his low-brimmed old felt hat, revealing that his graying hair had receded far up his forehead, giving him a noble brow. So my hair will probably go like that, Mangan thought, as his host went to the corner of the chamber and produced two enameled tin mugs, into which he poured stiff measures of gin. "Did you ever think you would become a priest?" he asked surprisingly, as he handed one of the cups over.

"No, I was never religious."

"Nor was I. Our strain in the Mangan family are all without the consolations of religion. Hell fire isn't what we're afraid of. I'll tell you what we're afraid of. We're afraid that we'll be forgotten. Am I right?"

He smiled at Mangan. "What I meant about being a priest was that you've come here for my confession." He smelled the gin in his cup, then drank. "God, that's good. It's been a long time between drinks. Sit down, will you?"

He sat himself on some sacks by the fire, drawing his old Wellington boots up under his chin, rocking to and fro, savoring the gin. Then he took out Dinny's envelope and pulled from it several sheets, handwritten on both sides of the paper. "I have a full report on you here," he said. "He must have been a long while writing it. So Kathleen has been your downfall."

"What do you mean?"

"That's what Dinny says. And although he's my son, I wouldn't say he has it in him to invent a yarn like that." He stared at Mangan. "God, you're the image of me when I was your age. As I was of my uncle Dan and Uncle Dan was of James Clarence himself. How much do you know about all this?"

"Not anything, really."

"This letter says you found a photo in Canada. Do you have that photo on you by any chance?"

"Of course," Mangan said, and took out the daguerreotype, passing it over to his double, who took it almost with reverence and went with it to the window, holding it to the light. He said nothing, for what seemed a long time, and when he turned back to Mangan, he seemed unsteady, as though he had experienced the exact feeling Mangan had when first he looked at the photograph.

"My God," he said, "where did you get it, did you say?"

"It was among my grandfather's papers. He emigrated to Canada in 1892. His people came from Drishane and he had a book by a Father Drinan claiming that Mangan had a son who settled in Drishane. My grandfather believed he was a descendant of that son. Look at the back of the picture. There are initials and a date."

Mangan watched his double turn over the daguerreotype and saw, with amazement, that he made a grimace of surprise which was just like one he would have made himself. "My God," his double said again. "J.M. That would be a couple of years before he died. You know, don't you, that he was not christened Clarence? He began to use it as a sort of pen name, at first. He signed his lighter pieces as Clarence. You know that?"

"Yes, I know."

"Of course you do." His double drank the remainder of the gin in his cup. "Of course, you've read the biographies." He picked up the daguerreotype again. "The trouble is, Drinan's is the only one which claims that Mangan married. And it's largely discredited. Or was, until now." He held up the photograph. "This changes things, I'd say."

"Why's that?"

"Because I also found a photograph, the only known photograph of James Clarence Mangan. And it is a photograph of this man, taken around the same period. And if your grandfather had this photograph in his possession, a daguerreotype, an original, the only one of its kind, then it must have been passed on to him through the Mangan connection. The link is forged. Wait till I show you."

He went to his shelves and eased out a large volume in a handsome binding. "When I saw this in Trinity College Library in Dublin I promptly pinched it."

Mangan opened to the title page and read:

TRINITY COLLEGE DUBLIN
A History
By J. K. McManus and Prof. R. McHugh

"As you'll see, it's a book about the university itself. You know Mangan worked in the library there for a time. As a cataloguer. And he haunted the place all his life. Now, look at this."

He opened the book to a plate. There was a soft-focus photograph of library stacks, with, before them, four men facing the camera. Two of the men sat on high library stools, one stood, and the fourth man was perched halfway up a ladder in the background. The inscription read:

PLATE XI
This early calotype photograph shows the library's "Fagel" room in 1846. Of interest are these habitués of the room including T. Stubbs-Heath, the antiquarian and historian (with beard). Extreme left is the historian J. R. Mitchel. The man on the ladder is believed to be the poet James Clarence Mangan. The fourth man is not identified.

"Here," said his double. "This will help you see better." He took from its green leather carrying case an old-fashioned magnifying glass, which Mangan then focused on the photograph. The man on the ladder wore a long shapeless cloak and peered nervously at the camera. At once Mangan had the sensation of seeing himself in fancy dress. The magnification of the glass showed the photograph's soft-focus surface as grainy and strange. Nevertheless, the face, purged of its normal lines, stared back at him large and familiar. It was his face. It was also the face of the man in the daguerreotype. It was also the face of his host. Mangan took up the daguerreotype again and scanned both photographs with the magnifying glass. The hair was the same length in both. The hairline was the same. "Eighteen forty-six," Mangan said. "This picture in the library was taken one year before the daguerreotype picture."

"Three years before he died," his double said.

Their eyes met and held. In the silence, broken by the distant crash of waves, a crow flying over the tower began its loud harsh call. "Kah! Kah! Kaaah! Kah!" They looked into each other's face as a man will look at his image in a mirror, searching for its secret.

"It's like two pieces of a puzzle that fit together," his double said. "The photo in the book and that photo of yours. Until now, I still had a little bit of doubt. What if I just *happened* to look like Mangan? But now you've brought the transatlantic evidence, so to speak. And not only that, there's your own face. My face. And you write poetry, I am told?"

"I did, once."

"I know what you mean," his double said. "I stopped myself, for a while. I lost heart. But now I am back at the writing. It is the only thing left for me. And I know now it was always the only thing."

The crow, wheeling high over the tower, cried, "Kah! Kah! Kaaaah!" The sound seemed derisive. "And what about James Clarence Mangan's poetry?" Mangan asked. "Do you like his work?"

His double smiled. "I know. Times change and tastes

change with them. But he has a certain power. And he's remembered."

"Remembered," Mangan said. "But for what? Certain poets are remembered for the lives they led, not for their poems."

"His poems are remembered." His double poured two more drinks. "Of course the life was colorful. He was a doper and a drunkard and died a pauper, alone in a charity ward. He went to an early grave. But that's all part of the mold, isn't it? Remember Joyce said that Mangan's was an exemplary life for a certain type of artist."

"The *poète maudit*," Mangan said. "And he was the prototype of that sort of poet. Before Baudelaire or Rimbaud. Before the term itself was invented. Yet he wasn't a great poet like Rimbaud or Baudelaire."

"But he *is* remembered," his double said. "His statue stands to this day in Saint Stephen's Green in Dublin. There are books written about him, as you know. And his poems are still read. Children learn them in National School. In the long run, what else matters? Whether he was a saint or a wastrel is secondary, I say. What counts is what a poet writes. And today, thanks to you and to that photograph, I feel certain at last that I am his blood and his genes carried into this generation. As you are yourself." He smiled and raised his tin cup in salute, then asked, "By the way, where did you get that bash in the face?"

"Two characters attacked me in a pub in Bantry."

"Did they knock that tooth out?"

"Yes."

"Astonishing," said his double. "I lost my own upper tooth in a brawl in Bantry. I was drunk. Is drink a trouble for you?"

Mangan shook his head.

"But you are a *maudit?* You must be."

"Why?"

"Because we all are. You and me and my uncle Dan, all the way back to James Clarence himself. It's in our blood. Are women your trouble?"

"I don't know. Maybe. Tell me about your uncle Dan. He was a poet, wasn't he?"

"He was, God help him." His double rose, went to the bookshelves, and took down a book. It was in a Victorian binding on cloth boards, with a fading gilt-scrolled cover. The title page read:

TALES OF THE WEST

by
Daniel James Mangan

P. Healy, Booksellers & Printers
Eyre Square
Galway 1891

Mangan turned the page and saw a listing of some fifty poems. "They will not be to your liking," his double said. "Although in their day they had a fair following. I remember at home in Duntally I found a lot of write-ups from the newspapers at the time this book appeared. Good notices, most of them. He was a contemporary of Wilde and Synge. He claimed to have met Wilde and to have been friendly with Synge. Maybe true, maybe not. He was a bit of an embroiderer when he told a story."

Mangan looked at a verse, then read it aloud:

"Thou sayest that fate is frosty nothing,
But love the flame of souls that are.
Two spirits approaching and at their touching,
Behold an everlasting star."

His double smiled. "Yes, I know. As I said before, times change and tastes change with them. But I'm afraid that if Uncle Dan is remembered at all, it's not for his poems. Did Dinny tell you the story?"

"No."

"Well, Uncle Dan's main claim to fame, I suppose, is that, because of his death, a man was hanged in Cork in 1916."

"Nineteen-sixteen. That was the time of the Troubles, wasn't it? Was it the British who hanged him?"

"It was the British, all right, but the man was hanged for ordinary murder. It was drink that did it. Uncle Dan was a heavy drinker with a bad tongue on him. It seems he was drinking in a pub down in the markets in Cork and he insulted some character, who asked him to step outside. Well, when he went out into the markets, this other man followed with a friend, and when Uncle Dan saw there were two of them and that they were both coming at him, he ran over to a butcher's stall and picked up a meat cleaver, thinking to frighten them off. But they were mad drunk, those fellows. They grabbed the meat cleaver off Uncle Dan, and then one of them swung at him with it and cut his throat from ear to ear. Butchered him like a pig."

In the silence that followed, the crow cried: "Kah! Kah! Kaaah!" as in terror at this news.

"That was my uncle Daniel," his double said. "Your kinsman. Would you like to see his picture?" He went to the shelves, pulling out an old photograph album, shuffling some photos which were lying loose in its back pages. "Here it is." He held out a photograph framed in passepartout, showing a young man wearing an academic robe, holding a sheepskin in his right hand, smiling at the camera. The young man had very short hair and a small mustache, but the mustache did not disguise him. Again, Mangan felt that giddy sensation. It could have been himself at twenty.

"He took his B.A. at Cork University. Apparently, he was a fair Greek scholar. He taught school for a while, until drink got him the sack. And wrote poems. All his life he wrote poems."

"You knew him" Mangan asked.

"No, he was before my time. I remember my father talking about him. He showed up once at our house at Christmastime. He was drunk for six days. I think he frightened my father. He frightens me. As he should frighten you. We are the same, all of us. We look the same, we write poetry, and we come to a bad end."

"A bad end?"

"Yes. Let's start with James Clarence Mangan, died of drink and drugs and malnutrition, a solitary, miserable life. Then Daniel James Mangan, a drunken wastrel, butchered in the markets like a pig. And myself crippled and destroyed and hiding from charges that could put me in prison for years. And yourself, I don't know about. But you have some trouble, I'll bet. Otherwise, why did you come?"

But Mangan did not heed the question. Crippled? And what crime had *this* man committed that could bring him years in prison? As he stared uneasily at his older face, the face smiled as though it understood his unspoken questions. "You know nothing at all about me, do you?" the face said. "And you've come here to find out, God help you. Well, you're the only man in the world that I'd want to tell my story to. For I think, now that I've laid eyes on you, that you are probably my only true kin."

As he spoke, he stood up and kicked a fallen clod of turf back from the lip of the hearth. The dogs, which had lain as if asleep, rose at once and stood watching. "But first let me go and see to a few lambs. I'll leave you here. I work for a German and he has a lot of sheep out on these heads. When I come back I'll tell you my story." He looked at the dogs and at once they went out. "As I said before, eat something if you're hungry." He reached into a tin box and took out a slice of cooked meat, which he tore at and chewed like an animal. "I'll be back," he said, and went through the opening, his rubber boots making a flopping sound on the winding stair, leaving Mangan still sitting with the passe-partout-framed graduation photograph in his hand.

He looked into the eyes of the young man in the photograph, that young man with his high, old-fashioned shirt collar, striped tie, the rented academic gown on his shoulders, his hair slicked down, his smile obedient to the photographer's command, posing with his academic sheepskin, ribboned and sealed. Myself on degree day in Notman's studio in Montreal. In the foul-smelling latrine of the pub in Bantry he again saw the tall lout loom over him, felt his lapels caught, felt the head butt into his face, the blood spurt from his nose. Long, long ago his other self drunk, seeing there were two of them set against him, seized a meat cleaver from a butcher's stall. And had his throat cut with it. And a man hanged on the gallows because of it. He put the photograph down and picked up the history of Trinity College, Dublin, opening it to the plate showing the man "believed to be the poet James Clarence Mangan," a ghostly figure in a long theatrical cloak. And at that moment he remembered the passage which had impressed him so much that he had read it aloud to his father and Margrethe in that snow bound cottage in Quebec:

In that gloomy apartment of the institution called the "Fagel" library which is in the innermost recess of the stately building, an acquaintance pointed out to me a man perched on the top of a ladder, with the whispered information that the figure was James Clarence Mangan. It was an unearthly and ghostly figure in a brown garment; the same garment, to all appearances, which lasted to the day of his death. The blanched hair was totally unkempt; the corpse-like features still as marble; a large book was in his hands, and all his soul was in that book. I had never heard of Clarence Mangan before, and knew not for what he was celebrated, whether as a magician, a poet, or a murderer; yet took a volume and spread it on a table, not to read, but with a pretence of reading to gaze upon this spectral creature upon the ladder.

There in the photograph, peering nervously at the camera, was the spectral creature on the ladder, the person "believed to be the poet James Clarence Mangan." And, again, in the daguerreotype, identified at last, the same face. And there, in a studio portrait, wearing an academic robe, that face reincarnate in a later time. That same face which had just left this room to tend some lambs. And which sat in this room now, come from America to find himself.

He put aside the photographs and stood, going out of the chamber down the winding medieval staircase to the ill-smelling lower room, to come out and turn down toward the cliffs in front of the tower. Wild long grasses were flattened by the wind like an angry cur's pelt. He walked over them, right to the rim of cliff. He looked vertiginously down sheer gray stone worn by deep crevices and sea caves. Gulls floated on air currents, dipping down along the edge of these impenetrable walls, diving far down to the rocks below, rocks wet with the dash of white spume. It seemed to him that he had come to the end of his journey, that something more than chance had made him find the daguerreotype the very night that Beatrice died, that something more than chance had given him access to her money, permitting him to undertake this search and find this poet who bore his face, his true spiritual father. He sat on the edge of the cliffs for what seemed a long time, staring at the white water far below. He heard a flapping of wings and, turning, saw the two crows take off behind him, flying over him like black spies. "Kah! Kah! Kaaah!"

But the crows had not come to spy. They were in flight from the sheep dogs, which now vaulted up on the court-yard wall. And in a moment his double appeared, his felt hat pulled low over his eyes, peering out toward the cliffs, looking for him.

It was the end of his journey. There could be no turning back. He rose and went toward the tower.

_____ *"Gin, will it be?"*
his double asked. "We're well fixed for it. We have a full
bottle and one half full. But we don't want to get polluted,
do we?"

"No," Mangan said as the other poured two drinks into
the tin cups, then settled himself on his heap of sacking
beside the fire. "There's a gale out there on its way to us.
I heard it on the wireless this morning. I moved some sheep
off the end of the German's head just now. I think we can
take it easy for a while and have a real yarn together." He
pulled off his hat, revealing again his gray-white hair.
"Yes," Michael Mangan said. "The minute I laid eyes on
you this morning—I was up there above you, watching
you come down the head—I couldn't see you close, mind
you, but I said to myself, That's not a tourist nor a journalist nor a policeman. That's somebody who was sent to me.
I'll not say I was waiting for you to come someday. That
wouldn't be true. But it is true that I've thought many's
the time that there might be one of us in America. I knew

that my father's brother went out there. And, years ago, there was an American came to Drishane saying he was related to the Mangans and asking about Mangans. But he never got in touch."

"That must have been my father," Mangan said excitedly. "He came with my mother, but she got sick and they had to go back to Cork."

"Did he look like you, your father?"

"No, not at all."

"And do you have brothers? Or does he have brothers?"

"No, I'm the last of the line, if that's what you mean. In America, at least."

"Here, too," his double said.

"Wait a minute. What about Dinny and Con?"

"Poor Dinny will never marry now. And that wee scut, Con, is a bumboy. Did you know that?"

"No."

"He is. Proven fact. He's been had up twice for interfering with young lads. Oh, we're a nice family, at this end of it. I'd say the line will carry on through you, if it carries on at all. It skips about, this special face. Uncle Dan never married, but his face showed up in his brother's family. In me. And my son doesn't have it, but it has showed up on his cousin in America. Which is you."

"And wanting to be a poet," Mangan said. "That goes with the face?"

"It does. And the bad end. Don't forget the bad end." His double reached for the gin bottle. "We'll have one more," he said, "before I start my story. But I don't want to get drunk, mind. Don't let me drink any more."

"All right. Give me the bottles, then."

But his eyes in the other's face met his own eyes in distrust. "You don't have to do that. I'll be careful."

Mangan nodded, took the bottles, set them down between his feet, and waited for the story to begin. But the other seemed unwilling to start his tale. Instead, he gave a low whistle, and at once the smaller of the sheep dogs rose and, tail wagging, came over to lie at his feet, curving its neck in ecstasy as he reached out and tickled it behind the ears. "You've met my wife, haven't you? Eileen?"

Mangan nodded.

"She thinks I'm dead and it's better so. If I were your age again, I'd not make the same mistakes. She is eight years older than I am, and God forgive me, I only married her because I had this notion of becoming a poet and she wanted to help me. You may not believe that, but it's the truth. You see, Eileen was an only child. The mother died when she was very young and she was brought up by her father. He was a neighbor of ours. Our house was Gorteen, up where Con has his caravan now. Their house was Duntally, down the road. Our fathers were good friends, for they were both farmers whose wives had died, leaving them with young children to bring up. So Eileen was like a cousin to us. And then when she was twenty-four, her father died, leaving her all he had. She got a hired man with a family to run the farm, and moved them into the main house at Duntally, while she lived alone in the wee cottage in the back. And six months after that, it was my father's turn to die. My older brother, Fergus, got the farm. I was in my last year at school at the time. I had started writing poems already and I even had one printed in a little mag that was put out in Galway. Oh, I'd great hopes for myself. I wanted to go on to university, but I got no scholarship and Fergus had no money to spare to help me. Gorteen was never much of a living, mixed farming and a few sheep. It began to look as if I'd have to find work as a laborer in England, and I was nearly shipping out to London when Eileen, of all people, said she would stake me to four years of university in Cork so that I could get my B.A. Well, I don't have to tell you her offer was music to my ears. Of course I promised her I'd pay it all back when I got my degree. And the next thing I knew was that Eileen began coming into Cork City every week to see me. She had her own car, and she was lively and liked going to dances, and anyway we had a good time together. And then in my second year at University College, Cork, I had two of my poems printed in a Dublin magazine. I have the magazine to this day. Eileen was bursting out proud of me and telling everyone that I'd be another James Clarence Mangan. That or better, thought I. Anyway, the upshot of it all was that in my final year I asked Eileen to marry me and we got married the month after I got my B.A. I landed a teaching job in a little place near Youghal, so we moved there, and the second year, Eileen had a baby. That was Dinny."

He paused to stir the fire with a piece of wood, then turned to Mangan. "And she went mad. Right after the baby was born, she went mad. It happens to some women. The doctors will tell you that. She went right around the bend and I had to put her into the asylum in Youghal. She was there three months. I had to get a woman to look after the baby, and even when Eileen came home, she was not herself. She'd changed. Nothing would do her now but that we go home and live on her farm in Duntally. She said she'd help me farm it. She said she had extra money and that she'd buy cattle like her father before her and she promised that I'd have plenty of time for my poetry. Well, to tell you the truth, I'd found out that I wasn't that keen on schoolmastering. So I said yes and we went home to Duntally and Eileen had the land rented and we took it back and moved into the main house. She had a great head for money and when she bought and sold cattle she was just as cute as her father had been at that game."

He paused. "Just about that time, Radio Eireann asked me to read some of my poetry on a program about young poets in the west of Ireland. I thought I was made. I thought it was just a matter of time until I'd be invited to read my poetry all over the place. Anyway, eight years after we moved back to Duntally, we had a second child. We weren't expecting it, of course. A baby girl. And the exact same thing happened. Eileen went mad again. This time I tried to look after her at home, but it was no good. I had to commit her to Our Lady's in Cork. And when they let her out, she was ten times worse than she'd been the first time. That little cottage behind Duntally—the one she and Dinny live in now—she half moved into that little house. At night, as soon as the children were asleep, she'd leave the big house and go down and spend the night there. What I'm saying is, she never slept with me again. It's understandable, I suppose. She was afraid to. And she changed in other ways as well. She was no company any more. She stopped reading, and she never talked about books or my work the way she used to. I'd show her something and she'd say it was good. That was all. It was good. She had no more interest in it than if it was a football. And she that used to be so interested.

"Anyway, I'm telling you this because I'm trying to explain that there's a reason for things that happen. There's a reason people do what they do. I was all those years alone in that house living like a monk. And I was a young man, remember. I was writing poetry and I went to Cork now and then and met a few people I'd known in my university days. But, ah, I never knew the people that counted. Poetry is a bit of a racket, as you know. You need to know the right people, you need to be able to get yourself talked about. I was stuck away on a farm with two kids and a depressive wife. Maeve, my daughter, was growing into a big tall girl. By the time she was twelve years old she was as tall as a full-grown woman. And pretty, too. And the upshot is that I began bothering her. Her mother never knew, but Dinny did, although nothing was ever said. Anyway, I used to get into bed with her now and then. And it went on, right up till she was twenty-one years old."

As he said this, he lifted his head, glaring at Mangan as though waiting for a blow. But when he saw the shocked, sickened look on Mangan's face, he looked away, his gaze dull, his eyes searching the fire as though trying to remember the end of a story told him by some other person. "I said twenty-one because she was twenty-one the year my brother Fergus died up at Gorteen. He had a heart attack while he was backing up his tractor and he fell off it and it ran over him. It was a terrible mess of a death. And the strange thing is that, just like our father before him, he died a widower, leaving two children. And they were Conor and Kathleen. And as you know, that wee Conor is next thing to a midget and no good for anything, so I had to go up there and try to keep the place in order until it could be sold. My son, Dinny, couldn't help, for two years before, he had started working in the Allied Irish Bank in Bantry."

"Dinny was a bank clerk?"

"He was, and a good one, it seems. Anyway, to tell you my story, I went to Gorteen to give a hand, and there was Kathleen." He paused and again looked Mangan full in the eye. "She was twelve, the same age Maeve was when I started with her. And Kathleen was beautiful. I hear she still is. I know, I know, there's no excuse for me, but one day, when I caught her changing her clothes up in her bedroom there in Gorteen, I made a grab at her. She was upset, but I was nice to her and promised I'd buy her sweets and things. I warned her to tell nobody, not Con nor anybody. Anyway, I calmed her down, so I thought it would be all right if I didn't touch her any more. Nor did I. I stayed away from her. I was only with her once. That's the truth, now. I only got in with her once.

"Well, anyway, it was about two weeks after that that this other thing happened. One night I was at home asleep when Maeve came into my room. She said she'd had

300

a bad dream and that she was afraid. I should have been warned that something was up, for she never came into my room. I always went to her in her own room. But that night I took her into my bed. And she was not the way she normally was. When I kissed her she kissed me back. I should have known, but anyway, I had her nightdress up and I had a cockstand and the next thing I knew she was holding it. She never did that before. She made me stiff as a board. And all of a sudden—she must have hidden it somewhere—she out with a big sharp kitchen knife in her other hand and made a chop and cut right through it like she'd cut off a chicken's head. And then she said to me in a very quiet voice—I'll not forget that voice—'Now you won't be able to spoil Kathleen like you spoiled me.' Christ, I was bleeding like a pig. I grabbed hold of the stump and held it tight trying to stop it. She paid no attention. She got off the bed and left the room. And do you know this? She took with her both the knife and my cock. Christ, I was certain sure I was going to bleed to death. But I never called out or anything, because Dinny was asleep in the next room. I got on my trousers and a jacket and into my boots and went dragging downstairs. It was the middle of the night. Of course, Eileen wasn't in the house. She was asleep in the cottage. We had no car then. Dinny had a little Lambretta motorbike but I didn't have the keys. And of course I was wondering where Maeve was. But when I got out into the yard I saw a bicycle lamp up on the road above, going up to Gorteen. I'll bet she's going up to tell Kathleen, I said to myself, and I was right. For she went straight up to Gorteen and ran into the child's room in the middle of the night, frightening the life out of her, with the big knife in one hand and my cock in the other. And threw the bloody thing on the bed. And I heard tell that what she said was: 'There. Now he cannot do it any more.' And that Kathleen let out a scream to wake the dead.''

In the bedroom the naked girl screamed, cowering under

301

Mangan. He looked at this brute, who looked back at him with his own face. "And you," he said. "What happened to you?"

"I got as far as the crossroads between Drishane and Bantry, squeezing what was left there, holding it tight, the blood dripping between my legs. It worked like a tourniquet, the doctors told me later. Anyway, it half stopped the bleeding, and the next thing I saw up on the road ahead was one of those big international trucks. I held up my hand and he stopped. I told him I'd been kicked by a horse and asked to be taken to Bantry if that was on his road. So he took me and let me off at the hospital there. When they rushed me into the emergency room I was half fainting and not thinking, so I made the mistake of giving my own name and address. And told the doctor who examined me that my prick was an occasion of sin to me and that I'd cut it off. I was hoping to make him believe that I was some sort of religious maniac. That was my second mistake, for by saying that, I made them treat me like a lunatic and so the hospital phoned the police and reported what I'd said. And the next thing, the Guards were over to Duntally, asking what had happened. And in the meantime there was holy murder on the home front. Kathleen's screaming had wakened Con and he brought both of the girls back down to Duntally and then the whole story came out. And all of them, including Eileen, went out to look for me, thinking I'd be bleeding to death in a ditch someplace. And by morning, when they hadn't found me, they were all sitting around in Duntally wondering what to do next, when in walked the police. And young Kathleen was still hysterical, and right off she let the cat out of the bag. That put the police in an awkward position, do you see. By rights they should be charging Maeve with assault with a weapon. Dinny, of course, was anxious to keep it hushed up and not interfere with his job at the bank, so he got on his motorbike and off to Bantry to see me. That was quite a meeting between father and son, I can tell you. Of course, I'd known all along that I could get seven years for having intercourse with a girl under thirteen. It wasn't only Kathleen I was afraid would testify against me, but Maeve as well. Dinny got me to discharge myself from the hospital and packed me off on a train to Dublin. He and I made a deal. He promised to support me for as long as I'd stay in Dublin and lie low.

"So I went there and got treatment in Jervis Street Hospital as an outpatient and lived in a roominghouse down behind the quays. It was my first time in Dublin since I was a boy, and I went to see Mangan's statue and all the rest of it. The thing was, as long as I couldn't be found, the police couldn't bring charges. Back home, of course, the story had got out. That drunken scut Con never could keep his mouth shut about anything. He even told some newspaper fellow, and the next thing, it was in those English dirty newspapers. Maeve had gone off to England and the newspaper tracked her down to a convent in Manchester where she was living and working as a lay sister. It was an enclosed order of nuns and so the paper had a whole yarn about vows of eternal silence and so forth. Of course, it was poor Eileen and Dinny who were the main victims. The scandal did him no good at the bank and he was miserable, thinking everyone was whispering behind his back. So he quit the bank. He tried to farm Duntally and failed, and now the land is rented and he works for the County Council on the roads as a laborer. Anyway, to get back to me, I got sick of living in a roominghouse in Dublin. I wanted to come home to the west of Ireland. So Dinny came up to see me and we worked out a scheme. He told the rest of the family that I'd passed away of a heart attack the same as my brother Fergus had. He even got a priest to write a letter to Eileen about it. She'd been off for a spell in Our Lady's after the incident, did I tell you that? Anyway, I don't know how he managed the letter from the priest expressing condolences and so on, but he did. He was always very thick with the priests, Dinny. And that's it. My confession. I live out here alone on these headlands and I look after the German's sheep and I go down to the German's place once a week for a bath and to see if there's any post for me. And once a week I walk all the way to the town of Butler, where I down a few pints and buy the papers and talk to people. In Butler, they think I'm a spoiled priest, an educated man like me herding sheep, what else would they think? As for women, I am no use to them any more." He smiled ruefully. "That is my penance. She robbed me of my abilities but not my desires. Well, I'll tell you the truth. I have written love poetry but I have never really loved a woman. Poetry is all I care about. I'm still writing under my own name. I send things out now and then, but I've been getting the usual runaround. In Ireland it's not what you do, it's who you know. If there was any poetic justice, which there's not, I'd be as well known as James Clarence himself. But I suppose you could look at it another way—and I do. Genius—the real thing, not the imitation—is hardly ever recognized in its own time. Take Schopenhauer. Take Stendhal. And yet the mark of true genius is that it can't be discouraged. Its time will come. You know, when I read Dinny's letter and saw you here today, the first thought that came into my mind was that here, at last, is my link with the past and with the future, a man with my own face, a poet, a younger me. I keep thinking that perhaps, although you don't know it, you are my moment and you have come. Do you understand me?"

The face was now trying to win him over. He looked at that face, saw it set in his own winning smile; an older me, a vision of myself in hell. He did not speak.

"No, how could you?" the face said. "Well, let me explain it to you. You could be the means of getting me out of here. You could be the way I'd see my fame in my own lifetime."

"Get out of here?" Mangan asked. "But there are no charges against you, are there? All of this happened years ago. Your daughter is living in Manchester. And Kathleen isn't going to make trouble for you, if she finds out you're still alive."

"You're right. But who is to say the police will not file charges against me if I go home tomorrow? And I can't go home, don't you see that. Why should I go back to a place where all they can see in me is a shame and a disgrace, where men and boys would be sniggering at me in pubs and asking to have a look at what I don't have any more. Why would I go back to a wife who never was a wife to me, a mad-woman who's in and out of the asylum? I'm far better off here. I live in a Norman tower, like Yeats himself, thirteenth century this one is, and with a grander view than ever Yeats looked out at from his at Thoor Ballylee. No, you misunderstood me. I don't want to leave here. Someday this place will be like Thoor Ballylee, there'll be tourists tramping over the heads to look at it and a plaque up on the wall saying it was where I lived and died. No, when I said I want to get out of here, I was speaking of my work. I want to get my work out, don't you see? There's always the chance that my work will be passed by in the future as it is being passed by today. I said to you that all the biographies show that men of genius can't be discouraged. But what of all the geniuses who were never discovered, the ones whose biographies will never be written? Maybe they weren't discouraged, either. Maybe they persevered against all odds all their lives, and for what? To die unknown. No, what I'm telling you is, suppose my poems could be published *now* in America. I'd only leave here once in a while to give a reading in London or in New York or somewhere. I'd not give up this place. That's what I mean by getting out. To get out just long enough to be properly discovered. Now, you're a poet yourself, you know the ropes over there. Listen, what I'm asking you plain and simple is: Will you help me get my poems published in America?"

"I find it hard enough to get my own poems published there."

"But mine will be a different story," his double said. "You'll see what I mean when I show you a few. But let's have a drink first. We've had confession. Now let's have a little benediction." He held out his hand for the bottle, and when Mangan took it out from between his legs and handed it over, his double rose, poured gin in both tin cups, served Mangan, then, addressing him, held his own cup aloft, smiling. "A toast to you!

> "My sovereign power, my nobleness,
> My health, my strength to curse and bless,
> My royal privilege of protection,
> I leave to the son of my best affection,
> Ross Faly, Ross of the Rings,
> Worthy descendant of Ireland's Kings!"

He drank and said, "That's from James Clarence. It's one of the poems he Englished from an old Irish one. 'My royal privilege of protection, I leave to the son of my best affection.' That could be yourself, for don't you look as though you are my son? Those photographs today, the one you brought and the one I have? Don't they make it a red-letter day in both our lives? For they're proof positive that you and I and Uncle Dan all descend from the man himself. Proof positive! The same man with the same face, the same gift of poetry passed on, and the pain that has been passed on as well. Lives filled with troubles and injustice and neglect. And yet aren't we proud of that heritage, both of us? I drink to you now, son of my best affection. Ah, it's a great day in my existence to see you come before me now, like a vision. And you will help with my poems, I know you will."

He smiled as he spoke, smiled with a strange mixture of arrogance and entreaty, and Mangan, looking at him, was filled with a premonition that he was looking at what he himself might one day become. It was as though in the recital of this sordid, horrible tale his double, like some scabrous sufferer from a dread disease, signaled that his listener was also infected. Mangan felt his skin prickle as the other crossed the room, seating himself at the rough table, self-importantly sorting the school exercise books. He watched him open and peruse one book, and then, wanting to look away from that sight, he glanced down at the photographs strewn on the hearth before him.

Daniel James Mangan, the author of *Tales from the West*, looked up at him. Himself at twenty, a newly won diploma in his hand. And himself, older, wearing a strange long cape, a spectral figure in the Fagel Library in 1846. And his familiar, the companion of his journey, eyes glittering greenishly in the shimmering light from its delicate copper surface. As always, it was this first and last image which brought that giddy feeling, that self, the sight of which had brought him to this island on the far side of the Atlantic Ocean, to an eighteen-year-old girl cowering naked in the corner of a bedroom, to this ruined tower and the last, most disquieting double of all, this foul, fawning child molester. His hand shook as he reached out and picked up the daguerreotype, the object which had inspired this unlucky search, seized irrationally by the idea that if he got rid of it now it would be a first step toward his escape from this net of unnaturally close resemblances, sordid family history, and unnerving hints of prophecy. "By the way," he said to his double, who was still rummaging through his exercise books, "I was thinking that I'd like to leave you this daguerreotype as a gift. You said, didn't you, that you think of it as the transatlantic evidence that you're really related to Mangan the poet."

"Yes, it's the corroboration of what I've always sensed

to be the truth. I'll tell you what. You leave it with me and I'll send it back to you later on. I'd like to look at it again."

"But I don't want it back," Mangan said. "I'm glad to let you have it."

"Well, thank you, then. There's a poem here I'm looking for, a short poem I think is the best thing I've done so far. You could say it's my masterpiece. It's here someplace. I want you to read it."

Above, rain began to beat again on the tarpaulin roof. Mangan remembered the long journey back to his car as a prisoner recalls the route home from his jail. To run now from these hated self-images strewn about him, and above all, from this mutilated passport of future decay. But surely I have never been this person, this foul old swill. And at that moment, as he looked again at his double, there entered into him a rage more powerful than any he had ever felt against another human being. If, at that moment, someone were to hand him a knife, he felt certain he would plunge it in that back bent over the rough table. Hatred clouded his vision. He felt dizzy, as though the blood had drained from his head.

"Here we are," the hated voice said. "This is the one. This is the one I want you to look at."

A ruled exercise book was opened and thrust at him. Obedient, he stared at the handwritten page, but his hand shook in an angry tremor and the words danced like imps before his eyes, gibberish in his furious brain. And in that moment, like a knife handed to him, he saw his escape and his revenge. He stared at the words, then put down the book.

"Well?" asked the eager, anxious, boastful voice.

"It's not good."

"What did you say?"

"I said it's no good. Show me something else."

The other looked at him with a sudden surprising stare,

then, without comment, turned and went back to the table, picking up exercise books and single sheets, rejecting them, going on with his search, until at last as in inspiration he turned to his bookshelves and took down a small, yellowing magazine printed on cheap paper: *Dublin Poetry Journal.* He opened this and handed it to Mangan.

FOR MAEVE
Michael James Mangan

Four stanzas, the poet as father writing wishes for his child's protection. Maeve. Now the words no longer danced in gibberish. Mangan read the verses slowly, stiff with contempt, remembering Yeats's prayer for his daughter, placing these thin lines alongside a great poet's work. He put the poem down. "Yeats said it much better."

"Maybe. But has it merit? It is work from my younger days."

"I don't think so. I can't see any merit."

In silence the other picked up the poem from where Mangan had laid it, put it back on the shelf, and went again to rummage at his worktable. A poem for Maeve, the daughter he "protected" by incest, whose anger had mutilated him for life. How can he have the nerve to show me that! But now the other came back with a long sheet of foolscap in his hand. "All right, then," the hated voice said. "I want you to read this. I just don't want you saying that it's no good or something like that. I want to know *why* it's no good. Or if it's good, tell me why. This is new work. It was written last winter, here in this tower."

There was no title. The poem was still in working manuscript form, with deletions and small changes in the lines. The foolscap was thumbed, dirty, and creased, as though it had been carried about in a pocket. Mangan began to read, but as he did, a sudden guilty doubt filled him. How could he, in his hatred of the man, fairly judge his work? Wasn't he filled with loathing and fear when he looked at this, his foul older self? Didn't he want above all to wound this specter of his future degradation, this sad, disgusting climax to his search for his forebears?

He read on, and as he did, became peripherally aware of the other's awful nervousness. From the edge of his eye he saw the Wellington boots shuffle on the stone floor and heard the man's harsh, anxious breathing. The poem was a meditation on death and at once he thought of the Symbolists, remembering the books he had seen earlier on these shelves: translations from Mallarmé and Rimbaud, the verses of Wilde. He read it, then read it again, and this time better understood what the poem was trying to say. The stanzas were filled with muffled hints about the sexual "follies" of the poet's life, and the poem ended with a denial that they weighed in the balance when set against the poems, his life's work. It was a testament, and as he read it again, his anger was so great that he no longer was capable of seeing it as a poem. He read the last lines:

> Alexander, Nero, Christ,
> Are words on paper, at the world's end.

And handed back the foolscap in silence.

"I asked for your opinion."

"I don't think I can give it to you."

"Why not?"

"I can't judge it. I'm completely hostile to its content."

"Why would you dislike what it says?" His double held up the foolscap, his hand shaking. "Isn't it true what it says? Isn't that what all history comes down to in the end? Words on paper, words in books, a handful of books, isn't that it? The thing that matters about my life is there on the page. If it's no good, then I don't matter. And if it is good, it's *that* that is my life, not the troubles I've had or the good or bad I did to those around me. You're one of us, you're a poet, you said. You should know better than anyone what I'm talking about. What is this like as a *poem?* That's what I'm asking you. It's the only question I have for you."

And again, confronted by that staring face, Mangan felt that he looked upon himself, a self he wanted to destroy. "It's a poem," he shouted suddenly. "Do you hear me? It's only a poem. Besides, you've been reading the Symbolists and it shows."

"How does it show?"

"Oh, for Christ's sake, what does it matter! It's only a poem and it's an indifferent poem. But even if it were a good poem, that doesn't get you off the hook. You're talking about two different things. All right, in the end, history comes down to words. But, before that, it happened. And words that try to change what happened are lying words. You bastard. You and your poem for Maeve! What you did to Maeve can't be wiped out by a few lines you scribbled before you screwed her life up. And what you did to Kathleen won't earn absolution because you sit here writing verse, imitating Yeats in his tower."

"Ah, so that's it!" the other said, his face lit in a smile of blazing anger. "So it's a little moral man we have here, a little priesteen giving out with his sermons and his penances. Infernal bloody cheek, you pretending to be a fit judge of poetry when you care as much about poetry as my dogs do. Well, it's good news, in a way. Yes, good news! To think that for a minute there, because you have my face and you call yourself a poet, I was trembling before the judgment seat and cast down by your arsehole pronouncements about my work. Indifferent poem, is it? Symbolist imitation, is it? It will be read aloud, year in and year out, when the dust has scattered you and every bloody thing *you* ever wrote."

As the man shouted, his dogs rose up, barking, excited by his voice. In the room with its tarpaulin roof, the barking and the screaming, angry voice resóunded as in an echo chamber, the sounds deafeningly loud. He thrust his face close to Mangan's, his rage so virulent that Mangan found himself clenching his fists as though at any moment he must raise them to defend himself. "Now get out of my house!" his double yelled. "Get out, and take your bloody bottles with you and get your arse back to America and get your prick stuck into some girl, because the only way you'll carry on our line, you sad fucking ape, is if you pass the seed along to someone who's worthy to stand up and call himself one of us, one who'll be, as I am, the true heir of James Clarence Mangan."

Knowing he should hold his tongue but made reckless by rage so that he could not hold himself back, Mangan shouted into that hated face: "Oh, for God's sake, you stupid old fool, who in hell do you think Mangan *was?* Nobody ever heard of him, outside of a few English professors and the people who live here on this godforsaken island. Mangan's not a world poet. He never *was.* He's dead, buried, and forgotten. Second-rate, rhyming jingler, doing translations from languages he didn't understand, and all of it derivative, dull, and pathetic, just like the crap you showed me today."

"Get out! Get out!"

"I will," Mangan said. He turned away from the suddenly raised fist and the barking dogs and went through the opening in the tower wall and down the winding medieval stair, his footsteps hammering on the narrow winding stone steps, the man's voice above him suddenly calling out to the dogs. "Be quiet. Down! Down!" In the silence that followed, Mangan crossed the filthy lower chamber, his feet sinking in the sheep dung and nettles, and came out into the ruined grassy courtyard of the castle. Above, the sky was shifting from rain to sunlight, light blazing suddenly through the clouds. A gull circled above. Involuntarily, he looked up at the slitted Norman window in the second story of the tower. But no one was there. He went across the court-yard and climbed the stepping-stones in the wall, going to-ward the wild, steep, grassy incline of the headland beyond.

But as he stood on top of the wall preparing to descend, a bottle crashed and splintered on the stones behind him. Mangan looked down and saw slivers of glass, smelled the juniper of the gin on the stones of the wall. He turned and looked back up at the tower. On the topmost battlement his double stood, his face in shadow as the sun struck his back, silhouetting him. "*Mangan* is no good, is that what you said?" the hated voice cried.

He saw the other raise his arm as though to throw some-thing, and hastily putting distance between himself and his enemy, jumped off the wall, falling on his knees on the long grass as something struck the top of the wall behind him. "That's yours, too," the voice yelled. "I want nothing of yours."

He looked down and saw the scrolled brass frame and in it the fragile plate of the daguerreotype smashed into splin-ters, its pieces mixed with the broken glass, myriad tiny jewels of copper, the face that was his face shattered be-yond any possible repair. He stood and went toward the steep narrow track which led back to the German's farm. And as he did he heard the voice, high above him, distorted, bellowing in the wind.

> "O, the Erne shall run red,
>   With redundance of blood,
>   The earth shall rock beneath our tread,
>   And flames wrap hill and wood . . .

"Do you hear me, Yank? Can you write lines like those?"

There was a crashing sound on the stones behind him. He turned and saw the second gin bottle fragmented on the grass. He looked up at the top of the tower. There was no one. A crow flew out from the battlement, its wings moving like heavy fans, going out from the tower as though fleeing a danger. He heard the dogs bark. Then all was silence save for the high wind as he climbed up and up, until the tower was small in the scale of landscape far below him.

Stumbling, out of breath, half running at times, he was still on the headlands an hour later, having reached the German's farm and gone on down the private road which led to the sight of his car alone in the empty landscape beneath him. Like a compass needle he had flickered closer and closer to this morning's encounter and now, his true north destroyed, oscillated wildly, his bearings gone. His pace slowed to a walk as a decision began to form in his mind. When he reached the car he drove off, retracing his route of this morning, through the town of Butler, away from the main road that led on to Shannon, going back on the road to Drishane.

And so, driving all through the afternoon, he came along the great arm of bay, up through Bantry and down the lonely winding peninsular road which led to the land's end of the country, down through Durrus to the crossroads at Drishane, the church spire rising ahead of him, and far out on the horizon a solitary sword rising from the gray sea, the lighthouse on Fastnet Rock. And now as he turned up the familiar, twisting road with its high blind hedgerows, out to the rim of road running along the mountainside with its sudden view of Drishane below, its church spire, and the bay curving out to a headland. He drove on, taking the fork which led toward Duntally. And as he turned into the fork, he saw ahead of him a man walking on the solitary ribbon of road, a familiar figure in worn serge suit, heavy boots, head bent, his pace the steady accustomed tread of the countryman. As the car drove up behind him, he turned and raised his hand in greeting. It was Dinny.

"Hello there," Dinny said.

"Do you want a lift?" Mangan asked.

Dinny got in. There was a ring of perspiration around his collar and his forehead was wet. "I asked off early from work," he said, "because I wanted to catch you before you go. Did you see my father?"

"Yes."

"And how was he?"

"All right," Mangan said. Ahead, as they came over a hillock in the road, he saw the high slate roof and faded pink walls of Duntally. Dinny slewed around in his seat, looking at him aslant. "It must have been a shock for both of you."

Mangan said nothing.

"He told you the whole story, did he?"

"Yes."

They had reached Duntally. Mangan drove the car into the empty courtyard, past the shut, empty house where a twenty-one-year-old girl had used a knife concealed in her nightgown and by that act changed these lives. Dinny reached across the gearbox and put his hand on the wheel. "Can we stop here for a second?"

Mangan stopped the car.

"Thanks. I don't want to talk in front of my mother. I wanted to ask you. What are your plans for young Kathleen?"

"What do you mean?"

"She is saying you promised her her ticket to America. Is that true?"

"Yes."

"If you are wanting to buy her a ticket, you would do well to give me the money and let me buy it for her. Money given to her or to her brother has a way of going into a pub and not coming out again. She's only a young girl, but she knows more than is good for her, if you follow me."

Mangan nodded, not wanting to look Dinny in the eye.

"I hope I'll not offend you by saying this, but if you are still thinking of taking her with you, I would advise against it. Now that you know the story. I mean, the sight of you must remind her of my father. I think there would be no happiness in it for either of you."

Mangan started up the car. "Have you finished?"

"Yes. I hope you won't take offense at what I said."

Mangan shook his head. He drove into the little lane which connected Duntally with the cottage behind it. Smoke came from the cottage chimney, and although it was not yet dusk, a light shone in the kitchen window. He drove into the yard and parked in a fluster of hens. At once, hearing the sound of the engine, Kathleen came to the door wearing her long white dress, smiling in pleasure at his return. Her hair was braided up, as he had not seen it before, and she seemed to him more perfectly beautiful than ever.

"Jim!" she called out. "Where were you? Oh, you're a rotten rat to run away like that." She came toward him and put her arms about him, kissing him, embarrassing him, in view of the old woman who stood in the shadows of the doorway and Dinny, who was behind him in the yard; mother and son watching again this living tableau of an old nightmare.

"Where *were* you?" Kathleen asked again as he disengaged himself. "Something about the car, Aunt Eileen said."

"I had to go to a garage in Bantry," he told her. "It was because of the car-rental people. Their depot is in Bantry and the repair took most of the day."

"And you took the gin with you," she whispered in his ear. "And left me here without a drop among these holier-than-thous."

The old woman, coming out into the yard, seemed to hear what was whispered. "Never mind, now, you slept the most of the day," she said to Kathleen. "And it was a good job for you that you did. You're a different girl with a good sleep in you. I told you this gentleman would be back. I told you, and here he is." She looked at Mangan. "Dinny says you're leaving us?"

"I am, yes."

"Will you have a cup of tea? You'll be tired from your journey."

But Kathleen looked up at him and gave a tiny peremptory shake of her head.

"No, I think I'd better be getting on, thanks," he said. "I have to go up to Gorteen to get my bags."

"But you can sleep here tonight," Dinny said. "You have no place to sleep, have you?"

"I can sleep up at Gorteen. I'd prefer that, thanks."

"At Gorteen?" Dinny and his mother exchanged glances.

"Yes, at Gorteen," Kathleen said. "And I'll give him his tea when we get up there." She stared defiantly at Dinny and his mother. "Are you ready, Jim?"

He nodded, turned to the old woman, and shook her head, saying, "Thanks very much for all your kindness." And added, foolishly, "It's been nice meeting you."

The old woman looked up at him. "God bless you," she said, and to his surprise pulled him down toward her, kissing him on the cheek. And he, knowing now why the sight of him had frightened her so, held her awkwardly in the darkening yard.

Dinny, waiting his turn, put out his hand. "Goodbye, Jim. And a happy life to you in America."

He gripped the rough hand of this, his unhappy kinsman. "And a happy life to you," he said.

Now it was time to go. Kathleen had seated herself in the car. They stood waiting, the old woman in her man's tweed jacket and boots, the former bank clerk with his earth-stained hands and workingman's hand-me-downs. They waved to him as he drove out of the yard, stepping forward, coming down to the gate like actors to the footlights for their final bows. And he waved in return. They were his kin, whose strange lives had intersected with his. Yet he knew the curtain had come down. He would never see them again.

The girl beside him sat silent until he switched on the headlights. As the beam struck the dark track ahead, a rabbit leaped in the lights, its white thumb of tail disappearing in a yellow gorse bush.

"Would they have rabbits in America?"

"Of course," he said.

"They have snakes. I'd be afraid of snakes. There's none in Ireland, that's a well-known fact."

"Yes, I know."

"Did Dinny tell you not to give me any money?"

"He said you might spend it all in a pub."

"He's a right old woman, that fellow. Is it true what he said, though, that you're off to America in the morning?"

"Depends."

"Do you remember, yesterday, you asked me to come with you? And you remember I said no."

He did not answer. She leaned forward and put her hand on his knee. "I'm trying to tell you that I've changed my mind. I've been thinking if I have to write to my aunt and wait for her letter back and send her letter to Dublin to the American embassy, it will take ages. But I could go with you now on a tourist visa and say you're my cousin and you're paying my holidays. We could be gone out of here by the end of this week."

He did not speak.

"There's only one thing," she said. "I'd want you to put in my hand before I go with you a return air ticket and a hundred quid. Just for insurance, in case you change your mind about me once you're back in your own place." She leaned forward, peering ahead. "No, don't stop here. We'll go up to the caravan directly. There's drink there and I can make us a ham tea. Would you like that?"

He accelerated, passing the yard of the house, going up the last slow incline to the yellow blob of caravan in the semidarkness of the field at the mountain's ridge. "Well, Jim, what do you say? Two hundred—did I say two?—anyway, two hundred pounds in my hand and my ticket before I leave."

He said nothing.

"Is that too much, then? You told us you were rich."

"No problem."

"Good man. Good man yourself." She laughed and jumped out lightheartedly as he parked the car at the entrance to the field. Her dog ran from under the caravan, fawning in welcome. And again, like a child she ran at the dog, picking it up, cuddling it, holding it like a doll in her arms as she ran to the caravan steps. He followed, thinking of the dog. What would she do with the dog and the caravan if she went off with him? He watched her set the animal down, shooing it away from the steps, then run up the steps and unlock the caravan door. Within minutes she had the lamp lit and the fresh bottle of whiskey out, a kettle on the stove, and was tossing back whiskey from a tumbler and talking excitedly about going to Dublin for her visa. "Have you ever been there? It's big. We could stay in a hotel—there's monster-big hotels there. I was in the Gresham Hotel once, a fellow took me in for a drink. I was scared to death at first. I was shy as shy. Are you hungry, or will we have another jar before I make our tea? We have sliced ham and I could fry you a couple of eggs if you like. Listen—is that a car?" She ran to the caravan window, peered out, then ran back to the table and extinguished the kerosene lamp.

"What's wrong?"

"Wait." She ran to the door, opened it, and he heard her footsteps on the caravan steps as she went down into the field. He listened and thought he did hear a car engine in the far distance, but when he looked out of the caravan window he saw nothing. He then went to the door and, looking down, saw her standing in the field peering toward Gorteen.

"What is it?"

"It's the Guards," she said. "I saw the flasher going as they turned in the yard there. It'll be us they're looking for."

"Why would they want us?"

"It must be a summons. They'll be needing us in Cork for the trial. Do you remember, we told them we spent that day with Con?" She turned and looked up at him in the moonlight. "Shut that door and come on down." Her dog was frisking around her in the field, and now she kicked it savagely in the ribs. "Get out of that," she said in a low, angry voice, and the dog slunk back under the caravan. Mangan also did as he was told, shutting the caravan door and joining her in the field. "Think they'll come up here?" he asked.

"Of course they will. They're just looking there because that was where they found you before. Come on." She took his arm. "We'll go in the back of the mountain. I know a place where they'll not find us."

"But supposing it isn't a summons? And supposing it is? What about your brother?"

"He can look after himself," she said, dragging on his arm, leading him up the slope behind the caravan to the rocky bluff where he had seen her emerge that morning in company with the old postman. "He got himself into this, didn't he? We're going to America, aren't we? Then let's keep clear of the Guards. If they serve a summons on us tonight, we'll not be let out of the country till after the trial is over. Come on, Jim. Hurry!"

But Mangan hung back, looking down the slope. He saw

a bright-purple roof flasher revolving in the yard of the house below. It was the police, all right. He was hiding from the police. "Follow me," she said, and went around the rock and out of sight, looking like a wraith in her long white dress. The police. For the first time in his life he was running away from the police. He went after her. Hidden on the far side of the rock was a small cave strewn with straw and grasses. She was in it. "It's my hidey-hole," she said. "Come and sit in here and keep quiet. They'll be up at the caravan any minute."

He remembered his car. "But my car is out there. They'll know I'm here. They'll know it's my car if they check the license."

"But they'll not find *you*," she said, as though she were explaining to a very small child. "And tomorrow we'll be in Dublin. Come on in. Listen!"

He heard the sound of car tires skidding on the cobblestones of the yard below. The police would come up here and check his car and know he was avoiding them. He was hiding from the police.

"Look," he said to her, "at the very worst it's only a summons to appear in court. We could probably make a deposition. Anyway, I don't like hiding. It's not right."

"Get down," she whispered, pulling on his arm. "You wet bloody Yank, will you listen, do you want me in America with you or don't you? Make up your mind. They're coming."

And they were. He could hear their car growling in low gear as it came up the rise to the mountaintop. The police, who were hunting him while he crouched in a cave staring at her angry face. The car stopped at the top of the road. She put her finger to her lips, her face changing from anger to a smile of conspiratorial glee. And at that moment he rose up and backed out of the cave. She reached out to stop him, but he evaded her and, turning, ran around the rocky bluff just as the two policemen got out of their car and began to walk across the field to the caravan, their flashlight beams dancing ahead of them in the wet grass. The dog ran out from under the caravan, barking. Mangan went to meet them, and as they came up, one shone a flashlight in his face. "Sorry," said the policeman. "But are you Mr. Mangan?"

"Yes, I am." He gestured back toward the rocky bluff. "I was just taking a leak."

"Right," said the policeman who had spoken. "Are you staying in the caravan, here? Can we go in a minute?"

"Of course." He led them up the steps. Inside, he found matches and lit the kerosene lamp. The policemen were both younger than he and had the purplish windburned skin of the Irish countryman. They waited respectfully until he had finished with the lamp, then one of them said: "We've been trying to get in touch with you, sir, one way or another, all day long. We were up here earlier, but you were out."

"Yes, I was in Bantry."

"They have been telephoning you from America," one of the policemen said. He reached in his tunic pocket and took out a notebook.

"Canada," the second policeman corrected him.

"That's right, Canada. There was a lady called this morning to the Sceptre Hotel in Drishane, very urgent. Then called back asking for the police, and so the matter was referred to us in Skull. You see, your caller couldn't trace you, because it seems you never stayed at the Sceptre, did you?"

"No."

"Anyway, she's called again a couple of times since. It's very urgent, she says. I'm sorry to tell you, now, but this is the message." He began to read from his notes. "It's a Mrs. Mangan and she said your father is very ill with a stroke and wanting to see you, most urgent; he's very anxious to speak to you about some matter. And she says if we find you, can you telephone this number at once. It's a hospital." The policeman took a slip of paper from his notebook and passed it over. "There's a phone in Drishane. We could take you down there. But then, you have your own car, don't you?"

"Yes," Mangan said. "Yes, I'll take my car. Thank you very much."

"Not at all, not at all," the policeman said, beginning to move toward the door. "We're sorry now to bring you such bad news," one said.

"The phone is in the Sceptre Hotel," the second policeman said. "The hotel does be open till ten and the switchboard to the exchange is open all night. Will you be coming down directly?"

"I'll just close up here first," Mangan said. "Thanks again."

He watched them recross the field and get into the police car. When they started the engine, they turned off the purple flasher. As they drove off down the steep road, he looked up toward the rocky bluff behind the caravan and saw her emerge, ghost-white in her dress, coming toward him, not watching him, but with her eye on the police car's headlights as it wended its way past Gorteen and around a lower bend in the road. Only then did she turn to him. "It was the summons, wasn't it?" she asked angrily.

"It was a message for me."

"What message?"

"My father is very ill. I have to get to a phone."

"Ah, Jim," she said, and came up the caravan steps to him. "I'm sorry, now. Weren't you right to go out and talk to them. Come on. There's a phone in Drishane. What's the matter with him?"

He told her about the message as she blew out the lamp

323

and locked the caravan door. They hurried to the car, her dog running and barking behind them as the car started off down the steep road. He drove recklessly, only half answering her questions about his father's age and what he did. What could it be that his father so desperately wanted to talk to him about? Would his father be able to speak to him on the phone from his hospital room? Were there night planes from Shannon? How long would it take to drive to the airport? Six or seven hours?

At the entrance to Gorteen he veered right and drove up to the front door. "Just be a minute," he said and, jumping out, found the door key, and knocking over tin cans in the dark corridor, he made his way upstairs to the bedroom. As he lit the lamp and began to throw his things in the bag, she came up onto the landing, looking in. Her face seemed frightened. "Do you mean you might have to go home right away?"

"I don't know," he said. "He's very ill."

He blew out the lamp and followed her downstairs. For a moment as he passed the shut door of the ground floor he paused, thinking of the portraits and photographs, the recorded images of all the Mangans in that room, a mute parliament of the dead, waiting for his father to join them. "Are you ready?" she called back, her body silhouetted against the moonlight in the front doorway.

"Coming." He hurried out, slamming the front door, and drove off with her, the car headlights illuminating the roller-coaster dips in the narrow road ahead. It was just after seven o'clock when they drove into Drishane. Its shops were shuttered and the only light was from the pubs, from which the noise of talk and laughter spilled into the dark street. He went into the Sceptre Hotel. At the front desk sat the same old woman he had met the first day he had gone in there. When he asked if he could use the phone for a long-distance call, she said: "You'll be the American, the one they were ringing up for. Did you get your message?"

The telephone was in the front hallway, in sight of the bar, where a few fishermen and farmers sat over black pints of porter. The local operator passed him to the Skibbereen exchange. "Hello, Skib, is that Skib? Skib here. What number? Hold on please, I'll call you back. Hang up, sir, we'll call you back."

"It's very urgent," he told the operator. Kathleen was standing behind him. He put the phone down. "They'll call me back," he told her.

"Will we go into the bar, then, and wait?" she asked, but he shook his head.

"You go. I don't want to miss the call."

She smiled up at him and took his arm, leaning into him, waiting with him there in the narrow hall, a waif-like figure in her bedraggled long white dress, her red hair tangled by the wind, her face reflecting his anxiety. From the nearby bar came a rising tide of talk, breaking in a muffled roar of laughter. What could his father want to speak to him about? What if his father was already dead? Images of his father smiling, then serious, then shaking his head came back to him in dim memory. But he could not remember his father asleep.

The telephone rang. Kathleen looked at him worriedly as he picked up the receiver. "You're through now," an Irish voice said, and he heard a phone ringing somewhere, ringing in the familiar American tone of home.

"Hello?" It was Margrethe's voice.

"Margrethe, it's Jamie."

"Oh, Jamie. Oh, I'm so glad they found you. We tried everything. Your father has had a stroke and he's in an intensive-care unit. He's very anxious to talk to you about something, but the trouble is there's no phone in there where they're working on him. Listen, I think you should come. He wants to see you very much."

"What does the doctor say?"

"It's serious." She seemed about to cry. "Apparently with a stroke it often takes two or three days before they know. When could you get here, do you think?"

"I could drive to Shannon in about six hours, but it depends on when I can get a flight out to Montreal or one that connects with Montreal. Maybe, by sometime tomorrow. You don't think he could speak to me on the phone?"

"I told you, he's in an intensive-care unit and there's no phone there. Besides, his speech has been affected. It's hard to understand what he says."

"Okay. I'll come at once. Tell him I'm coming. And, Margrethe? Have you any idea what it is he wants me for?"

"No. He just keeps asking for Jamie. And says it's important. He keeps saying, 'I must tell Jamie. Where's Jamie?' "

"Okay. I'll try to phone you from Shannon as soon as I have a flight."

"Good. We'll meet you. I'll get Don or someone."

"Right." He hung up, and as he did, Kathleen's pale face moved in front of him. "You have to go?"

"Yes. Right away."

In the bar, the murmur of talk rose, then fell. He looked into her face, saw that there were tears in her eyes. "It's the end of us, then," she said. He put his arm around her shoulders and walked her past the bar and into the tiny front lounge of the hotel.

The old woman at the desk looked up. "Did you get your call all right, sir?"

"Yes, thanks."

"They'll be ringing back now, with the charges," she said and got up, going down the hall to the telephone, leaving him alone with Kathleen in that little room with its desk and chair, its rack of picture postcards, its wall clock and calendar, and a green plastic-covered sofa bench. He led her to the bench and sat her down, himself beside her.

"Listen," he said. "This is what I'm going to do." He took out a book of checks on which were printed his and Beatrice's names and the Fifty-first Street address. He wrote a check payable to Kathleen Mangan, tore it out of the book, and gave it to her. "That's your fare," he said. "And some money to get you started. And if you want to stay in the States, you can give my name and the address that's on that check and I'll write a letter, or whatever, to act as your guarantor."

She read the check and looked at it blankly. "You're joking me. This is a joke, isn't it? How much is this in pounds? Jesus, if I bring this into a bank they'll throw me out on the street."

"No, they won't," he said. "The check is good. Two thousand dollars is about a thousand pounds. And it's not a loan, it's a gift. You can do what you want with it."

Down the hall the phone rang. The old woman picked it up.

"A gift?" Kathleen gave a shaken little laugh. "You're serious?"

"Yes."

"I feel as if I've won the Sweep. God, you must be rolling in it. Do you always do things like this with girls you just met?"

The old woman came up. "That will be eight pounds and ten pence, sir."

He handed her a ten-pound note. "I'll just get your change now," she said, and went to her desk. He turned to Kathleen, who looked again at the check and then at him.

"*I'd* better give you some change," she said. "If I take all this, I'll be robbing you."

"There you are, sir." The old woman handed him a pound and ninety pence. "Thank you," he said, and turned to Kathleen. "Don't worry about the money. You're not robbing me. I didn't earn it. It was given to me."

"You're sure?"

"Of course, I'm sure." With the old woman as audience, he took Kathleen in his arms and kissed her. "I have to go now."

She hugged him. "I hope all will go well for your father. And thanks, Jim. Thanks. God, aren't you the great fellow altogether."

"I'm not. I wish I were."

PART THREE

_____ *Mangan left Ireland*
on a rain-filled morning, flying up the mouth of the Shannon River toward the Atlantic, the plane rising high above a winter storm. He flew to New York, landing in another rainstorm, and caught a flight to Montreal. And so he arrived home eighteen hours after he had first spoken to Margrethe, not knowing whether his father was alive or dead.

As he stood in the Montreal terminal waiting to clear customs, he saw, rising above other waiting heads in the outside gallery above him, Don Duncan, his father's old friend, dressed in a heavy sheepskin collared coat, waving to him; a comic figure, but also a figure of dread, for in his face Mangan could read neither hope nor sorrow. And so, as he went out to meet Don, who bulled his way through the crowd, coming toward him, he felt a premonition that the news would be bad, that his father had died, that what his father had wanted to ask him or tell him would never be said. His face must have signaled his fear, for Don, joining him, at once embraced him in a bear hug, saying: "Good you got here. He's still hanging in."

For the first time since he had heard the news of his father's stroke, he wept, tears on his face as he went with Don out into the snowbanks and freezing winter winds, a winter landscape unchanged in the weeks since he had left Montreal. "How is he? Is he able to speak?" he asked, and Don said yes, his speech was affected but he could speak.

And then, when they were in the car and driving out of the airport entrance, Don turned to him and said: "Did Margrethe tell you? It's a bad stroke. He could go any time. It's a slow thing, a stroke. It may take two or three days before it goes either way."

Mangan, staring ahead, saw the steaming exhausts of other cars, the high dirty slabs of shoveled snow, the cleared lanes of traffic racing in the smoking Arctic air: a landscape of death. "Is he still in intensive care?"

"No, he's back in his own room, now."

"So, he's a bit better."

"Not necessarily. I asked the doctor about that. There's not a lot they can do for a stroke victim. They just have to wait and see if he'll pull through."

"How's Margrethe?"

"She's a great girl," Don said.

The hospital, the Montreal General, was familiar. Mangan had visited it years back, when his mother was operated on for a benign tumor. His father was on an upper private floor. Don showed him the way, pointing out the room, then shaking hands. "I'll be back after supper," Don said. "It's right there, number 423."

The sign on the door said NO VISITORS. Mangan did not know whether to knock and so decided to push open the door. When he did, he saw Margrethe sitting in the room. His father, lax in the bed, seemed to be asleep. Margrethe, her face drawn, wearing no makeup, dressed in a long woolen sweater and gray flannel skirt, rose, smiled at him, and came outside to join him in the corridor.

"How is he?"

"He's much the same. Oh, I'm so glad you managed to make it. Was it a terrible flight?"

"Is he asleep or what?"

"He dozes most of the time. His breathing is difficult. Anyway, he's going to be very happy that you're here. Look, you go in now and sit by him. He'll wake in a while. Maybe when he sees you, he'll manage to tell you whatever it is that's worrying him. It's hard to understand him. You have to listen carefully."

"Aren't you coming in?"

"No. I'm going down to the cafeteria to get a coffee. I think it would be better if you were alone with him. I'll be back. I'll check with you, okay?"

He nodded and watched her go off down the corridor, her straight back, her lithe walk, this thirty-year-old bride of his father's last years. He wondered if his mother had been told. But, of course, they would have told her. She might even be here. He looked along the corridor again. Margrethe was standing by the elevator, waiting to go down. She waved to him. He waved back and then, fear in his mouth, pushed open the heavy hospital room door and went in.

In the room, the overhead lights had been switched off and a light was lit over his father's head, its beam like an aureole behind the long thinning locks of gray hair which straggled around his ears. His father's eyes were closed and his breathing was stertorous, labored, as though each breath were being torn from unwilling lungs. In the white hospital robe his father's neck seemed particularly bare and vulnerable, an old child in a nightshirt, the skin pale, almost translucent, as though its normal ruddy color had been drained out. To Mangan's surprise there was no heart-monitoring machine, nor were there any intravenous plastic tubes attached to his father's arms. He lay in the bed, solitary, linked

333

to no technology, as though his case had been considered and abandoned.

Mangan tried a small, throat-clearing sound as he sat in the chair vacated by Margrethe, but as he did, he realized that the loud, labored breathing in the struggling chest of the ill man must shut out all other noise. One hand lay lax on the sheet, discolored by bruises or the marks of needles. Mangan reached out and took that hand in his. At once, his father opened his eyes, turned his head, and looked at him, at first seeming to see nothing, his eyes blinded by the labor of gasping for breath. And then, with a sudden cough, his father said: "Jamie—it's you. Jamie."

"Yes, it's me." He rose up and, as he had rarely done in his life, kissed his father on the brow, felt clammy sweat on his lips. He sat again. "I came from Ireland this morning."

"Ireland." His father said the word perfectly, then nodded. "Tracing . . . your . . . double." His eyes sought the ceiling as though he were summoning up his strength. "Any . . . luck?"

"I don't know if luck is the right word," Mangan said. "But listen, Dad, Margrethe said you wanted to talk to me. You wanted to tell me something."

His father nodded. His breathing seemed to stop, then started again. Mangan noticed rivulets of sweat running in the corded gulleys of his neck. "Yes," his father said. "I'm glad you . . . came before I . . . kick off."

"You're not going to kick off."

His father shrugged his shoulders in a painful parody of his usual noncommittal shrug. "Maybe," he said, at last. "But . . . *if* I die . . . I'm in a . . . mess, Jamie. My . . . fault." He turned his head and tried to smile, then reached out his hand as if to hold Mangan's hand. Mangan took the offered hand, felt the old man's fingers grip him tightly, then lie loose in his own.

"What is it, Dad?"

"Margrethe," his father said, gasping again. And then

said something Mangan did not hear, the words slurred to unintelligibility. "You see?" he added.

"Sorry, I didn't hear that. What was it?"

"I said . . . she's . . . pregnant," his father said. "And I don't . . . have . . . savings. House is . . . mortgaged, has been ever . . . since . . . your mother . . . got divorce. She . . . needed money . . . then. And I . . ." Suddenly, surprisingly, he smiled. "I over . . . extended."

"Don't worry, I got money from Beatrice. A lot."

"So . . . you said on the . . . telephone. Before you . . . went to . . . Ireland." His father stopped and gasped painfully for breath, gasped and gasped until Mangan was sure he was having some sort of attack. Then suddenly he said, "It's not . . . fair to . . . ask you but I'm . . . asking. She'll need . . . help." Again his father stopped and labored to breathe. "At least . . . until she . . . mmmarries . . . again." He coughed. "And the . . . child is going to . . . need someone for . . . longer. That's what I . . . wanted to . . . ask. Will you keep . . . an eye . . . on it?"

"Of course. Anyway, you're going to be all right."

"Well . . . maybe," his father said. He added something which was so slurred Mangan could not hear it.

"Sorry, Dad? What was that?"

His father shook his head. "Doesn't matter. This bloody . . . speech. Your grandfather died . . . just like this. Couldn't . . . speak. Anyway, we've . . . managed to talk. Thanks. And listen. Will you . . . phone . . . your mother? Margrethe's been speaking to . . . her. I spoke to her on the . . . phone. I told her . . . don't come. But, will you . . . call her?"

"Yes, don't worry."

His father coughed again and gasped for air. "A child," he said. "It will . . . be a son. I . . . feel it."

Mangan nodded and smiled.

And then his father closed his eyes, still gasping. "Just

a . . . minute," he said in a slow, slurred voice. "Just . . . a rest."

"Yes, of course. Rest," Mangan said. He watched the old man's chest expand and contract painfully, listened to the constant tearing sound of his breath. *A child.* He's going to have a child. And I, flying the Atlantic, wondered what secret he wanted to tell. And it was then, watching his father try to rest, watching his pale sweating face, his long, lank, thinning gray hair, his childishly awkward white neck, that he knew his father would die. A stroke is a slow death. He bent his head and rested his cheek against his father's hand. The old man opened his eyes. "You . . . all . . . right, Jamie?"

"Yes, I'm fine." He lifted his head and looked at his father. "I'm very fond of you, Dad. Do you know that?"

His father, breathing laboriously, raised himself, looked at him, then said, "Were you . . . in a fight over . . . there? You . . . lost a tooth."

Mangan nodded. Through his father—who knew nothing of Gorteen, Duntally, Norman towers, and lonely headlands—the uncanny facial resemblance, the poetry, the wild blood had been transferred across the Atlantic Ocean to this cold winter land, to this, his father's harsh native city in which he now lay dying. He looked at his father's face and wished that those features were his own.

Someone had entered the room. He turned and it was Margrethe, carrying a plastic cup of coffee. "All right?" she whispered. "Is he still asleep?"

"No," his father said suddenly, his eyes still shut. And added in a slurred voice, "We . . . had . . . a . . . talk. Good . . . talk, eh, Jamie?"

"Yes, Dad. Now take it easy. Rest."

Silently, Margrethe offered the coffee, then went to sit at the other side of the sick man's bed. They sat in silence, watching him labor to breathe, watching him die.

TITLES IN SERIES

J.R. ACKERLEY Hindoo Holiday
J.R. ACKERLEY My Dog Tulip
J.R. ACKERLEY My Father and Myself
J.R. ACKERLEY We Think the World of You
HENRY ADAMS The Jeffersonian Transformation
CÉLESTE ALBARET Monsieur Proust
DANTE ALIGHIERI The Inferno
DANTE ALIGHIERI The New Life
WILLIAM ATTAWAY Blood on the Forge
W.H. AUDEN (EDITOR) The Living Thoughts of Kierkegaard
W.H. AUDEN W.H. Auden's Book of Light Verse
ERICH AUERBACH Dante: Poet of the Secular World
DOROTHY BAKER Cassandra at the Wedding
J.A. BAKER The Peregrine
HONORÉ DE BALZAC The Unknown Masterpiece *and* Gambara
MAX BEERBOHM Seven Men
STEPHEN BENATAR Wish Her Safe at Home
FRANS G. BENGTSSON The Long Ships
ALEXANDER BERKMAN Prison Memoirs of an Anarchist
GEORGES BERNANOS Mouchette
ADOLFO BIOY CASARES Asleep in the Sun
ADOLFO BIOY CASARES The Invention of Morel
CAROLINE BLACKWOOD Corrigan
CAROLINE BLACKWOOD Great Granny Webster
NICOLAS BOUVIER The Way of the World
MALCOLM BRALY On the Yard
MILLEN BRAND The Outward Room
JOHN HORNE BURNS The Gallery
ROBERT BURTON The Anatomy of Melancholy
CAMARA LAYE The Radiance of the King
GIROLAMO CARDANO The Book of My Life
DON CARPENTER Hard Rain Falling
J.L. CARR A Month in the Country
BLAISE CENDRARS Moravagine
EILEEN CHANG Love in a Fallen City
UPAMANYU CHATTERJEE English, August: An Indian Story
NIRAD C. CHAUDHURI The Autobiography of an Unknown Indian
ANTON CHEKHOV Peasants and Other Stories
RICHARD COBB Paris and Elsewhere
COLETTE The Pure and the Impure
JOHN COLLIER Fancies and Goodnights
CARLO COLLODI The Adventures of Pinocchio
IVY COMPTON-BURNETT A House and Its Head
IVY COMPTON-BURNETT Manservant and Maidservant
BARBARA COMYNS The Vet's Daughter
EVAN S. CONNELL The Diary of a Rapist
ALBERT COSSERY The Jokers
HAROLD CRUSE The Crisis of the Negro Intellectual
ASTOLPHE DE CUSTINE Letters from Russia

For a complete list of titles, visit www.nyrb.com or write to:
Catalog Requests, NYRB, 435 Hudson Street, New York, NY 10014